PRAISE FOR JACOBO'S RAINBOW

"A beautiful novel set in the past but perfectly, scarily, relevant to our current moment." —Gary Shteyngart, author of *Lake Success*

"*Jacobo's Rainbow* is a sweeping examination of the unique buckle in time that was the 'Sixties,' told from the perspective of the ultimate outsider—a young man who was born and raised in the tiny New Mexico town of Arroyo Grande, a town so isolated it didn't even legally exist. Jacobo's journey takes him from that remote enclave to a college campus, where he becomes immersed in the Free Speech movement, and to the battlefields of Vietnam. His insights and observations about society, his peers, bigotry, and anti-Semitism are both trenchant and currently relevant to the culture wars and threats to free speech we see on our college campuses and in society at large today. *Jacobo's Rainbow* is a deeply moving, sensitive, and profound novel—a definite must-read." —Marcia Clark, author of *Blood Defense* and *Final Judgment*

"Blending together historical events and wonderfully imaginative settings, David Hirshberg explores the American Jewish experience in this evocative novel of self-discovery, belonging, and the complexities of identity." —Shulem Deen, author of *All Who Go Do Not Return*

"Although set in the 1960s, David Hirshberg's *Jacobo's Rainbow* is infused with prescient relevance today. This hero's journey shines a light on activism and protest on a college campus as well as the idea of patriotism and serving in the army. Most profoundly, it depicts a search for identity as young Jacobo Toledano struggles with the blurry distinction between who people are and how they present themselves in public. I loved this novel for its timeless message: that building a home of one's own means leaving the safety of childhood and being resilient to the knocks the world hands you, true for an individual as well as a tribe."
—Jeanne McWilliams Blasberg, author of *The Nine* and *Eden*

"*Jacobo's Rainbow* is a powerful, electrifying glimpse into the life of a young student advocating for the Free Speech Movement and protesting the Vietnam War. It's a story about truth, loyalty, tradition, and the shortcomings of human perception, an all-too-often occurrence for those who haven't yet experienced much of life. Hirshberg's keenly nuanced characters will remain with the reader long after the last page." —Crystal King, author of *The Chef's Secret* and *Feast of Sorrow*

"David Hirshberg propels the reader into the mix of the turbulent 1960s, as if this novel were constructed from personal conversations between the characters and the author. They are all agents and witnesses of their times with intersecting ethnicities, religions, races, genders, languages, and ages. Characters in this captivating narrative hide, discover, and reveal their true inner selves as they interact with events and one another. This is a saga that drops bread crumbs for the discerning eye and gratifies the reader who recognizes them and revels in the *aha moments* when the pieces come together. Hirshberg is immensely skilled at conjuring plausible events that serve the narrative. He captures the essence of anti-Semitism experienced by Jews of different hues and origins. The author represents with imagined accuracy the experiences of young men and women caught up in the Free Speech movement and in the jungles of Vietnam."

—Debbie Wohl-Isard,
Editor, *La Granada*

"In *Jacobo's Rainbow*, as he did in *My Mother's Son*, David Hirshberg explores that stunning moment when youth gives way to maturity—and uncovers the lasting effects of that profound transformation. The year is 1963, and Jacobo, who was born and raised in a sheltered, idyllic New Mexico village, enrolls in a university and quickly becomes embroiled in the turmoil and passion of that one-of-a-kind decade. As he begins to find his voice and take stock of his individuality, he also sees, in surprising fashion, how truly connected we all are. A highly original novel by an inspired chronicler of fact and fiction that reveals our darkest instincts while celebrating our innate humanity."

—Barbara Josselsohn,
author of *The Lilac House* and *The Bluebell Girls*

ALSO BY DAVID HIRSHBERG

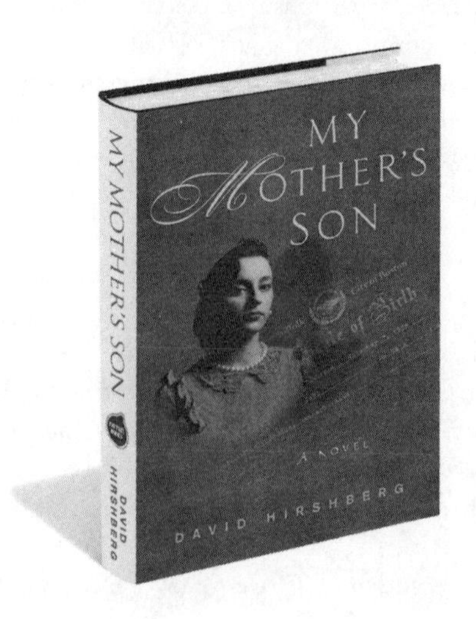

JACOBO'S RAINBOW

JACOBO'S RAINBOW

A NOVEL

DAVID HIRSHBERG

BEDFORD, NEW YORK

To Ann

Published in the United States by Fig Tree Books LLC, Bedford, New York

www.FigTreeBooks.net

Jacket design by Asha Hossain Design, LLC
Interior design by Aubrey Khan, Neuwirth & Associates, Inc.

Library of Congress Cataloging-in-Publication Data Available Upon Request

ISBN 978-1-941493-28-1

Printed in the United States

Distributed by Publishers Group West

First edition

10 9 8 7 6 5 4 3 2 1

CONTENTS

PROLOGUE

It seems as if anniversaries have a way of letting spirits loose, and they don't respect boundaries any more than viruses do, so the only way to fool yourself into thinking you can control them is to make others believe that they can see them as well. A conjurer uses sleights of hand, feints, and misdirections, which can succeed because you're willing to suspend visual disbelief. However, an author only has one dimension to work with, as well as a disconnected audience, which can be a disadvantage. But on the other hand, there's no one to say that what you're reading is false.

Today marks the fifteenth anniversary of a momentous event in my life—the day I was sent to jail. It's the obvious time for me now to tell my story. My guess is that you're going to believe this is fiction; that would be a delusion.

Jacobo Toledano
Arroyo Grande, New Mexico
June 10, 1980

CHAPTER 1

Speaking is silver,

silence is gold

Until 1960, all of us in Arroyo Grande were ignorant of electricity and automobiles, were unaware of plastic, steel, or homogenization, hadn't been exposed to vaccines, x-rays, or Freud, weren't acquainted with Shakespeare or Hemingway, had never listened to Gershwin or Mozart, couldn't have imagined Les Demoiselles d'Avignon or The Starry Night, didn't know what JFK, DNA, SOS, IBM, CIA, or RBI stood for, were uninformed of the existence of George or Booker T. Washington and assumed that England, France, Spain, and Portugal were still the most powerful nations on earth. We used sassafras roots as toothpaste, made paper from pulp and colored it with plant dyes, played the lute and the lyre, and used percussion instruments made from animal skins. And we never went to sleep without our parents saying, "Then all shall sit under their vines and under their fig trees and none shall make them afraid."

This is what I wrote in 1962, word for word, as the beginning of the essay part of my admission application to the University of Taos (commonly referred to as UT), close to the Colorado border. It came out of an assignment from a creative writing project in our remote, small school, in which we were asked to reimagine our family's history in the form of an introduction to a novel. The part about the vines and fig trees wasn't fiction. That's what my parents, Aarón and Raquel Toledano, and seven other families who together comprise the entire village of Arroyo Grande—the Ávilas, Córdobas, Pontevedres, Gironas, Alicantes, Lisboas, and Firenzes—say each night as the kids are put to bed.

There was more than a kernel of truth at the heart of this fiction, so to disguise it, I resorted to hyperbole, which found favor with the admissions office. They published the essay along with my photo in the UT newspaper on the day I registered, as an illustration of achievement from a member of the incoming class. It caused a sensation, especially since it included a picture of me wearing a colorful Navajo shawl, with a scruffy red and blond streaked beard, and gray-marble eyes.

Waiting in line, I heard an echo of a muted howl that was picked up by a few others around me. It became a chorus of soft bays that I figured was some sort of musical conversation, one of many things I was going to have to pick up on if I wanted to fit in seamlessly. Within a few minutes, they were interspersed with shorter yelps, the cacophony similar to the sounds of the red wolves I'd hear late at night when I slept outdoors in Arroyo Grande. After a bit, the student closest to me tapped me gently on the shoulder and said, "*Lobo rojo, lobo rojo.*"

Red wolf, red wolf. From then on, I was sometimes addressed as *lobo rojo*—unless someone turned out to be my friend, in which case he or she pronounced Jacobo with the J as H sound, *Hacobo*, the typical way in Spanish, notwithstanding the fact that it should've been said with a 'ja' sound, as in Jake.

Eight families had lived in Arroyo Grande in the west-central part of New Mexico since 1677, having arrived there after a five year sojourn that began in Constantinople and worked its way to Mexico. At the outset, they put down roots far from others, and only in 1867 when a Navajo Indian group set up camp a few miles away did they begin to assimilate. They thrived in the high altitude and benefitted from the remoteness of their existence; the community had never been breached by plagues of war, disease, or fear. Their seclusion contributed to their self-reliance and was something that was handed down and practiced without aforethought. Food, water, clothing, shelter, entertainment, and medicine were omnipresent. They'd opted to preserve a segregated way of life as a method of community survival. Initially interacting with the Navajos and then later trading with settlers, ranchers, and prospectors who'd traveled down the Rio Grande, they gradually become acculturated into the American way of life by the nineteen thirties.

Not that they were fully integrated.

There were no telephones or electricity or paved roads. None of that was a hardship. Several ancient cars and trucks were used within the village (not that anyone had a driver's license). There were no prohibitions against using modern conveniences such as battery-powered tools and radios, and we'd accumulated so many books that a library was built right off the central plaza. No one had a social security card, registered to vote, or served on juries. The truth is that Arroyo Grande legally didn't exist. You couldn't find it on a map, there were no records in the county archives, and we buried our dead without permits, up on a hill, from which you could see both the mountains to the west and the Rio Grande to the east.

My father ran the general store, which was constructed at the easternmost part of the village. It was nearest the road the WPA had built in 1936 in order to enable trucks and personnel carriers to have unfettered access to a new army base that was being built on the western side of the river. That's where the higher elevation would preclude flooding in the spring when the heavy melt would flow south and cut off communities, sometimes for up to several weeks at a time.

The store was universally called The Trading Post, especially after Joseph Deschene, who was commonly referred to as Navajo Joe, opened an Indian boutique within it, where he sold blankets, other woolen goods, carved figurines, and silver jewelry to tourists, army personnel from the base, and then to new-age seekers who increasingly flocked to remote parts of New Mexico to align with nature and seek out those spirits that welcomed their embrace.

The arms that the founders of our village had brought with them hundreds of years earlier—unused muskets, lead balls, and knives of assorted lengths and shapes—testaments to the great victory of the community's isolation, were prominently displayed in alcoves in the back, perched above the two massive fireplaces on the opposing side walls, and hung down from massive hand-hewed rafters that supported the ceilings.

My father enjoyed greeting customers in an effusive manner, finagling them to tell their stories to a perfect stranger. He was adept at using the anecdotes he'd just heard to then steer someone to an item that hadn't been in consideration when the person had walked into the store.

Aarón Toledano was an imposing figure, the tallest person in Arroyo Grande. He moved with a grace that was uncommon for someone of his height. Although one would say his hair was red, it was more appropriately defined as red*dish*. If you looked at him straight on, you'd notice streaks of different red hues forming a rainbow-like impression that culminated in the bun that knotted it all together, a common style worn by many of the adult men. His beard was long and full, and his moustache hung down over his upper lip, concealing his smile, which had the unintended effect of some not being able to determine his mien—not a disadvantage when he acted as the unofficial leader of Arroyo Grande.

After dinner on Friday nights, my father would tell stories to me, my older sister Débora, and my younger sister Nohemi. We'd sit, legs crossed, with our backs to the great fire, listening to him raise and lower his voice, watching him standing, walking around the room, hearing the wood crackling, seeing ashes floating in space, noticing shadows flickering in an otherwise darkened room. When the stories got too scary, Nohemi would crawl inside her blanket, roll to where she was touching my legs, and peek out, turtle-like, only when there was a pause for a transition from one scene to another. When she was really petrified, we'd hear a loud uuuuuuuuuum, uuuuuuuuuum and would see the blanket move up and down, side to side, which wouldn't annoy anyone except the cat who'd settled in for a snooze in one of our laps.

The stories would all start out the same way: a group of three children, one boy and two girls, all related, would sneak out of their house at night, go into the woods and dig up dirt, clay, and loam, and fashion the materials into a person twice the size of a normal man. The giant creature would spring to life as they poured hot coals over it, then the children would throw water to cool the figure and watch it form hair, eyes, fingernails, and toes. The children would stick twigs into the head and then blow air into the space when they pulled the twigs out, giving life to the creature—or Holyman—as my father called it. Then the children would reveal to the Holyman the terrible situation that they were in and how the Holyman should seek revenge on those who'd harmed them. The stories always took place on a cold, windy night filled with danger in the fields, woods, and alleys. The children would be pursued by pirates and wizards, then would be assaulted with words and attacked with weapons. They'd be forced to admit crimes that they hadn't committed, sins they weren't guilty of, and made to believe that they'd never see their parents again or witness the sun to rise that very day.

Then—the Holyman to the rescue!

The creature, who couldn't talk but who could see and hear, would materialize from the shadows and instantly spring into action, absorb taunts and insults, fend off musket balls, knives, and lances, retrieve those strapped to the rack, tied to the stake, shackled by chains attached to horses, or hoist up those who had their heads forced under water, in which case he'd breathe life back into the child, knowing that the very air that he blew would empty his own lungs and cause his own death. In the end, he'd always die, without a sigh or trace of any emotion, and simply melt back into the earth to be recalled again on another Friday night. Then we'd go to bed, to dream of the Holyman who'd always be there for us when we'd need him most.

The first time I decided to write and illustrate a story was after one of these Friday nights, when I did my best to recreate the evening in what would now be called the style of a graphic novel, but back then was simply referred to as a comic or funny book. I'd sketch a cell, in which I tried to capture both the imagination of what my father had been describing as well as the scene itself, with my sisters in rapt attention, or huddled under a blanket, or drinking some lemon-flavored water with a *burék*, a pastry filled with cheese and eggplant, a favorite late-night snack. By the time I was sixteen, I had a large notebook filled with these pages, so it was natural that I'd call upon this ability to compose and draw as part of the college application.

On the day I left Arroyo Grande for the UT, Navajo Joe handed me a going away gift. More colorful than anything he'd displayed at The Trading Post, it was an intricately woven shawl with a large opening, through which I poked my head, spread my arms wide, and pirouetted around so that everyone else could see the appreciation I felt and the honor I acknowledged. He motioned for me to accompany him, and we walked down to the water's edge.

In this part of New Mexico, the Rio Grande is magnificent. Sunlight illuminated the striated rainbow-like threads of currents that alternately competed with and calmly nestled alongside each other, giving the impression of a race between elements to find out which could claim dominance. We could see unusually far up and downstream, past a sharp bend in the shoreline, cinched at the tip by a large rock promontory jutting out into the river like an exclamation point as if to indicate the presence of the Navajo village directly up the hill to the west.

He pointed to a ring of large stones that appeared to be a map of the constellations we'd see in the wintertime. He didn't say anything, just moved his head slowly around the stones, nodding, encouraging me to do the same, silently leading me to take it in, to understand the simplicity of the representation. I can't say I understood what it all meant at the time, but later, on a return trip, it served as a beacon to two bedraggled, wearied young men who were just learning about the circle of life.

At the bottom of the hill, the land leveled out as if in a gesture to enable the Rio Grande to change course without offering resistance, a symbiosis of land and water that reflected the ageless history of time. I stood there, mute, absorbing the sights and smells, a minute that was both singular and intimate. A little later, it was time to say goodbye. I hugged him, making sure I didn't catch either his long black hair, which was twisted into a braid that went half-way down his back, or the pendant that he wore around his neck—a five-pointed metallic object in the shape of a star—that could cause you to blink if it caught the sun just so.

I approached my father and reached for the door of the 1939 blue Plymouth. It never occurred to me to ask what would happen if the police were to pull us over and find out that he didn't have a driver's license.

We drove for almost ten hours until we caught sight of Taos Heights on the east side of the river, on a hill above the old mining breakwater islands, the commercial fishing ship wharves, and the pleasure boat piers that spread like the extended fingers of a hand hopelessly reaching out to bridge the expanse of the bay. At the edge of the eastern shore, a large multi-colored house sat perched over the water with a deck that jutted out over the river. Who knew that this house would be my refuge in a storm unleashed upon the land.

We went directly to a café, this being my father's last stop before saying goodbye and then returning home. He introduced me to the proprietor, an older man named Ben Veniste. I was struck by the faint odor of fertilizer, a dank, musty aroma that reminded me of the still air of the cistern, dug from the softer clays near the farms out on the western part of Arroyo Grande. Ben Veniste's long hair was trapped within a fishnet helmet, over which he placed a chef's hat, giving him the appearance of being much taller than he was. He manipulated his cane with such dexterity that you wouldn't have been surprised to learn it wasn't necessary, that it was just a prop. He had what can only be described as larger-than-life presence, made all the more striking by his hearty laugh and his predilection for thumping the cane in dramatic fashion against the floor to underscore a pronouncement he was making or to gently nudge unruly customers out the door by using it to playfully tap the back of their legs.

He kissed my father on both cheeks before he left, a warm gesture that I didn't expect.

Outside the café, my father put his hands on my shoulders, looked me in the eye, and told me not to forget the *Pequeño*. I gave him my assurance. And I meant it. On Saturday nights, just before I fell asleep, I recited it, sometimes out loud, other times silently.

Then he said, "*La palavra es de plata i la kayades de oro.*" *Speaking is silver, silence is gold*—an admonition to me to not reveal any of our secrets.

We embraced and he gently tugged at my shoulders, a signal that he wanted me to bend over a little so he could kiss the top of my head. It reminded me of my last conversation with my older sister Débora: "It's going to be difficult for our parents, you not being here, especially since you've taken on so much responsibility with chores, helping at the festivals, and with Navajo Joe at The Trading Post," she noted in a way that shifted the hurt to others, an easier sidestep that allowed her to start without outwardly revealing her own fears.

"I'll be back before you know it," I responded.

She was silent. I knew what she was thinking.

This is your home, but you might not return.

"I could barely accept when you soared past me in height," she said playfully, "but my fear is that when I see you again, you'll have grown in stature too. And, well, you know, you could be different, could view us in a strange way. You'll have found new customs, new friends, new ways of looking at the world."

"I'm scared, too. You're almost nineteen, and when I get back there's the chance, actually a strong likelihood, that you'll have found your *amor*, and where will that leave me? No more chances to snuggle up with you on one side and Nohemi on the other under the blanket in front of the fire."

My mind raced through a series of faces recalled from those young men a little older than I who could possibly be satisfactory to this smart, vivacious, beautiful young woman, and I acknowledged silently that none of them could measure up to her talents or expectations. I kissed the top of her head. We both laughed and wiped our tears.

My father leaned his arm on the roof of the car. He said, "*Kuando el padre da al ijo, riye el padre, riye el ijo.*" *When the father gives to the son, the father laughs, the son laughs.*

We both teared up, as neither of us had practiced for this moment despite having had ample time to prepare for this gift he was giving me. I thought about my mother's goodbye back at our house; she held me for a full minute or so without a word, her embrace getting stronger by the second. When Madre let go, she pulled my head down to her level and kissed my cheeks and forehead. We laughed softly as relief washed over us, our anxiety overcome.

"*Kuando el rio de la padre yora el padre yora el ijo,*" my father added. *When the son gives to the father, the father cries, the son cries.* I understood through my blurry vision that I was giving my father a special gift—the knowledge that I was ready to seek out uncharted territory as our forebears had done in 1677.

He pulled a shiny metallic object out of his pocket that, when pulled apart, revealed a mirror. He handed it to me. The surface was dazzling, and the child in me opened and closed the mirror repeatedly, much to his delight. I slipped this precious gift into my pocket.

Then my father said the words he'd say on Friday nights when he gathered the three children together:

"May I bless you and guard you;

May I make my face shed light upon you and be gracious to you;

May I lift up my face to you and give you peace."

And we'd all say, "Amen."

CHAPTER 2

I noticed the similarity

of what I was reading

to what I'd just heard

"Faith is a commodity that doesn't fluctuate with supply or demand."

I said it matter-of-factly in response to one of Myles' harangues on economics in which he'd disguise a question as a pronouncement in order to get your goat or to keep a rant going or, as Claudia thought, simply as a means of keeping himself on center stage. He could do this easily from his position as the gifted orator and critical thinker, augmented by his vantage point six inches above the floor on the platform that'd been installed behind the cash register of the bookstore on Broadway Avenue. He'd ring you up, bag what you bought, comment on your bearing, engage you in a dialog, or fill up a void with a soliloquy, neither spilling a cup of coffee nor letting the ash drop from his ever-present hand-rolled cigarette. It was a performance, and it went on every weekday at 2:00 p.m. and lasted until 8:00 at night, when he'd whisk away some girl who'd come in near closing time. We'd never see her later at night after he joined us out on the sidewalk in front of Ben Veniste's cafe, where we'd get stuffed with bowls of mushrooms, white beans, eggs, and onions as well as rants about the war, poverty, discrimination, civil rights, and free speech.

We were drawn to Myles by a force as mysterious and seemingly as powerful as gravity, yoked into his orbit by the very invisible hand that he so denigrated for its role in the marketplace. He was six years older, and looked the part of a young professor with his ever-present tweed jacket and his ability to lure you into an intellectual corner and leave you there wearing a dunce cap and feeling embarrassed. To us, he was a world apart. He told us he'd been on the buses in Mississippi for the first freedom rides, harvested lettuce in the San Joaquin Valley, picketed the induction center in Albuquerque, witnessed the speech at the March on Washington, attended the first SDS national convention at Pine Hill, New York, and been hosed down protesting hearings of the House Un-American Activities Committee in San Francisco.

"Everything of value is priced by greed," he'd said to no one in particular and everyone within the store, and that's when I piped in with the thing about faith. It just came out, unexpectedly, not in opposition to what he'd said but rather as a means of offering an exception to the rule. It hung there like the trapeze artist who reaches the zenith between swings, where for an instant you're not sure if she'll grab the bar or fall to the floor, when everyone sucks in their breath, swallowing all the noises for that split second in which life itself seems to disappear.

Myles moved his palms up and twitched his head from side to side, which meant I'd derailed his train and ruined his evening. A girl left the store by herself, so we walked together in silence, north on Broadway then east onto Stratford and up the stoop into his apartment on the first floor. I noticed that Myles' shelves were filled to the gills with books and especially plays—Shakespeare, Shaw, Wilde, Miller, and Williams among others. There were almost as many works crammed into his modest space as we had at the library in Arroyo Grande.

Most evenings, Myles and his entourage met at Ben Veniste's café. In good weather we'd sit outside, excitedly conversing about the major issues of the day: the buildup of troops in Southeast Asia; discrimination against Blacks and Native Americans; poverty in the land of plenty; the right to express oneself in public. And minor ones as well: grade grubbing; what to say to girls; suitable clothes to wear; how to pass a toke. As we'd walk home, I'd feel as if I were marching behind a soldier—not one of arms or fortune but one of opportunity. In those days, prospects seemed limitless for well-educated young adults who adopted a kind of manifest destiny in which ideas based upon reason and logic would triumph.

What amazed me was that this optimism wasn't shattered following the murder of President Kennedy. The shock of the assassination had an unexpected impact on Myles, who worked through his grief to affect the changes that the president had set in motion. Time had become his enemy. Each tick that wasn't accompanied by action was a moment lost that could never be recovered. He'd tell us about his efforts to march for civil rights, to protest the growing involvement in the war, to lobby for the end of the draft, and to demand that eighteen-year-olds get the right to vote.

In the fall of 1964, Myles came back for his third year of graduate school after the Freedom Summer, energized about the possibilities, angry about how much had yet to be accomplished, and guilty that he wasn't on the front lines once the fall term began.

He was a gifted storyteller who could both charm and harangue simultaneously. He painted a picture with words, at times like a portrait, so that we had distinct images of people in our minds. It was as if we were listening to an impressionist giving us lay of the land or sometimes an abstract expressionist mixing a jumble of things that, up close, we couldn't decipher but in context, putting the image further away, we could actually feel what he was describing and almost eavesdrop on the original event.

We'd met the first day when I was waiting in a line to register for classes, wearing the wrap that Navajo Joe had given to me.

Myles approached and asked, "Are you Native American?"

Having been born in New Mexico, I didn't hesitate to respond affirmatively. "I come from an out-of-the way village in the west central part of the state."

"Stop by my apartment tonight," he practically ordered and handed me a business card with his name and address on it. I had no idea who he was or what I was getting into; nevertheless, "okay" came out of me without thinking if it was prudent or foolish. That evening, I met Claudia and others he'd recruited from his sweep around the campus.

On his rolltop desk were portrait pictures of old, unshaven men on porches, corncob pipes in hand, their feet shooting out of denim overalls like the tips of corn breaking free of the sheaths. Hung on the walls were blurry photos—action shots—where the camera had been unsteady from the photographer running or having been pushed by deputies who didn't want the world to see what was happening when outside agitators came in to ruin the way things were...the way things would never be again.

I noticed a girl with skin like a young western honey mesquite. She had green eyes that looked like the buds on the trees that would explode each spring after the short deluge that brought water to the cisterns of Arroyo Grande. She approached me at Myles' suggestion—one Indian should meet another. She slid into a language that was new to me.

"I'm sorry, I don't understand you. Do...you...speak...English," I asked, enunciating each word slowly and carefully.

"Of course," she said in that exquisite way that girls have of demonstrating their superiority without covering you with a blanket of shame. "It's Hindi," she said. "Myles told me you were Indian." Her English was British.

"Ah," I said, "not *that* kind of Indian. Not *your* kind. I get it. I see, he, Myles, thinks I'm an *American* Indian, you know, because I'm wearing this shawl. It's Navajo, a gift, a going away present from a real American Indian. I don't speak Navajo. Jacobo. Jacobo Toledano," I said with a hopeful smile.

"Oh, Mexican, or should I use, what is it, how're they now saying, ummm, oh, oh, I remember: Hispanic."

"It's Spanish, yes, the name."

"You speak it, of course, yes?" she asked. "Spanish, that is, at home?"

"I, we do, yes, but not all the time." I was concerned that she was going to dig a little deeper and was relieved that she pivoted back to herself.

"My name is Mir," she said. "We came here when I was little. From a village on the west coast, near Cochin. Have you ever heard of it?"

Before I could answer, we heard the rapping of an opener against the side of a bottle, so we turned the same way that ducks all pivot their bodies in one direction when the current changes. Myles had hopped onto a chair at the far side of the room.

Speaking in a manner that seemed practiced, Myles gave us a first-hand primer about the Freedom Rides—buses filled with Anglos who'd descend upon a town in the south and attempt to integrate diners, restaurants, barbershops, department stores, and public benches. I listened to accounts of people my age challenging poll taxes and literacy tests, trying to convince Black people to accompany them to the registry to fix their names to the lists that would make them eligible to vote. I listened as he described how the National Guard had to make sure that Black kids could go to school with white ones.

"It's universal," he said sadly, "you find it all over. A fear of the *other*, the outsider, the ones who look different, whose customs aren't familiar, whose beliefs are at odds with the majority—those folks in power who want to protect their way of life. Make no mistake about it, fear breeds hostility. So don't be fooled by someone who says frightening things then apologizes when caught. It's what they say in unguarded moments that expose their true beliefs. That's when you can attack them for revealing their real motivations.

"Imagine," he continued, "how you'd feel if you were drafted into the army but couldn't vote, couldn't go to a university, couldn't even eat at the lunch counter at the Five and Dime. What would you be thinking if you," he pointed to me, "had to step out of the way of a white person, maybe tip your cap, bend a little at the shoulder and waist, give a weak smile and call the man you're being deferential to 'sir' while he calls you 'boy'? Let me know how your parents," now he singled out Mir, "had to deal with not being able to get a loan to buy a house. But wait, what does it matter?" he asked. "You can't accumulate any money for a down payment anyway because the only job you can get is shining shoes or cleaning someone else's house. And when you," he gesticulated to an African American student, "see a pretty girl, you can't smile or wave if she's white, no sir. Why, that can land you in the pokey where they feed you slops you wouldn't give to farm animals, for which you'd have to express your appreciation or they'd slap you on the face, pull your hair, and call you nigger or sambo."

Several people gasped. Myles didn't seem to notice, not skipping a beat.

"Imagine that you'd hear the same things from your parents and their parents and *their* parents, people who lived at the time of the Civil War." I scanned the room and saw everyone nodding, some with tears in their eyes. "And despite there being the three amendments to the Constitution, three pieces of paper that said you were free and that everyone had equal protection under the law and that you could vote, regardless of your race or color, well, for the most part, they were just words on a page. Here they are."

He thrust three pieces of paper out in front of him that I found out later were the thirteenth, fourteenth, and fifteenth amendments to the U.S. Constitution, turning them so all of us could see them, as if, by magic, our acknowledgement of their existence would manifest change.

"Freedom," he continued, his voice rising, "freedom is what we hold dear; freedom is what we say we have; freedom is the cornerstone of our democracy."

Myles continued to read from an invisible script, staring over our heads. He was on stage and building to a crescendo.

"They teach us that in school. They teach us that right here. We're 'the land of the free, the home of the brave.' How brave is it for a sheriff to hose down a group of Black kids wanting to go to school? To *school.* Imagine that. How brave is it to be a nightrider with a shotgun going after a Black kid walking along a country road? How brave is it to falsely accuse someone of a crime, say a robbery or a rape, when its design is to cover your own misdeeds. How brave is it to watch someone rot in jail or work himself to death on a chain gang? How brave is it to live your life unaffected by your participation in this or by your willingness to pretend that it doesn't happen or by your delusion that somehow *they deserve this.* That must be what they think as they wave their flags at the Fourth of July parades or say the pledge of allegiance at the Friday night football games or thank the Lord on Sunday morning, these good brave people."

We erupted into sustained applause and foot stomping. Myles put both hands out in front, moving them forward and backward a few inches, a maestro orchestrating his instruments.

He'd been running his hands through his long stringy hair, which hung down over his face like the bars of a prison cell, making it appear that his speech was coming from a victim trapped within the system.

He continued as if he'd memorized it all, no word out of place. Looking back later, it became clear that this was perfected in advance. But even when I had a better understanding of Myles' persona, it didn't diminish the power of what he had to say.

"Bravery," he continued, "on the other hand, is an eighty-year-old man in coveralls with a cane, agonizingly making the trek up the courthouse steps to make his mark in the ledger. Bravery is that same man being spat upon, taunted, and threatened yet not stopping the forward momentum of his feet, even when confronted with the patronizing police chief positioned in front of him brandishing his billy club, admonishing the old man. 'Boy,' he called him, 'go on home now; don't cause no trouble, ya hear.' I watched as the old man said nothing, imperceptibly but relentlessly moving his feet forward, inch by inch, until the brim of his hat pushed against the chest of the officer. To me, he was Moses leading the Hebrews through the desert, only this time, he got to see the land of Canaan."

Myles had warmed up, but he was no opening act for the headliner. He was the connecting wire, and he sent the electricity to each of us. We'd capture it and fling it back to him without any diminution of energy. It appeared that he could feed off the psychic nutrition we provided.

For the most part, this night was devoted to his own experiences. He told us he'd spent that summer, 1964, in Mississippi, registering Blacks to vote, along with students from the north—some Black, mostly white. They'd been warned about the violence that was sure to come. And come it did. The deaths of Chaney, Schwerner, and Goodman bewildered me. Why were they were killed for simply trying to get people to vote? I was in loud dialogue in a dream that night, first yelling at the police to find their killers and then going back in time, begging their parents not to let them leave home. It reminded me of when my younger sister Nohemi would awake in fits and come scampering into my room accompanied by her blanket, a nightmare having been caused by one of the stories of the Holyman. She'd sleep on the floor between my bed and the wall; it was a barrier against my leaving, to ensure that I'd be there to protect her.

Little did I know at the time that the police were corrupt and that nothing would've prevented these three young men from going on this mission.

Scattered around Myles' apartment were pamphlets, posters, buttons, and stickers as well as reprints of articles and newspaper clippings from the cities and towns where the events had unfolded in what was only then first being called Freedom Summer. At the end of the evening, the pamphlets, posters, buttons, and stickers were stacked neatly into boxes to be hauled off in the supermarket pushcart that was on permanent loan from the local store. Myles asked for volunteers to bring the materials to the tables that would appear early each morning on the Worthington Strip, a part of Broadway Avenue, the street that starts at the UT in the north and ends at the section of Taos Heights that was called Oak Land. It earned its name from the hundreds of trees whose planks became the floors, mantels, and moldings of the houses of the wealthy residents of Taos Heights. Once most of the trees were gone, the debris from the clear cutting was fashioned together to form the shanties where the Blacks made homes between the giant stumps that rotted away over the decades, providing an enormous layer of rich compost that generated the fruits, vegetables, and flowers that were then sold to the whites.

Instead of leaving with the pushcart, I lingered by Myles' bookcase, rifling through some of the news articles and open books that contained stories and essays on the various subjects that Myles had been speaking about. I noticed the similarity of what I was reading to what I'd just heard, but it didn't register with me until after the mêlée.

Claudia stayed behind as well. Her pot-induced smile was punctuated by greater-than-normal spaces between her teeth, which gave her a jack-o-lantern-like face. I'd find out later that, under different circumstances, it'd be lit from within by a fiery caustic speaking style which she'd use with rapier-like skill to eviscerate friend or foe alike, mostly by demeaning thrusts. What saved her, in Myles' eyes, I guessed, was her intelligence, dedication to his causes, and voluptuousness. To me, it was obvious that their relationship wasn't limited to shared interests in political and social outcomes. Not that I ever saw them kissing or exchanging tender words. No. It was more akin to what lawyers call circumstantial evidence—noting the frequent times when they were both unavailable, after which Claudia would sometimes reappear shaken or even bruised, while Myles was often especially acidic toward her.

The next day at dawn, I wasn't at the Worthington Strip with Myles, Claudia, and the pamphlets. Instead, I was at the edge of the Bay, where I'd see Herzl, with whom I'd train and row and otherwise spend time with practically every day; that is, almost every day until I was arrested and put behind bars.

CHAPTER 3

Even a blind man

can see it

The morning after I was at Myles' apartment listening to him speak about the Freedom Summer, the morning after I smoked a joint for the first time, the morning after I got out of lugging the pushcart filled with pamphlets, posters, and buttons, I missed the confrontation that occurred on the Worthington Strip when Claudia and Myles found out that they were banned from setting up tables and distributing posters and leaflets on activities related to voter registration drives, the Johnson and Goldwater campaigns, military recruitment on campus, draft counseling, school and housing integration, poverty, free clinics, and job discrimination. I'd been approached by a man who'd asked me if I'd like to try to row. His earnestness and encouraging affect had me agreeing to meet him at the boathouse without giving it any real thought.

It was about three miles to the river from the main part of the campus. The bus took me south on Broadway Avenue through Oak

Land, then made a ninety degree shift directly west to the bay. The boathouse was surrounded by thick greenery, and when you stood on the deck that jutted out over the water you would have a panoramic view of the brown mesas, yellow cliffs and purple flowers on the other side of the Rio Grande. The double doors welcomed us into a high-ceilinged room arranged around a pool table with a fireplace mustachioed by a mantle of cut stone blocks set in mortar. It smelled of moist carpet and pine that long ago lost its resin. Only the kitchen had been retained for its former use; bedrooms had been turned into workout spaces, dining areas refashioned into storage rooms for towels, liniments, and bandages, and the downstairs sitting area was home to racks of shells, oars, and replacement parts. The shells were stacked neatly, one upon the other, as if this were a furniture warehouse outlet and you could walk through the aisles and point to the one you wanted. Where elegant screen doors had once opened wide to invite guests to drink and eat on a wooden veranda suspended over the shore, now a series of glass doors slid on metal tracks to enable easy portage of shells from casements across a wooden deck that lapped the water's surface.

It was my shape—sinewy they said, at six feet four inches and in the neighborhood of 185 pounds—that was responsible for my name being on a list of rowing prospects. If I'd been approached first by the geology or political science club, I probably never would've known the pain and exhilaration of pushing myself to the limit of endurance, and I would've ended up a different me.

I was told what I was going to learn on the first day. Initially, I'd be introduced to the boat. Then, I'd be shown the indoor training tanks, and finally, I'd be taken out onto the bay. There was never an assumption that this was an opening chapter that wouldn't have an ending. I was going to row; I had the physical attributes and that was that.

This was the day I met Herzl. He was a grade ahead of me and already a rowing sensation. He was a champion single sculler whose exploits were covered not only by the *Albuquerque Tribune* but also in sports pages throughout the country. A picture of him on the river wearing a red bandana with muscular arms about to pull on the oars—a twentieth century reimagination of the famous Thomas Eakins painting—had been captured by a student photographer and became the centerpiece of the front cover on the UT's yearbook.

Herzl had me by an inch and was thinner, his shoulder blades cut through his shirt in such a fashion that when he ran, you got the impression that he could sustain lift, and you wouldn't be all that surprised to see him flying around ahead of you. Mounted onto his skinny frame were momentous sculpted biceps and thick wrists, disproportionately out-of-whack with the rest of his physique, the result, he informed me, of years of arm wrestling.

Herzl told me he'd been tortured as a kid by a couple of boys who'd mocked his appearance. They called him "Bones," and this got nastier as they got older. On Fridays at the school cafeteria, they would become especially hostile.

"You want to know what it's like to be a Jew?" he asked. He didn't wait for an answer. "If you can believe it, these guys took out their antipathy toward fish on me," he said. "And recess was something to be feared, as they'd wait for me and pummel me with food and fists. On Tuesdays and Thursdays, I got picked up from school early to go to Hebrew class, having to go through a gauntlet of insults and missiles. You wouldn't believe what they'd say, Christ-killer and all that."

How, I wondered, could Herzl have been guilty of killing Christ? After all, he was only a year older than I was.

"I knew I couldn't take these kids on, fight them. They'd kill me, but my Hebrew teacher told me that I could humiliate them, and that would shut them up. This was crazy. I mean, you think these guys could understand shame? Please! Anyway, he told me about arm wrestling, and I have to tell you, I thought he was nuts, *loco*. What, with my skinny arms, I was going to wrestle these kids?" He ran his hands over his arms which were sinewy and taut, muscle built on muscle, and I had a hard time visualizing them as thin and weak.

"He knew I'd lose a fight with my whole body for sure. You can see that, but if I concentrated on one part, my arms, say, in one particular way—arm wrestling—then I could take them by surprise. There are tricks, you know, to arm wrestling, it's not just brute strength. Well, that's part of it, but not all. Here, let me show you."

He positioned his right elbow on a table and, just like that, my arm was on the table, prone, defeated. I was embarrassed. "Not as simple as it seems," he pronounced. "My Hebrew teacher told me that there were five things that were important. I wrote them down on a piece of paper and studied them. Want to know what they are?" And with that, he whipped out a folded piece of paper and showed it to me. I read the five things that he'd been taught: the angle of the arm, the angle of the grip, the strength of the bicep, the strength of the wrist, and the ability to wrestle with the weaker arm. "Although it's called arm wrestling, it's really wrist wrestling, you know?"

He continued. "The teacher gave me an exercise that I could actually do when I was studying Hebrew. No kidding. My arm would be the fulcrum. I'd lift massive texts up and down while my eyes concentrated on learning the intricacies of reading the letters without any vowels from the texts on the desk."

I was intrigued and wanted to know how it all turned out, so I asked him to continue.

"I could do this for hours," he went on. "It was trickier for the wrists. I had to work on them when my teacher was out of the room. I'd grab the Torah scrolls. They're wrapped tightly around two dowels and held together by a strap. With one hand on one of the dowels and keeping my arm in the position I'd take when wrestling, I'd slowly rotate the scrolls with my wrist to a horizontal position, back and forth, keeping my arm rigid. I'll show you how back at my room. At first, it was excruciatingly painful, really awful, but after a while, I got the hang of it.

"That's how I learned. So one day, after maybe six months, I challenged the other kids in my bar mitzvah class. It was no contest. I killed them," he said excitedly, then quickly added, "that's a figure of expression, you know that, don't you?"

"Yes, go on."

"Okay, so then I knew I was ready for the punks at school. A few days before Easter, one of the tougher kids put on this dramatic scene in the cafeteria: he dabbed ketchup on the inside of his wrists and staggered over toward me, pretending to be in a death scene with his arms outstretched as if on a cross, wailing in agony, the other kids egging him on as he stumbled over to my table. They'd taken up a rhythmic chant, 'Jesus, Jesus, Jesus,' and formed a circle around me. The kid with the stigmata—"

"Stig what?" I interrupted.

"Stigmata. You know, red marks on the wrists, like blood."

"What are you talking about? One of the kids had blood on his wrists?" I asked incredulously.

"No, not actual blood. It's supposed to represent the wounds where they nailed Jesus to the cross," Herzl said. "I thought you'd know about this."

I shook my head.

"Anyway, this kid thrust his pretend-bloodied hands toward me, and I grabbed his left hand with mine, elbow down on the table. I challenged him. To an arm wrestle. You should've seen his face. I wish I had a picture. Really. He laughed and whipped his head around to the other gentile kids—no offense—who were now whooping it up. They shifted their chant from 'Jesus, Jesus, Jesus,' to 'pin, pin, pin,' while the kid looked around the room waiting for the signal to crush me. Someone yelled out, 'On the count of three,' and as God is my witness, it didn't take a second for his arm to be slammed to the tabletop when I heard the number three. Naturally, he shot up and yelled out, 'Cheater Jew! He jumped the gun; it's a kike trick, and anyway, I'm a righty.' I willingly obliged, put my right elbow on the table, grabbed his hand, then hesitated a second after the number three was again shouted out. Our right hands were locked tightly in a vertical embrace. His whole face lit up in anticipation of victory as he scanned the room for approval, something I let him feel for a moment, knowing his defeat would be all the more humiliating. And it was. I slammed his arm down so hard I thought one of his knuckles would break. Ha, ha! He then came up with all sorts of excuses. You know, his arm had been bruised and the cheating thing again. He told me we should have a real fight outside after class. I ignored him. He moved to the back of his crowd and hurled insults at me, like kike, Jewboy, heeb, yid, all the regular things, but I didn't care, I was taking on all comers: other hoods, athletes, and kids two or three years older. The results were the same. I have to tell you, I never had any problems after that with these guys, although I didn't kid myself, to them I was still a rotten Jew."

He paused then added matter-of-factly, "So I thought I could row," staring at his wrists.

It was then that I began to realize that this Herzl guy was something special.

THE SHELLS WERE wooden with high-topped basketball sneakers that were bolted into the hull. In the back were two wooden handles, some ropes and a megaphone that worked not by amplifying your voice but by focusing it. The boats were sleek, ranging from about thirty to sixty feet long, yet less than two feet wide. I sat delicately on the seat that slid on a rail, my thighs tightening as I pushed back, generating continuous ripples in my muscles. I imagined that I was rowing, two hands making tight circles in the air, turning my wrists at the proper time to ensure that the pretend blade would slice into the water with the least resistance.

The seats were so narrow that if I would've sneezed I could've toppled over. I stayed attached to the dock, the oars tucked tightly to the side of the shell in the same way that the Canada Geese lazing out in the bay would retract their legs when they cruised after paddling. I moved the seat back and forth to get used to the slide. Without any resistance, it was easy. I recognized that out on the water it had to be done in unison. I learned that the shell had a rudder, but could also be nudged by putting a greater amount of pressure on the oars on one side. They showed me how the rudder is connected to a tiller rope that had wooden handles, called knockers, on both sides of the cox. They were used to adjust the steering, as well as to keep the stroke by hitting them gently against the gunwale so the oarsmen could feel the beat.

I was intrigued after spending some time with Herzl. The challenge of working in precision with others was intoxicating and, well, maybe it was the complete novelty of it all, an organized sport on a river, a far cry from made-up games on a dry plateau.

I started a routine. Every day, I'd take the bus to the boathouse, undertake warm-up exercises, get drilled on some ever-increasingly sophisticated techniques, learn about race strategy, and then take the step from dock to shell, an amphibian-like transition for which I seemed to have been naturally selected.

Later, I'd remember the pain, the tension, and the disquiet. I knew of nothing so rigorous as training for rowing. With rowing, there's no margin for error. Your blade must hit the water just so. Too early or late, you could be out of the race, maybe even into the river. The shell is that narrow, and the balance is that precise; you don't get another chance. After all the training including pulling on the machines in the tanks and practicing, if you make the slightest error, all might be in vain.

The pain would radiate from my wrists, forearms, biceps, then to my back, upper and lower, and continue down to my rear, which had to get used to being numb (you can't shift your weight around to give your fanny a breather, or you'd upset the delicate balance), and finally down to my legs, where my thigh muscles twitched annoyingly in pace with my pulse. While the workouts helped to reduce the physical pain, no regimen that we knew of could prepare us adequately for the searing, stabbing, throbbing sensations that caused our skins to bristle and our brains to seek refuge in a less hostile skull. We never had a break, an opportunity to relax. Every second mattered. Each stroke had to be perfect.

Stroke! The cox would call out, accenting the beat with the smashing of the knockers. I had to follow the exact pattern I'd practiced. Above the exhaling and grunting, the noise from the seats squeaking, the wind rustling, and the water hitting the blades, I had to keep a sharp ear out for his calls; the pace could change in an instant, and I never knew when. The anxiety could be as great as the physical pain. But wait! I also had to adjust for other boats and currents and waves and wind and temperature and rain. *Please let me do everything right. God, I don't want to be the one to screw up. My head is killing me.*

Many times, I thought I was going to die after they'd pushed me to the limit. I'd get to a point where I thought I was going to collapse, when all of a sudden, the pain would go away. Like that. Gone. I'd stare at everyone in front of me, watching them in perfect unison, rowing effortlessly. The boat would take off and fly down the river, there'd be no resistance. I could row through exams that I'd gotten poor marks on, past dreary encounters with girls, beyond interminable meetings, boring lectures, disappointments in what I'd said to someone or how I overreacted to others. I could row over my life, remembering and savoring incandescent times: my father's eerie Holyman tales; Navajo Joe's mysterious incantations; Madre's lessons on how to bury and recover plates from the yard; my younger sister dancing and pantomiming her stories. It was during these fleeting instances that I wouldn't feel the blood blisters squishing up against the oars, the hollowness in my triceps, or the anvil that'd descended upon my chest, preventing my diaphragm from moving my lungs. I wouldn't sense any of it. I'd be liberated from everything except freedom. And then: boom! It'd be over in a flash. Pain would replace blood, replace memory, and I'd wonder if this feeling had really happened at all. How long could it've lasted? Only a moment. That's why they have a special name for it: a moment of swing.

A COUPLE OF weeks after I'd heard Myles' dissertation on the Freedom Summer, I jumped off the bus and made a beeline to Ben Veniste's café. I asked him if I could borrow a colander and a five-pound bag of sugar. He asked if I wanted them to use as a weapon, and I laughed, explaining that I wanted to use it to strengthen my wrists.

"Why in the world would you think I'd need a weapon?" I asked.

"For the confrontation up on Broadway Avenue," he said. "Where've you been?"

"On the river. What're you talking about?"

"A riot. You missed it. The cops came. It was practically a battle. They used their nightsticks on your friends Myles and Claudia, where they set up their tables. The noise was so loud, I heard it from the café. Thought there was a fire, what with all the sirens. Then I knew something else was at hand when I saw some of the cops were on horses and had shields."

From the start of the school year, Myles, Claudia and others had been using the Worthington Strip to heighten awareness of what was going on with voter registration drives in the south, with increasing troop deployments to Vietnam, and with the local racial hiring and housing discrimination in both Taos Heights and in Albuquerque. "Something for everyone," Myles had said, a remark that displayed his prescience for publicity, knowing that he needed to sweep as many people as possible into a wide net.

"It's time," Claudia said to me on one of my visits to Myles' place, holding her own court, "to get the word out on Vietnam. The domino crap. It hasn't gotten the headlines because of the Freedom Summer," she said. I detected a note of jealousy.

"Most newspapers," she noted shrilly, practicing as if she were out on the Strip, "are covering the South: Freedom Riders, sit-ins, marches, attack dogs, the murders of the three guys. That's important, for sure, but let me tell you, while we're looking within," here she meant the U.S., "the army's all of a sudden got twenty-three thousand men on the ground in Vietnam, and who's to say there won't be ten times that number within a year or two? Huh? I'm telling you. It could happen. Once these army guys smell war, they can't stop. Don't bet against it." She was in her element, oblivious to the fact that she was only talking to me. My guess was that it was a warmup, a practice run, much like I'd be doing on the river, so I couldn't criticize her for rehearsing. "And who can believe that nonsense about the attack on our ships—it's just a pretext, the second coming of the sinking of the Maine."

While Myles was in Mississippi in June struggling for equality, Claudia was in Albuquerque gearing up for battle with the *Albuquerque Tribune*, which had aligned its editorial policy to be in lockstep with whatever the Defense Department or the president said.

"The facts be damned, William Randolph Hearst-like," she said, smug in her ability to bring a newspaper analogy to a newspaper story.

"Why, you would've thought that the Rio Puerco Bridge had been attacked," she said sarcastically, reading the tributes in the paper, then proceeding to mock the report of what'd happened in the Gulf of Tonkin in early August.

"Glad I am not a boy," she added.

She'd spent the better part of the summer of 1964 picketing the induction center in Albuquerque, writing letters to the editor of the paper (that were never published), writing, editing, and printing flyers with instructions how to beat the draft and how to boycott stores that advertised in the newspaper, and swiping copies of the *Tribune* from lawns, porches, and mailboxes that had been delivered by the newsboys early every morning when she was already up working on her third cup of coffee. It was Myles' pamphlets and Claudia's flyers that became the honey that attracted all the other protest bees to the Worthington Strip.

At first, the bigwigs at UT paid little notice. The tables were orderly, the stray papers were picked up at night, the air was cordial and, while there was the occasional spark, there was nothing so combustible that it couldn't be contained easily. As the days went by, the voices became shriller. It became apparent that the realities of a war would necessitate a large increase in ground combat troops. ROTC students in uniform came in for harassment, the placement office was targeted to prevent the CIA and other government agencies from recruiting on campus, and petitions were signed to be delivered to the chancellor of UT—petitions that started to look like phone books, they contained so many names. Shop owners near the Strip complained to UT officials that the noise and general tumult was hurting business, and newspaper reporters from the *Albuquerque Tribune* came to Taos Heights, assigned to write stories denigrating the unruly students, highlighting some of color, calling out many as communists. In interviews with the paper, UT officials flicked their wrists to swat those few rabble-rousers and malcontents while characterizing the vast majority of students as a homogeneous group, one that existed only in their minds, recalling reveries from the early post-World War II years.

Then they banned anyone from setting up the tables on the Strip. The backlash was instantaneous. The crowds that gathered on the Strip grew, class attendance fell, more pamphlets were distributed, cars had to be rerouted as that section of Broadway became a pedestrian mall. Shop owners engaged in confrontations with student demonstrators, emerging red-faced with blue veins bulging out of white necks, an inspiration for a talented student artist who painted a caricature of them onto the body of Uncle Sam and pasted these posters onto the shop windows before dawn the following day. An irate shop owner confronted a group led by Myles, who extemporaneously cupped his hands around his mouth and shouted out, "We *don't* want you!" lunging forward in a mock Uncle Sam pose.

Claudia was not to be outdone. "Two, four, six, eight, shopkeepers discriminate!" she hollered, and the crowd that was conga-dancing down the sidewalk picked this up. She then alternated with, "Three, five, seven, nine, the *Tribune* sings the party line!" Two motorcycle cops who'd been drawn to the scene by the backed-up traffic on nearby streets raced their engines in neutral to get everyone's attention and told them to clear out of the street to let traffic pass. Myles had the shrewdness to realize that the cops were neither there on orders nor were looking to confront the students, as evidenced by their leaving the scene as soon as a few cars were able to pass. Within a few minutes, the shop owners had drifted back inside, and the students were back to their usual activities around the tables, both sides spent and feeling victory.

"It was over," Ben Veniste told me. "A kettle that got hot but didn't reach a boil. The rest of the morning was uneventful. Your friends at the table, pamphlets, a little proselytizing, nothing aggressive. At noon, some of the students even drifted into the stores. Lunch, magazines, that kind of thing. Then, all hell broke loose." He said that it just so happened that there was a Board of Regents meeting that morning at UT, and they were getting firsthand reports of what was going on at the Strip. "You can imagine what these guys were thinking when they heard about what was going on: communists, anarchy, riots. For them, they think about the days leading up to the fall of the Bastille."

"What do you mean by that?" I asked.

"See, Jacobo, the chancellor doesn't want to lose his job; the newspaper chief is afraid of what'll happen to advertising if stores close; the ex-congressman doesn't want a blemish on his record if he tries for the Senate, that kind of thing. For them, it has to be stopped. It can't get out of hand. They have to show overwhelming force to prevent it from happening again.

"Want some iced tea?" he asked, interrupting himself.

I took it and squeezed a lemon into it, thinking about the lemon-flavored water we'd drink in Arroyo Grande, musing about how life was so much more complicated, *difficult*, here in Taos Heights, and, I guessed, anywhere outside of our village.

He took a swig himself and started up again. "So just after lunch, I took a stroll up there when everything had calmed down. Then the cops show up. Some on horseback, can you believe it? Maybe some Wild West kind of thing. Cavalry. Who knows? Behind them are more cops with shields and nightsticks. The head honcho has a bull-horn and tells everyone they have five minutes to take down the tables and get out of the area. Five minutes, out of the blue, when everything was practically back to normal. Well, you can envision what happened. The kids were full of swagger. They went right up to the cops. They taunted them, calling them pigs, jawing at them, screaming their lungs out. I was astounded. The cops didn't move. Maybe they'd been warned about looking like the police in Mississippi, I don't know."

I was reminded of Myles' speech at this apartment.

"Anyway, when there were thirty seconds left, the guy with the bull-horn forcefully told them to get going, to take down the tables and leave. You know what they did? Nothing. No one moved. Not a one. It was really tense. At precisely five minutes, the bullhorn cop turned to face his men and gave the order to proceed. And just like that," Ben Veniste snapped his fingers, "the cops moved forward, practically touching, at least their shields. You should've seen them: helmets crouched below the tips of their shields, hands on their clubs. They meant business, I'm telling you."

I was absolutely entranced. This was a scene out of a novel, and it was hard to believe it was real. I wished I'd been there so I could've drawn it and created cells illustrated with cloud words.

He continued. "There was an uproar so loud. Screaming from the kids together with the neighing of the horses, the yelling coming through bullhorns, the whistles being blown either randomly or in some sort of signaling sequence, I'm not sure which. The metal tables and chairs were being scraped on the sidewalks. You know the sounds they make?"

"Like fingernails on a chalkboard? I asked.

"The same but worse. And the car horns, although to tell you the truth, I couldn't tell if the horns were being blown in sympathy with the cops or the kids. Anyway, there was complete chaos for about fifteen or twenty minutes. In the end, the cops plucked some of the kids and got them into a couple of paddy wagons. Then they moved out, leaving the shop owners to clean up the mess."

I didn't know what a paddy wagon was, but I got the point.

"You could sense that the kids had savored their first experience with battle."

"What about Myles? And Claudia? Were they arrested? Were either of them hurt?" I wanted to know. "Do you think it's over?"

"No, they weren't. And over? You mean the protest? Today, for sure, finished. No more cops and no more kids on the Strip trying to save the world today. But over, over? No, no, not by a long shot. My bet is that Myles and Claudia are planning act two right now."

"Do you know what they are going to do?" I asked hopefully.

He gave me a look, then turned around and mumbled what I thought might've been, "*I un siuego lo ve,*" *Even a blind man can see it.* But I wasn't sure, so I let it pass.

I bolted to Myles' apartment, where he was surrounded by lieutenants who'd tasted battle for the first time and were eager to return for a second assault, not having been wounded. The scurrying about seemed purposeful, as if assignments had been given out, and there'd be a quiz in a few minutes so they'd better be prepared. I spotted Mir, so I wended my way over to a corner of the room where she was stacking rolls of film into a box.

"Can you take these to the bookstore?" she asked and I said sure. I was aware that they processed film in a darkroom downstairs, the room where Myles would make out with girls who came in at closing time. I wondered if Mir had been one of those girls, if she'd spent time with him there. I was angry, resentful that I was being banished from the war room and sent on an errand. This was my first interaction with jealousy, and it came over me as if I had a fever. I was burning from head to toe. Was this my punishment for missing out on the events while I was miles away rowing in the bay?

"It's very important," she said, "that we get these developed quickly. Wait for them and bring them right back. We'll select the best ones and take them to the U," using the shorthand for the UT paper. "They'll use what they want and then send the others out over the wires. Hurry, go on, we've got to get this done soon." She was all business. I was out the door, running to the bookstore, feeling at least a part of the group but not dismissing the idea that Mir and Myles had been together in the darkroom.

When I came back with the developed pictures, Myles was putting the phone down. He thanked me with a slight head bob, which I reciprocated with a thumbs up but kept pivoting my head from him to Mir, searching to detect that special moment when locked eyes transmit as much intimacy as whispers.

I didn't know how much I was revealing to her. I'd never had more than a friendship with a girl. I was unmoored. It reminded me of how off-kilter I'd been when I first arrived at UT. I'd been bewildered when I was told to go get a shot by my dorm counselor. I nodded, but only to avoid embarrassment. I knew about shots from guns and that photographs were sometimes called shots. I had just learned that "being shot" was a synonym for being exhausted, and I kind of got the context when someone offhandedly said, "give it a shot." But *go get a shot*? I mulled this over for a while, not sure of which humiliation—appearing to be stupid or naïve—was the best way to proceed.

I sidled up to a senior in my dorm and asked, "Hey, can you tell me what a shot is?"

"You mean like a drink?"

"What? A drink? That doesn't sound like what the person was getting at."

"A photo, then?"

"No. I was told I need to get one, but I don't understand."

"Polio?" he inquired.

"I don't have polio," I said.

"No," he laughed, but not in a condescending way. "I wasn't thinking you were sick. Maybe you need a polio shot, to prevent you from getting it."

"I guess so," was all I could manage.

He walked me over to the infirmary and, after speaking to the receptionist, confirmed that I needed to get a polio vaccination. I thanked the senior, perhaps a bit too much, and shook his hand too long.

Culture becomes ingrained in us in parallel with learning language and understanding interpersonal relationships. It's an acclimation process that insiders take for granted, much to the detriment of the outsider, who's frequently the target of disapprobation under the assumption that he or she is somewhat dim.

I wanted to avoid that with Mir at all costs.

MYLES RELAYED THE news to the group that the Regents had officially declared the Strip off limits to students for the purpose of setting up tables, distributing literature, and holding court. Gatherings of more than ten students would require a permit, effectively shutting down their right to campaign for their causes. Myles was livid. "Whatever happened to free speech?" he snarled, tapping his index fingers rapidly on opposite sides of his head, increasingly harder, prodding his brain to do double duty: to come up with a response and to inflict some pain to counteract his anger. When he stopped, you knew he had a plan. "Tomorrow," he began, "we stay away from the Strip in the morning. Let them think they've won. Back to normal. No tables, no literature, no demonstrations, nothing. And no one talks to the U. Got that?"

Everyone did. No one was going to miss his points or go against what he was saying. He looked for confirmation expressions and, when he was satisfied, he began again.

"The Regents will talk to the *Tribune*, they'll say everything's fine, that they've broken our backs, that the outside agitators have gone away, that UT has the right to act *in loco parentis*."

Claudia took advantage of a tiny hesitation and chimed in, "These guys are going to go on and on that shop owners have the right not to have their businesses suffer, that the overwhelming majority of students are peaceful and want to go to class, that we're rabble rousers, disrupters, communists, anti-Americans. You've read all this before in the *Tribune*. It's BS."

"So Claudia," Myles called out, "who's not here?"

She scanned the room, calling out acronyms when she noted a representative, "CORE, SLATE, SNCC, SDS." She grabbed a piece of paper and a pencil and started to jot down the names of organizations and people who weren't there. She knew the price these folks were going to pay: expulsion from King Myles' court.

Myles continued, scanning the room, making eye contact with each of us, making us each feel special, connected. "At five o'clock, tomorrow, we—all of us who're here—will set the trap. Let's make sure all the groups appear on the Strip at five sharp with tables and materials. For now, store them in cars, hide them in the alley on Stratford, put them in the park. Don't let anyone see them. Don't hang around.

"Mir, do you have the pictures?" he asked, his mind racing from one detail to another with no time in-between to lose. He thumbed through the stack of photos the way a speed-reader goes through a book and seemed satisfied. "Take them to the U." He gave instructions to others, and within a minute, the apartment was empty except for Myles and me. All the assignments had been given out. There was nothing left for me to do. Other than having dropped off and picked up the pictures, I was feeling left out. Myles rummaged around in a drawer. I decided to leave quietly. As I turned the squeaky handle, he picked his head up and asked me where I was going.

"Close the door," he ordered, "I have something for you." He handed me an empty spiral-bound notebook with perforated pages that he'd found in his desk. "Here," he said, handing it to me, "I want you to record everything we do, everything we say, who says what to whom... Don't leave anything out. Put in all the names and dates and times, draw maps, sketch things, and be sure to leave room for pictures. Mir will be taking pictures. Stick with her. The two of you will get it all. I'm counting on you—on the two of you." I grasped the notebook and reached out to shake his hand. He was startled but shook it, nevertheless.

"And one more thing," he warned. "This is very important. You can't imagine what's going to happen, so you have to watch and listen closely, very closely but—and this is a critical but—you can't get involved. Do you understand? No involvement. Even if you're on the parapets with us, you're not *of* us. "*¿Entiende usted?*" he asked in Spanish. I nodded yes, that I understood. He put his arms up on my shoulders, almost a blessing. I knew not to object. "I've seen what can happen. In Mississippi, throughout the south, trying to register voters, trying to *eat*—can you imagine?—to eat at a diner when it got ugly. Police, dogs, bullwhips. For God's sake, how's that for an image refuting emancipation? Hoses and boots kicking those who've gone limp, not resisting arrest. We need someone here to get it all down, to write and draw and tell the real story so as to be able to rebut the fiction that'll come out of the *Tribune* and the Regents. We need you to stand back, to be able to put it in context so that the world will be able to comprehend this war. I know you can do this, Jacobo." I preened. He gave me final instructions and told me where I should meet Mir the next day.

I had much to do: I'd go to class in the morning, take the bus down to the boathouse to start practice midday with Herzl, then get back to the Strip before five so I could be ready when Myles gave the signal. All the while, I'd be thinking nonstop about Mir. I imagined a photo of the two of us emerging from the shallow pan in the darkroom of the bookstore, our heads side-by-side, peeking out at the new world all around us. I saw us kissing in the tank at the boathouse at night, then walking down to the river, playfully daring each other to jump off the dock into the chilly waters. I saw us observing the conflagration that was going to happen on Broadway Avenue—where I was to write and draw, she was to snap photos. Together, they would be a recording of the events that would change our lives in ways we couldn't predict.

CHAPTER 4

Open sesame!

I took the bus from the boathouse, then sprinted to my room to get the notebook. When I got near the Strip, it was quarter to five. I wandered off to the corner of Alta and Vista where I found Mir taking pictures of the mounds of pamphlets and the collapsed tables and chairs that were stacked against the sides of the buildings, partially hidden by garbage cans, scraggly old hedges, and the assorted trash typically littered around commercial driveways. She looked relieved when she saw that I was carrying the notebook.

"I've been to all of the holding stations and photographed everything I could, as well as all of the students who're going to storm the Strip at five," she said.

"Take a picture of me," I requested, posing with an idiotic smile.

"Didn't Myles tell you not to get involved?"

I nodded. She snapped one off anyway. She gave a slight hand wave and said, "See you later."

I watched her walk away. I couldn't take my eyes off of her. It wasn't just her looks. She had a way, different from so many of the others but similar, I thought, to my older sister: poised and sure of herself without being arrogant. I smiled as a thought quickly came over me: *did I have a shot?*

As she turned the corner, I started my assignment, beginning to draw a map of the area, marking the locations where everyone was getting ready. There were no crowds. People were milling about, and I wondered which ones were preparing for the protest and which others were simply walking around. I was worried for Myles and Claudia that the turnout would be modest, that their passion wouldn't translate to enough other people to make a difference. A small showing wouldn't only galvanize the opposition, it'd be a singular setback for what they were referring to as the "Movement," a word that was gaining in currency. And Myles was perceptive enough to know that the Movement needed symbols—visual and audio cues to reduce complicated issues into simple paradigms that could make a convincing case for strangers to come to his aid or to otherwise support his position.

Myles had told us that in the nineteen-twenties and thirties, John L. Lewis had had little luck in organizing mine workers by making speeches using deductive logic, winnowing down from the broadest concepts to the most specific problems facing the average mine worker. Lewis would stare out from a raised platform outside of the gates to a mine, within sight of the management goons hired to disrupt his union organizing activities. He would see the blackened faces of the exhausted men who'd spent the day—ten hours or more—underground, with pickaxe and shovel, filthy overalls and hardened deposits of coal under their fingernails, in their ears, noses, and throats. They were barely able to stand and were hungry to get home to eat a meager meal and go to sleep. Lewis' message of the benefits of the unions was lost on these undereducated men of the Appalachian and Allegheny mines, his abstractions not distinguishable from the reality of the landscape. Lewis was losing his fight.

Then, one day, after having no reaction from the crowd, no support from men who couldn't comprehend their own exploitation, Lewis did something different. He picked up a twig and held it high above his head with each hand at one end. He said nothing. He showed the stick from one end of the throng to another. Then he snapped the twig in half and threw the pieces on the ground. He uttered not a word, made no facial gesture. He bent down and picked up three twigs. He repeated the showing to all and, with some effort, snapped the three twigs, then also threw them on the ground. Finally, he grabbed ten twigs. He wrapped his hands around the bunch at both ends and, with all his might he tried again to break them, his face in contortions, cheeks red, eyes nearly shut, and with his torso rocking back and forth. He couldn't break the twigs. He tried again and failed. Then he lifted the twigs high above his head and with a deep, resonant voice, shouted out one two-syllable word that made the connection: *union*! And the men erupted into a chant: union! union! union! stomping from one foot to the other, like a racecar driver revving the engine in neutral, just waiting for the green light so he could hit the accelerator.

Myles needed a Lewis-type symbol for the Movement much as Dr. King had taken advantage of photos of Bull Connor in Birmingham, Alabama, with police dogs and fire hoses; much as northern liberals had responded to the pictures of the gravesites of Chaney, Schwerner, and Goodman; much as William Randolph Hearst had needed the headlines about the sinking of the *Maine*; much as Lyndon Johnson had needed the Gulf of Tonkin incident, which Claudia had noted with a sneer.

Mir had told me where the other holding sites were, and as I started to head toward them, I realized that it'd be better for me to get the whole lay of the land. With students hunkered down in alleys and back lots at more than a dozen places, I hoisted myself up on a trash can and grabbed the pull-down fire escape on a building that overlooked the Strip. It was rusty. A few of the steps were bolted onto only one rail, and it swayed from side to side as I ascended. I scrambled over a four-foot wall at the edge of the roof, which enabled me to hunch down and get close to the edge without anyone on the ground noticing. I could see for several blocks down Vista and Broadway where the gatherings were turning into crowds. I sketched the area, noting the date and time and the estimates of how many people were at each location that I could see. On the streets and specifically on the Strip, there was nothing unusual. No police, campus or city, were around. It was a beautiful day. Pizza smells emanated from a vent on the other side of the roof. I looked at my watch. It was a minute to five. In the alleys, tables were now hoisted on backs, boxes of materials were gathered in arms. It was quiet. Heads peered down at watches.

At five on the dot, everyone moved at once. As they walked down the street, they were joined by others who appeared as if by magic from doorways, cars, and on bicycles. Within a few minutes, dozens of tables had been set up, boxes of materials had been unloaded, and a crowd of about a hundred were hawking their free wares to those who came to protest. The energy was palpable even up on the roof. More than a few of the students were gesticulating in a manner like a drummer, pounding the air with a snare, kicking the bass like a dance step, yelling out some orchestrated speech. Occasionally, when the wind was favorable, I could hear either a practiced or an extemporaneous rant—I couldn't tell which—competing with others in an attempt to attract passersby to a particular cause. As the noise picked up, it seemed to invite more students, store patrons, and owners, as well as the curious. By five fifteen, there were more than five hundred, if my calculations were correct. People streamed in from the campus, past Kettys-Burg Hall, where the president, provost, and deans had their offices, named after two early benefactors: C. Wainwright Kettys and Hopkinton

Burg. No matter that C. Wainright's family name was pronounced Kett-*iss*, the four-story limestone building was invariably referred to as Kett-*ease*-burg.

Something caught my eye. Glistening in the late afternoon sun were a couple of flickering lights to the north. There were some men on the roof of Kettys-Burg Hall. As they moved around, a flash reflected off metal. I held my hands on both sides of my head to deflect light and squinted through this makeshift tunnel. There were three men, two of whom were in uniform. Police. One cop was setting up a tripod, and the other had a large camera; the sun ricocheted off this equipment. I made a note and drew a picture of the building with the figures and the camera. The third man was older, wearing a suit. I was pretty sure that they didn't see me.

By half past five, you could hardly see a spot where there weren't people jammed together. Girls were hoisted on boys' shoulders, looking like totem poles set to joust. Banners appeared, sprung from pockets and newsboy bags, homemade signs in bright colors, as people gravitated to where they indicated like-minded individuals would assemble. While there was defiance, the gathering seemed festive. A few came in costume, on unicycles, juggling balls and slicing through the crowd. I made a quick sketch of the jugglers. I looked for Myles and Claudia and Mir to no avail. The three men on the roof across the street were still there, pointing and taking pictures.

I was feeling left out and was tempted to go down to the street when I noticed some figures on the roof of the building directly across from me, over some stores that faced the pizza parlor. There were men in uniform, crouched down behind those taller parts of the wall that made the roof line look like a medieval castle from the street. All had clubs, handcuffs, and guns attached to their belts. My first instinct was to stand up and wave to the crowd in the street, but no one would've noticed me, no one except the police across the street or the three men on the roof at Kettys-Burg Hall. Within a minute, I could see cops creeping along many of the other rooftops, and when I ran to the back side of my roof, I could see them congregating far down on both sides of Broadway on Vista. My head started to pound. I could hear my heart from the inside of my ear drums. I started to sweat and found myself unconsciously wiping my brow every few seconds in order to prevent any drops from falling on my notebook, in which I was furiously jotting down my observations and making sketches.

I was all set to move down and make my way back to my first vantage point overlooking the Strip when I noticed several of the policemen on Vista, disrobing. They put their police shirts and pants in a pile and put on chinos and T-shirts, then broke away from their comrades and made their way around the block to where the mass of students now numbered in the thousands. I watched as the disguised cops slipped into the crowd and picked up the particular beat of those in proximity, just more folks who'd joined the protest. And that's what it had now become, a protest, more than a rally. The noise became uglier, something that startled me in a way that prompted me to close my eyes to determine if what I was seeing was influencing what I was hearing. There was organized chanting and serendipitous raving, mouths twisted into contortions, and pieces of paper from the pamphlets and the single sheets torn into shards and flung into the air and at the ground, contemptuously, defiantly, provocatively.

All of a sudden, one guy leaped on the trunk of a parked car and, without hesitation moved to its roof, seemingly unaware of the precariousness of his position. He had a megaphone, battery-powered I could tell, because I could hear the voice above the roar of the crowd. He knew not to try to get their attention by asking them to quiet down; that would've been a hopeless cause. He started to speak, said a few words, then the car honked. This happened again. And again. Word, word, horn, horn, word, word, horn, horn. Repeated and repeated. The jumble of the crowd seemed to inch closer as if the bullhorn were a kind of magnet attracting the steel resolve of the initiated, leaving the slag of the onlookers and the fence-sitters out on the periphery.

I tried to see where in the crowd the cops were who'd exchanged their uniforms to blend in, but at this point, they were indistinguishable from the anyone else. Abruptly, the wind shifted, and I could now hear the two words, *free speech*, that were being repeated, separated by the double beats of the car horn, a kind of punctuation that didn't have the frivolity of an exclamation point but wasn't as declarative as a period. Peering over the wall, perhaps a hundred and fifty feet on the horizontal from the honking, it sounded like an audio semaphore, and it seemed to have the same effect on the crowd that the buglers' notes had on the soldiers when they heard the music of chaaaaaarge. *Free speech*, they chanted, the sounds ricocheting off the walls of the buildings a split second after the fact, the way we'd anticipate the splash a moment after we'd watch the stones we'd hurl into the ponds that had formed in the spring after the rains pummeled Arroyo Grande.

My head hung over the edge, and I caught a glimpse of a guy near the edge of the crowd. He was wearing chinos and a blue shirt, indistinguishable from many in the crowd. He was striding through the throng, purposefully keeping himself erect, not giving way to anyone. He clipped shoulders and backs, cutting a straight line, oblivious to bodies in his path and giving equal inconsideration to men and women, old and young. This was antagonism, confrontation, premeditation, and fascination. He'd filed his flight plan and was determined to stay on course. Bodies were bumped, thrown off stride, knocked to the ground. The people in his wake were universally pointing to his back from their positions on the ground or on one knee, but with the commotion of the rally, no one ahead of him had any warning of what was coming. A middle-aged woman who'd been knocked down had attracted the attention of a kid on a unicycle who pumped furiously in the direction of the walker, pedaled in front of him, leaned toward the center of the moving circle, centrifugal force keeping him in orbit until the walker made a sudden move and knocked him off the seat with a rapid chop of the back of his hand. Enraged, the unicyclist grabbed the big wheel and flung it at the walker, clipping him high on the back but missing his head. With the impact of the wheel, the walker spun around and attacked the cyclist. He was soon joined by others in chinos and colored shirts who materialized out of the crowd as if on cue. One of them looked like a policeman I'd seen changing out of his uniform far down the street on Vista. Aha! There it was: a setup, a provocation, a "Remember the *Maine*," a Gulf of Tonkin ruse Claudia would say to the press afterward. A dirty cheap trick to me, fifty yards away and powerless to intervene, to stop it, to warn others, to tell them what was going on. I grabbed my notebook and set the stage, drawing the path of the walker, the bodies rudely shoved out of the way, the unicyclist, the flying wheel, the confrontation, the emergence from the crowd of the other plain-clothed cops.

I saw blue hats on the roof opposite, bobbing as the cops crouch-walked toward the fire escape. I focused on the three men on the roof of Kettys-Burg Hall, furiously taking pictures. It was about to get ugly. My instinct was to get to the street and start to warn the crowd about the cops. But then what? I'd turn up on the street at the same time as a hundred cops with guns. Standing on the roof and waving wouldn't do any good; no one down on the street was looking up in my direction. The only people who'd notice me would be the cops on the roof at Kettys-Burg Hall.

I took out my copper-encased mirror, the one my father had given to me as a present. I held it in the palm of my hand; as I opened it, the sun glanced off the mirror and stabbed my eyes, causing me to squint and turn my head rapidly to the side. Absentmindedly, I played with it, aiming the reflected rays down on the sidewalk below: on the collapsed unicycle, on the mêlée with the incognito cops trying to corral a group of a dozen or more protesters, and finally on the three people on the roof of Kettys-Burg Hall, primarily just to see if the beam would travel that far. If it did, I imagined that I could hear their conversations, which would be carried back to me on the invisible light wave, giving me magical powers like the ones possessed by the Holyman. My aim had to be precise, and my first few tries had the light bouncing irrelevantly off the yellow-lit cornice or the orange roof. Finally, I caught the glasses of one of the policemen on the roof of Kettys-Burg Hall. He flinched, looked around, and reset his head behind the camera. I kept the beam on his face, enjoying his annoyance, getting pleasure out of seeing him swat at an invisible intolerance, upsetting the rhythm of the process the trio was undertaking on the roof. Perhaps this aggravation would preclude him from getting the one picture that he'd need to submit his evidence. Somehow, I had to participate in the act without, of course, violating Myles' strict admonition to remain part of the audience and not get involved in the drama. I had to warn the guy on top of the car with the megaphone that the cops were descending from the roof across the street, that other cops were filming everyone, and that undercover cops were disrupting the rally in the hopes of generating an out-of-control backlash—a reason, naturally, for the cops to restore order. I angled the mirror to blaze into the eyes of the guy standing on the car, not an easy feat, as he was jiving excitedly to the pulsating beat of the noise from the crowd.

He swept the megaphone across a hundred and eighty-degree arc, scooping up passion and sending it back through the same device, not as a diatribe but as a brief, an indictment against a policy wall that had to be reduced to rubble. The crowd had settled down, except for the fringe where the altercation with the unicycle was taking place, eager to listen to the articulation of their grievances. It was easier now to pick up some of the words, depending on the orientation of the megaphone and the direction of the wind, which, too, had seemed to calm, as if it knew to lower the anxiety of the frenzied students in the crowd.

The guy on top of the car held up a pamphlet in his right hand and spoke through the megaphone at a slow pace, alternating his gaze from the pamphlet to the crowd. He began to read. "Congress shall make no law respecting an establishment of religion, or prohibiting the free exercise thereof; or abridging the freedom of speech, or of the press; or the right of the people peaceably to assemble, and to petition the government for a redress of grievances. *Free speech*," he shouted, shaking the pamphlet vigorously. "The right to assemble peacefully," he continued in a defiant pose and made a sweeping gesture with his arms, palms down, as if he were blessing the whole assemblage. "The right to petition for a redress of grievances," he declared, emphasizing the word grievances.

The crowd went wild and picked up the chorus of *free speech, free speech, free speech*. I signaled my approval and applause by manipulating the mirror to flutter the light to his face. The guy on top of the car turned, instantly, toward the light, holding the pamphlet over his forehead as a visor, and that's when I realized that it was Myles standing on top of the car, leading the crowd! I should've known. I stood up and gesticulated wildly, pointing to the three men on the roof of Kettys-Burg Hall across the street. At first, Myles just stared at me waving wildly to him, but after a moment, he picked up on the repetitive jabbing with my fingers toward the building across the way. He turned to look at Kettys-Burg Hall, peering under the pamphlet to see the three men on the roof. With that, the convergence of three events took place: Myles' loudspeaker bristled with the newsflash that the cops were on the roof of Kettys-Burg Hall filming the rally; the altercation with the unicycle unleashed the fury of the crowd on the undercover cops who were clubbing people indiscriminately; and the police in uniform emerged from fire escapes and stairs down to the street and began to march, shields in front, nightsticks up, toward the thousands at the rally. Myles leapt off the car and began to run straight through the crowd toward Kettys-Burg Hall. A seam opened in front and closed as he approached the building and then ascended the steps. I watched the folks who'd come to the aid of the unicyclist become surrounded by uniformed cops, nightsticks raining down on their backs and steel-tipped boots kicking men and women, boys and girls, whomever was in or near the fray. Other cops began to form a cordon around the entrance to Kettys-Burg Hall. I could make out Claudia pointing excitedly to people she knew in the crowd, who hurriedly scrambled up the steps then disappeared through the doors before the cop barrier had completely circled the building. There must've been seventy-five or so culled from the crowd this way. Although I recognized a few of the boys from the times we listened to Myles in his apartment, I didn't see any of the girls he'd walk home from the bookstore after closing hours.

I ran to the edge of the roof, reached for the fire escape rail, and took two steps at a time on the way down, more concerned that my forward momentum could send me careening over the landing than aware of the jouncing and the sway of the rickety old structure. The protesting sounds it made was all the less noticeable because the squeaking and groaning that I'd experienced on the way up was masked up by the noise from the riot on the street. I made it halfway down, past the turn when it suddenly gave way, man and metal in free fall, the mortar blown out of the wall where bolts lost their footings, flinging slivers of brick in all directions. It could only have been a few seconds before I hit the ground and a few seconds more that I lay there, patting myself with both arms, starting with my chest and working the way to my feet, instinctively doing a first-pass triage to feel for pain. My head throbbed. Specks of mortar and brick swirled around me. My left foot was caught underneath a step. It was positioned in such a way that I couldn't free it. Wriggling didn't help. I leaned on an elbow and tried to twist my leg, but it was impossible to move. I started to panic. I was panting. A lot. I put a palm on each side of my head as if to keep it from splitting apart. I started to spread the debris around me, looking for my notebook. Nothing. Such a failure.

"You're a damn lucky guy," I heard someone say as he put his hand on a large chunk of rail that had plunged straight down into the macadam of the alley just a yard or so away. I hadn't noticed it previously, but looking at it then, I started to dry heave.

He bent down and placed his hands on both steps, then, with a wince, was able to move them just enough so that I could squirt my leg out.

I managed to respond in short bursts between exhales. "Thank you...can't believe...just gave way...like that...was half way down."

He smiled and made the boxer's stance, moving his bulging biceps up and down, which got me to emit a small laugh. Then he offered me his hand. He had to use both to get me upright. I was probably a good six inches taller than he was but likely the same weight. His blond hair was cut short behind a front row that stood straight up from the application of stick'um, which was so different from the way our hair fell down over our foreheads.

"You okay? I'm telling you, I saw it, thought you were done for. I don't see any blood. Can you stand by yourself?"

"My notebook," I said woozily.

"What? Hey buddy, you all right? Upstairs?"

I turned my head in the direction of the fire escape, dangling from the top-most bolt that was the only thing keeping it from completely disengaging from the building.

"I, I lost my notebook, I've got to get it. Myles. Will kill me."

"Well, you're not gonna die from whoever Myles is, but you've got quite a welt on your forehead."

I touched it gently. The pain was excruciating. I ran my fingers through my hair and beard, then held my palms up close to my eyes to see if there was blood. Just a couple of scratches on my right hand from where it scraped against some gravel.

"You've gotta get some ice on it," he said. Come on. Let's go."

I was woozy. And nauseous. Slowly, he guided me across the street to a luncheonette. It was empty. Which was good because the thought of food made me want to puke.

"Sit. Over here. There's ice."

I sat on a stool as he leaned over the counter, grabbed a handful of shavings from a bucket, wrapped them in a dish towel, and held the makeshift bandage to my forehead.

"Are you gonna throw up?"

"I don't think so," I said, lowering my head to the table and placing my arm underneath as a pillow, thinking I actually might.

"Okay then. Stay here for a while. Don't move. Keep this on. Pressure. Don't get up too fast. If you have to, find a place to lie down. When you feel better, go get checked out. I've gotta go."

Keeping a grip on the dishtowel with one hand, I gave him a thumb's up with the other. It was only then that I noticed the guy's chinos and blue T-shirt.

After a few minutes, when the saliva stopped filling my mouth, I lifted my head slowly, spit into the sink repeatedly, then grabbed a glass, scooped some ice, and stuffed some into my mouth. It felt good. On my second try, I managed to stand upright for more than a few seconds. My clothes were filthy. Mortar and brick dust. With one hand, I brushed off as much as I could, which didn't have a big effect. In the mirror behind the counter, I could see the red welt that made me look like a cyclops. I put the dishtowel on the counter, filled it with fresh ice, then wrapped and tied it like a bandana around my forehead, the pressure and cold having a positive effect.

When I walked tentatively out of the luncheonette and saw the fallen fire escape, I panicked again. I crossed the street slowly. I was afraid to go under any part of the fire escape. Tentatively, I used one foot, then the other, to sweep away dust and bricks, scanning the area for my notebook, castigating myself for being such a loser. I alternatively cursed my feebleness and urged myself not to give up. It had to be here. When I saw a bit of spiral sticking up, I was ecstatic but bent down too quickly to retrieve it and had to sit on my knees to regain my strength and composure.

It was an effort regain my strength and composure as well as to retrieve the notebook. Finally, I began to walk hesitatingly, toward Kettys-Burg Hall, where I could see thousands of students milling on the outside of a police ring around the building. I took my time getting there. As I approached the crowd, I was astounded to be greeted by Mir, who launched into a cross examination to make sure I'd witnessed and written down everything I'd seen from my vantage point on the roof. While she was thumbing through my notebook, she talked so fast I could hardly understand her, what with her accent and her moving quickly down the street. She was almost running, the way wild turkeys do, in between the waddle and the flight. It was hard to keep up.

"I've been taking photos, been into and around the crowd," she said excitedly. "Did you see the undercover cops running down people and beating up the guy on the unicycle?"

"I did," I said wearily.

Her cameras bounced against her back, tethered by the straps around her neck, and her hair flew out in disarray behind her, a comic book frame of whirlwind motion. She was headed somewhere, and I followed, slowly regaining some strength and responding to questions that were designed to fill her up with enough information so that she could spread out a frosting upon the cake of the pictures that she took.

I followed her lead to the bookstore. She burst through the door, sweeping aside the black curtains that hid the enclosure where the door led to the darkroom. An intermittent glow from a flashlight on low battery was enough for her to remove the film, set up the equipment, pour the chemicals into the trays and gently move the paper through a series of pans with tweezers. There was no sound in the room except for her hands splashing in the liquids, determined to finish quickly; she was on a mission. She was so absorbed she didn't notice me staring at her, watching what appeared to be a bas-relief of her against the blackened, shadowed wall—an image that would sustain me in dark hours in the future. She moved precisely, with confidence, occasionally interrupting herself with comments meant for no one in particular. She took a series of photos out of the last bath with the tweezers and hung them on a wire with clips protruding every eighteen inches or so. She was impatient, stomping around and ducking underneath the pictures murmuring, "Come on, come on …," gently blowing on the photo, checking her watch, running her fingers through her hair, encouraging the pictures to develop faster. As images began to emerge, she began to pull them from the clips. When she was satisfied that she had enough, she ran out, all but forgetting that I was with her, leaving a few partially developed pictures swinging from the breeze of our exit. I'd assumed that she was going to make a beeline for Myles' apartment, but instead she headed toward Ben Veniste's café. Before I could embarrass myself by telling her I wasn't hungry or even feeling too well, she said that Myles' apartment might be under surveillance and that she'd use the pay phone at the café to speak with the student reporter at the paper.

As was the case when she spotted me in the crowd, she gave no salutation or introduction when the receiver was picked up at the other end. The outpouring came fast, her descriptions of the events so accurate, her remembrances of my jottings so precise that it seemed superfluous when she hung up and said she had to deliver the pictures, pronto. For the first time, she looked at me squarely in the eyes, then jerked her head back as if she'd received a punch.

"You look funny. Not haha funny. You okay? Your clothes are filthy. And what's with the bandana?" With this, she reached up and, in one motion, pulled it off. I winced.

"Oh my God," she said when she saw the welt. "What did they do to you? How could they beat an innocent bystander? Those bastards with their billy clubs."

"I'm okay," I said. "Really. It probably looks worse than it feels. The ice helps. And the pressure."

"I'm so, so sorry, I thought it must've been some Mexican thing, you know."

She went into the kitchen and came back with a soap-filled paper towel to daub my forehead gently, then made a new cloth napkin bandana filled with ice that she promptly tied, asking me, "Is it too tight? Too loose? Are you sure?" as she adjusted it with my responses. I sat on a chair as she walked around me, brushing more dust off my clothes and, I suspected, making sure there were no more apparent injuries.

When she finished, she pushed up on her toes, touched my shoulder, and leaned her lips against my cheek. Yes, it was a goodbye peck and a thank you, but I reinvented it as an invitation, one that I needed to RSVP to although not at that very moment. I realized that I needed to acquire the alphabet of intimacy which can't be learned from a book. She waved to me and Ben Veniste.

He got a glass of cold water and handed it to me along with two aspirins. He looked at me the way my father would and said, "Two things to say. One, don't be a hero. If the pain becomes unbearable, you've got to get yourself to the infirmary. Got that?"

I nodded.

"And two, forget about revenge. You'll never find the cop who attacked you. There are other ways to win."

If only he knew, I thought to myself.

He asked me to fill him in on the riot, and when I got to the part about Myles getting into Kettys-Burg Hall, he put his hand on my arm. "Come with me," he said abruptly and a bit alarmingly. "We've got to go."

"Where? Where to? What are you going to do? Where are we going?" I asked and slipped the notebook down my back, tightened my belt and covered it by blousing my shirt loosely over my jeans.

We left the restaurant, walking slowly away from the action. We could've been a father and son out for a stroll on a beautiful fall afternoon. We traipsed north on El Camino then turned east, headed straight for the tower which housed the bells that rang out over the campus every fifteen minutes. We were at a point that if we looked straight ahead, we'd head directly for the tower, but if we turned right, we'd pass over Blueberry Creek via the campus gate and end up not too far from Kettys-Burg Hall. We could hear the uproar that was fast becoming a conflict.

"You okay?" he asked.

"Better, thanks," I said.

"All right then. Listen. Your Myles is not going to let the cops on the roof go free, uh-uh. They are his bargaining chips to get the police surrounding the building to back off," he said. "The longer they're up there, the more tension there's going to be. Your pals will make their demands more stridently, leaving no room for compromise. Mark my words. This is going to create a dilemma for the cops on the outside, who'll be pressured to take some action, to restore order. You can bet on it. For all we know, while we've been walking, the big honchos who work in Kettys-Burg—the president and the deans—have been detained as well. If that's the case, watch out. You're going to see fireworks, that's for sure. Stress leads to explosions. And you know what happens then?" he asked. He didn't wait for an answer from me. "The hardliners seize control. Compromisers get branded as weak. Wait, you'll see. It's an old story."

He said this with resignation, and yet there seemed to be a purpose for him telling me this, for wanting me to accompany him on this tour, which was distracting to me, for I wanted to be with the crowd a couple of blocks away. Yet I stayed with him, out of deference and respect, although truth be told, I'm not sure I was hiding my feelings well. We turned right and started to approach a red brick walkway that led to the campus gate. Ben Veniste guided me a little bit east, where the lush colors of the andromedas and the giant rhododendrons lined the slopes that descended the banks to the culvert that was once Blueberry Creek and now carried an occasional spring runoff down from the hills to the east. It was quite a chore for him to lead me down to the bottom of the embankment. He'd move his cane further out front and pivot his left leg in a semi-circular motion, then bring his right up to meet the left. He'd established a routine that took a lot of energy and concentration. We got to a spot where the spruce trees were packed so tightly that no one could see us, though we were only ten or so feet below the level of the walkway. Impatience was about to take root: what were we doing here, and why was this so important to show me at this precise time? I took a deep breath to calm myself. We could hear the tramping of sneakers, flip-flops, wing tips, and the scraping of moccasins and loafers making their way through the gate above to join the crowd that was leaving me literally stuck in the mud. Ben Veniste looked me squarely in the eye and then said softly, "Follow me, and be as quiet as possible," moving his index finger perpendicular to his mouth. We were in the deepest part of the depression, right under the gate. Follow him, sure, but where? There was no place to go. He wended his way around a clump of trees, dropped down into a crouch, reached through what appeared to be a knothole in a wide tree and gently, quietly and firmly tugged at the wood with his hand inside the hole. It moved as if on a hinge, not just the one strip of wood but its neighbors as well. It was a door, disguised as a tuft of trees, probably made out of the debris of a long-downed spruce. It wasn't full height, as could be seen when he bent down and stepped through, motioning me to follow.

As I entered, I inhaled a mushroom waft, dank and cool yet not unappealing. Once inside, there was plenty of room to stand up. It was cavernous, perhaps two dozen feet wide. He withdrew a flashlight from his pocket. Down the middle was a row of upright railroad ties, every ten feet or so. All along one side were earthen beds bordered by ancient railroad ties, stuffed with mushrooms. I kneeled down, snapped a mushroom from its root, rubbed the excess dirt off and bit into it, gently, tepidly, savoring its subterranean flavor. On the side of the mushroom beds were the tools of the trade—spades, hoes, tunnel compost, and satchels. He explained that he would come here very early in the morning with his Mexican kitchen helpers and tend his underground garden, leaving just before light, the satchel filled with what he'd serve that day. I wondered how much pain he had to endure to accomplish this daily task.

"How'd you find this place? When did you start? Does anyone know about this?" I inquired, for a moment forgetting what was going on above us.

"When they built the trolley tracks, the ones that used to run on Broadway up from Oak Land, they dug a trench on the eastern side. It was done to facilitate the horses," he replied authoritatively. "Originally, this was a horsecar line, a single horse would pull the tram one way."

I wondered if this was going to be a lecture with a follow-up quiz.

"That's where they'd switch horses and bring the one that'd just pulled the load down a gentle embankment, near where we went through the door, into the trench, where there was water, a blacksmith, and a barn with some hay where the horses could be groomed. They needed a place to cart off the manure. You could imagine the amount from a day of hauling from thirty or so horses. So they made the trench wide; it's more than twenty-five feet in most places, and it goes on for about 250 feet or so."

That was why I couldn't see to the far end.

"Then they decided to switch to electric trolleys."

"That was probably pretty popular. I mean, no more manure—up there," I pointed. "So how'd they end up with this place?"

"They debated what to do with the trench. Some wanted it left open, as it could be a safety valve for any overflow from Blueberry Creek, but the plans were already underway to fill in the creek and to divert it through another part of Taos Heights. There were proposals for an elevated walkway with a storage area underneath. They couldn't agree on anything. Welcome to city government."

"So how did it become your mushroom garden?"

"They laid the ties horizontally over these upright ones down the middle of the trench. Up top, they dumped tons of dirt that came from the excavations of the new houses that were going up in the hills. So, today, all you see is grass. Lawn. No one knows that there's a universe down here. I heard the story from an old timer and, honestly, I wasn't sure I believed him, but anyway, I came down here one night and had an inspiration."

"Pretty cool," I said politely, trying not to appear antsy. I mean, was there a purpose to this jaunt? Especially at this time?

We walked the entire length of the tunnel with Ben Veniste using his cane in the manner of a blind person crossing a street, sweeping it in front of him in a wide arc. At the far end, there was a wall of railroad ties. I turned around and started to walk back. I'd found this a diversion of sorts that I would've been more attentive to on another occasion, as he could hold my sway in the manner of my father. I asked him what time it was. Six thirty, he said, fully forty-five minutes since I'd fallen down from the fire escape. I wanted to be polite to Ben Veniste, but I had to get back to see what was happening. Had the confrontation turned ugly, bloody as he had predicted? Had he kidnapped me to preserve my virginity from the events that were unfolding above?

"Wait, Jacobo," he said. "Come back here." He was standing next to the railroad tie wall, one hand leaning against it. "When they finished putting the railroad tie roof over the trench," he went on, watching me squirm as I wasn't in the mood for a continuance of his history lesson, "they went to shore up this far end where the wall was sloped and loosely packed."

I found myself rapidly muttering, "uh-huh, yeah, oh, okay" in the vain hope that this would jumpstart his story and bring it rapidly to conclusion.

"In order to make sure that the dirt wouldn't cascade down upon the railroad ties, breaching the integrity of the supports, they used pickaxes to remove the rocks and debris from the slope."

"Uh-huh, yeah, oh, okay, I see, got it, yeah."

"Now here's the thing: when they did that, one guy's axe blade broke a large rock, and when it tumbled down, it exposed a foundation." Was this a cue that a dissertation was coming on nineteenth century building materials? I had to keep my exasperation in check. I hesitated for just a second, then saw his fist disappear into a depression within one of the railroad ties. I saw his hand tighten, and he grimaced as he pulled on what turned out to be a handle tucked away in the railroad tie that allowed a door to swing gracefully on an iron hinge, revealing an opening through an ancient mound of building rubble.

"Open sesame!" he exclaimed triumphantly and strode through the arch with the self-satisfaction of a man who didn't have to look back to know I'd be following him immediately and that he didn't have to explain a thing to me. I knew instantaneously that we'd just secreted ourselves into the basement of Kettys-Burg Hall.

CHAPTER 5

The calorie-less food

of euphoria

We proceeded slowly, fingering the walls, feeling moisture, splinters, and cobwebs. It was crypt-like, with a decayed rodent aroma and eerily quiet in contrast to what must've been going on above. Ben Veniste's flashlight was on its last legs. We could still make out the dimensions of the room, probably ten by fifteen feet. There were no human footprints in the layer of dust except for the path that we made hugging the wall to the other side. My expression signaled that there didn't seem to be a door; he once again put his index finger to his lips then gently leaned his shoulder against a section of the wall on the opposite side and pushed with his hands. He asked me to assist. Slowly, quietly, a heavy metal pocket door started to slide. When it had opened a couple of feet, he turned sideways and motioned for me to shuffle through. I followed his order. "This is as far as I go," he whispered. "A storage room, old, probably been out of use for years, but there's another pocket door over there. Never opened it."

I was on my own.

"Thank you," I said as I extended my hand, an apology for the impatience that I hoped he hadn't noticed.

"Jacobo, I just want to tell you that when you open that door," he pointed to the far side of the room, "you'll be crossing a threshold that's more than a physical demarcation. Do you know what I'm saying?"

"I think so."

"Sometimes we're faced with a decision as to whether or not to cross a line, you know, to get into an area—that doesn't have to be physical, by the way—and we're not prepared for the consequences. In most cases, to be honest, we've rarely thought about this beforehand; we just take things in stride. That can be okay. I'm not saying it's good or bad. Just that you don't know how it's going to turn out, that's all."

"And this is one of these cases?"

"It is. I know you're pumped up about what's going on with the demonstrations, but just understand that you could be caught up in something that's going to drown you when you don't even know you're in the water, let alone struggling. So be careful."

"I will," I said, interpreting that as watching out for physical danger.

"Just keep your eyes and ears open, and know that sometimes the king does something that his subjects don't fully appreciate until it's too late. Okay?"

"Okay, thanks. Really. I'll keep my eyes and ears open. I just," here I paused and nodded to the door on the other side of the room, "can't thank you enough."

He gave me the okay hand gesture and disappeared back through the opening. I heard the door make a soft, dull thud against the jam. The pocket door was virtually invisible, just a metal slab in a section of a room filled with old gray metal file cabinets, roll-top desks, wooden chairs with right arms, wastepaper baskets stacked inside one another, an ancient carpenter's tool kit, cardboard boxes stuffed to the gills with used erasers, pencil sharpeners like organ grinders, broken rulers, and color-coded canvas maps of the world.

Wary of making noise, I made sure I didn't trip over anything and found the door on the opposite wall. It slid open easily. I peeked out through a slit as I opened it a bit. A linoleum floor led to a staircase covered by a carpet that looked like it'd been stitched together out of welcome mats. It was thick, dirty, and well-worn. As I took the steps two or three at a time, I could hear muffled rumblings ahead of me. The staircase joined to a landing with a door. I could hear voices on the other side. Rather than a conversation, it was a symphony without a maestro orchestrating the individual voices into a unit of sound. I opened the door enough to slither through and stepped into the hall. I quickly shut the door and blended in seamlessly, no one having noticed that I'd sprung from this part of the basement. The doors were closed at the entrance to the building from the street, guarded on the inside by a few guys who were making sure that the police couldn't get in. I could see out the tall windows where the cops were wearing helmets and had their nightsticks out, thrashing at kids trying to get in. As I made my way down the hall, there were similar confrontations at every first-floor window. When I got to the top of the landing on the second floor, I felt a breeze and saw an open window where a couple of guys were coming through.

I made my way up to the president's office on the third floor, where Myles was sitting on the desk, his feet dangling off the edge, speaking rapidly into the phone. Claudia was at the window, a human surveyor, pointing out to anyone who'd listen what was happening outside, naming names, yelling instructions, admonishing the cops. Her tone could change from advisory "...go limp, don't give them an excuse to beat you..." to threatening "...I'm watching you, Officer Tall with the tattoo on your right arm..."

I slipped my hand down the back of my pants and withdrew the notebook, grabbed a pencil off the desk, and began to add to the diary of the day, drawing a map of the route: from the rooftop overlooking the demonstration, to the photo lab at the bookstore, to the café, to the walk with Ben Veniste toward the gate, to the tunnel that housed the mushrooms, to the basement and the storage room of Kettys-Burg, to the mob scenes in the building and outside, up to the third floor where Myles was now standing over me waiting for me to look up. I'd finished the drawing but hadn't yet had a chance to start writing when I sensed his body less than a foot from my face. My first thought was to apologize for being there. After all, he'd instructed me to not get involved, but his body language wasn't confrontational.

"No time for dress up, Cochise," he said.

I lifted up the bandana.

"God bless it, Jacobo. You weren't supposed to get involved. That was the deal. Observe, write, draw. If you stay out of it, they can't get their hands on the notebook. Do you understand? Let me see it."

I handed it to him, then pulled the bandana down to cover up the bruise. He began to read.

"This is good. Just what's needed. Now take *this* down too," he said, sweeping his hands around to take in what I assumed to be everything going on in the building. "All of it. The words, the music, the pictures." He put his free hand on my shoulder. "I mean it. Don't let them get it, you understand?" I did. Who knew that the consequences of that simple exchange would be so profound?

I didn't ask him what he was planning to do or even about the status of the cops on the roof. I didn't ask him what he'd do if the cops outside stormed the building or what his negotiating points to solve the crisis were. After all, he was the leader. He was the one who'd been on the buses and the marches. He'd faced down hoses and the taunts from crowds. He'd goaded the community to publicly express its outrage, and he'd made the decision to invade Kettys-Burg Hall. The continued presence of his palm on my shoulder conveyed a trust that was rich in symbolism for the others in the room—others who had by now turned to observe our dance.

I was flushed with pride at having been included and welcomed. I was amazed at the spirit and determination of those who wanted to affect change. It was all so admirable. By the same token, I was troubled, for as much as I saw the good in so many of my fellow students, I'd also witnessed the anger, physicality, and, well, hatred, from the police and the counter-demonstrators: clenched teeth and fists, venom from the deepest part of their bodies, contempt for those with an opposing view. It was as if there were a finite amount of righteousness, and each side wanted to deny the other any part of it, otherwise it would reduce the amount each side felt it was owed. I found this difficult to accept. I looked upon the world with envy as to the material things and general health that most people enjoyed, yet it seemed to me that those things were taken for granted, like sufficient oxygen to breathe and clean water to drink. Freedom is a wonderful state of affairs, for sure. I wondered: doesn't it come with responsibilities to respect and protect the rights of others?

Myles called out to Claudia, "Pow-wow time," and within a minute, a group whose members I recognized from Myles' apartment materialized in the room. Everyone else left the president's office. I stayed, unobtrusively in the corner, pencil in hand, notebook at the ready. All told, there were eleven of them.

"All right everyone. Take a deep breath. We're all safe here. Especially since we've got a *hero* in our midst," he said, in a tone that was strangely equally sarcastic and salutary, jerking his head in my direction and pointing to his own forehead. Everyone looked at me for a moment. I gave a sheepish smile, then dropped my eyes to the notebook.

"The three cops are still on the roof. The door from the fourth floor's been blockaded. There's no way they can get down," Claudia said.

"Ropes," someone asked, "What if the cops surrounding the building have ropes?"

"Impractical," another remarked. "You're not going to get guys in their fifties to descend forty feet, hand over hand, and, anyway, we've got control of every window. We wouldn't let them down."

"Fire truck," offered another, and this was a cause for concern. He went on, "The ladder could be hoisted at an angle to be far enough away from any window."

"Get them off the roof," Myles instantly commanded. "Now. Put them in a room on the fourth floor, take the phone out, and listen up: kid gloves, okay?" The phrasing was an *ask,* but the intent was an *order*. A short kid with thick glasses and sideburns got up and hustled out the door, taking the order as a figurative baton that was going to be passed to everyone else inside the building.

"We take the high road," Myles said. No one questioned this approach.

"I've got four things," Myles continued and everyone was rapt. "One, what are our demands? Two, how do we handle negotiations? Three, what are our contingency plans? And four, what do we do with the hostages?" I wrote this down verbatim. "Oh, make that five," he added. "Don't trash the place. Don't open a desk, look at a file, read a piece of paper. Make sure everybody knows the rules. Got it?"

Claudia strode to the door, nodded to the room and left.

"Okay, now. First. Demands?" he asked and made eye contact with everyone, sweeping from left to right, even locking in with me for an instant before moving to another set. All sorts of lists emerged, some handwritten, some extemporaneous. Folks had their say, mostly about restoring the tables on the Strip, allowing anyone to proselytize without restrictions. People were logical and very analytical. There'd be a trade-off, the group seemed to agree: the de-occupation of the building for the restoration of students' rights. They'd anoint Myles to negotiate with the campus authorities and get back to normal. Everyone would leave the building, the cops would recede and go back to their regular assignments, and classes could resume immediately—the next day, in fact. There was agreement all around and a feeling of accomplishment. They'd reached consensus, rapidly, on the demands. There was no need for a contingency plan, and the hostages—well, they weren't *really* hostages—they'd leave when all the students left, hopefully in an hour or so. There was satisfaction, accomplishment, and victory in the air. The battle was won, the war was going to be over, the treaty was about to be signed, and it was time to live in peace.

I closed my notebook and shoved the pencil inside. The pandemonium in the rest of the building seemed to have subsided. The crowd outside had quieted. There was no one shouting from the windows, and the phones weren't ringing. All the energy that had manifested itself in furor had been spent. People were hungry, tired, and thinking about what they had to do the next day. There was homework to be tackled, classes to prepare for, lives to be lived. In that split second before the explosion, a whirlwind of images had flashed through my mind: how and where would I next see Mir, would Herzl and I meet to run together or take the bus to the basin, was I prepared for my next class? When the bomb came, it was so unexpected that people didn't move at first, despite being blown off their feet by the percussion waves.

Myles shot up from his chair. His thighs hit the table so fiercely that it was lifted a couple of inches and slammed back down. The crash was made worse by the cascade of shattering drinking cups, eyeglasses, and trays reverberating on the tabletop and landing on the floor scattering shards, ashes from Myles' extinguished cigarettes and drinks onto people whose spastic motions exacerbated the noise and chaos that'd instantly enveloped the room. Standing erect and leaning forward with his palms down on the newly located tabletop, Myles' face filled with blood from chin to the forehead as fast as my mother filled pitchers with tomato juice for our Friday night dinners. His intensity was strong enough to parch our throats, to take our collective breath away. We expected a scream, a shout, a yell and were caught short by the upbraiding that came barely above a whisper:

"If we were in Philadelphia a hundred and eighty-eight years ago," he started out, "this is the group that would've said something like, 'Just give us judiciary powers, remove your soldiers, stop taxing us unless we agree, allow us to have trial by jury and, in return, we'll stop this process of severing our ties and go back to being loyal subjects of the crown.' Am I right?" he asked rhetorically, then continued when no one said a word. "Would you've been the ones who would've advised Lincoln to negotiate a new set of relationships with the southern states following the shelling of Fort Sumter? I'd bet on that. Uh-huh. And maybe you would've suggested that Dr. King should've kept his dream to himself. I mean, you don't want to ruffle too many feathers now, *ya hear*?"

The room was quiet and most people had lowered their heads to avoid making direct eye contact with Myles. He was just getting going. He started slowly, then revved up his engine, the better to drown out or steamroll any opposition.

"Listen up, everyone. A simple axiom of politics is that you don't get what you want unless the other side actually fears that it'll lose. Not thinks offhandedly that it *might* not win." He paused and then spit out, "Do...you...understand?"

Scanning the room, I could see that this had a powerful impact, as heads were now raised, eyes locked on Myles, a realization that his words carried meaning.

"You know you're going to win when you can feel that ache, that heartbreak, those feelings that boil up inside you when you start to think you can actually see that the current order will be broken, smashed, and changed forever, not just disturbed like a rubber band that eventually snaps back into place."

I drew a rubber band that was stretched to the breaking point in the notebook. Myles wasn't finished. Curiously, his gaze was above everyone's head; it was as if he were now making a speech to an invisible audience.

"When the other side comes to terms with the idea that the band's going to be cut and that it can't be reassembled in the same way, then and only then will they negotiate, in the vain hope that they can save at least part of what exists. But what they don't realize—and what hasn't been recognized in this room—is that it's already been lost for them. Before the negotiations have taken place. Gone. Their world can never be the same. I know it. When will you?"

He paused, looked directly at those in the room, and assumed a lighter, mocking tone. "Unless, of course, we give them their world back. Give it to them, free and clear—here, take it, go on," he pretended to give it away by thrusting his hands out to a few people directly in front of him. "And you know what it'll be like if we allow this to happen? Huh? Anyone? Let me spell it out for you: it'll ensure they win, we lose, and no one—not a single soul who ever thinks about stretching that rubber band will do so again in the future, mark my words.

"So, I guess if that's what you all want, then that's what we'll do," he mocked. "I'll write the surrender note on some of the lovely stationery here inside the president's desk and place it on a platter when I walk out of here to hand it to the cops."

I drew a picture of a platter with a note folded over on it. I kept my eyes firmly downcast on my notebook. There wasn't a sound in the room: no talking, coughing, shuffling papers, squeaking wheels on the floor, rolling pencils, clearing throats, foot tapping, or knuckle cracking.

Just as it was beginning to get unbearably uncomfortable, Myles' voice filled the void.

"I've got four things," he repeated as if he'd never said that previously, "One, what are our demands? Two, how do we handle negotiations? Three, what are our contingency plans? And four, what do we do with the hostages."

There was no sarcasm; the mocking tone was gone. And just like that, the buzz was restored to the room, potential demands erupting spontaneously, gushing out so quickly that they overflowed one another, making it difficult to concentrate on one thread. Each idea was designed to capture Myles' attention, his favor, as if to obliterate any remnant of shame for not stretching the rubber band.

Claudia re-entered as Myles asked, *What are our demands*, and she seized upon several ideas then reformatted them into a plan that she offered up to Myles. She proceeded to tick them off, one by one, reading from a set of notes:

"One, the trustees will issue a statement that UT subscribes wholeheartedly to the First Amendment and that all members of this community have the right to free speech, the right to assemble, the right to petition the trustees without fear of recrimination, and the right to have unfettered access to the press." She glanced around the room to ensure she had the group's approval, which was signaled by nods and comments in agreement.

All eyes were on Claudia except for mine. I was looking at Myles, trying to discern his reaction. His face gave no clues, but his body language was relaxed. I sketched him standing, leaning against the desk, his legs crossed, his shirt open-necked, his tie knot about two inches below his neck, cigarette dangling from his partially opened lips.

"Two," she continued, "UT will not allow the local police to enter the campus at any time unless there's probable cause that a crime has been committed, as evidenced by a warrant enabling them to do so, signed by a city or state judge. And a corollary to that," she quickly added, looking around the room, "is the police will withdraw immediately from the outside of this building, and those members of the police department who've deliberately taken actions of force against innocent students and other passersby will be brought to trial to face criminal charges for assault." With this last declaration, the room erupted into sustained applause, especially since it was an extemporaneous remark that Claudia had added when she had felt support waves from those assembled. She went back to her notes.

"Three, anyone who participated in the peaceful demonstration and non-violent occupation of this building will be exempt from any disciplinary actions from the UT or Taos Heights police." As this was essentially a self-serving remark, the crowd made no comments.

"Four, UT will de-authorize the U.S. armed forces from recruiting on campus by the end of the year." With this statement, there were cheers, whistles, chair banging, foot stomping and lots of exuberant replies. It took a few seconds for the room to quiet enough for Claudia to continue.

"Five, UT will hold a referendum—one person-one vote—on the subject of shutting down the active ROTC program at UT." This was met by sustained applause.

"And last," she said turning to me, "we unanimously request our battle-scarred scribe to insert these demands and write up my off-the-cuff remarks so that we have a permanent record of everything that's going to be communicated to the cops, assuming, of course, we all agree." We all correctly interpreted that to mean if Myles was on board. She held up her notes high for all to see, walked over to me, and deposited them on top of my notebook with a flourish.

As I gathered her notes, I was impressed that she'd been able to put them together during the time she'd been spreading the word throughout the building about taking the high road.

At that point, one of the assembled stood up and addressed her with a nervous agitation. "Claudia," he began respectfully, his voice partially cracking at the realization that he was going to pull against the tide when he knew it was controlled by gravitational forces as strong as the moon. "Point one, about the issue of free speech and assembly…that's what's practically guaranteed. I mean, if we got a lawyer, we'd win that one for sure. No disagreement. But the business about the warrant being required? We can *ask*, but that's really another legal issue that, even if they say 'okay,' well, it's really up to the courts, don't you agree?" Although this was phrased as a question, he left no room to countenance a response as he slid into his next point, his pitch lowering and phlegm evaporating. "I agree that they won't give us a hard time—your point three—as long as we leave the place as we found it," he continued, here making eye contact with others in an attempt to garner support. "But no recruiting and removing ROTC, sure, we're all for that, but we've got to be realistic; that's not something the other side could give in on, and even if they could, it's dependent upon the army to get in line, and we'd be here for months before that'd ever get resolved, one way or another. So I say, let's stick with what's reasonable, okay? Let's not lose sight of why we're here. Remember, it all started with the pamphlets and free speech."

Before he had a chance to sit down—before what he said had registered with the audience—Claudia sneered out the word *quisling* and then launched into a tirade.

"You're a Menshevik when a Bolshevik is necessary, a republican when a Robespierre is required, a Sun Yat-sen when a Mao is needed. Get *out*!" she screamed.

With his reasonableness having been confronted with unbridled contempt, he bolted from the room, leaving his jacket slung over his chair, which marked his absence like an x-ray—a ghostly reminder of his former self, vaguely familiar but ultimately unrecognizable. While Myles' theatrics had the magnetizing effect of bonding, Claudia's histrionics generated repulsion, as they were seen to be inauthentic, a device to project the aura of leadership, a synthetic attempt to demonstrate power. Yet, without disapproval from Myles, she had the privilege of his protection, and the crowd supported her, openly jeering at the jacketless student who left in a huff.

What ever happened to free speech? I asked only myself, knowing that I'd be booted out in a similar fashion if I actually asked the question out loud.

I checked my concern, and took everything down, beginning with the rights of free speech (although I added the word *irony* with a question mark in a parenthesis), assembly, petition, and press, putting them in the notebook which now had more than fifteen pages of jottings, drawings, quotes, and demands. I found time to flip to the end of the notebook to start sketches that would serve as placeholders afterward when I'd have more time to complete finished drawings.

I handed the notebook to Claudia who reviewed both what she'd given to me as well as what I'd added. She placed the notebook in Myles' hand, a gesture that those who didn't know her could misinterpret as a supplicant offering an indulgence to a superior. He glanced at it, folded the corner of the page that housed the demands, walked back to the desk, opened a drawer, pulled out a list of telephone numbers, then called the police. He never said who he was or what he wanted. Within a minute, he started talking softly. We dared not stir, we didn't want to miss the half of the conversation we were privy to, as this would make our interpretation of what the whole conversation was about even more difficult. After a minute, we could see him reading from my notebook; then there was silence.

"No," he said firmly when he was finished reading, "none." More silence. "I understand fully," he continued. "Do you?" he asked, not imperiously but with confidence. More silence for an extended period of time. "Until then," he said and hung up.

"They're giving us until noon tomorrow," he indicated as he turned to face us, "and if we don't surrender, leave on our own, release the three cops, they'll come in—with force he said, whatever that means.

"I don't know about you, but I'm hungry," he continued in a segue so smooth it took a moment for us to take its measure. "Is there a kitchen in the building or vending machines?"

Now I must confess that until that very instant, I hadn't thought of food, but within seconds, my stomach was growling, and saliva built up in my mouth. What I wouldn't do to bite into a soft tomato or a hard-boiled egg from Ben Veniste's café and wash it down with ice cold lemon-flavored water. The report back from the kitchen was that the meager provisions had been consumed, and that the vending machines had an inventory of Good & Plenty and Jujyfruit candies. There was a suggestion for a trade of one of the hostages for some food, but this was dismissed by Claudia with a flick of the wrist that, if captured on film, would've represented a remarkable visual definition of disdain. I made sure I captured the image.

I knew that anyone walking out the door of Kettys-Burg on a mission to get provisions would be detained or worse yet, arrested. In any case, it wouldn't result in our getting any food. Myles wouldn't consider bargaining for it. I started to calculate how long we could realistically last, consuming exclusively the calorie-less food of euphoria, and came up with a rather bleak forecast: a day and a half. I hadn't eaten since breakfast and most of the others were probably in the same position. It struck me that the cops and the administration would figure that as well and could wait out the siege until our lack of coals couldn't stave off the hunger chill. We'd then become irritable and brittle, and the unity of purpose would crack. The answer was food. The question was how to get it. I stood up and absentmindedly sniffed under my arms, conscious not only of the lack of food but also of the possibility of odor. My shirt smelled of mushrooms. I reeked so much of a dankness that I wondered how anyone hadn't noticed. Well, to be sure, the events of the day sure were of more concern that anyone's attention to hygiene.

Then it hit me. I made for the first floor, pivoted to see that no one was watching, then opened the door that led to the part of the basement through which I'd come. I went down the staircase so swiftly that I landed on the linoleum floor with a clunk, fearful that someone in the hall above might've heard. I stayed in a crouched position for a moment, then proceeded to the far end of the room, opened the well-camouflaged pocket door and found myself back in the cement-floored storeroom that housed the rejections of school years past. I walked carefully to the far wall, leaned my palms against it and pushed to the right, adding my left shoulder and knee on instinct as the wall slid slowly. On the other side of the room, I turned the handle on the door, and I merged into the mushroom cave. It smelled like me.

CHAPTER 6

No problem.

I can do it.

Just give me the signal

I made my way through the tunnel carefully, neither wanting to careen into any of the railroad support pillars nor stumble into the precious mushroom beds. At the far end, I peeked through the opening and scrambled up the Blueberry Creek embankment around the rhododendrons, hesitated for a moment at the top, dusted myself off, made sure my bandana was still positioned directly over the welt, then took the circuitous route back to the café.

As Ben Veniste was preparing a fresh cloth napkin with ice to my forehead, I told him that the pounding had lessened—which was true. I filled him in on what was going on. I needed no histrionics, left out ancillary details, and focused on the situation at Kettys-Burg Hall: the cordon of police surrounding the building; Myles' demands; the absence of food and drink to sustain the movement; and my secret flight to the café. Within a moment after my last word, he reached for his cane, tapped the floor in what appeared to be a code, waited for his kitchen helpers to arrive, gave them some instructions, then told me to shut the front door and to put the "Closed" sign in the window.

Within a few minutes, the counter was filled with stainless steel bowls and pitchers. Ben Veniste put me to work. By midnight, we'd moved tables together in clusters with all the chairs neatly stacked up to one side. By 1:00 a.m., all the cardboard boxes that'd been stacked up outside of the rear door had been placed on the tables, and we were filling them with tomatoes, cucumbers, peppers, lettuce, carrots, olives, radishes, onions, hard-boiled eggs, several different kinds of cheese, as well as breads and flat crackers. The vegetables were sliced to perfection, the result of Ben Veniste's wizardry with a knife, or knives I should say, his collection of cook's, paring, slicing, carving, breading, and boning instruments made me think that he might need a license to operate these weapons.

At 2:00 a.m., the two young Mexican men proceeded to lift the boxes and take them out back, stacking them next to their bicycles that they'd ridden from their homes in Oak Land. Effortlessly, they strapped a wooden pallet over the metallic rear tire covers with rope, in such a way as to create a cart, made level by putting a brick underneath each kickstand. Ben Veniste told me to stand between the bicycles, now thrashed together as a unified machine, to prevent it from tipping over, while the young men made repeated trips to the tables and brought the cardboard boxes of food through the kitchen and onto the pallet. When we agreed that any more weight would jeopardize our ability to control the vehicle, I said, "*Vamonos, mis amigos*," to the two young men, but before we could mount up, so to speak, Ben Veniste motioned to me to come inside with him. I was hoping I wouldn't be getting a treatise on food or bicycles or the two accomplices who were going to help me get the provisions into Kettys-Burg Hall.

"You still okay?" he asked, not waiting for me to answer before he gently lifted the bandana an inch to inspect the welt. "It's purple, a good sign," he noted. "What about inside?" by which he meant the administration building.

"Everyone's behaving, if that's what you're getting at."

"I'm just concerned that there'll be an eruption of some sort. The longer this thing goes on, the more likely that it becomes like a pressure cooker, a volcano, and I don't want to find out that you get caught up in the debris, the ash. Remember Pompeii?"

"It's under control, really. Myles is in charge. He's got a plan for how to calm everything down with the hostage cops and let everyone get back to normal. It's all going to get settled, really," I said.

"Remember when I told you about the king? Right before you entered the basement?"

"Uh-huh. Does this have something to do with Myles?"

"It does. Look, I have no way of knowing what Myles is actually up to. His motives may be pure. I'm not saying Myles isn't genuinely trying to defuse the *situation*. He's in it up to his neck, like all of you. But remember, he's got six years on you, came here in fifty-eight when *he* was eighteen, and took the campus by storm."

"Myles? Why, were there other demonstrations? Things like what's going on now?"

"No, no, nothing like that. Myles was the BMOC."

"What's that?" I asked.

"Big man on campus, the hot shot, the guy everyone recognizes. He was the lead in all the plays, had all the girls swirling around him, asking for autographs—on a college campus no less, how about that? He'd get an article about him and his picture in the paper at least once each semester. Everyone knew who he was: the leading man, the star. Not the athlete. The guy on stage. Couldn't walk around without the other kids staring at him. Every guy envious.

"Jacobo," he said looking me squarely in the eye, "he's an actor, through and through. First and foremost. Don't forget this, be on the lookout."

"Are you saying he's playing a role?" I asked. "Are you…uhmmm… is this what you're thinking? Honestly?"

Even as I was saying this, my mind was flashing back to Myles standing on the rise behind the bookstore, offering a soliloquy to any and all who happened to be browsing or checking out. Myles back at his apartment, in front of the bookshelves filled with famous plays, with perfectly cadenced and enunciated speeches holding us in sway. Myles on the roof of the car out on the Strip, giving us history lessons and urging us to take action. Myles in command at the president's desk in Kettys-Burg Hall, giving orders to those both in and out of the building. I didn't know how to interpret what Ben Veniste had said to me.

I'd been exposed to a charismatic leader back in Arroyo Grande—my father. That Aarón Toledano was the person to whom others would look for direction was a blessing. He was the head of the *konsilyo*, the council of ten men who set the rules, but they had no legal authority. An outsider would've called him a village elder, not so much because of his age but because he was the guiding spirit of our souls. It was Aarón the fair, the wise, the unselfish, the modest captain who'd steer us out of harm's way with that soothing voice, commanding presence, and inescapable logic. A man who listened and learned. It was through these qualities that he gained the respect of his peers so that they accepted, willingly, his proposals to adjudicate, to resolve, to prepare, and to guide, without prejudice as to family or friends. No one ever had to question *his* motives.

"Thanks for the head's up. I appreciate it, I do, and I have to say I really like the way you look out for me. Honestly, thank you again," I said to Ben Veniste as I extended my hand, not actually knowing what I would be on the lookout for.

Ben Veniste rapped his cane against one of the back tires, the signal for the three of us to take off with the bicycles loaded down with provisions from the back of the café on a roundabout route that would take us eventually to the depression that was once Blueberry Creek. We couldn't take the chance of going the shorter route directly to the gate, as there'd be a risk of being spotted by a campus cop or a city policeman. And anyway, how could we explain what we were doing as we lowered boxes of food from the gate down the embankment to the long-forgotten door to the hidden tunnel that ran directly to the basement of Kettys-Burg Hall? I whispered in Spanish to my companions that by going far east to the start of the creek bed depression and up the hill that we'd then be walking the bicycle contraption down the incline of the creek bed and would be out of sight two blocks before we got near Kettys-Burg Hall. Although Ben Veniste hadn't told them the purpose of the mission, I informed them that if we were stopped before we got to the dry creek bed, we were to say that we were on the way to the stadium further east where the rowing team was preparing for an early morning run.

My position was between the handlebars of both bicycles, keeping them parallel so that the front wheels were aligned. The two young men were behind the pallet in the back, holding it steady with one hand gripping the middle of the pallet and the other on the cardboard boxes, preventing them from toppling over—which they easily could—each time we went over a pebble or let a little space get between the front tires of the two bicycles. Notwithstanding the turmoil several blocks away, we didn't run into any police, our only encounters being with an occasional student who didn't seem to notice us and a couple of guys who lived in the Preserve up toward the hills in the east who did, fending them off with some offerings that were heartily received. When we approached the start of the creek bed, we slowed our pace, as the momentum from even the slight decline would exert a disproportionate force that could quickly cause the bikes to pick up speed and possibly tip over. We made it down safely and parked them just underneath the old wooden door hidden by the rhododendrons. A conga-like line moved the cardboard boxes inside and to the far end, picking up mushrooms by the dozens. By 3:30 a.m., we'd made it to the top of the stairs that led to the main floor of the building. It was quiet but not noiseless. We could hear bustling outside the front door and distant or muted conversations that'd occasionally spike but that we couldn't interpret, like when I'd fiddle with the dial on the radio at home late at night and get muffled static until I'd pick up KGGM in Albuquerque in English or KOBE in Las Cruces in Spanish with some entertainment or news.

We carried the boxes up the steps into the kitchen on the second floor and unloaded them onto the counters. I bit into a tomato as if it were an apple, the seeds and meat spilling down my beard, causing the three of us to laugh—conspiratorially so as not to wake several slumped students whose heads were awkwardly inclined on their arms, bent at angles on the tabletop. The three of us returned to the basement door unseen, and I told them to take the boxes back to Ben Veniste's café, making sure to cover up the door to the outside, to retrace their steps in reverse back through the Blueberry Creek depression and to keep their conversations to a minimum. I shook their hands longer than was necessary and started to give the first one a hug. When he backed away from me, I understood instantly that this had been a task—something that Ben Veniste had paid them to do, for probably two or three times their usual wage and that they'd been eager to comply, the hour of the day notwithstanding. Whereas I was on a mission, they were on the job, completely unaware of the purpose of sneaking food into a campus building, something that they'd simply attribute to the *loco* behavior of college students that had no effect on them whatsoever.

Feeling proud and contributory, I waltzed into the president's office. The lights were off. No one was there. I sat on the deep leather chair and leaned my head on the soft cushioned armrest, making it easy for me to drift off, the throbbing contusion having subsided a bit. I imagined seeing Mir scurrying in the street, then racing down the steps to the basement of the bookstore to develop her photos. I watched her eyes squint as she saw the bruise on my forehead. I heard her tenderly saying, *Oh my God* when she saw the welt. *What did they do to you? How could they beat an innocent bystander? Those bastards with their billy clubs.* I didn't replay my *I'm okay, really. It probably looks worse than it feels.* I'd made the permanent record reflective of a better me, which, over time, would obliterate the original version as completely as a new recording would erase the previous words on a tape cassette. I was the only one who knew it was a fake.

I heard some noises that I couldn't associate with Mir, try as I might. A man's voice. A woman's. A rapid back and forth, punctuated by clapping sounds, followed by short exclamation bursts that may or may not've been words, I couldn't tell. They were coming from the other side of the wall. Intrigued, I put my ear to it. No luck; it was too thick to distinguish the voices. I moved along the wall, hoping to find a place where it was thinner. Nothing doing. Toward the corner of the room, I spotted a door, which, to be honest, I'd never noticed before because it was covered by three laminated diplomas showcasing the academic credentials of the president. At first, I thought there might've been a secret powwow going on in the adjacent room that was becoming feverish and hesitated to enter, as the folks on the other side may've been there on an invitation-only basis. When I heard a muffled clap followed by a distinct *goddammit,* I turned the door handle slowly, curiosity having overwhelmed my reticence to interfere. Luckily, it made no sound. I opened it just enough to fit my head through. My body was behind the door so the only thing someone inside could've seen was my forehead and eyes. It suddenly occurred to me that if someone were to burst into the president's office and either turn on the lights or start to speak that I'd be exposed. Yet I couldn't take the chance to close and then re-open the door, so I held my position in the still manner of a deer that would stand motionless when my little sister Nohemi and I would come across it on the mesa out west in Arroyo Grande.

A small amount of moonlight peeked through the partially opened Venetian blinds, enabling me to see Myles and Claudia—both naked—she with a joint in her lips, he with a bottle of beer in his hand. Snippets of venom went back and forth rapidly—it was an argument. About what I couldn't say. Myles jabbed a finger an inch or so from Claudia's face. She swatted it away, hissing *gofuckyourself*, which was immediately followed by Myles saying something like, *that'dbebetterthanwhatIjusthad*. Claudia turned her body away from Myles. I presumed she was going to gather her clothes that I could see in the moonglow, draped carelessly on the sofa. Myles nodded his head in the manner of someone thinking, 'Sure, walk away, you know I'm right.' Claudia pivoted as swiftly as the ROTC guys who practiced drilling on the football field and sucker punched Myles in the gut. Bam! Wow, she coldcocked him, causing him to double over and grab his abdomen. It happened so fast he never had the chance to contract his muscles, so the blow was twice as effective. Myles coughed and grunted as he regained full height and put his hands up, both palms facing her, the signal for a truce, a time out, a "let's go to our respective corners and take a breather from all of this." He put the beer bottle down. Claudia gave a nod, and when she turned to look for her clothes, Myles slammed his palm down on the back of her head. His blow knocked her over the sofa, where I could make out her frantic efforts to escape, crawling on all fours, crab-like, toward a table under which she could seek safety. Myles went after her, whacking her rear repeatedly. She let out a moan/grunt/scream with each blow. Then, unexpectedly, she stopped crawling, turned with lightning speed, and sunk her teeth into his ankle. Myles cursed wildly. He spun around and I thought he might've caught sight of the narrow slit of the opened door. As I stepped back from the wall, I noticed a framed pen and ink drawing of Kettys-Burg Hall covered by glass that reflected my image.

I was a witness to something for which I'd never know the beginning and wouldn't be privy to the ending, the middle portion being the only part I'd seen. Now, tell me, if you walked into a movie or had a book thrust in front of you under those conditions, would you be able to discern what was really going on?

I left the president's office.

An hour or so later, I came back and saw Myles behind the desk subconsciously rubbing his ankle. Claudia wore a green, yellow, and red striped knit hat pulled low over her forehead that I'd seen on an African American kid previously, covering up what must've been some bruises. A couple of familiar faces were gathered around the conference table. If I hadn't peeked in on what had gone on in the other room, I wouldn't have noticed anything different about Claudia's demeanor, except that she wasn't making eye contact with anyone, which could easily have been ascribed to weariness.

I was suddenly struck by the remembrance that the angle of incidence equals the angle of reflection, which meant that if Myles had been looking toward the door when I'd been about to leave the office where I was eavesdropping on him, he more than likely would've seen a figure through the picture-frame glass. If that were the case, I hoped that he couldn't have made out who it was.

In as normal a voice as I could bring forward, I explained to Myles about the tunnel, the dry creek bed, the bicycles strapped together with pallets, the two young Mexican men, Ben Veniste's coming to the rescue, and that no one saw or heard us so that our secret would be safe and our ability to restock would be guaranteed. Myles nodded, then told me to write down everything I'd been through in the last few hours, jerking his head toward the notebook that I'd left on the table. I couldn't detect if his matter-of-fact orders were the result of his knowing I'd been the one who'd observed his fandango with Claudia.

The room was quiet. Each person seemed to be self-absorbed. I went to the kitchen, pulled out some of the food that had been moved into the refrigerator, and leaned against one of the counters.

I couldn't stop thinking about what I'd witnessed. I wondered if it would affect my feelings about Myles and Claudia. On the one hand, I rationalized, it had nothing to do with the confrontation between students and police. Their sexual activities and intimate personal interactions were entirely within their province. Who was I to judge? Perhaps it wasn't what I thought it was. After all, Ben Veniste had said Myles was an actor, and this might've been a scene in a two-person play that they put on for themselves. Or Claudia could be a masochist or Myles a sadist or maybe there was no *or* involved. I could debate it back and forth, but in the end, there'd be no resolution, as I'd never have the requisite evidence to present to the jury of my mind. Yet, it did bother me. I couldn't simply dismiss it. It was as if someone dropped a new variable into a previously answered equation, and now it wouldn't solve for any outcome that made sense. The Myles and Claudia of before were different from the Myles and Claudia after. Or, it's just as likely that this was a point at which the Jacobo of before was different from the Jacobo of after. There are always events that we mark in our memories the same way we use lines on a doorframe to record heights, and it was becoming clear to me that this was one of those incidents.

As I ate, I reviewed my notebook. Sketches illustrated scenes, quotes captured the language, comments added color. Energized by my involvement and thrilled at having made a contribution, I was suddenly struck by the fact that I might've been the progenitor of it all. I was the one that had manipulated my mirror in such a way as to carry the light into Myles' eyes to warn him that the three policemen on top of Kettys-Burg Hall were photographing him and the other ringleaders of the Movement. Was that what catalyzed his reaction to storm the building? Was all of this somehow my doing?

Pulled out of my reverie by an approaching set of voices, I peeked out of the kitchen and was startled to see Herzl facing Myles, engrossed in conversation, coming toward me. To my knowledge, this was the first time these two campus celebrities had ever been face-to-face. There was no doubt in my mind that each knew about the other. Rivals keep tabs, don't they? Myles had to have known about Herzl, whose victory in the intercollegiate single sculls rowing championship had been splashed across the front pages of the UT paper and the *Albuquerque Tribune*, and noted in a *Sports Illustrated* feature. They say that ink has no weight and makes no sound, yet its repercussions can change behaviors and minds more than heavy loads and loud voices.

I fell in behind them as they passed, giving a ridiculous wave to Herzl. I could tell he had seen me but was so absorbed in his conversation that to acknowledge me for even a moment would've jeopardized his time with Myles. I followed them along the hall, then upstairs. They headed to an office on the fourth floor where the policemen had been brought after their forced descent from the roof. It'd been easy to capture the trio of cops; they were older, out of shape, and hadn't been carrying any weapons. Most likely, they were specifically chosen for their assignment because they weren't capable of engaging in street tactics with agitated demonstrators. Taking a few pictures from the roof of Kettys-Burg Hall was the equivalent of a day off and a chance to embellish their involvement in the riot with grandchildren in later years.

What amazed me was that Myles showed no effects of what I'd seen in the room behind the president's office. I assumed he and Claudia had structured their relationship in such a way as to mask emotions when others were around to avoid exposing vulnerabilities—something leaders tend to do to ward off challenges, something they strive to preclude at all costs.

I watched them walk briskly, with purpose. Claudia suddenly materialized, as if a telepathic message had been given to her to enter their space so she wouldn't be relegated to an exterior orbit around these two rotating suns. She pranced in front and in back of them, arms flailing, head bobbing, fingers jabbing, contributing her two cents, while Herzl, a head taller, pivoted his neck to take in both of them, a judge observing the histrionics of attorneys playing for the benefit of the jury. When the three of them reached the office door, Myles put his palms in a vertical position and the ruckus stopped.

"Open it," he commanded to a student standing outside a door, who took a key out of his pocket and turned the handle. Myles entered, nodded to the three cops, glanced down to see that I still had my notebook, told me to enter, closed the door, and lit a cigarette. Claudia and Herzl were left in the hall. Although the cops were tied to chairs, bound hand and feet, I was frightened. My fear was not from a physical danger. Rather, it was from the simple anxiety of not knowing what was going to happen. Unanticipated vehemence can emanate spontaneously from the flimsiest provocation. Would there be an evolution from a demonstration of democrats seeking reasonable rights into a mob of radicals initiating a reign of terror that no one could predict in advance? Were we in the presence of a Jefferson or a Jacobin? Would I witness some unspeakable punishment disproportionate to the crime of spying, or would the seeds of a deal be sown and reaped right in front of me?

I sketched the three cops whose hands were tied behind the backs of the chairs. Myles pulled up a stool and swiveled a bit to-and-fro while lighting up a smoke. From behind, he appeared older, his jacket being the standard of choice for full professors, tweed with worn patches on his sleeves. The cops gave me an initial glance, then ignored me as if I were an inanimate object.

"They're coming at noon," Myles said softly, exhaling a puff above their heads. No explanation as to the meaning of the pronoun was necessary. "So, you're the ones who're going to stop them," he said, somewhat briskly. One of the men in uniform gave a harrumph and rolled his eyes. The cop in plainclothes ignored his colleagues, leaned forward and requested that the knot be untied.

"Maybe later," Myles responded.

"The thing is..."

"Myles."

"Look, Myles," he said, choosing his words carefully, "this is going to get out of hand. It is already. You have no idea the kind of trouble you're in. You don't want to get in deeper. Untie us, we get out. I already forgot your name. Leave the place, you get back to school, we go about our business. I'm sure there's a way for the tables to be set up, you know, the pamphlets, that kind of thing. We can work it out. You look like the kind of guy who doesn't want trouble. You don't want your record to have a blemish. It's over. When they come in, they'll use clubs. They've got helmets and shields. Someone's going to get hurt. You don't need this. Untie us, we shake hands. I mean it. No kidding. No hard feelings."

With that, he looked at his colleagues who grimaced, yet nodded in assent.

"The pamphlets," Myles spit out, "you'll let us set the pamphlets out on the tables?"

"As long as it doesn't block the access to the shops. That's fair," the plainclothes cop negotiated. "Otherwise, you know, they have rights too."

"Pamphlets."

"Yeah, pamphlets, signs, what have you, okay with us, even the clowns, you know, the guy on the unicycle, that sort of thing. Okay with us as long as everyone can get to the stores. Like I said, we'll forget about this, pretend it never happened, get back to normal, okay?" he said rather jovially, showing signs of enjoying the tête-à-tête. He appeared almost jaunty.

With that, Myles swiveled, snatched the notebook from my hand and continued his orbit until he stopped precisely where he'd started, face-to-face with the plainclothes cop. In that rotation, the what—three or four seconds it took him to spin around?—I could see a change in his body language. Myles' spine straightened, adding a half a foot to his height. His face lengthened, taking on a tomahawk look. The fingers on his free hand tensed, forming a whitened fist with red knuckles. Then he abruptly and menacingly leaned forward at so sharp an angle I thought he was going to butt heads with the plainclothes cop, who jerked back to avoid a collision. He succeeded, save for the ashes that fell on his lap.

Maintaining this slant over the inclined plainclothes cop, Myles appeared from behind to be a jackhammer drilling into his adversary without the attendant noise, as his voice never lifted above normal, which, paradoxically, added to the pummeling he was giving. In this awkward position, arching over the man in the chair, with one hand holding my notebook open, Myles read from it with all the venom of a snake:

"One, the trustees will issue a statement that UT subscribes wholeheartedly to the First Amendment and that all members of this community have the right to free speech, the right to assemble, the right to petition the trustees without fear of recrimination, and the right to have unfettered access to the press.

"Two, UT will de-authorize the local police from entering the campus at any time unless there's probable cause that a crime has been committed, as evidenced by a warrant enabling them to do so, signed by a city or state judge. And a corollary to that, the police will withdraw immediately from the outside of Kettys-Burg Hall and those members of the police department who have deliberately instigated actions of force against innocent students and other passersby will be brought to trial to face criminal charges for assault.

"Three, anyone who participated in this peaceful demonstration and non-violent occupation of Kettys-Burg Hall will be exempt from any disciplinary actions from the UT or Taos Heights police.

"Four, UT will de-authorize the U.S. armed forces from recruiting on campus by the end of the year.

"Five, UT will hold a referendum—one person-one vote—on the subject of shutting down the active ROTC program at the UT."

As he got to number five, he straightened out and was now looking directly down onto the near horizontal face of the plainclothes cop. With his free hand, Myles reached to the desk and lifted the receiver from the phone.

"Call," he ordered. "Call them and tell them. Read it to them. Here, from the book. Call. Now. Do it."

"No way," said the plainclothes cop, defiantly. "Nope. I'm no stooge. Listen to me, pal," he hissed and tried to right himself to be more of an equal to Myles. "You're in big trouble, young man, way over your head. Cut the crap and untie me, us, now. Schoolboy games are over. I'm saying that when they come in here and find us tied up like this, there's no telling how berserk they're going to go. And you know what? Know what I'm going to tell them? Huh? Know what? Nothing. I'm not going to tell them nothing. Because I'm not going to have to. I'm going to enjoy them beating the crap out of you and your gray-eyed, red-haired, long-nosed, hankie-on-his-forehead creepy friend there with the notebook and all the pantywaists who invaded this building."

With that declaration, the other two cops became emboldened and started insulting us, making a racket by lifting themselves off the floor then slamming down their chairs with full force. I was taken aback, not sure of what to do. I looked to Myles for guidance either from what he would say or how he'd react. With the hubbub, Claudia and Herzl burst through the doorway and, for an instant, I could see the semblance of a smile, condescending for sure, that suggested she knew what was going to transpire. The three policemen kept up their chair dancing, hurling slurs and curses, their faces contorted with fury. It almost looked choreographed. As Claudia's smile widened, I became calmer, though still smarted from being called creepy. Herzl was unabashedly excited. Myles nodded to him, said "get it," and my friend bolted from the room. Claudia started to clap in rhythm to the beat of the chairs stomping on the floor, a mocking act that sucked the energy from the three policemen who were clearly starting to get tired. Then she turned her attention to Myles, all but completely ignoring the cops. As their slights bounced off us, leaving us unscathed, Myles and Claudia clearly relished the upper hand. Herzl reappeared with a rope. Myles inspected the strands of the rope, said it looked good to him, then went to the window. Herzl followed him and opened it. Myles turned back toward the plainclothes cop, pointed in the direction of my notebook, still opened to the page with the demands, and told him to make the call.

One of the other cops spat at Myles. Claudia slapped his face so furiously that her ring left a splotch of white within an emerging reddened area, leaving me mesmerized for a second as it reminded me of the unfolding of the purple and gold flowers on the rainbow hedgehog cactus that could be seen at first light in Arroyo Grande. I was amazed that I could recall such a sweet moment during a time of distress and uncertainty. I didn't know then that I wouldn't be able to do it later when confronted with a more personal torment.

Myles withdrew a handkerchief from his trouser pocket and wrapped it around the eyes of the cop who'd spit at him. He tied it so tightly that the cop started to complain that it hurt. Claudia approached the cop's face so closely I thought she was going to kiss him. Instead, she pulled up phlegm with an exaggerated snort and spit massively onto his lips and nose. We were all stunned. Since his hands were tied behind his back, the cop was powerless to clean himself off, which must've added to his humiliation. Myles reached for a sheaf of paper on the desk, crumbled three or four sheets together, molded them into a ball, and proceeded to shove it in the mouth of the plainclothes cop, whose head was held still by Herzl's vise-like wrists. Myles repeated the procedure twice more until the shouts and curses were nothing more than primitive sounds that signaled the onset of fear as the cops strained at the ropes knotted to their wrists and ankles. Herzl took the strands of rope, which I could see now had been the cords cut off from some Venetian blinds, braided to give them additional strength, and weaved them through the backs of the chairs, individually. The cops were too consumed with the paper in their mouths and the restraints on their extremities to realize what was happening as Herzl worked quickly from behind. When he was finished, Claudia handed the phone to Myles, who dialed a number and spoke to the three cops before the connection was made.

"You've left me no choice," he said matter-of-factly, not caring whether they were even listening. He winked to indicate that there was a voice on the line.

"No," he stated flatly, "we haven't changed our position." He listened then began again, "I, we understand. But before you come, appreciate this: there'll be consequences." He fell silent again; we imagined he was being lectured. He was patient, nodding, not in agreement, rather more like marking time. His civility was remarkable given the scenes that had just played out on the street the day before, in the president's office the previous evening, in the room next to the president's office with Claudia, and here in this room on the fourth floor. On top of a car, he'd been less a rabble-rouser and more a troubadour with a megaphone, coalescing a large crowd with divergent interests that could've easily fractured into street violence. He'd led a group into the administration building that suffered no broken glass, no overturned furniture, no stripped files during a night of occupation. He'd prodded his minions to recognize the power that they possessed, and was in the process of demonstrating how to use it to their advantage.

"Our demands are reasonable," Myles continued into the phone. "You'd be wise to hear me out." After a few seconds, he looked up at us.

"'Save your breath.' That's what he said. Can you believe that? He hung up."

The three cops started to laugh, muffled, derisive hardy-har-hars through the stuffed paper in their mouths. It stopped abruptly when Herzl yanked the chair with the strapped-in plainclothes cop by the braided Venetian cord across the floor to the open window. Instead, panic coursed through the veins on the side of the cop's neck, and I wondered if his heartbeat drowned out his own garbled words, which we all imagined were an entreaty that he'd agree to Myles' demands that he read from my notebook. Myles ignored him.

Herzl straddled the sash and leaned out to pat the bough of an ancient oak tree—one of the refugees rescued from the deforestation of Oak Land planted too close to the side of the building, its fingers denied entry into the rooms by the annual trimming. By this time, the sun was up and members of the crowd rushed immediately to a spot directly below him, formed a circle and locked their hands on the diameter, forming a target for Herzl, in anticipation of a jump. Electricity radiated outward through the crowd and pulsed back in the form of blankets offered to form a better landing zone. Police barricaded the area; walkie-talkie static buzzed through the near noon air. Herzl tightened his grip on the ledge, simultaneously grabbed the bough, and then swung his legs outside, his body floating above the crowd, rhythmically swaying back and forth, secured by the trust in his muscular wrists and biceps. He tucked his knees under and began to swing, a signal to the crowd that their initial impression was off the mark: he wasn't contemplating a jump. As each arc gathered height and speed, the crowd applauded. A voice through a megaphone told him to get back in the building, an order he ignored with a flourish, letting go of the branch, his body dangling from the sash by his left arm, his legs riding an air bicycle parallel to the building. His defiance energized the crowd, the applause melding into a metronomic clapping with each rotation of his legs. After a minute, his left arm contracted and, in an instant, he was back on top of the sash, then into the room. The roar of the crowd almost drowned out his pronouncement.

"No problem. I can do it. Just give me the signal."

CHAPTER 7

I had no idea

how significant

this would turn out to be

Other students reported to Myles on sightings of police activity from vantage points on every floor. The cavalry had arrived and were dispersed within a ten-yard perimeter of the building. Squad cars barricaded the Strip, blocking the business district from the campus. Out back, where Herzl had performed his high-wire theatrics, dozens of cops had nightsticks in hand and leaned on transparent plastic shields that looked like they'd been salvaged from old motorcycles. To the north, crowds had gathered in front of the gate. Corralled behind double layers of sawhorse barricades, students chanted, thrust homemade signs in the air, and launched constant verbal assaults at cops who stood shoulder-to-shoulder, wearing helmets and sunglasses. Out front, in a concession to appear nonconfrontational, only a few cops wandered about, some in plainclothes, checking their watches every thirty seconds or so—a tic that suggested both excitement and anxiety customarily seen when a thoroughbred is locked into the starter's gate.

The phone rang, and the voice requested that Myles meet him at the main entrance. There was no belligerence, even a tone of hopefulness. The man he met at the front door of Kettys-Burg came by himself. He was middle-aged, hair parted prominently in Robert McNamara fashion, tie clasped over a too-tight Oxford cloth shirt allowing an undershirt to peek through in two places, looking as if another set of eyes were trying to fathom this new world. He smiled professionally and extended his hand, keeping it suspended in that split second when Myles was rationalizing a decision whether or not to grasp it. He carried none of the gruffness that Myles had experienced when it was only a voice on the other side of the line. "George Townsend," he said, explicitly cleaving off his police chief title, perhaps because it was unnecessary, perhaps because it might've induced Myles to respond with a sarcastic, "Rebel leader," in order to strike a balance.

We were all listening in, having opened the windows on the upper floors of the front of the building.

"I thought it might be better if we could meet, talk it out, just you and me," he said, ignoring the dozens peering through the windows. They were standing directly in front of the middle of the three casement window doors, flanked by the five-story Ionic columns that defined the building, much as overgrown incisors characterized a saber-tooth tiger.

"The thing of it is," he began, recalling from the script he'd created or that had been drilled into him, "what we've got here is a real predicament, okay. And it's the same for both of us, you know. I've got people—you know who they are: the chancellor, president, trustees, and whatnot. People with a lot of pressure on them, too, from the governor and the shopkeepers and the papers. They all want this settled. Nobody wants anyone to get hurt. I certainly don't, and I don't believe for a minute that you do, either, though that's what some of those people think. You've seen what happens when things get out of hand, like on the buses, the bus rides, and the lunch counters in the South. Now, no one wants that here, no siree."

He paused to assess his impact as measured by Myles' expression. When he saw none, he continued.

"You know about the point of no return, don't you? When the plane hitting headwinds approaches the midpoint over an ocean. What do they do? The map says it's shorter to keep on course, but there's a chance they'll burn up so much fuel they won't arrive safely. Do they turn back? They may be wrong about the wind. Or maybe it's the fuel indicator. You know, those things aren't always reliable. Could be a little sputtering in an engine. Myles, can I call you Myles?" he asked rhetorically.

It was a good cop feint that could metamorphose into bad cop animosity as quickly as the light touch of a finger could set off the detonation of a catastrophic bomb. Myles nodded.

"You see, Myles, this plane I'm talking about? We're both on it together, my friend. Same plane. With headwinds or a bad dial. Now, we don't have the kind of engine trouble with the thick black cloud coming out of it like you see in the movies when someone's been blasted out of the sky in a dog fight. Not that kind. Can't do anything about that plane. It's a goner. But our plane doesn't have that black smoke. Oh, it's wounded all right, maybe low on gas and all, but it can still land, uh-huh. And you know why? Well, on account of the pilots, that's all. Yup, the pilots. Two of them. Sitting side by side, working together. Using all of their training, all of their experience to bring that baby home. That's what they learned in flight school. What to do when something happens. Something they didn't anticipate. Something that's not in the manual. 'Cause they can't anticipate everything. But they talk with each other, give each other ideas. And maybe they disagree. I'm sure they do. One guy wants to do one thing, the other guy says, hell no, that won't work. But they know they're responsible for the lives of fifty folks, say, and if they can't get together on this, well, sure as the sun comes up in the east, they're going down. Then that would be the real tragedy. Yup, if the plane went down because these two pilots were too proud to listen to the point of view of the other and to consider that, well, maybe the other guy has a point, you know? And can you imagine if you're back in the control tower and listening in to this crap? You can see what's going to happen, and you're screaming into your microphone, but it's as if they've turned off the sound. They don't want to hear from anyone else, let alone the other pilot, goddammit!"

As the chief of police was talking, the two of them had wandered, together, weaving between the columns and the steep steps. Unbeknownst to Myles, the telephoto lens of the police photographer was snapping away, and the hidden microphone squirreled behind George Townsend's ostentatious tie clasp was transmitting without interference to a tape recorder in the back of a police van parked on Stratford. The intent was to have the pictures developed quickly, then unite them with the transcriptions of the secret recordings and the notes of the reporter into a news article that'd make the editorial staff of the *Albuquerque Tribune* proud.

Freedom of the press, the editorial director would then toast, clicking glasses with the news director at a pub that afternoon, unwittingly celebrating its demise. *The Fourth Estate*, the news director would retort, leaping to his feet to cement his alliance with the editorial director, the incongruity of it all having as much resonance with him as the head of the beer that he blew off with the same disdain he expressed for the Myleses and Claudias of the world. The article that appeared in the *Tribune* the next morning carried the dignified photo of the police chief extending his hand to Myles in that very instant when Myles hesitated, an appetizer that came recommended with the front page lede entrée on the starvation of the hostages and was topped off by the editorial dessert lambasting outside agitators, all designed by the paper's master chefs who catered to their owner's fancies.

While the newspapermen of the *Tribune* were gorging on self-congratulations, Mir had taken the photos that'd been developed in the darkroom of the bookstore on Broadway Avenue to the UT paper and had written an article based upon her personal observations of the fracas on the Strip. Myles understood that if the *Tribune*'s views were to stand unopposed, the confrontation would be defined in terms of unruly hooligans, communist dupes, and ungrateful privileged children, not on the issues of freedom of speech and assembly. And, too, he knew full well that these abstractions couldn't marshal public support in the absence of concrete symbols, any more than *Taxation without representation* wasn't a galvanizing rallying cry until the actions of the Boston Tea Party brought its meaning home to each New Englander's hearth.

It was Mir who was charged with this extraordinary responsibility to define the situation with visual, written, and audio cues. Wrapped around her photos of the activities on the Strip (described as a riot in the *Tribune*), she put the demonstration in the context of a larger issue—a societal fault line that would demarcate positions on race, war, poverty, access—that would require individuals to stake a position on one side or the other.

In her breakthrough photo journal article that was published two months later in *Life Magazine*, she wrote "As I typed, I felt enveloped by the still lingering reverberations of the sway of the crowd, the surging currents of electricity wired to my nerve endings, the memory of the physical jostling from exuberant elbows, arms, boots. My eardrums throbbed. Boom, boom, boom. I inhaled Myles' sermons back in his apartment; boom, boom, boom, I pulsed with the beat of the free speech-honk-free speech-honk cadence that preceded Myles' address to the crowd the day before. Boom, boom, boom, I captured the swarm to Kettys-Burg Hall with the police on Myles' tail. Boom, boom, boom. My fingers worked independently, my bystander eyes sparkled with approval, my mouth mimicked the words louder and louder, impervious to the stares of moth-like colleagues attracted to my fire. They gaped at this whirling dervish who was channeling the momentum from the demonstration. When I finished, I ripped the page out of the typewriter, grabbed the previous pages and pictures, then bolted down the hall where production would typeset, ink, and press. As I passed the publisher, a fellow student two years older broke in behind me, pad in hand and asked what the title should be, would there be a subhead? I'd heard free speech chants, seen surges, jostling, and swarms, observed the crowds move, be moved. I continued on for several more steps, not responding, then made a full twirl without breaking stride, and in that second when I was face-to-face with the publisher, I echoed the bellow that was erupting from within—*Free Speech Movement!*—and picked up my pace down the hall."

While Myles and George Townsend, chief of police, were having their tête-à-tête and while the chief was quietly celebrating his electronic eavesdropping of Myles' words and facial expressions, the wire services were pulsing with the story of the Free Speech Movement, replete with pictures of what had actually happened on the Strip the day before. Managing editors across the country were re-blocking their front pages to lead with the eyewitness account. Afternoon editions would hit the streets by 3:00 p.m., and evening newscasts would carry pictures with voiceovers supplied by local affiliates. The UT paper would print a special edition, and Mir would be outside Kettys-Burg with her camera and portable tape recorder, set to interview students, professors, police commanders, university officials, and shopkeepers.

Mir's words captured the storyline of the previous day and the events that led up to it. It was one of her pictures, however, that channeled that narrative, much as John L. Lewis's demonstration of union power by holding unbreakable sticks had brought the message home to the uneducated miners two generations earlier: a young man in tweed jacket with patches on his sleeves, standing on top of a car, feet planted as if he were to hail a taxi, right arm thrust in the air, holding what the caption said was the First Amendment to the

Constitution, megaphone in his other hand, facing thousands of people rapt in attention.

"You see where I'm going, Myles?" the police chief continued. "Safe landing. Touchdown. No lives lost, not even any broken bones. That's what I want, what we want. And you too. I know you don't want any trouble either. I'm one of the pilots, and I want to work with you, co-pilot. Let's work together. Let's make sure the plane lands safely and no one gets injured. Okie-dokie?"

While this was patronizing to Myles, he let it pass without even a nonverbal response since he knew that this was all cop foreplay to the police sex act, something that'd played out many times the previous summer in Mississippi. He'd told us about one such time when we were all sitting at the conference table in the president's office. He reached into the inside breast pocket of his tweed jacket, pulled out a typewritten page and read it to us.

"Invariably, it started with the finger jabbing to our ribs by the younger troopers, egged on by contemporaries gnawing on a pinch that they spat out more frequently than their dogs would lift a leg. Their hostility was overt, inbred, and communal, suffused with a patriotism and religiosity mocked by flag lapel pins and dashboard statuettes. They tossed out *nigger*, *kike,* and *faggot* as effortlessly as they brandished a nightstick or made a lariat out of rope that no longer was simply a prop. They laughed as if they were imitating a car trying to start on a cold morning and were imploring us to provide the spark that would ignite their engine. That they were in the right was never open for discussion. This is what they'd learned at home, something that'd been passed down like clothing and family stories. It'd been taught that way *because it was*, shorthand for because it was in the good book. And no one was going to defame the good book, now, *heah*?

"I warned my fellow Freedom Riders of what to expect and how not to resist. I knew that when the exuberance of the young troopers was spent, the older officer would appear, telling his reports to calm down, we don't want our *viz-a-tahs* to get the wrong impression of our southern hospitality. And appear he did. He asked for chairs and if we were interested in a glass of cold water. He never used offensive words and feigned respect, condescendingly offering to ask, as an aside, if the young black man next to me was offended when the trooper used the word *sonny*. At that point, the hat came off, and he took a laborious drink of a glass of cold water, to the point of exaggeration. He then held up the empty glass as if it were Yorick's skull and offered some lamentation for the days gone by when there weren't any outside agitators to stir up the locals, 'if you get my meaning.' Then he offered us an escort service to the county line, as if that intangible barrier would serve me as a deterrent to the cause. I accepted his offer and pledged not to return, a commitment that was as hollow as the officer's farewell: 'I'm glad we reached this understanding, and as God is my witness, I wish you no harm.' And I understood that the officer's disappearance was the signal for the troopers to manhandle us all the way to the sign on the road that told us we were leaving the county, 'You come back and see us sometime, now, ya'heah'?"

GEORGE TOWNSEND KNEW it was time to pause, to let Myles respond so that he could assess the situation to avoid implementing any hasty battlefield command directives that could jeopardize his mission. He needed to get the three officers out safely, to ensure that the integrity of the building's contents hadn't been compromised, to disperse the students and have classes resume, and to restore public order so that commercial enterprises could reopen. His entreaty to Myles was a key element of the peace negotiation that invariably is convened during battlefield engagements—not so much to actually generate a cessation of hostilities but rather to determine by probing if there were a new set of circumstances that could yield an advantage that could subsequently be exploited once a resumption of the struggle was initiated.

Later, when I was in jail, I read an interview with the chief that in which he indicated that this process wasn't new to him. He'd been an aide-de-camp in 1952 to Admiral Charles Joy at the armistice talks to end the Korean War that were held at Panmunjom, straddling the 38th parallel. He'd witnessed, first-hand, the North Koreans play for time when their troops were advancing, profess disarming innocence when the subject of POWs was brought up, and act as gracious hosts when Western cameras were turned on. He was also there when these same negotiators would criticize the UN forces for not moving fast enough when battlefield conditions were worsening, become overtly hostile when torture was put on the agenda, and refuse to establish dates for future meetings, necessitating the continuation of the misery.

The irony in all of this was that George Townsend in 1964 was co-opting the very tactics of his despised enemy, the communists, while railing to his minions that the reds were the behind-the-scenes operatives fronting for student dupes.

With the good cop pause, Myles knew he was obliged to respond. Yes, he knew where the chief was going. He was attempting to lure Myles into a position to see the situation as a contest between groups with equivalent competing goals for which Myles and the chief had the joint responsibility to determine the outcome. There'd have to be give-and-take on both sides. Compromise was the key operative word. You certainly couldn't have the pilot pulling up on the throttle while the co-pilot was pushing down. Nobody would win that game. A game in which people could be injured or worse would be a win for neither side. Myles flashed an acknowledgement smile accompanied by a vertical head bob that resembled the last ten seconds of reverberations from the face atop the sprung jack-in-the-box. At that moment, George Townsend believed his training had begun to pay off.

However, he wasn't anticipating receiving compensation that he wouldn't be able to bank.

"Mr. Townsend," Myles began respectfully, "I appreciate your personal involvement. I do. Thank you. I'm in a hundred percent agreement that I don't want any violence, or for anyone to get hurt. No one does. So, what do you have in mind? I mean different from what you told me over the phone last night."

"It's time to call it a day, son," the police chief said in a fatherly way. "Protest is one thing, signs, banner waving, that kind of thing. But this—taking over a building, holding hostages, shutting down the university—these things won't do. You can make your points another way. Got to stop. Right now. You've got to get my men down here, pronto, then leave the building. Right away. Everyone out. That's for starters. Once they're out, safe and sound, well then, we can talk about what happens next."

"Let them out first, then we discuss what happens to us, that's what I understand you're offering."

"That's the way it has to be, uh-huh, yup."

Myles waited a full ten seconds before responding, ten seconds in which the chief was calculating how he was going to physically transport the building occupants to the police station and trying to determine if it'd be better for him if he were to allow Myles to be hauled off in handcuffs.

"George, may I call you George?" Myles asked.

"Yesiree."

"I was hoping to hear something different, George. I was hoping that as my co-pilot, you could see the situation from *my* seat. You want the *situation* taken care of," Myles said, holding up two fingers from each hand and putting figurative quotes on the word the *situation*. "You see the situation as the hostages, the takeover of the building, the school shutting down, shopkeepers not doing any business."

"And the outside agitators, the communists," the chief interrupted, "trying to wreck our way of life. They start with helping you, son, making signs, leading marches, that kind of thing. Then they take over. That's what they do. They sneak in, gain your trust, then it's all over in a flash. And, well, I don't want to offend, so don't take it this way, but they trick you. That's why, you know, they say you're dupes. No offense."

Myles' impatience upon hearing "dupes" caused him to talk over "no offense" and to change his tone to one of exasperation. "Chief, you see this as a series of events, actually crimes of some sort, like disturbing the peace, not having a permit, trespass, false imprisonment. Technically, you're right. March us up in front of a judge and the gavel comes down: guilty. If we were a bunch of guys invading the building to steal things or to rifle through records or had some preconceived idea to injure the cops who were spying on us, I'd be on your side. Throw the book at us. Common criminals, thugs, guilty.

"But that's not what's going on here. This isn't a battle of occupation and hostages. It might seem that way to you and your men, but it's not. It's a battle, sure, but not a battle with guns; it's a battle of ideas."

"Commie ideas, Myles," the chief interjected.

Myles stepped back a half a step, as if to gain a better vantage point from which he would hurl his word bombs. He shook his head slowly and deliberately before he resumed speaking, the chief not recognizing that a chastisement was coming his way.

"Chief, you're on the wrong side—the losing side—of a war about our way of life. We're battling for ideas about what we can say, what we can think, what we can demand, where we can demand it. It's the American way." He paused and then unloaded with a sharp, "Don't tread on me," a double entendre rebuke that infuriated the chief, whose body stiffened as if he'd been shot through with an electrical jolt.

Myles' demeanor had changed. He now lectured George Townsend. "We're not co-pilots, Chief. We aren't working together because we've got different versions of how the plane should land."

The chief tried to interrupt, but Myles waved him off.

"I gave you our demands last night. Five things. Five demands that you haven't responded to, said you weren't going to. You gave me until noon to surrender. I know you're planning to come in, swinging batons, your guys hiding behind shields, running wildly into rooms, beating, smashing, yelling, kicking, taking the stairs, looking for three cops, trampling, cursing, all because you wouldn't negotiate with me as a co-pilot when you had the chance. *I gave you the opportunity to bring the plane down safely, and you ignored me, threatened me.* Now you come, all pleasant, 'let's get through this, work with me.' Too late, Chief. No dice. We're staying. We're not coming out until our demands are met. Oh, and by the way," he finished his *touché*, "you're not coming in at all. Ever."

He turned quickly and reentered the main door, only partially hearing the chief sneer, "You'll pay for this in ways you can't imagine," and not privy to the order given in the van by the man listening to the conversation via the chief's tie clasp microphone, "Get set, prepare for orders to move in fifteen minutes."

Myles took the stairs two at a time and headed for the room where Herzl and I were watching the three cops, still tied to their chairs. The three cops were sweating profusely from a combination of the stuffiness of the room, their incapacitation, and the fear of their fate as the noon deadline approached. The crowd hadn't quite settled down, still abuzz from Herzl's ape-like swinging in midair. Everyone outside knew that the cops were poised to charge. Myles had told Mir of the noon deadline when she called to tell him about the story that she filed. I spotted her, camera in hand, making her way through the mob, filling requesting hands with copies of the UT newspaper, which would cause spontaneous groups to form, listening to a reading of the main story and jockeying for position to see the pictures that Mir had taken the day before. We could see the cops out back gather into formation and had reports that similar maneuvers were occurring on all sides of the building. The cops were poised to move as soon as the chief gave them the order. Claudia reappeared and told Myles everything was in place. Myles motioned to Herzl, who approached the strapped-in plainclothes cop who was still tied up in the chair by the braided Venetian cord and slumped next to the open window, drool oozing out of the sides of his lips from the effect of the ball of paper Myles had jammed into this mouth.

The hullabaloo seemed to dissipate as if on cue. We could hear the horses snorting and their metal shoes clanging against the stone walks. The people reading the newspapers were doing so in silence. It was as if we were all waiting for a whistle or a trumpet or the noon-bell carillon from the tower to signal the start of the hostilities. Myles was straddling the threshold of the door, alternating peeking in to see the cops and the three of us as still as statues then peering down the hall. Suddenly, there was a ring on the phone that startled us disproportionately to its sound. We flinched in unison. Before the second ring, Myles flicked his right wrist into the room, the signal for us not to pick up the receiver. His left arm, outside the room, thrust forward, and within seconds, we could hear window sashes opening throughout the building. With the phone still ringing, Myles nodded to Herzl, who bent down to seize the strapped-in plainclothes cop.

Mir's pictures of what occurred that fall day in 1964 at Kettys-Burg Hall on the campus of the UT in Taos Heights, New Mexico, were carried by the wire services across the country for inclusion in the later afternoon runs of the big city presses. Her report was read, line for line, by one of the anchors on the evening network news. It was said that the president interrupted a reception at the White House to steal a few minutes in front of a TV, although we don't know to this day if that was true. What I can tell you is that Myles had positioned Mir perfectly to capture shots of the two events that catapulted the fracas from a local incident concerning pamphlets and protest at a university in the southwest to a national clash over First Amendment freedoms and the attendant issues of war and civil rights.

Simultaneous with the opening of the window sashes throughout the building, the curtains (which had been taken down from their rods) were draped as banners, inside out, threaded between windows. They'd been cut so that letters hung from them, like children on swings. Three words—Free Speech Movement—fluttered in the midday breeze on each of the four sides of the building. As the words became evident to the crowds, a great cheer went up, followed by sustained applause, then chants of "free speech, free speech, free speech," over and over again. Those at the forefront of the crowd pushed against the sawhorses with both hands in frustration as their compatriots further back raised fists and made tomahawk-like cuts at the air in tempo with the chanted words. The mounted police were focused on restraining their spooked horses. Those on the ground with batons at hand were waiting for the signal to storm the building. Claudia had informed us that the doors to the outside had been jammed, and the windows on the first floor had been blocked by massive oak desks piled high against the sills. It looked for all the world like a major confrontation was about to escalate into violence. Myles' boast that the police weren't coming in appeared to be just that, a temporal declaration to avoid the humiliation of the admission of defeat. Strangely, however, his face didn't betray his conviction. He was taking it all in: the rousing from the crowd outside, the hooting from those standing behind the drapes, the still-ringing phone that went unanswered. Herzl was staring intently at Myles.

Suddenly, without making eye contact with anyone in particular, Myles shouted, "Go!" and Herzl lifted up the chair with the plainclothes cop strapped to it in a fast clean-and-jerk, pushed it through the window and let it hang by the strength of his right arm against the side of the building. The police broke ranks and rushed to the spot directly underneath where the dangling cop was being pressed up and down like a barbell by the Torah-conditioned strength of Herzl's right arm. The other two cops in the room couldn't see that the plainclothes cop hadn't been dropped and were alternating red with rage and white with fright, squirming violently and coughing spasmodically as the saliva-soaked paper that'd been stuffed into their mouths worked its way to the back of their throats. Hundreds of people followed on the heels of the cops outside, still chanting and tomahawk chopping. At the very instant when Mir and the photographer from the *Tribune* were snapping as furiously as possible, as Claudia and I were peering out the window, as the two other cops were thrashing on the floor, and as the plainclothes cop was crying the Hail Mary, Myles picked up the ringing phone and said calmly in a normal voice, "Myles here."

George Townsend the co-pilot wasn't on the other end of the phone. Instead, George Townsend the seething, acrimonious police chief who'd been bested by a graduate student in front of the president of the UT, the mayor, and the governor was launching a diatribe with dead bullet ammunition. Myles let him rant.

When George Townsend was spent, Myles said, "Chief, we've provided you with our five demands. They haven't changed." The profanity-filled response was heard by Claudia and me as we huddled around the phone that Myles angled outward from his left ear. When it was over, Myles said nothing. There was silence. After a few moments, the line went dead.

The siege never materialized. The police were told to stand down and gathered beneath the cop hanging out the window. They dared not taunt Herzl. Out in the crowd, we could hear several variations of, "Did you see what that asswipe Jew was doing?" from a number of cops, which Mir told us later that she'd also picked up on her tape recorder. Upon a signal from Myles, Herzl retracted the plainclothes cop through the window and deposited him and his stink on the floor. Myles asked me to retrieve some paper towels from the men's room and a pitcher of water and a bowl from the kitchen on the lower floor. He asked Claudia to leave, had Herzl close the window, and then Myles explained to the now-subdued cops that he'd remove the paper balls from their mouths and allow them to clean themselves, one at a time. Physically and emotionally exhausted, they sat slumped and offered no resistance.

"Let's eat," Myles announced buoyantly and led us back down a flight, the room now being guarded by others.

We sat around the president's desk, gorging ourselves on the tomatoes, cucumbers, peppers, lettuce, carrots, olives, radishes, hard boiled eggs, cheese, onions, breads, flat crackers, and mushrooms that I'd brought into the building surreptitiously the night before.

When we finished eating, Herzl motioned for me to come to an unoccupied room with him. "I'm sure you heard 'asswipe Jew,' from some of the cops outside." I nodded. "I wasn't surprised that some had yelled it out. What really bothered me was that no one in the crowd had the inclination to use some of their energy to shout down or shame the cops who were saying it. Neither Myles nor Claudia has made mention of it. You don't score points standing up for a Jew," he said. "Unless, of course, you're a Jew yourself." He paused. "We take care of our own, you know. And by the way, that's not selfish. It's self-preservation."

Back in the office, Myles told us his plan: the Free Speech Movement would have to enlist the support of a wider audience in order to sustain itself and avoid settling into a run-of-the-mill student vs. police battle that could be turned into a privilege vs. hostage fight that they couldn't win.

"We have to maintain the high ground," he noted. "Hanging the cop out the window was a necessity in order to avoid a pitched battle, but it won't play well in the paper if we're associated with violence, especially against cops. There was never any intention of dropping him, but we had to convince the cops that we would. In the future, when all this dies down, we need to get the word out that it was a stunt.

"Herzl, bring the three cops down to the conference room on the second floor. Have some food brought to them and take off one of the arm restraints for each of them. Be careful, make sure to station people at the windows and the door of the room. They're cops, and although they don't look like they're in great shape, we need to outnumber them three to one, okay? Let them talk to one another. But let them know that we expect them to be on best behavior. Otherwise, tell them it's back to the full restraints and the paper down their throats. Claudia, come with me."

Myles knew that with the three hostage cops, it was unlikely that the building's electricity would be turned off or the phone line cut. He sensed that the police chief had his own set of problems, not the least of which was going to be pressure from the UT to resolve the crisis so that the school could get back to normal operations. He also understood that having the cops as hostages was an embarrassment to the police department. After a conversation with Mir, Myles understood how the situation was being depicted on television and in those newspapers with the most influence on elected officials throughout the country. He knew that the Free Speech Movement had to be seen as a continuum of the Freedom Summer, the Freedom Rides, and the March on Washington. He asked me if he could read my notebook, which I handed him eagerly. He huddled with Claudia for a half hour, spoke with Mir for half that time, then went back to an office and sat down.

I made my way to the room where the cops were being held just as they finished eating. Claudia appeared and took a seat in a chair facing them. She reintroduced herself, formally, extending a hand to each and exchanging names. All that occurred was in the past, she said, and she didn't excoriate them for spying or apologize for having them tied up. Her tone was businesslike but not unpleasant. She asked them if they knew why they were there. "Not by choice," one of them responded quickly. She asked the question slightly differently.

"Do you know why you're *still* here?" she tried again.

They seemed dumbfounded and couldn't answer.

"You're still here because they *want* you to be here," she said.

They were incredulous, dramatically exhaling sounds that weren't words but which carried straightforward meanings.

"If they wanted you out, they would've negotiated your release," she said evenly. "We made some requests that they didn't even deign to negotiate."

"Demands," the plainclothes cop snorted.

"Yes, demands," Claudia replied, "but still...," she trailed off, watching their expressions. "You know how it works," she picked up. "One side asks—makes *demands*—and the other side counterpunches, maybe agreeing to some points, suggesting changes to others, perhaps denying the possibility of a few. But the key point is that they're engaging, they're negotiating, they're attempting to get a solution for a problem that'll work for both sides. It's part of the give-and-take. Both sides—your chief and Myles—know that despite what's in the papers, they're not going to get a hundred percent of what they demand, what they want. Everybody knows that. We know that. It's the unwritten rule."

I was struck by how out of character she seemed; this was a new Claudia to me.

She could see that despite her being thirty years younger and a *girl*, no doubt, she'd made an inroad. Not a highway yet, but a start.

"Something to think about," she said.

She and I left to rejoin Myles. She plopped down into a large brown leather chair, flopped a leg over the side and went to sleep. Myles asked me to read from my notebook, occasionally asking for clarification or color or another way of thinking about what I'd witnessed. He wanted it all, from the beginning, from the observations on the roof where I witnessed the scene on the Strip the day before right through to the most recent notes scribbled almost unintelligibly in the room upstairs with the three hostage cops. However, I never put in anything about the collapse of the fire escape, my head injury, or the kindness of the police officer out of uniform who'd freed my leg and taken me to get ice to put on my wound. Myles motioned for me to show him a sketch and to explain what I meant by a particular representation or notation. Reading and showing him the sketches, I felt like a maestro playing legato with one hand and staccato with the other. This exercise went on for more than two hours, nonstop. At a certain point, he paused and leaned back in his chair.

"It's coming to me," he said.

Claudia awakened with a snort, and we laughed, the first private moment we shared in more than twenty-four hours. There was no outward manifestation of change as a result of their encounter. How quickly boiling water loses its steam when the flame is turned off.

I was wondering if Myles had recognized me in the reflection of the glass. If he had, he wasn't letting on. I was edgy. He began to pace around the room. I'd never seen him particularly worried before. I had no idea what was going to happen next and wondered if he did either. Was he formulating a plan or going to wait until the other side made its move and then counterattack? Was he rethinking the wisdom of anything he'd done? Did he have an outcome in mind, and if so, was he merely playing out all the chess moves in advance? At one point, I thought about asking but stalled, like an airplane at the top of a loop the loop, not sure that the question would elicit an answer that I'd find comforting. Part of it was that I didn't want Myles to think that by virtue of even asking a question I was somehow unsure of the righteousness of the cause. And part of it, too, was that I didn't want him to squeeze me out as Claudia had done to the guy who'd left his jacket on the back of the chair in the president's office the night before when he bolted from the room. Originally through luck, I'd been swept into Myles' field, and I enjoyed the special status it conveyed. Others showed deference and Claudia's sneers were never directed at me. Perhaps they needed me for the notes and the sketches. If that was the price of admission to this exclusive club, it was something I was willing to pay. It also enabled me to have a connection to Mir, although I hadn't seen her recently except for glances through the windows.

On what might have been the tenth revolution around the room, Myles suddenly stopped. "They're not going to cut them; they'll tap them," he muttered, articulating the conclusion of a conversation he'd been having with himself. He filled us in so that this seeming non-sequitur had a context.

"They haven't called, and God knows they want this thing to be over. There's no question they'll negotiate. They'll give on the first demand, free speech and all. It's really a restatement of the First Amendment.

"I agree," Claudia said.

"The second, sure, that too. All it means is they need probable cause—something any hack will give them. A warrant won't be a problem, so they'll go for that as well."

"Completely," she added.

"They'll agree to three, the thing about prosecuting any cop who contributed to the riot. I'm pretty sure they'll say okay to it, because, you know, in the end, they simply won't be able to find those responsible, so that's an easy one for them to give in on."

"Yes, you're right," she said, as if she were now assigned the role of cheerleader.

Myles didn't seem to acknowledge her confirmations.

"It's four and five that they can't do and won't even be able to negotiate: no army recruiting and getting rid of the ROTC."

"That's because they don't have the authority. That's why they haven't called you to negotiate," Claudia chimed in, her voice rising. "They're trying to figure out what their position should be and maybe more important, how they can make our demands sound unreasonable. So we can be portrayed as spoiled children, communists, anti-Americans, unpatriotic, you know how they think."

"Precisely," Myles replied. "And what better way for them to prepare their side than to find out what our real positions are so that they can then negotiate with this knowledge in hand.

"So, you see?" he looked to me for confirmation but continued on without my response. I could just as easily have been a mannequin. I started to think that this was either a set piece or the result of their spending so much time together that they instinctively knew what the other was going to say. I wondered if this was something that they'd discussed in the room next door that had somehow degenerated into the violence between them after sex.

Myles went on, "Originally, I thought they were going to cut the lines, deprive us of contact with the outside world. But if they did that, they'd make us martyrs, something they're not going to do. They're waiting for us to make a call—a call not to them but to someone else, and they'll be on the line. They're going to tap it. They're waiting for me to call someone."

"So make sure you don't," Claudia admonished him in a harsh tone.

Myles looked at her as if she'd lost her mind. "What? What are you talking about?" he said acidly as if to scold either her inability to comprehend or her insolence.

She blushed and instinctively turned to face away from us, pressing one of her hands against the multi-colored knit hat she was still wearing, a temporary pressure bandage to alleviate the pounding. This rebuke caused a physical, and no doubt, an emotional reaction. She cowered, the opposite of what she'd done when I spied on her and Myles a few hours before. I was amazed. It struck me that behavior in the presence of a third party could be so different from what it would be in a one-on-one situation. And I was just a voyeur. I was thinking that if I'd not been there, this might've escalated into a physical fight à la the contretemps I'd witnessed earlier. This was the first time I recognized that people say and do things differently when they're in the presence of a group. Later, I'd witness a situation in which the dynamic of a group superseded the behavior of individuals, emboldening them to act in a reckless manner they wouldn't countenance if any one of them had been alone.

Myles picked up the phone, dialed the number of the UT paper, and asked for Mir.

When she got on, he said, "The cops are singing, loud and clear, you got that?" And he went on to explain how the police were first hiding on the roofs of the buildings above Broadway and how several cops stripped out of their uniforms into civilian clothes and prompted the confrontations, and how the three hostage cops were filming this from the roof of Kettys-Burg Hall. All of this was true, of course, but none of the information had come from the three hostage cops. It was all contained in my notebooks. He knew that the cops' plan had been to promote a riot that would result in mass arrests. He said that he was now aware that the police had created false signs, banners, and documents that would later be "found" on telephone poles and the Strip, which would link the protesters to the Communist Party.

He relayed this tale to Mir as having come from the three hostage cops, who, he indicated with a gleeful tone, were telling him everything about the operation in order to save their own skins, having been victim and witness to Herzl's ravings.

"No telling what this crazy Jew will do next. I can't control him," he said.

"What else would you expect from a Heeb?" Claudia chimed in, still staring out the window.

I was stunned. What was going on? Should I say something? Generic? You know, like derogatory comments about people of different faiths were really beneath them? Why, after all, did Myles say "crazy Jew" and not just "crazy guy?" And why did Claudia feel the need to say "Heeb?" What did Herzl's Judaism have to do with anything? Thinking back to what Ben Veniste had said to me earlier in the evening, I wondered if Myles was playing a role for the cops listening in on the line. Was it that he was mimicking what he'd heard from the southern cops the previous summer and trying a false ingratiation ploy allowing these cops to think that deep down, he was more like them? Or was this simply some sort of a signal to them? That he'd give up Herzl for them to prosecute as part of a deal? Or was it something far worse—an ingrained hatred for a people based on two thousand years of institutional prejudice stemming from the charge of Jewish guilt for the death of Jesus?

I decided to say nothing, but I debated whether I should bring it up with Herzl when I saw him next.

Myles told Mir that there was plenty of food in the building and they could hold out for weeks. Then he got to the heart of the matter, assuming an exaggerated intensity marked by a lowering of his voice and a measured cadence.

"This is just for you to know, Mir," he offered conspiratorially. He even cupped his hand over the phone as if a hidden camera were capturing his image, which would authenticate the very falsehoods he was saying. "I'll agree to negotiate with the police chief the next time he calls. I'll restate our five demands. In some form or another, he'll agree to discuss the first three, not agree to give in, but to negotiate."

There was a silence for a few seconds which indicated that Mir had responded in some fashion.

"You're right that he'll say that he doesn't have the authority to discuss the things about army recruiting and ROTC. The truth is he doesn't. But I'll tell him I don't believe him. In any event, we'll meet and start the negotiation process. He's going to be eager, getting pressure from the higher ups to free the hostages. Knowing this, I'll have the upper hand."

Silence again.

"Okay, I'll soften something, and he'll think he's on the way to a settlement. In his favor. That's when I'll change the demands. Jesus, he'll go nuts. I'll add one or make a new condition attached to an existing one. He'll charge bad faith. I'll counter by saying he must've not understood. He'll be furious. He'll have a temper tantrum. Go bananas. Things'll get hot. But I'm going to play cool because we have three hostages and the Yid who hung the cop out the window. I'm not sure the next time he won't go off the deep end. They don't listen to anyone, you know, except one of their kind. They call themselves, what is it?" he pivoted to Claudia.

"Stiff-necked people," she called out.

"Oh, yeah."

Back to the call with Mir. "Hey, by the way, it's too bad you'll be at your house tonight sleeping instead of here, taking pictures on the inside for tomorrow's paper." Then he hung up.

Heeb. Yid. Stiff-necked people. Well, at least he didn't say *kike*, I thought to myself.

"Will they take the bait?" Claudia asked, showing no signs of having been reprimanded just moments earlier. She either had no self-respect or possessed a skin so thick she could become desensitized to his criticism as rapidly as water evaporates from a puddle on a hot summer's day.

"Yes, I'm sure," Myles replied. "They had to be on the line."

"I've got to go back to the room with the cops," she said and bolted from the chair.

"Tonight, Jacobo, when you go to Ben Veniste's to get more food, bring Mir back with you," Myles said.

With this command, blood rushed through my system faster than water ran down the Rio Grande past the boathouse, and it seemed to flee my head and collect in my genitals. Appearing woozy, Myles assisted me into the chair that Claudia had just vacated. I pushed his anti-Semitic words to the back of my mind, allowing me to hope that this was part of a scene in a play that still needed several acts before I could figure out the true meaning of what'd been said.

A hint of a smile, perhaps it was a smirk, betrayed Myles' serious intentions and seemed to suggest that he was enjoying the game, especially as he was setting the rules. He asked me if I knew where he was going. I responded in a literal sense, "Up with Claudia to the room with the hostages?" which provoked a genuine startled roar of a laugh. "No, Jacobo, not where I'm going but where I'm headed, do you understand?"

"No, I don't understand…or know what you mean."

He put his hand on my shoulder, gave it a couple of shakes and said playfully, "Hey, didn't they teach you colloquial English on the reservation?"

He smiled. I did my best to suppress a wince. Then he launched into the explanation.

"Look, the three hostage cops aren't going to be harmed. I've seen too much violence in the South. For real. I agreed to your friend's window hanging stunt only because it was dramatic and would prevent the cops from storming the building. If they'd done that, there would've been a real riot. A lot of folks would've been injured." He looked at my bandana. "Like that, but worse. I want this to be a war of *ideas,* and I have to choose my battles carefully. This one—the Free Speech Movement—we've got to win it. Otherwise the war will be lost."

I imagined him beginning what could only be described as a dress rehearsal soliloquy, a practice run for his conversation with the Police Chief or any other bigwig that would take George Townsend's place. He gesticulated at the right time for emphasis with his arms, fingers, eyes, shoulders, neck, and mouth. Each twitch, each mannerism seemed coordinated with his words, and their tones rose and fell with an onomatopoeic effect.

Myles could see something that none of us had seen, as we were too wrapped up in the moment. I suspected that he had the capability to project into the future and analyze the current situation as it was playing out, thereby giving him a perspective that others didn't enjoy and an advantage that adversaries couldn't comprehend. I wondered what would happen if he lost this gift.

In addition to being an actor, was I witnessing the workings of a playwright?

He could detect that this was an instance that'd be labeled by a future generation, much as historians have characterized sixteenth century Europe as having been the Age of Reformation. Yet, those alive in Germany or England in, say, 1550 would've thought of themselves as living in Modern Times. Myles had told us that those who'd condemned Galileo for his heretical thought that the sun was at the center of the solar system could never envision a subsequent era in which he'd be praised as the first modern scientist. Yes, Myles was wise enough to know that the façade of the American Century had begun to show some cracks that weren't discernable to those whose eyes were at ground level, but that, when viewed from the future, would be as apparent as the blood spattered on Jackie Kennedy's pink Chanel suit in Dallas. He knew that the Free Speech Movement wasn't just about what was going on at the UT in a city in northern New Mexico. Rather, he understood it to be the label for a metaphor of the times that ultimately became known as *The Sixties*—a catch phrase that didn't describe a decade so much as it defined a dramatic shift in how we lived our lives and thought of ourselves as a people.

Myles also knew, all too well, that wars are won by generals, and he was intent on being the next five-star, regardless of how he got to that command pinnacle.

My imagination got the best of me and I envisaged Myles' next act of the Free Speech Movement: He'd channel "The Times They Are a-Changin" in substance and tenor. He'd recognize that "Come gather 'round people..." was a worthy successor to "When in the course of human events..." and that it was now time to resurrect the American Revolution that had ossified and left fossils of racism, poverty, and war that needed to be excavated and put in museums as relics of the past.

As if he were alone, he darted, pranced, leaped onto the desk, alighted on the swivel-back chair, squatted, sat cross-legged, lied down on his side, leaned against the wall, all the time starting and stopping, editing on the fly, twisting the corner of his mouth when he was equivocal, nodding vigorously when he approved, never stopping to catch his breath. He went on for a few minutes, not stumbling over any word, no hesitation, no cracking of voice. He stood behind the desk, wearing his tweed jacket and occasionally ran his hands through his hair. His fingers lightly touched the president's leather-bound ink blotter like a sprinter hovering over the starting line. After this warm-up, he walked calmly to the front door, opened it, planted himself on the steps, waited until the buzz of the crowd died down, walked up to the microphone that had been set up, looked straight forward and offered up a short speech delivered to the cops, reporters, members of the administration, shopkeepers, and everyone else who'd descended upon the entrance to Kettys-Burg Hall.

Yes, I saw him make this speech; I heard every word. And when it was over, I felt my fingers pressing so hard against the top of the desk that pains went up my arms to my shoulders. I looked over and saw Myles sound asleep in the big leather chair, having collapsed there after Claudia left the room more than an hour earlier. He'd heard nothing I'd just said, witnessed none of my conjuring, was unaware that I'd usurped his very essence to create a short speech that I then wrote down in my notebook with a hard-pressed ballpoint pen. I'd share it with him one day when my self-confidence would enable me to bear the brunt of his criticism.

In my exhaustion, I turned to the image of Mir, something that I'd been doing with great frequency. A feeling of warmth—my first love—had enveloped me, and I wanted to have a reminder of her with me at all times. I turned the page of my notebook, put down the pen, picked up a newly sharpened pencil, and began to sketch an image of her, using both the point and the sides of the pencil. I made her face me with a three quarter's view, one ear hidden, the other showing her favorite dangling earring. I shaded her high cheek bones and temples to reflect her bronze skin and showed her smile without teeth, which you could only see when she'd laugh. Then I made the decision to catch one of her eyes in a wink, which would always be a special signal meant only for me whenever I'd look at her. As I was about to close the notebook, I realized that this page shouldn't be read by others; it was too personal and had nothing to do with my assignment, so I gently tore it out along the perforation, folded it over twice, and put it in my rear pocket. I had no idea how significant this would turn out to be.

CHAPTER 8

It's all about Myles

I left Myles asleep and went upstairs to the room where Claudia had returned to speak with the three hostage cops. As I entered, one of the cops said, "Show me something first," and with that, coming up with a literal response to his question, she crossed her arms, grabbed the bottom of her T-shirt and, in one swift jerk, pulled her top off. The three cops were stunned that she did this and would now have something to tell the boys back at the stationhouse. Instantly, she wasn't the same person to them. She was just some twenty-one-year old girl with huge tits flapping near their faces. She betrayed no embarrassment at my being there and acted as if this were in the normal course of events. She put her hands inside her back pockets, leaned back on the desk, and said, "Now it's your turn." I was expecting each cop to disrobe, and for an instant I felt queasy, imagining that she was referring to me as well, since when she said the word *your*, it was at precisely the time she had turned to see me take a place at the side of the room.

She made no effort to put her T-shirt back on.

"We were supposed to take pictures of certain things," the plainclothes cop offered, breaking the silence, trying desperately to make eye contact with her so as not to be characterized by her as a pervert.

"Like what?" Claudia responded nonchalantly, moving forward a little so that her breasts separated from her body.

"You know, the crowds," he replied.

"What certain things?" she persisted. "What were you told to do?"

The plainclothes cop wouldn't look at his comrades and said wearily, "They wanted the confrontations, the fights. That's what the movie camera was for. Individual photos were for the leaders, you know, like Myles, up on top of the car."

"I understand the stills, but pictures of the fights, why was that important?" she pushed, her voice rising with impatience.

"They needed them. It was the most important thing we were supposed to do, that's all."

"Listen to me," she warned, getting up and approaching him. "You have a choice here. You can answer my questions, stay in this nice room, eat some good food, and practically lick my tits, or," she paused and leaned over him so close that his lips were within a hair's breadth from her nipples, "we'll take you back to the other room, tie you up again, stuff more paper down your throat, watch you gag and crap in your pants and hand you over to the *kike*, who'd think nothing of hanging you out the window again, only this time I'm not so sure he wouldn't let you drop."

The *kike*! She'd picked up the verbal baton from Myles and was running with it.

There was no doubt that I was going to make a sketch of Claudia naked from the waist up, a drawing that would somehow have to include her female animal-like exterior juxtaposed with her male ruthlessness. I recalled seeing drawings of Echidna in a class on ancient history, the half woman, half snake Greek god, an apt inspiration for what she represented, so I reached for my notebook to begin. It wasn't next to me. I freaked out for a minute, thinking I might have lost it, then remembered leaving the notebook on the president's desk as I tiptoed by the sleeping Myles to get here to where Claudia was interrogating the three cops.

"They needed them for the splicer," the plainclothes cop spit out. "Okay? Got it? That's all I'm gonna say," he said defiantly.

At this point Claudia glanced at me, I'm sure to indicate that she wanted me to get every word of this, then twisted her head back to the cop and practically shouted into the top of his head, keeping her breasts tantalizingly close to his mouth. I paid extra careful attention, trying to memorize everything that was being said so I could transpose it into my notebook later.

"They were going to splice your film of the crowd, how, to rearrange the sequence of events? To make it appear that whatever trouble there was came from the crowd, not the cops? Is that it? Is that what you were doing? Was that the plan? Huh? Yes? Tell me! Now!"

"Yeah, yeah! That was the plan!" he shouted, moving his head back so that his eyes were now locked with hers.

With that admission, she placed her hands firmly on the sides of his head and planted an open-mouthed kiss on his lips, then moved her body straight up and slowly brushed her breasts against his cheeks, his consolation prize for spilling the beans. She turned around, slipped her T-shirt back on, briskly passed me on the way out, gave me a thumbs up, then disappeared down the hall. I stood awkwardly in the room for a few seconds, then followed her out, replaced by the guys who'd been standing guard outside the room.

Kada gayo kanta en su kumash. Every rooster sings in its coop, I said to myself.

I went in search of Herzl and found him in a room next to where the three cops had been held originally, where he'd hung one out the window. He was sitting on the floor in the corner. Thinking he might be asleep, I tiptoed in and sat on one of the chairs the cops had been tied up in, imagining the frustration, anxiety, and fear they must've felt. With the shorter days and an overcast sky, there was little light in the room despite it being five o'clock. I'd have to wait until midnight to go back through the tunnel to get more food. I wasn't tired, but with the darkness, Herzl's soft rhythmic breathing, and the tension of the last thirty hours having subsided, I allowed myself to relax.

Herzl's head rested on a sweatshirt jammed up against the baseboard. His thick curly hair spilled down over his forehead and was parted in the front. His black beard was dense and bushy—a stark contrast to mine, which was uniform in length and predominantly red. His eyebrows were thick and angled like exaggerated circumflexes. His nose was long and straight and his mouth perfectly horizontal. All of which had the curious effect of making him look remarkably like the geometric representations of faces drawn by the Navajo women on pottery—a caricature of a primitive. The bulge in his biceps was made more prominent by the thinness of his waist. His legs accounted for a disproportionate percentage of his height, his sculpted calf definition merging into elongated, sinewy thighs. It was clear to see where he generated great strength and why it was difficult to keep up with him on water or land.

I was eager to ask him questions: would he have dropped the plainclothes cop if Myles had ordered him to do so? How had he gotten into the building (since I was pretty sure he wasn't part of the group that took control with Myles)? Why was he even there (he had shown no interest in any of the campus organizations that planned and executed the rally)?

There was no light when Herzl awoke. He ran his fingers through his hair and said he had to pee. I filled him in on what went on with Claudia and the three hostage cops.

"Look, Herzl, I really have to know. Would you, you know—"

"What do they think?" he interrupted.

"They think you're crazy."

"Then it did the job."

"Myles thinks you are, you know. He said 'nuts' and 'loon' too." I didn't mention any of the slurs. "Anyway, so how'd you get here?"

"I just came upon the scene more or less by chance from behind Kettys-Burg."

Why he wanted to get inside the building was not so straightforward.

"Impulse, that's all. I saw the crowds, the cops chasing them, the administrators rushing out the doors, windows opening, kids raising their fists and shouting. I'd never seen anything like it."

"But how'd you get inside?"

"Garden hoses. I connected a couple of them that were attached to a sprinkler and shimmied up the nearest tree. I wrapped the hose around a shoulder, then climbed out on the limb nearest the building and heaved the end to a kid in an open window. He yelled to me that he'd secured it to a desk. I tied off my end and swung across as if it were a monkey bar. No big deal."

"I was really surprised to see you here. Happy, but kind of amazed," I said.

"Me too. I wandered about. Poked my head into rooms. Kids talking about free speech, opposition to the war, discrimination. You've seen it."

I had indeed.

"I didn't need to be convinced to show support for these kinds of issues. You have to understand, Jacobo," he said, "Jews believe passionately in the American freedoms. We shy away from war, having been its victims for so many years. If we're going to fight, let's find a just cause that we can win. That'd be good for a change, don't you think? Two thousand years out of the ring. We're rusty but not without some skills. I mean, enough of this martyr stuff."

I thought about his arm wrestling and smiled.

He went on. "We've fled from one country to the next with little on our backs but our clothes, scrolls, and children. The Jew haters say we're like a spider spinning a web, trapping our prey as we went to conquer the world. Conquer, ha! We've got no swords to kill foes or gold to buy prosperity. Nothing. All we carry is our collective memory, Torah, pride, patience, and yearning for peace. Oh, and misery, don't forget the misery. I'm sure if you could've measured the weight of all the things we carried, misery would've accounted for more than half.

"I have to go to the bathroom."

When he returned, it was as if he'd left a placemark in a book and returned to the same page.

"We spent hundreds of years in certain places, telling ourselves that we were locals, but knowing that at a moment's notice, like that," he snapped his fingers, "the king's henchmen would awake with something as flimsy as a vision and *poof*, here they come, raping and killing, squeezing dreams from us like water from a sponge until it becomes dry.

"And you know why?" he asked rhetorically. "For having killed Jesus, they'd say. That's what they think. And you know what? We wretched Jews would look at the blood, the deaths, and the stolen children, then quietly pick up our shattered belongings and tattered prayer books. Here's the pathetic part: the only thing we could say was, 'Next year in Jerusalem!' God bless. Enough.

"That so much expectation could come from such hopelessness." He sighed, trailed off, and went silent for a few seconds before starting up again.

"No one has to teach us, me, about the right to free speech. Don't need reminding about the hazards of state religion, of being a proxy in someone else's war or being prevented from practicing what I preach. I could take a test on those subjects today without studying. *Any* Jew could *teach* those courses without a syllabus.

"I'm starved." With that, he took off for the kitchen.

Al buen entendedor pokas palavras abastan: *To one who understands, only a few words are needed*, I said softly as he went out the door, then reproached myself for not sharing my thoughts with him.

While Herzl was getting food, I trotted down to the president's office, anxious to reclaim my notebook. It wasn't there. I turned the lights on and scurried behind each bookcase, table, chair, lamp, and sofa, becoming more frustrated and talking to myself. I lifted the blotter off the desk, uncovered magazines from the glass coffee table, checked behind the curtains, rummaged through the bookcase. No notebook. I retraced where I'd danced around the room when Myles fell asleep in the chair when I'd made my grand speech to the sleeping leader of the movement. My eyes darted to impossible places: the window ledges, the transom over the door, the chair rail. With inspiration, I opened the desk drawers; no luck. The wastepaper basket; no. I pounded the desktop with my fist. Once, twice, three times, berating myself for losing the record that Myles had requested I make and disappointed that I couldn't do the one simple thing he'd asked of me. *I'll look like a fool in front of Mir,* I thought. What'll she think of me now? What'll I say to her when I meet up with her after bringing more food in the middle of the night? I was crushed. Water drizzled out of my pores the way chickpea paste oozed from the linen bags Madre used to make the tapas paste for Friday night dinners. I could inhale the smells of her hearth and yearned to be back beside her warmth. I shivered and instinctively rubbed each arm with the opposite hand. I took one last turn about the room, opened the door, and aimlessly walked down the hall. I was despondent. I noticed a green light arcing out to the hall for about five seconds, accompanied by a soft buzz, followed by a click and a shuffle. Intrigued, I headed that way, began to turn into the room where the light and noise had originated and was startled by Myles, who exited and gave me a cheery greeting, perhaps overcompensating for my glum expression. "Hey, here's your notebook," he said, jamming it into my hands. "I'm off to see how Claudia's doing with the cops. By the way, when you go out to get some food, bring Mir back, okay?"

I raced to the room where I'd been talking to Herzl in order to jot down Claudia's experiences with the cops, including sketches of her, topless, in a variety of positions as well as to capture Herzl's ruminations on the Jews.

I was exhausted from conversation, writing, and drawing. When I was finished getting the notebook up to date, I fell asleep.

This time, when I turned the door handle to the room adjacent to the president's office, it made a squeak. Myles saw me, smiled, and asked me if I wanted to take a turn with Claudia, slapping her on her rear with one hand and opening his other palm the way Ben Veniste would indicate that a customer could sit at a particular table. Another time, it was Claudia who saw me first and began to scream at me to get out while Myles read a newspaper account of someone else's adventures in the south during the previous summer. The third time they both looked at me and said, simultaneously, whothefuckdoyouthinkyouareyouredhairedindianassholejewlover, then ignored me and continued their fight.

After a few hours, I awoke, left Herzl curled up in the corner of the room, quietly made my way down to the first floor and quickly slipped through the door that led to the basement and the undisturbed room that abutted the underground railroad tunnel. I pushed the door that opened onto the Blueberry Creek and ape-walked up the slight incline until I could see over the top, far enough away from the crowded sleeping bag encampment not to draw any attention. I looped the long way around to the café, walking slowly, head down. I went to the back where the pallets were stored.

"*Bienvenido, hermano*," came a voice from the shadows that startled me. I inhaled the fragrant aroma of one of Ben Veniste's cigars, something he wouldn't smoke inside the café. The closer I got to the sound, the more easily I could see, especially as he dragged on the cigar, the glowing tobacco leaves casting enough light to make out his silhouette and cane. I recounted what'd transpired during the last twenty-four hours for him and was so engrossed in the details I almost forgot the second part of my mission: to bring Mir back with the food.

She lived on the south side of the campus in a dormitory near People's Park—a complication for easy access that would require me to have my story straight, because the police were now using the park as a staging ground, information that Claudia had wheedled out of the hostage cops. Everything I came up with seemed convoluted. Realistically, what was I doing up at three thirty in the morning when there was a tense hostage situation involving students just four blocks away? How could I bluff my way into Mir's building if asked by hostile cops what I was doing there since I couldn't prove I lived there? After unconvincingly trying out several scenarios that seemed okay with the first anticipated question, but which broke down upon further examination, Ben Veniste came up with an idea that made sense in its simplicity and plausibility. He ambled over to a wooden chest underneath pegs where students hung clothes when they entered the café and retrieved an unclaimed dark blue hooded sweatshirt that had the word UT in golden italicized script arched over the word Crew over the left upper part of the front.

"You're on your way to pick up a teammate for an early morning run followed by a workout on the river. Spend a few minutes and write down some of your rowing commands, so you can show them that all you're doing is practicing your homework."

He handed me some ledger paper, and I immediately set to the task of following his suggestion. I sketched an eight-oared shell and circled where the cox would sit, penciling in Mir's name, as the jig would be up if I tried to convince a cop that she could pull an oar on an equal footing with us, who averaged almost six feet four and a little less than two hundred pounds. I put in some notes about the sequence of the number of strokes throughout a typical race, the length of the sprints, the goals in minutes and seconds for each kind of sprint, the number of strokes per minute we'd practice, and the training methods we used to increase our breathing capacity and stamina.

Keeping my head down while staring at the piece of paper containing my sleight of hand and with the hood of the sweatshirt creeping down my brow, I passed a cop who didn't give me a second thought. Standing in front of the house where Mir lived, I suddenly realized that I neither knew her last name nor which floor she lived on. Peeking into windows or scaling a trellis to gain access by bypassing the locked front door were out of the question, what with police bivouacked all over the area. There was a settee on the front porch filled with blankets that would serve as a refuge for me to gather my thoughts and anesthetize the bite from the pre-dawn autumn morning. In one motion, I lifted a blanket, lowered my shoulder, and started to roll onto the bench when I was startled by a muffled cry, then momentarily shocked as the blanket began to move. "Ow! What the! Get offfffff! Hey!" came the distressed sounds, accompanied by uncoordinated arm and leg squirming. I leapt up immediately, apologizing profusely and hoping the noise wouldn't attract the suspicion of a patrolman disassociated from the pack, out for a smoke or a nip from a hidden flask.

Mir jerked her head out from underneath the blanket and ran her tongue all around the inside of her gums, then broke into a wide smile when she realized who was standing above her. "Shhhh, Jacobo," she said softly, touching my arm and sending so much electricity through my body I imagined I was brighter than the streetlamp outside her dorm. She kept her arm there as she recounted why she was on the porch.

"I sensed that Myles was giving me a signal when he said it was too bad I wasn't in the building taking pictures. I mean, why would he say that if he didn't have a way to get me in and out with my camera? But I didn't think it would be you! How did you get out? And how is it that they have enough food? None of us could figure that out."

I told her all about it as she got up and started to walk with me back to the Café. It was quiet. There were few people milling about. I was startled when I heard a voice that appeared to come from directly behind us.

"Everything okay?" the voice asked.

"What's it to you?" Mir shot back, neither breaking stride nor turning around.

Something about the voice. I stopped. My heart rate exploded. I turned around. It was the cop who'd rescued me from the fire escape, now in his uniform but without his hat, the brush cut still standing at attention in the middle of the night.

"Yeah, yeah, I'm, we're fine, just needed to get some air."

"Get that checked out, okay?" he said, pointing to my bandana.

"Sure, yeah, I will, thanks." I said and gave him a thumb's up in front of my chest so Mir couldn't see it.

"All right, then," he said, then looked at Mir when she started to walk away and made the boxer's stance, moving his bulging biceps up and down so that his shirt uniform rippled. I nodded and smiled.

"What was that all about?" she asked.

"Some cops, you know, are all right, I guess," I said.

She gave me a look that said *are you kidding?* then put her arm around my waist and leaned into me.

At this point, guilt was competing with shame for my attention. I'd gone past the opportunity to come clean with Mir, Ben Veniste, Herzl, Myles, and the others inside Kettys-Burg Hall. The truth would've been so simple. It was nothing to be embarrassed about; it wasn't as if I'd tripped and fallen down like a clumsy ox. Mir was talking, but I wasn't really listening. Instead, I was carrying on a conversation with my conscience. I tried to convince myself that I hadn't lied. I never said that I'd been attacked or participated in the riot. Others had seen the bandana as evidence of what they'd imagined. People do that. So I just let it pass. Harmless, wasn't it? *Well, no, it wasn't*, my other self was telling me. And now I'd compounded the problem by allowing it to go on, realizing that I was in the position of having to keep up the pretense as an admission of my failure to tell the truth at the outset. Was it out of defiance against Myles' admonition to stay out of the fray? A rebellion against authority? A desire to be admired? Even if any of this was true, couldn't I have seen this as fleeting, of having no intrinsic value?

"Oh boy," I said, at first thinking I'd said it in my reverie.

"What? Oh boy, what?" Mir said, nuzzling against my arm.

"Ah, nothing, sorry, I don't know where that came from."

Another lie.

I did notice, with racing heart, that the closer we got to the café, she maintained her pose without prompting from me. Ben Veniste greeted her warmly, winking at me when she was out of eyesight, eliciting a smirk that gave my feelings away. Pallets piled high with food were loaded onto two bikes at the back door. We started out in wagon train fashion, each of us paired with one of the young Mexican men primed to inform any who might ask that we were taking breakfast to the crew team, who'd be conducting an early morning running workout at the stadium. Inside the tunnel, we added mushrooms to the containers, transferred the pallets to the basement and into the second room, then unloaded them quietly before making several trips up the stairs into the first floor of the building. We arranged the containers on a table in a large room on the first floor. Immediately afterward, Mir loaded her camera with film, fiddled with the various lenses, buttons, and levers, pronounced herself ready and took off as if she was already familiar with the place. I found Herzl fast asleep where I'd left him in the room on the third floor. My nerves were too jangled to sleep. I made new entries into my notebook, augmenting the summaries I used on my outing to retrieve Mir by making sketches of her sleeping on the porch and of us walking arm and arm.

At 5:00 a.m., Mir was positioning Myles and Claudia in various poses and grabbing passersby from the hall when a particular setup needed balance or depth. She shot Myles from below to accent his command, from above, standing on her tippy toes on a desk to make a portrayal of a lecture, arranging students on chairs, on the floor, and leaning against door jams, all eyes on the leader. Through the window in the door of the room where the cops were lounging, she took pictures of Claudia, engaged in serious discussion, all of them looking like they were taking a seminar together. She caught candids of Myles tapping a pencil to a private beat against the president's desk, of Herzl dozing, of me writing and sketching in my notebook, of others reading books as if it were simply time to prepare for a class, of a few sitting around a conference table eating the food we'd snuck in via the tunnel, of well-behaved young people in tidy rooms debating and writing. She captured the ordinariness of what was going on inside Kettys-Burg—a necessary counterbalance to what was being said by the cops and the administration, who had the ear of the press.

Public opinion was being formed based on the limited amount of information available and the established credibility of those with institutional authority. Myles understood that he needed to preempt the formation of hardened negative opinions by demonstrating the humanity of those inside the building. It wasn't good enough to pummel ahead with the righteousness of the cause, a construct that would be lost on a public smarting over the disruptions of normalcy brought about by the Civil Rights Movement, the opposition to the war in Vietnam, and the emergence of the feminist cause. Mir's photos were one part of the solution to this problem. He appreciated how quickly and earnestly she worked, saluting her with an imaginary degree: *summa cum diligentia,* while he gently prodded the two of us down the steps toward the secret tunnel, concerned that she'd be exposed if she left after dawn.

He never knew that it was Mir who'd taken the photo of Herzl on the river that adorned the cover of the yearbook. I wondered if he'd known if he would've allowed this princess entry into his court.

Just before I poked my head through the opening to the creek, Mir tugged at my shirt to get my attention. "Come here," she whispered, not letting go of my shirt, pulling me toward her. "Closer, I have to show you something." Considering that there was no light from outside and I wasn't going to strike a match, I started to say that it would have to wait, when she tugged me with both hands on my hips and kissed me on the lips. I froze. She tilted back and instructed, "You can open your mouth, you know." With that, she introduced me to a world as alien as Taos Heights had been to me when I first arrived. I couldn't control a tremble. My head gently butted against hers. I let out an "ouch." She laughed, ran her fingers above my bandana, and snuggled against my chest. I kissed the top of her head. She let out an uuuuuuuuuum, something I hadn't heard since my little sister Nohemi would nuzzle with me listening to the Holyman stories.

"You have to go," I said tentatively, kissing her cheek repeatedly and fumbling for the camera to remind her why she couldn't dally. The door to the creek closed, and I impulsively snatched a few mushrooms, cleaned them by swiping them against my pants and started to go back inside, enveloped by the dank fungal cloud.

Yes, Mir's pictures and accompanying captions were one part of the solution to the problem. But how else was Myles going to turn the tide? Other than the hostages, what leverage did he have? And at what point did holding men against their will become more important than the nobility of upholding and protecting rights? Myles had to know that these men had rights as well and that the public's infatuation with Myles and the Free Speech Movement could be as fickle as the wind. What, in fact, did Myles really want to achieve? He'd told us he knew the demands for no army recruiting and getting rid of ROTC would never be satisfied, his goal was not to occupy Kettys-Burg Hall indefinitely, and the hostages would have to be released, unharmed, quickly. Under what circumstances would he claim victory? I pondered these questions alternatively with others, such as: Why is my pulse banging in my ears? Will Mir always taste this good? Was this a "thank you" kiss she'd shared with many others or was I special? When I saw her next, would I be able to savor her tongue?

I didn't have long to wait for answers to the first questions. Upstairs in the president's office, Myles laid out his plan for me when I burst through to tell him that Mir had made her way safely out of the tunnel with her camera intact.

"Jacobo, we're going to release a hostage at seven thirty, in less than two hours. On our own. Before the cops call. No prompting; no strings. A goodwill gesture on our part. Mir will be out front. It'll be early and there won't be more than a few folks out there. She'll take a picture quickly and get back to the paper, where she'll add it to the story she's working on. It'll go out over the wires by 10:00 a.m. and will make the afternoon papers all over the country. The headlines will focus on our generosity, our selflessness, our initiative at breaking through the logjam and ensuring a demonstration doesn't turn into a crisis."

"Then what?" I asked uncharacteristically.

"Then we get the call," Claudia replied for him, yawning from where she'd been resting on the sofa. "That's when they'll want to negotiate. They'll think we're squeamish, that they have us on the run, that letting one cop go is a sign of weakness."

"Isn't it, without getting anything in return?" Herzl asked, ambling in from his den upstairs, absentmindedly fiddling with his mezuzah that hung on a slender silver chain around his neck.

"We still have two more, and the game isn't played just with Taos Heights police or UT's administration," Claudia responded without turning to face him.

"Let's get the group together," Myles stated flatly, and Claudia went off to round up those who'd been in the room when the five demands had been created. Once assembled, Claudia behaved as a parliamentary whip, browbeating those around the table. Her cudgel was her special relationship with Myles, and she wielded it indiscriminately toward anyone whose proposal or thought differed from Myles' plan. Some acquiesced, others seethed, no one challenged to any extent. With banishment the penalty for disagreement, the possibility for rebellion was cut off at the knees. This, too, went into my notebook, along with my observation questioning the need for the others if the decisions had already been made by Myles and Claudia.

The plan was clear-cut: when the cops eventually called, Myles would ask for a gesture from the other side, offsetting the release of one hostage. The implication was that after a conciliatory gesture on the part of the cops, there would be another hostage release. While the specifics weren't spelled out, a path forward was being set: Myles would gain the upper hand with the release of the first cop, and the late morning stories which would begin to appear over the wire services about the goings on the inside of Kettys-Burg Hall would be presented in a favorable way.

Just before dawn, Myles asked Herzl to bring one of the cops down, then opened the front door of Kettys-Burg. He maneuvered into an exaggerated bow, not righting himself until the startled policeman realized he was free to go. Sitting on top of the parapets that'd been arranged against the windows, we watched the cop scurry down the steps, lose his balance while gaining his freedom, and tumble safely by tucking his head inside his shoulder, taking the blow on his upper back.

When the call came, it was almost noon. Myles felt vindicated; the other side agreed to the demand, in writing, that the UT had deauthorized the local police from entering the campus at any time unless there was probable cause that a crime had been committed, as evidenced by a warrant enabling them to do so, signed by a city or state judge. From the second and third floors, whoops and hollers echoed to the outside, escorting the local cops who retreated from their positions around the building and walked or rode back out of sight. They were replaced by two dozen or so campus police, middle-aged men moonlighting from the fire department or post office—gun-less, baton-less—and eager to avoid confrontation any more controversial than reprimanding a student who might've been carrying an open bottle of beer. Myles knew that it'd taken several hours for Taos Heights cops to have made their case to the UT administration, the mayor, and the city council.

He asked for suggestions for their next move. No one spoke up, fearing that his request was rhetorical and that Claudia would vitiate any response with a withering retort. "I'd hold off on the release of the second cop," someone interjected at last, as much to restore the semblance of a group participatory effort as anything else, "until we see how this all plays out, you know, with the newspapers and the reporters. We have to determine if it was worthwhile."

Myles nodded, making eye contact with everyone, a connection that helped to reestablish a façade of unity.

"We wait," Claudia said to no one, which had the effect of clearing the room.

The next time the phone rang, it was someone at the campus newspaper, informing us excitedly to turn on the radio, to listen to the all-news station. First, we heard the facts, the release of the cop in exchange for the pledge not to invade. Then came the speculation that the crisis would be resolved. Finally, we heard the description of the pictures that Mir had taken the night before, recounted by Mir herself. She was on the radio! Calmly, she narrated an invisible view of life inside Kettys-Burg, her British-inspired English providing a professional veneer of authenticity to a reporter a thousand miles away who was looking at the pictures she'd taken under Myles' direction to make a favorable imprint on the American public. Myles' plan was working to perfection. Within a few hours, those pictures would be printed on the front pages of afternoon papers all over the country, followed by their appearance on the three broadcast television evening news programs. We could only imagine how the cops and the administration must've reacted to the pictures. We guessed that heads were on the chopping block for being unable to answer the simple question of how we were able to get the pictures out. Later, they speculated that one of us went to the roof at night and quietly dropped film canisters to a conspirator on the ground. How someone would've been able to approach the building that had been cordoned off was never discussed; certainly no one ever assumed that there was a hidden tunnel out to the Blueberry Creek.

At 7:00 p.m., Myles called George Townsend with the request for the police chief to initiate a conciliatory gesture. Within an hour, the call was reciprocated, and the chief notified Myles that the trustees had just issued a statement that the UT subscribed wholeheartedly to the First Amendment and that all members of this community have the right to free speech, the right to assemble, the right to petition the trustees without fear of recrimination, and the right to have unfettered access to the press. Within a few moments, the second slip of paper, signed by the UT president—in whose office Myles was holding court—was slipped under the front door. Almost as soon as it'd been read, the second cop was released with little fanfare from within or outside. All that was left was the third cop—the plainclothes one who'd been hung out the window by Herzl.

Lounging in the president's office, the group started to grapple with the most selfish issue, the third demand, the one that would exempt them from any disciplinary actions from the UT or Taos Heights police. They all knew that they'd have to abandon the fourth and fifth demands that related to armed forces recruiting and ROTC. It dawned on me that Myles' insistence in putting them in the mix had been prescient, an act of foresight in a negotiation process that exposed his distance from us. We'd just been lurching from incident to incident without an understanding that we were actors in a play that had, in truth, already been scripted. Demands four and five had been included knowing that they'd be surrendered, so as to provide the other side with a partial claim to victory, an important lesson that I'd take away. Myles could play chess with his enemies, his maneuvers practiced in anticipation of myriad responses. His focus was on working backward from a desired outcome to identify the many divergent paths that he could take to get him there. He could then pick the one that would lead to success without the need to destroy his opponents. To have the ability to understand your adversary's attack plans in advance was a distinguishing characteristic of a leader, and a critical insight I took away from the siege of Kettys-Burg Hall that served me well in the future.

"The third demand," Myles intoned rather solemnly, "is one that can't be satisfied merely by the release of the plainclothes cop. They're going to need something more. They're simply not going to give us immunity from prosecution. If they give in on that, we win too much and heads—their heads—will roll. No, they need something in return. Any ideas?" he asked hopefully.

We sat there mute, like students who'd been asked a question by a teacher that revealed we hadn't done our homework or worse, that we hadn't internalized anything from the lecture we'd just heard. After some inane ideas were meekly put forward, Claudia offered something following what appeared to be an imperceptible nod from Myles.

"What about an apology of some sort?"

"Like what?" Myles asked quickly, perhaps as part of a choreography with her.

"We could say we were sorry for some aspect of what went on, not for the occupation and not for the demands, not that, but something else, something that might be critical for them for public relations purposes but that's not important to us," Claudia replied, a bit too energetically.

"Anyone?" Myles piped up, looking eagerly at our skeptical faces. A few suggestions were eventually coughed up: sorry for preventing the administration from doing their jobs; sorry for causing the local businesses on the Strip to suffer a couple of days of reduced income; sorry for having caused classes to be cancelled, that kind of thing. Claudia and Myles gently prodded, and it occurred to me that they'd indeed been in cahoots and had a plan, but they wanted the group to come up with it or at least to get on the right track, from which they could get it to where they wanted to go. I can't explain how I figured it out, but once it popped into my mind, I knew what they wanted. From there, it was a modest leap to the actual sorry they were determined to tease out of us and to present to the world. My pride in figuring out what they had in mind was offset by the betrayal it would engender.

I knew that they wanted Herzl to apologize for hanging the cop out of the third-floor window.

Such a statement would be the perfect act of contrition. It would be acceptable to the cops and, in Myles and Claudia's view, would come at no real cost to Herzl, who could simply say that his emotions had gotten out of hand and that he'd had no intention of endangering the life of the cop. Yes. All neatly tied up in a bundle and packaged for the press. But this ignored the fact that it'd been Claudia's idea executed under Myles' direction, and who knew if Herzl had ever had any notion of causing harm to the hog-tied policeman. What was more important was that Myles and Claudia didn't have any comprehension of Herzl's history of having been harassed and bullied as a kid, and, as a result, that he'd refuse to play the unctuous Jew who'd obligingly agree to serve as a foil to enable others to avoid responsibility for their acts. Far from being the sycophant who'd absorb the light from the glare of public scrutiny as the price to pay for not having his religion become the center of unwanted attention that could provoke anti-Semitism, Herzl radiated his Jewishness and dared others to confront him directly. Herzl had wanted the cops to understand that it was a Jew—a physically strong and confident Jew—in whose hands their lives were literally held. I knew that Herzl wouldn't agree to an admission of guilt.

"Herzl won't apologize," I blurted out, having made the connections silently, which caused everyone seated at the table to react in a puzzled fashion.

Accepting that I had correctly exposed their plan, Myles and Claudia exclaimed practically in unison, "Why not?"

"It's an easy way to proceed," Claudia said.

"Are you saying that a Jew won't take one for the team?" Myles asked.

That remark shot through the room like an arrow, and appeared to hit a couple of the other students who recoiled in shock, mouths agape. Perhaps they were Jews. The room fell silent.

It wasn't my place to reveal any of the intimacies Herzl had shared with me, and I wanted to get them to reorient their thinking in terms of an alternative solution. However, their persistence caused me to wonder if perhaps they'd already tipped off the cops that this was a deal that they could deliver and that there wasn't going to be any other resolution to the problem since the other side had accepted the arrangement. Why else were they being so insistent? Then, after much back and forth, they deputized me to bring the proposal to Herzl. They imagined that coming from me, it'd carry more weight and be more difficult for him to refuse.

Finding him up in the room where he'd been napping, I undercut Myles and Claudia's position by providing a detailed description of the conversation I'd had with them. Herzl was completely quiet. When I finished, he leaned forward, looked me in the eye, and said assertively, "Tell them I'll do it."

I was shocked.

"Are you serious? You'll do it? I can't believe you'd agree. Why would you do this?" I asked incredulously.

"I didn't say I'd *do* it," he retorted, easing into a wide grin. "I said *tell them* I'll do it."

He agreed with my speculation that Myles had likely signaled on a call that the cops were listening in on that he could deliver the goods or had explicitly arranged to provide for Herzl's apology in a private discussion with Chief of Police George Townsend. Either way, it mattered not one whit to him how this turn of events had become the *sina qua non* for the solution of the hostage crisis.

"You know," he said after a long pause, "it's all about Myles, mark my words."

"What do you mean 'it's all about Myles'?" I asked.

"You yourself told me."

"What? No, I didn't. What are you talking about?"

"Jacobo, you told me that the night you were at his apartment, after he mesmerized everyone with his stories about the Freedom Summer, you lingered by his bookcase and noticed news stories and articles on the very things he was telling you about."

"Yeah, so what?"

"Did it ever occur to you that he, well, cribbed a lot of what he said from those papers and books?"

"Do you mean copied?" I asked.

"In a manner of speaking," Herzl replied, "yes."

"You mean he never did those things he told us about?"

"I'm not saying he didn't go to Mississippi last summer. Maybe he did, maybe not. Let's say he did. Did he have all those experiences? Could've. But it's also possible that he read about them afterward and used those words—someone else's words—to get all of you energized. Look, I'm not saying he doesn't believe in the cause. Just think about it. And…"

"And what?"

"He's good, very good at what he does." A generous comment in the midst of an indictment was something I hadn't anticipated. "You know what I'm talking about?"

"His leading the movement," I said.

"Well, that may be true, but it's not what I meant. Come with me."

I followed him down the hall to a point where he stopped and turned on the lights. As my eyes adjusted, I saw he was standing next to a poster on the wall and made a slight head bob to me to look at it.

It was a poster from a student production of *The Third Man*, a one hour radio play that'd been adapted from the movie that came out in 1951.

"So," I said, "it's a picture of Orson Welles. What's that got to do with Myles?"

"Look closer," he said, and when I did, I saw that the young man wearing the fedora with the collar of the trench coat pulled up was in fact Myles, who'd impersonated Welles's stance and upward gaze to perfection. The overall effect was so flawless in mimicry that even when I deconstructed the poster and saw that it contained Myles' name and indicated that it was a radio show to be broadcast on Saturday, April 9, 1961, ten years to the day of the original broadcast, my impression was that I was still looking at Orson Welles from the original promotional shot.

"Keep in mind, Jacobo, that Myles has a unique ability to blur the lines between fact and fiction, you see?"

As I walked back to the room with Herzl, I noticed for the first time that in this hallway on the third floor there were a dozen posters honoring students and events but, Myles must've been indignant that his image was here and not on the cover of the yearbook—where there was the photo of Herzl.

It's all about Myles.

Just keep your eyes and ears open, and know that sometimes the king does something that his subjects don't fully appreciate until it's too late.

Myles has a unique ability to blur the lines between fact and fiction.

As I stood there, I wondered if it's all about each of us. Do we always put ourselves first, in the best light, regardless of the consequences, the impact on others, the effect on ourselves in the future? Are we always in competition even when it's not warranted? Do we consciously try to take advantage of those around us or is it innate, something we just do when our prejudices reign supreme? Is self-reflection the antidote to this kind of behavior, or is it merely a mirror that reflects and reinforces aberrant conduct?

And was I immune to this? My head was spinning.

Back in the room with Herzl, I tried to calm myself down by seeking refuge in the issue at hand.

"So what do you plan to do?" I asked, hoping that there could still be a middle ground that might work for both sides.

"I want you to go back down and tell them I've agreed, and I'll write out a statement that I'll sign."

"They'll want you to read it, out front, on the steps, before the cameras. They'll need to show a person, a face with expression."

"Contrition," he interrupted. "Tell them I'll do it. Whatever they want."

"I'm confused," I said.

"Look, if I say no, they'll badger me to death, then Claudia will browbeat me in front of everyone. I don't need that."

Or worse, I thought. I'd seen her face contort with a red ember that couldn't readily mask the hot coal that was always burning inside her. She'd lash out at the slightest provocation that ran counter to what she wanted to do, and her wrath could rain down indiscriminately on anyone at any time, without thought as to the impact it may have on that person or those within earshot. Even against Myles.

And if he said no, I couldn't imagine specifically how Myles would react, but somehow Herzl's Jewishness would be part of it, and this time, I was afraid, it could lead to a public display that might be picked up by others. An initial spark can ignite a fire that can burn out of control.

"And since the truth is I really won't do it," Herzl continued, "why should I put myself through that humiliation? I'll just say I will, everyone will relax, I'll write out the statement, even practice it in front of them, if that's what they want."

"A charade then," I said.

"You got it."

"So, what'll you do? I mean when the time comes, you know, to step outside the front doors and read the speech?"

He extended his arm and put a hand on my shoulder. "Jacobo," he started slowly, "I have to know that I can trust you completely."

In that split second before I responded, I ran through how different answers might alter our relationship. My first impulse was to agree wholeheartedly. On the other hand, I knew that declining his entreaty to share such an intimacy would sever our friendship—the one I cherished most since leaving Arroyo Grande. And there really was no third way. I wanted it all: the camaraderie of a best friend that wouldn't inhibit my offering candid advice that he might not be prepared to follow.

"You can," I said. "You can trust me, yes."

"Okay, so here's how it's going to play out in Myles' mind. You and I'll finish a draft of my apology. Then, we'll give the note to Myles and Claudia for review. They'll call the cops and make the offer to release the last hostage and let them know that I'll say I'm sorry for hanging him out the window."

"All this in exchange for the immunity pledge, I presume," I said.

"Yes, for sure, and the cops will agree, no doubt about it. They'll set up a microphone on the front steps. Just before that, Myles is going to tell you to get more food and to bring Mir back with you to take pictures of the preparations for the release and speeches."

"That makes sense," I said.

"Then he'll tell Claudia to fix up the plainclothes cop. You know, make sure his face and hands are clean, that type of thing. And to wipe any puke off his clothes. The plan will be that at a quarter to eight, Myles will open the front door, and that I'll get in front of the microphone next to him with Claudia and the cop right behind us. That I'll introduce myself, offer genuine regrets—that I'm not going to appeal for any special treatment—and that I'll say some nice words to Myles, like 'thanks for making sure anything didn't get out of hand,' something like that. That I'll turn around to face the cop directly and apologize, then I'll step to the side to make way for Myles."

"Then Myles' part of the plan is to have the last cop walk down the steps."

"A free man. That's when Myles will speak. He'll plan on saying something special. My guess is that he's prepared a lot for this. Remember, this'll be his time in the sun."

"You're right," I said. "He may never get a better chance. I mean, there'll only be a few hundred out front, but with the cameras, everyone's going to see this tonight on the news."

"Myles is smart. He's going to make sure it's going to be over quick. The last thing he wants is to go on and on. This is his John L. Lewis moment. A couple of sticks and everyone will get it. Big time. Then the plan will call for him to walk back in the building to all sorts of cheers and pats on the back."

"All very well and good, for sure that's what they'll expect, but that isn't what's going to happen."

"Up to a point, it is," he corrected. "Everything will go as planned, except that at a few minutes to eight when they're ready to go, they won't be able to find me."

"You can't hide," I said. "They'll tear the building upside down and find you. And if you think you'll go out by the tunnel, you can forget about that. I don't think they'll trust you at all. You're the 'crazy Jew' to them, after all."

It came out. Not planned. I decided to just plow on, not to make a big deal out of it and hopefully, it'd pass. It did. It shocked me, but later I realized that it was such a commonplace thing for Herzl that it was simply a part of life that he'd learned to ignore.

"They'll have people guarding the door to the basement. Remember, too, there's all the furniture stacked up against the windows on the first floor and you're not going to jump, what with double heights, even from the second floor, it's more than twenty feet, you'll break every bone in your body."

Satisfied that I'd taken his options away and smug in my belief that by sheer deductive logic I'd oriented him to the same outcome that Myles was anticipating, I was astounded when he matter-of-factly informed me of his escape plan.

"Jacobo, I'm surprised you haven't figured it out," he said, "although by not suspecting anything, it gives me comfort that it won't be discovered or even anticipated by either Myles or Claudia. Harebrained schemes are so named for a reason, I guess."

I must admit I was stumped and eager to hear how he planned to leave undetected. I gave him a look that encouraged him to go on.

"To me, it's rather obvious." He gestured to the window the way a magician's assistant poses for the audience to prompt it to demonstrate its appreciation for the last trick.

"You're not going to jump!" I exclaimed incredulously.

"Jacobo, remember when I swung out the window in front of the crowd?"

"Sure."

"Well, the tree is still there. The branch is right next to the window. Instead of holding on to the sill, I'm going to grab the branch with both hands and swing from branch to branch, from one tree to the next, invisible to everyone in their sleeping bags, out to where the edge of the trees borders the Creek. If anyone spots me coming down the trunk, they'll simply think I'm some kid who climbed up to get a look at what's going on inside the building."

Actually, it was rather obvious, now that he said it. And I had no doubt he could pull it off, what with the enormous strength of his wrists and arms, the coordination he demonstrated every day out on the river in the shell, and his prior experience swinging through the air.

He said "Well, it's time to write my 'I'm sorry' speech," which got me to rip out a page from my notebook and hand him a pencil. My tacit approval bolstered his spirits. He played with words out loud, wrote some down, erased many within seconds, and kept up a constant stream of patter that technically was a back and forth with me, but had I not responded, it wouldn't have changed in any way. My presence wasn't required for him to have a conversation. When he finished, he said, "Ta da!" We fell into an exaggerated silence.

I broke it by asking, "If you go out the window, then the whole scene you played out for me a few minutes ago about you and Myles in front of the building making the apology and letting the cop go won't take place, so what's going to happen instead?"

"I've thought about that. The first thing I'm going to do is give this draft to Myles and Claudia and let them make any changes they want. That'll keep them off guard. Second, I have to ask you something. Can you trust me?"

For a split second, I thought this might be a trick question; then it occurred to me that he might have misplaced the pronouns. "Can *I* trust *you*?" I inquired, hoping to elicit some clarification.

"Yes, can *you* trust *me*? I'm going to lay out the events as I see them unfolding and they'll come as a shock to you, so you'll need to have faith that what I'm going to tell you is likely to happen."

Well, I thought, if I could say "Faith is a commodity that doesn't fluctuate with supply or demand" to Myles at the bookstore, then I could have faith in what Herzl was going to mention.

"Okay, yes. Shoot," I said.

"Good. I'm glad you didn't say cross your heart and hope to die, by the way. Anyhow," he continued, "when they go looking for me, you know, to make the speech out front and they don't find me, they're going to think that you were in league with me, that you were somehow involved in my escape. But even if they think you didn't help me, they'll know that you didn't warn them, so whether or not you lifted a finger for me, you didn't do anything to prevent me from getting out of here."

He was right. I hadn't thought of any of this. By sticking with him I was headed for a collision course with Myles and Claudia. I'd seen firsthand what they'd done to those who were on the outs. I'd be banned from their group. And blamed if anything went wrong. But what if Herzl went into exile? Left school? Out the window and out of my life? It was a disorienting thought. The locus of my newfound existence was disintegrating before my eyes. My head started to pound again. Sweat emerged from every pore, seemingly pumped directly by my heart, which was racing so fast now that I felt myself slithering out of my clothes.

"It gets worse," Herzl said. "Think about it."

I was ready to throw up. I managed a weak, "How so?"

"If they don't get the apology from me, they'll look for something else to give the cops. That's the only way out of the mess we're in. Don't forget, they need *something*, otherwise Myles and Claudia and all the others in here don't get immunity, and they could be arrested and put on trial. What do you think would happen to them in a court with a jury of store owners, cop relatives, army people—you get where I'm going—who'd think nothing of putting a couple of rabble-rousers, outsiders, communists, whatever, in the clink."

My head was spinning. "Yeah, but they don't have anything else to give to the cops," I said.

"Jacobo, think, think. Once they turn their attention from me, they'll focus on something else that can get them off the hook. In fact, once they turn to what I'm getting at, they'll curse themselves for not coming up with this originally."

I was stumped. Clueless. My mind raced over all the faces that had sat around the desk in the president's office, reviewed all of what I'd heard in offices, hallways, and anterooms, played the pictures back of what went on in the room with the cops when they were tied up, in the other room when Claudia took her top off...nothing. Herzl leaned toward me, left fist in right palm resting against his chin, supported at the elbows by the arms of the chair. It was disconcerting. The intensity of his gaze was comparable to the mica-made fire that'd sustain us throughout the night when we slept outside in the fall, back home in Arroyo Grande. The memory from such a fire radiated over me suddenly and forced a spasm that expunged the chill I was feeling, even if for just a brief moment.

I forced myself to stare back at Herzl. Why wasn't he just telling me? Why was he playing a game? He wanted me to come up with the answer, but why? Did it have to do with me? What about me could be of importance to Myles? I was just the scribe. In fact, I was to be invisible. It'd been Myles who expressly told me not to get involved. I was the quiet one, the observer, who was only to jot down and draw what I saw so that there'd be a record of what went on. It couldn't be anything to do with me, I said to myself, confidently.

"Herzl, stop staring at me. It's not me or anything I did, I'm not Myles' solution. All I did was write everything down in my notebook..."

I never finished the sentence. As soon as I said it, I knew what Herzl was after. I had to hear it to understand it. The notebook! Of course!

"The notebook has everything that the cops want," I said, embarrassed that it'd taken me so long to figure it out.

"If it got into the wrong hands—let's say Mir took it to the UT paper and they published it, everyone would know that it was the cops who provoked the demonstration, started the fights, spied on the crowd, took photos, and were going to splice the roll of film to make it appear that the students were the cause of the confrontations," Herzl said.

"Of course, of course, you're right, a hundred percent," I said, still angry that I hadn't realized this myself. "And the notebook would show that the three hostage cops were given every opportunity to explain what they were doing on the roof."

"And it'd reveal that all it took was a little peep show to get them to spill the beans," he said. "And it explained how you smuggled food—"

"And Mir—"

"And Mir into the building through the secret tunnel—"

"And how Myles knew the line was tapped," I said.

"And don't forget that Myles told you of his private conversation with George Townsend, which is in there too."

"Yeah, wouldn't it be something if it were to get out that the tough guy head of the police was practically begging for a peaceful resolution," I said.

"At the same time, he was probably posturing—you can picture this—to his comrades about how harsh he was with Myles," Herzl said.

Our machine gun conversation bursts subsided as we let our conclusion sink in.

"I get it. Okay, I've got to hide it. Hide it and say I lost it," I said.

"They'd never believe you for a minute," Herzl said.

"I did lose it. I told you, yesterday, I couldn't find it. I practically went haywire."

"Yeah, but you found it right away. In fact, Myles had it. It wasn't really lost at all," he said.

While Herzl put the finishing touches on the apology note that'd never be read, I sat motionless in the chair, ruminating over the pros and cons of each option available to me.

"Herzl, here's how I see it," I said, the animated conversation having had the effect of making me feel almost normal. "Once you leave in the middle of the night, they'll come after me for the notebook, but they won't know we're a step ahead of them. They'll just say they want to review what's in there, you know, to make sure it's right. So I'd have to hide it first, and I could do that. I could bury it underneath one of the mushroom beds in the tunnel, it's so dark in there, they'd never find it. That could work. What do you think? And after I do that, I could go downstairs and in a pretend panic, start the search for the notebook, making sure I burst in to the president's office with a terrified look and ask them if they'd seen it. I could even get them to help me by combing every nook and cranny to look for it. It might work."

"They wouldn't believe you. And, well, I think you've got to consider this: they'd beat the crap out of you until you told them where it was."

He had a point.

"Okay. Well, I could leave when you leave. You go out the window, I go out the tunnel," I said.

"Except that, in case they get queasy feelings about me, they'll start guarding the tunnel pretty soon," he said.

"Then what do you suggest? Is there another option for me?" I asked.

"Look, you have to think of the worst scenario and then plan accordingly. If there's anything we Jews have learned in the last twenty years—why it hadn't been already pounded into our pious anemic brains for the 2000 years prior to that I'll never know—is to set our own course and not to depend on others for anything. Your worst scenario comes about with either some silly attempt to hide the notebook or to pretend that you didn't know I'd split. I'm not sure what they'll do to you, but whatever it is, don't think for a moment that you'd be spared something pretty bad. Okay, so it's the nineteen sixties, lucky you, you won't get the auto-da-fé. But my advice is keep your pants on; you don't want them to stick a totem pole up your Indian tush."

"What're you saying?" I was feeling hopeless again.

"I'm saying that there's no easy way out for you. You have to do what's best for you and, well, if I were you, I'd take the notebook and get out. Leave *before* me. Go on your food run through the tunnel, tell them you'll be back with the goodies, but hightail it and don't come back. While you're gone, I'll finish up the apology note and give it to Myles, then I'll come back up here. I'll tell them that I'm going to nap before the big show—they could put guards in front of the door, who cares—and a few minutes later, I'll go out the window."

"And then what?"

"I haven't figured that out exactly, so let's meet at Ben Veniste's. We'll have some time to catch our breath and think of the next step."

The idea was instantly appealing to me because Mir and I had agreed that she'd meet me there instead of her place that night. She was set to reprise her role of picture taking and interviewing during the night, then sneak back out later through the tunnel to print and wire her photos and stories.

"Okay," I said. "We leave, there's no notebook for Myles, no secret deal with the cops. What happens to him, Claudia, the others here, the Free Speech Movement?"

"For Myles, it's all about the spotlight. He'll figure something out. Claudia and the others? He doesn't really care. The cause? Well, he's already won, in a sense."

"How's that?" I asked.

"Jacobo, think about it. Newspapers all over the country have run stories about free speech, the war, and the draft. They're talking about it on TV and the radio all the time now. Myles lit the fuse. It may take some time before the explosion comes, but trust me, it's on the way. Maybe it'll be better for him if he's arrested. You know, the martyr thing. At any rate, you can bet that Myles has something in mind, something he's dreamed up, attention-getting. We'll see."

"You're prepared to leave Myles…" I started to say it as a declaratory statement but tempered it by raising my voice to generate some ambiguity that would allow him to hear it as a question.

"In the lurch," he completed my thought. "Myles in a lurch and Claudia in a tizzy. See you at the café." He slipped around me to make his way to the president's office. A few minutes later, I popped my head in to where Herzl, Myles, and Claudia were hunched over papers strewn on a coffee table, breezily mentioned that I was going to get the food haul, and paused just long enough to catch Myles' wink—his signal of appreciation to me for helping him through the crisis.

It's all about Myles, mark my words.

CHAPTER 9

Quite a time you had

with your eesh

I must admit that in my walk down the basement, through the tunnel, and along the creek, notebook in hand, I had no guilt with regard to my infidelity to Myles. My admiration for his passion was unchanged, and my alignment with his goals was unshaken. But at the same time, I'd been warned by two people I greatly admired—Ben Veniste and Herzl—that Myles may not be the person he presented himself to be, and I'd seen an ugly side of him that gave credence to their concerns. Thinking back on it now, this might've been the first time I'd experienced a situation in which I had to evaluate someone's motives as opposed to simply accepting their actions at face value. I was on that cusp between childhood and adulthood. I had to begin to think more deftly about people and events, otherwise I'd fall to the pediatric side of the ledge. Emotional maturity isn't something that automatically accrues to each child as a matter of course as he or she ages.

I had a snack at the café, told Mir what the plan was, and waited for Herzl. As soon as he came through the back door he asked, "Did you bring the notebook?" I filched it out from its place hidden underneath my shirt secured by my belt, and held it up triumphantly. Mir and Ben Veniste applauded.

I didn't ask Herzl if he'd had any trouble ape-swinging to his freedom from the window of Kettys-Burg.

"I thought I'd hide it here," I said to Ben Veniste, "in the back of the kitchen, on a high shelf, behind some cans."

"I have a better idea," he responded. "Why don't you take it to the man you call Navajo Joe? That way it'll be out of Taos Heights and in safe hands."

"How do I get it to him?" I couldn't imagine how this could be done.

"The two of you have to leave now," Ben Veniste said, nodding to Herzl and me, "and you have to take the notebook for safekeeping."

He filled me in on his plan. The two of us would ride the café's old bikes to a spot close to the boathouse, where they could be retrieved by his Mexican kitchen helpers in the morning, take a never-used old wooden two-seat shell that wouldn't be missed, row down the river at night, portage the boat up on the bank during the day and wend our way downriver to the Navajo village where no one would ever suspect to find us or the notebook.

"Not in a million years," was how he phrased it.

He reminded us to get rid of any clothing that had the UT name on it and suggested that I speak only in Spanish if approached by anyone, let alone the police. "Wait a minute, I'll be right back." We watched him place his cane on a nearby hook, navigate up the steps that led to his apartment above the café, right hand gripping the rail, left hand hooked around his left knee, acting as a hoist to lift his injured leg to the next step. He repeated this laborious process until he got to the top step, where he picked up a second cane and disappeared into a room. After a minute or so, he reappeared with two knitted caps and oilskin slickers. "Here," he said, triumphantly, after having taken a full minute to come back down, holding out the cap to me, "Keep it low over your brow. Don't let anyone see the bandana. We expressed our appreciation, despite the fact that the slickers were too short and pulled against our chests. We were grateful nonetheless, as we hadn't been prepared to face the elements on the river. I took off the sweatshirt with the UT logo. Mir told me she had to get back into Kettys-Burg Hall via the tunnel or else Myles and Claudia would determine she was part of the conspiracy with Herzl and me. Before I could think of how to say goodbye, she grabbed my cheeks with her fingers and kissed me, her tongue brushing mine. We stayed motionless, even as Herzl came in to get the bikes and as Ben Veniste filled knapsacks with enough food to last four days.

She told me she'd tell Myles that I wasn't feeling well and that I said I'd be along later, so she came back on her own. He'd have no reason to doubt her, and she'd take her pictures throughout the night, sneak back out, have them developed, and would still be there out front in the morning when Myles was supposed to let the plainclothes cop go free.

"But without Herzl's apology or my notebook, he'll have nothing to offer. There won't be an exchange and the occupation will go on. There'll be no resolution," I said, worried now that my selfishness would prolong the standoff and cause irreparable harm. That I could bring up the issue of Herzl's apology without speaking about my need to apologize didn't occur to me at that time.

"It's out of your hands," Ben Veniste said matter-of-factly, straddling two bikes.

"I wouldn't worry about it. It's never been about what it seemed to be," Herzl added.

At any rate, Myles has something in mind—something big and attention-getting. We'll see, was stuck in my mind.

Ben Veniste hugged me. "*Enbonora, hermano*," good-bye, brother, he said with warmth. Mir leaned her head into my chest and withdrew it only upon hearing the jarring sound of Ben Veniste's cane being whacked against a stool set up in front of the counter, his signal for us to get going. She squeezed me, then walked away without looking back, her camera slung over her shoulder. Herzl and I mounted up to start our ride down toward the river. I sensed an ache, a feeling that I'd never see Mir again. And it was compounded by the thought that I hadn't told her the truth. There are times I wished I hadn't said things that could be construed as either self-aggrandizing or hurtful; and other times, I regretted not having spoken at all, perhaps out of fear or not knowing how to correct the record without putting myself in a position of shame.

At the deserted boathouse, we quietly made our way without lights downstairs to the room that opened up to the dock and found the ancient shell affectionately known as the 'cedar speeder' tucked away in the crawl space, accessible through a half-height door. Without saying a word, we set it into the river, squeezed our knapsacks filled with food and clothing (and in my case, my notebook) where the cox would've sat and between the seats, then gently pushed off from the dock. Within a few minutes, we were under the bridge that I'd crossed to enter Taos Heights when I'd first arrived at the UT. We were able to do about fifteen miles, based on our knowledge of the current and our strokes, before we caught a wisp of dawn. We made landing, brought the shell up a slight incline, and parked it between a stand of squat junipers and a hollow that effectively kept us out of view from both sides of the river. We slept for a few hours. We woke up at the very moment when Myles was standing in front of a microphone giving a speech that historians would later call the defining moment, not only of the events of the day but also of what we now call *The Sixties*.

We spent much of the first day scaling high slopes of whispered conversation only to tumble down into depressions of self-doubts and anxieties followed by fitful attempts to sleep. We were exhausted, physically and emotionally. We tried to determine how best to cope with what would be a nocturnal existence, especially because we had to muffle our conversations and avoid using flashlights. We agreed to eat in spurts, only when we tied up on the shore, given the constrictions of space and inherent instability of the shell.

That night, we were fortunate that there was a crescent moon which reflected enough light for us to navigate but wasn't sufficient to make us an obvious target from the shoreline. I was struck by how the moon appeared to be leaking, a ragged sliver of white that seemed to drip onto the water, bubbling over a branch or some other debris that was desperately trying to keep up with us. Or was it pointing the way? Gently stroking behind Herzl, watching the moon, the light and the water, feeling the wind, it brought me back to when I said goodbye to Navajo Joe on the bank of the Rio Grande. He'd handed me a going away gift, a beautiful intricately woven shawl with a large opening, through which I poked my head, spread my arms wide, and pirouetted around so that he could see the appreciation I felt and the honor I acknowledged. He motioned for me to accompany him, and we walked down to the water's edge.

Without preamble, he spoke. "The river," he intoned, "it is the blood that runs through our bodies. The earth," he bent down and scooped up some red dirt, "the earth is the muscle." He closed his fist around a clump of warm, dust-covered clay. "The rocks are our bones." I glanced from the big gray boulders to the pebbles, taking it all in. He pointed up and said, "The yellow sun is our heart, beating as it comes up on the other side of the river and sets over the mountain, once every day." I took his cue, staring east past the river then turning slowly to the west. "And the wind," he finished, "is the spirit that breathes life into us, that sets the blood, the muscle, the bone, the heart into motion." I didn't know if he'd finished so I stood there, silently.

"You understand?" he asked.

"Yes," I replied, "I do," although not completely sure.

He placed each of his hands on my forearms and said something in Navajo. I shook my head in the affirmative, hoping this gesture would be taken as appropriate. I smiled. I admired the shawl. I noticed the greenish brown stripe that ran like an epaulet from the neck over each shoulder, separating the front and back red halves that were dotted with gray circles of different sizes that surrounded one brilliant golden sun with six coronas on the front. I searched vainly for the representation of the wind and not finding it, felt idiotic; it must have been there, and then I realized that it was invisible. It wasn't supposed to be represented at all. At that moment, I thought I really did understand: it was my responsibility to supply the breath of life.

This was the shawl that I'd worn on the day I'd met Myles and Mir.

Later, he'd tell me that when he grasped my forearms, he spoke the words of the Blessingway.

It was cold at night, with temperatures on the river hovering in the forties, made all the nippier by the wind racing down unimpeded from the north without obstruction. We wore our knit hats pulled down low over our ears and heavy sweaters tucked into dungarees, which I enjoyed staring at ever since Mir had told me that originally the fabrics had come from Dongari in India. Our boots were packed into our knapsacks, and our feet, customarily sockless in the shell, were appropriately covered and tucked into the foot stretchers—open-toed sneakers that were fastened securely by tacks. They provided an anchor that improved our efficiency, but this was looked upon as a two-edged sword, as it would hinder us from escaping if the shell were to flip. Our compromise was to lace the high tops through the eyelets but not to make a bow at the top. When we felt the wind picking up, we put on the slickers, expecting rain, but shed them when it became clear there'd be no precipitation. On land, we placed them on the ground to smooth out the pebbles and avoid direct contact with ant colonies, then rolled over to have them encase us to provide extra warmth.

We replayed some of the events of the previous days and enjoyed a few moments of levity, but for the most part we were fidgety, rapidly switching subjects, alighting on them with tenterhooks, then bouncing off to another topic, always coming back to the justification of our actions, the contrivances of our escapes, and our assumptions that somehow, it would all work out for us and Mir.

"We're running away," I said matter-of-factly. "I'm not sure it's the right thing to have done."

"Second and even third thoughts are okay, Jacobo. It's better to have doubts and to work through them. It's not a sign of weakness, you know."

"Isn't it selfish? I mean, we're fleeing to save ourselves," I said.

"A very wise rabbi once said, '*If I am not for myself, who will be for me?*'"

"Okay, sure, I get that, but the effect on others…who knows what that could be…."

"I'm with you, Jacobo, believe me. I'm not suggesting that we think only of us. That same sage also said, '*If I am only for myself, what am I?*' But there comes a time—and this is one for me and likely for you as well—when we have to do something that saves our skin so we can live another day, fight another battle, win the war."

I was silent for a while. I appreciated how Herzl was trying to get me to work all this through, neither resorting to bullying nor playing games, which is how I thought Myles or Claudia would've handled this situation.

After a few minutes, Herzl said, "I'm reminded of those Jews who professed Catholicism outwardly but who secretly practiced Judaism—their loyalty was to themselves, their community. Conversos. Spanish, by the way."

I felt comforted with Herzl at my side. This gave me consolation far beyond what the circumstances would outwardly suggest.

We skirted the topic of our impetuousness, the implications it could have for us, and how we'd explain it in such a way to our families so that they'd be proud of our actions. I offered that, on the assumption the occupation was indeed over and things would get back to normal in Taos Heights, we could go back in a few days and resume our studies and our lives, albeit without Myles and Claudia. If this were to come about, I reasoned, our parents would never know about our escapades, and it could be something that we could share with them at a later date, safe from recriminations.

"Don't be so naïve. There's no going back. We've got to figure out how to reach the man you call Navajo Joe. First things first."

Once we put shore on the second day, I began to think about the brusqueness of what he'd said and the force by which it hit me. We'd been so consumed with our exit strategy and getting the notebook into safe hands that I hadn't thought about what we'd do when we'd finally gotten it safely hidden. I'd imagined a settling down of the crisis, after which we'd resume our everyday lives, but Herzl had disabused me of this notion by a simple "There's no going back." We were no longer students—we were fugitives who needed to get to a place where no one would find us, where we could be sustained without imposing on anyone, where we'd have time to decide what to do on our own terms.

I rested the side of my face on a smooth stone and wrestled with this problem, turning over from side to side, aware that the slicker squeaked each time I moved and hoping the sound wouldn't be noticed. I struggled with how I'd have to explain what'd happened to my parents. I turned on my back, and up in the sky I saw their faces. They were speaking to me, their mouths open. Was I seeing contortions, strained necks, exaggerated hand motions, representations of anger, admonishment, and discontent? They were speaking to me all at once: 'How could you do this, what were you thinking, you were sent to the UT for a purpose, what will we do with you?' Did I hear them say, '*Bien de los cielos mal de la terra,*'—*you have spoiled a good opportunity by your inappropriate behavior*? I looked down below on the lower part of the riverbank where Herzl was comfortably encamped underneath a thick piñon. A part of me wanted to tussle his shoulder, rouse him, and have him explain what it was that my family was saying to me so he could help me deal with my torments. Herzl, wake up, get up, see, see *my* demons, listen to them, shield me from them, tell them to go away, speak to them on my behalf! I rolled to one side and then another, tucked my legs into a fetal position, wrapped my arms around my chest, pulled my shoulders together to make me smaller, to diminish me from the evil eye, to lessen my significance to the moment. I could feel my body temperature rise then fall precipitously, sending me into alternating spasms of heat and chill, lessening the pain from my headache coupled with an abdominal cramp. I had alternating visions and choruses, pangs and nausea. I craved sleep to enable me to break free. Rest is what I desperately needed. Sleep, sleep, sleep, let me gather my strength. Instead, I was poked by the bristles of the sagebrush I'd nestled against. I moved yet was poked again. And again. I squirmed, yearning to rest. And again.

"Jacobo," I heard them whisper to me, "Jacobo," again and again, just my name, was it my father, mother, sisters? I couldn't tell. The poking stopped. I felt a warm hand on my neck, so peaceful, a gentle rub. Mmmmmmm. So tired, I reached around my back to embrace the hand, I knew they would understand, yes.

"Jacobo," the voice said, now much closer to my ears. The rubbing became insistent, translating to more of a maneuver. I was being lifted up, closer to the voice.

"Jacobo!" it insisted right outside my ear. Startled, my eyes opened to Herzl hunched over me, his expression going from worry to humor in a split second. "You were doing some heavy dreaming," he said softly. "I've been rustling you for quite a while. You were out of it, talking in your sleep, carrying on a dialog with someone, thrashing all about, quite a sight to see. Take a leak, and let's get going." He went down the bank to gather his knapsack and to check again on the makeshift hideout he'd constructed for the shell from the brush, branches and grasses he'd gathered when we put ashore.

I got up slowly, contorting my face, moving my jaw and rubbing my cheeks in an attempt to reconfigure my face, which must've taken on the shape of the stone my head had been resting on.

In a few minutes, Herzl returned with some fruit and a canteen filled with water from the river. He turned to me with a mouthful and said, "Quite a time you had with your *eesh*." He laughed softly and crept back down to add more dirt, stones and branches to better hide the shell, as he'd noticed from a new angle where it could be spotted from above. Was it a ghost? An angel? A demon? A recollection? I leaned on my left elbow and, with my right hand, set the stone that my head had been resting upon from a horizontal to a vertical position, a commemoration of something I'd never be able to know.

CHAPTER 10

Oh, more than one,

*you owe me**

"Anyone seen Jacobo?" Myles asked to no one in particular. "Get Herzl," he said to Claudia. "We need to go over what he's going say one more time."

"Not just what he says," Claudia added. "How he's going to say it and his body language. It's all got to come together."

"I'm hungry," Myles said. "Jacobo, food!" he called out theatrically.

After a few minutes, Claudia came back and exclaimed breathlessly, "Herzl's nowhere to be found. Not in the room upstairs; no one's see him."

"Christ almighty. The basement?" Myles asked.

"No, Jacobo went down alone to get the food, he should be back soon. The door was guarded, no way Herzl followed him."

* Helen Karlstein, *The Dimming of the American Enlightenment Bulb: lights out due to anti-Semitism?* (Albuquerque: Enchantment Land Publications, 1968), 142-144. Reprinted with permission.

"Then where the hell is he?"

"On the roof?" someone suggested.

"That's idiotic," Claudia snapped.

"Maybe he's sleeping somewhere else, in another room," someone else offered encouragingly.

"For God's sake, go find him," Myles ordered, and a couple of guys split up to go through every room in the building.

At 3:00 a.m., after the building had been scoured, and neither Herzl nor Jacobo were to be found, Myles realized that his plan had fallen apart. He knew he'd been hoodwinked by Herzl. But Jacobo? Where was he? Had he joined up with Herzl? Why? Because they were teammates? *That wouldn't be enough,* he thought to himself. Jacobo had thrown his lot in with the Free Speech Movement. He even went so far as to disobey orders and get involved, becoming a hero, suffering a wound in the fracas with the cops. Something wasn't right.

He motioned to Claudia to join him in the room adjacent to the president's office, where they'd had sex and a post-coital fight the night before.

"Listen," he said when they were alone, "no Jacobo means no notebook, nothing with which to trade for, and if Herzl doesn't show up, we don't even have the apology. God*dammit*."

"We hold more cards than you think," she said.

"What are you talking about?"

"Look, the longer we stay, the better our bargaining position."

"What?" Myles asked with a facial expression that was designed to antagonize Claudia.

She let it pass.

"We've shut down the university and the town. Nothing's happening," she said. "The press is going to get all over them. For the cops starting the riot, for businesses being shut down, for a couple thousand kids not being in school, and all for what: having some pamphlets and shouting about the war and civil rights? They'll turn, you'll see." She paused and then came out with, "Don't be a pussy."

"Look, Claudia," he said, lowering his voice and speaking deliberately, lecturing her as if she were a child. "No notebook, no apology—no resolution. Oh, they'll turn for sure, but *against* us. The national journalists will start to paint with that yellow brush you often talk about. Privileged pansies. Draft evaders. And wait for the lies to start. About how we've trashed the place, stolen files, made free love, miscegenation, you name it. It'll be relentless. This little *skirmish* will become a *war*, and you know who's going to win that one. I don't mind fighting, but I'd at least want to go into battle with some ammo."

"Don't go outside to meet him. Let him sweat," she said.

Myles began to walk around the room.

"What?" she said.

He didn't respond. Likely he didn't hear her, as he was having a conversation with himself. He was sitting her out, so she realized that she'd have to cave a bit if she wanted to have some input.

She began calmly. "All right, all right. You go out to meet him. But let's make the two pricks pay. With no notebook, the cops don't know that Herzl wouldn't have dropped the cop. So you say you had to intervene to stop him from letting the cop fall. From killing him. You're the hero. One for you, minus one for the *bar mitzvah* boy."

"Okay, okay," Myles responded calmly. "I'll have the chief make sure the plainclothes cop is taken to the hospital. They can say he's being held for observation from the trauma or something like that."

"Not good enough. Have the chief announce that the cop's had a heart attack. Leave it like that. That's what the world will think. Remember, it's the first thing that someone says that gets all the attention. No one ever checks afterward to find out if it's true."

"I'm pretty sure the chief will buy in on that. When he asks about Herzl, I'll reply with something about *Judas*. That'll get his attention. He'll probably pat me on the back after that."

"So okay, after the release of the third cop, you've got nothing to offer. That's when you hike up your sissy pants," she sneered, "and reiterate the two demands—no army recruiting and no ROTC—that you know he can't agree to. Leave the chief hanging. Make the next move his. Whatever it is, we'll know his plan, and then we can act accordingly. Yes?"

"Sissy" stung him like a bee, but Myles knew this wasn't the time for a rebuttal, physically or verbally.

At 6:00 a.m. Myles called Chief George Townsend. It was arranged for Myles to meet him at the front door at 8:00 a.m.

CHAPTER 11

Two 'Free Speech-niks'

Sought by Police

Today's Smile

ALBUQUERQUE TRIBUNE

Good Morning

85th Year — Friday Morning, November 20, 1964 — Price 15c

Two 'Free Speech-Niks' Sought by Police

Communist Dupes Charged With Assault
Of Police Officer & Document Theft

Taos Heights, New Mexico (UPI)—

An All-Points Bulletin was issued early this morning by Taos Heights Police for the arrest of Herzl Schneider and Jacobo Toledano, former UT students who were leaders of the illegal occupation of Kettys-Burg Hall, the UT's administrative building.

Schneider is wanted for endangering the life of plainclothes Officer Charles Webster by hanging him out of a third-floor window. Webster is being treated at Taos Hospital for what has been described as a mild heart attack.

Toledano is accused of stealing documents from the office of the president.

Police Chief George Townsend praised graduate student Myles Bradford III for assisting in the peaceful end to the confrontation that rocked the campus and unsettled nerves throughout the land.

CHAPTER 12

A piece of paper

in my back pocket

The plan was simple: row down to the Indian village, stash the notebook with Navajo Joe where cops could search all day and night but not find what they were looking for, then have him drive us to Arroyo Grande.

We walked for a mile or so until Herzl spotted a phone booth near a gas station. "I've got to get in touch with my parents. They'll have a conniption if they call me at school and no one knows where I am. I'll tell them that I'm on my way to a Jewish retreat in Arizona and will be back at school in two weeks."

"We're sitting ducks, just standing around," I said.

"Yeah, you're right, two guys our age, height, and with beards. I'd like to read the APB they must've put out on us—the paragraph with the description of us as desperados on the lam and a statement, like 'armed and dangerous,' that kind of thing," he said smiling and giving me a knuckle sandwich.

"Maybe you should've said swarthy and intellectual," I said, which caused us both to enjoy a hearty laugh, something we hadn't done since before the seizure of Kettys-Burg Hall.

We moseyed down the street, passing an auto body shop, a diner, a few abandoned buildings, several open lots with the detritus of the neighborhood splayed all over it, and one-story buildings with broken windows and streaks of rust.

I froze.

"Herzl," I whispered.

As he turned around, I put my forefinger to my lips and pulled him into a narrow driveway alley between two cinderblock buildings.

"A cop," I said, "up ahead a couple of streets. Coming our way. Slowly."

We both looked to the end of the alley and saw that it was closed off with a high chain-link fence topped with wire.

"Just our luck," I said.

Without saying a word, we both pulled our knit caps down lower over our foreheads.

"Forget about luck," Herzl said. "Life's not a game of chance. You take the initiative, make it on your own terms. If something extra happens to your benefit after that, well, then, I guess you could call *that* part of it luck."

"Yeah, okay, but we've only got a couple of minutes before he gets here," I said, "What are we going to do?"

"Knock him out," Herzl said.

"What? Are you out of your mind?"

"Remember when I told you about the arm wrestling? How I built my arms up to be able to take all comers?"

"I remember, but so what?"

"What I didn't tell you was that I broke the kid's wrist."

"Seriously?"

"Yeah, the Jesus thing. He mocked me so much that when I finally got him to arm wrestle, I slammed his wrist down. Bam!" he said, too loudly, then started up again more softly as I motioned with my fingers. "Again and again I smashed it repeatedly on the table. He whimpered. I stood over him and said, 'Any more takers?' and they parted for me when I left the lunch table as if I were Moses at the Red Sea."

"So, what, you're going to go up to the cop and arm wrestle him to death?" I said sarcastically, still processing the image of skinny Herzl towering over the other kids, now having assumed the superior position, taunting his tormentors.

"Sucker punch him."

"For God's sake, you're talking about assaulting a cop."

"You want him to arrest us?"

"We don't know if he even *knows* about us."

"But in case he does," Herzl said.

"There's got to be a better way. We're grubby," I said. "Practically look like bums. Let's walk out together, have a nonsense conversation, real chatter, pretend laugh. We'll just walk right by him. He'll never suspect anything."

"Maybe, maybe not. Here's what I'll do: give you a couple of taps on the arm. I'll bend over and tie my shoe, then you break up as if I've told you something that's a riot, play some pocket pool, and when we get near him, say something like, *Was she as good as she looked*?"

"Who're you talking about?"

"Jacobo, say anything, for God's sake. It doesn't have to make any sense. Stupid is good, for once. I'll say something back that's equally dumb. Just play along. Let's go."

"But you won't attack him," I said in a tone that begged for agreement.

He didn't respond. I was wondering what else he'd withheld from me. I started to get angry until I realized that I hadn't exactly been truthful with him. The difference, of course, was that my issue wasn't going to get us arrested for assault and battery, on a cop no less.

I played along, hoping I could gain control of the situation. We walked out of the alley doing our best imitation of a couple of goofballs. Was the cop searching for us? Or just a patrolman making his rounds? If he stopped us, would Herzl actually fight with him? Would I run? I was fidgety. I had the same dry heaves as when I'd hurt my head falling down the fire escape. Rapid heartbeat. Starting to sweat. Trying to remember what Herzl had said. He was chattering away. Words, but I couldn't distinguish one from the other. Drowned out by the beating drum. We're goners. God knows I wasn't an actor. How Myles did it, I couldn't fathom. I tripped, practically stumbled.

"That's good," he said facing me, thinking it was a spontaneous move when it was a physical mirror of the clumsiness of my emotions. As we got closer, I suddenly had the feeling that my discombobulation might appear to be the effects of alcohol, and the last thing we needed was to be rounded up for public intoxication. So I began to straighten up, walking normally. I adjusted my pants and remembered about pocket pool, worried now about getting trapped in my underwear. It took my mind off the cop for a few seconds. I saw him out of the corner of my eye. Light blue shirt, dark blue pants, and a blue pointed cap with a silver badge that contained a number. This was it. We were ten feet away. I looked at Herzl, who was mumbling something, but I wasn't listening. What was it that Herzl had said previously? 'You take the initiative, make it on your own terms.' I wasn't going to have us get thrown into jail, so I approached the cop.

"Good morning, officer," I said, forcing an exaggerated smile.

He stopped.

Herzl stopped. And gave me a *What the hell are you doing*? look.

I stopped. Partially between Herzl and the cop, trying to make sure that this wasn't going to get out of hand. I could never go to jail.

"You boys know where I can get a good cuppa joe?" the cop asked cheerfully. "I need a kick before I start my rounds early in the a.m., and this is new territory for me."

"Ah…well…like…here's the thing," I said in a staccato manner, not having any idea of what I was going to say before it came out.

"First time...for me, well, us...here...too...you know...just visiting...so's I wish I could help ya...but that's the way it goes." I began to nod as I was talking, a faux nervous tick that fit perfectly with this false way of speaking, my whole persona having taken on the trappings of a guy who really was down and out. I looked at the cop and was struck by what I now could see on the silver badge on his hat: an eagle with spread wings atop an oval that said U.S. Post Office Letter Carrier.

"Okie dokie," the mailman said, and we parted in opposite directions.

It was all we could do to hold it together for a few paces, before our pent up tension released into uproarious laughter. It was one of those fits that you can't stop; the more you try, the less you succeed. It took a full ten minutes before we could get back to a semblance of normality.

"How'd you come up with that whole way of talking?" Herzl asked.

"I don't have a clue," I said, "it just came to me."

"A spontaneous adaptation," he said, matter-of-factly. "Something like what we Jews do. Instinct inbred over a hundred generations."

"I'm just glad you didn't cold-cock him," I said. "Let me ask you: if he *was* a cop and he was looking for us or at least knew to be on the lookout, would you've hit him?"

"Maybe. It wasn't my plan at school to break the kid's wrist, I just seized the moment. It all depends."

"On what, circumstances? Hunches? Moods?"

"I don't know. Maybe a combination. I can't pinpoint it. It's just that all of a sudden, in a moment, you get a feeling. It's there. You can't describe it, but you sense it, and you know you have to act on it," he said.

I'd see Herzl's impulsiveness again.

And mine.

"I'll tell you this," he said. "About the cop I hung out the window? I would've dropped him if he would've called me an asswipe Jew or something like that. No hesitation."

Now *that* would've changed things.

"Let's go back down the street, get some food and then some rest," was how I responded.

What I took away from this was that Herzl had suckered punched me.

We walked briskly past a guns and ammo storefront, finally finding a bodega, where I picked out some fruits and nuts and made small talk with the proprietor in Spanish. I took advantage of the opportunity to ask if there was a park nearby, and, obligingly, he walked out to the other side of the street, where the vantage point enabled us to see a playground with benches and trees, both of which had seen better days. There must've been a school nearby, as we saw a group of kids—seventh or eighth graders—kicking a soccer ball on the field adjacent to the playground.

Herzl amused himself by swinging from the monkey bars, starting out slowly, then picking up so much speed I thought he'd smack his head against one of the supporting rails. His strength and coordination were impressive. He motioned for me to join him, but I demurred, indicating that the incline of the slide was comforting, especially with my slicker as a pillow under my head and the metal reflecting whatever heat it could trap into my legs and back. I was asleep within a few minutes.

"I'm back," I heard Herzl announce, not knowing that he'd gone anyplace, but based on the sweat dripping from his forehead, I realized that he'd likely been doing some heavy exercising. "We ought to go back, down the bank, lie low."

I sat up, stretched, and reached down for my knapsack.

It was gone!

At first, I assumed that Herzl had picked it up but quickly saw that his was on his back, and he wasn't holding anything else. I scanned the rest of the playground; maybe I'd absentmindedly left it near the monkey bars or the swings.

Nothing there.

I glanced at the field where the kids had been playing soccer. They were nowhere to be seen. My notebook! Everything I'd written down, the record of what really happened at the Free Speech Movement—gone! I put my right hand into my pocket and grabbed the copper-encased mirror that I'd received as a going away gift from my father at Navajo Joe's village, the only possession I now owned save the clothes I was wearing, my yellow slicker, and a piece of paper in my back pocket.

Indignation and embarrassment competed to steer me in a direction of finding the knapsack, enabling me to fly down the street, lifting lids from trashcans, rummaging through them, kicking them over, engaging in a too-loud soliloquy—"It's got to be here. The knapsack I understand, but they'd just trash the stuff inside. What? A towel, some food, socks, bandages, a notebook"—moving on to a dumpster, a pile of junk next to a parking lot, a clothing bin on the corner…approaching the few people on the street too closely to ask breathlessly if they'd seen a dark green knapsack, assuring them it was okay if they had it, I just wanted the notebook, witnessing them flee from me, unable to process this unnatural force of tension, aggression, and panic, their repulsion causing me to be suspicious and to stare at them as they departed, looking for a tell that would generate an eruption alongside an exhortation to Herzl to join me in catching the thief.

Herzl forcibly pulled me away from a slow-gaited man aimlessly traipsing behind a shopping cart, who swiped at me with what looked like a shepherd's staff. I must've been nothing more than a wolf to him—a predator hungry to steal his sheep. I'd merely wanted to scrounge through his cart to see if he'd picked up my knapsack or just the notebook from any of the bins on the street. While he was wildly gesticulating at me as I backed off, I kept up a belligerent pose that distracted him long enough for Herzl to signal to me that my goods were not in his cart.

I put my hands on my knees and felt I might vomit, so Herzl guided me slowly to an empty lot next to the bodega where he bought a bottle of carbonated water for me. My pulse raced, sweat oozed from my forehead, behind my ears, my underarms. I sat on a dilapidated webbed chair and lowered my head to my knees, slightly bobbing up and down, spitting the eruption of a stream of saliva, keeping my eyes shut. I cursed my carelessness in falling asleep in a public place, allowing myself to become a victim, failing to guard my knapsack, now wondering how I could recover my prized possession.

"We've got to make a decision," Herzl said, lowering his head to my level, an attempt to get me to focus on what to do next, to prevent me from consuming myself in guilt. "We can't hang around here much longer, especially during the day. Maybe go up and down the road a mile or so each way, searching out bins where someone could've thrown the contents away."

What he didn't say was, *But the odds are, we're not going to find anything*. Or *Don't get your hopes up*.

We agreed to go in opposite directions for a half hour, then double back and meet in an hour. Individually, we went into stores to ask if anyone had come in with a knapsack or had dumped things into a wastepaper basket. No luck. At our rendezvous outside of the bodega, we exchanged shrugs and sideways head swivels, words would've been needless incursions. We both knew that we had to get back on the river. Herzl showed me some items he'd bought for me: a blanket, sweatshirt, flashlight, packaged crackers, ripe and dried fruits, nuts and cans of juices. We made our way back down the embankment. Once it was dark, we uncovered the shell and started downriver again.

The air was warm, the slight breeze was from the north, making our rowing easier. Honking geese caused us to look skyward. We were transfixed watching their inverted V formation, seeming to fly right below the moon.

We didn't speak for at least an hour. Then, Herzl started up with, "It was a dark and stormy night."

I laughed, the first time I'd experienced a pleasant feeling since I woke up on the slide early in the day.

"Sounds like the start of a Holyman story," I said.

"Tell me one," he said.

"You first," I said.

"I'm not good at fiction."

"So give me some facts," I said.

He nodded, then started up, in short exclamations, as if each staccato burst was timed to the exhale after each stroke.

"My father was born in Prussia.

It no longer exists.

It's vanished.

One stroke of the pen.

Poof and it was gone.

Like the Pale of Settlement.

Disappeared.

Who's even heard of it today?"

He pulled up both oars through the locks and rested them on his thighs, looked straight out the stern, waited for a few moments as if to check that I was still rowing, then started speaking again.

"My mother was from Austria. She was a Cohen. That means descended from Jewish priests when they had them, before there were rabbis. A couple thousand years ago. Stop me if you know any of this, okay?"

"Go on," I said, stroking rhythmically in a groove.

"They used to say they could trace Cohens through history by their superiority. *Uppitiness* my father the tailor would say. *Schneider*—that's German for tailor—my mother would sneer. She'd really get his goat with that. It was all about her being from the line of the high priests while he was someone who added extra fabric to my pant legs so the cuffs could be unrolled as I got older. A put down, you know, but not mean-spirited. Fun. It was part of who they were.

"They met in Vienna. Just before the Anschluss—you know about that, don't you?"

"I do."

I had to duck when Herzl spit three times over his shoulder into the water as he mentioned the Germans.

"They left everything except what they could carry. They drove first to Budapest, stayed there a few weeks, but it wasn't much better than Austria. Once Jew-hatred comes out of the shadows, it gets accepted. I'm not kidding, even by people who aren't anti-Semitic. It becomes part of the way it is. People like to go along with the majority; you don't stand out if you do. Life's easier that way.

"They ran low on money, so they sold their car when they got to the border with Yugoslavia and joined a caravan of Gypsies. It must've been a deal. You know—watches, jewelry, maybe a few coins, whatever they had left.

"They ended up in Trieste on a fishing boat which took them across to Venice, where my mother had a cousin. When the Americans came after the Italians switched sides, my father acted as a translator, which got him a visa to the States in 1949, and the rest, as they say, is history. Technically, I'm Italian, which means I can't ever run for president. Ha ha!" he exhorted.

"We were the lucky ones who got out with nothing but some books and schemes."

I was eager to hear the rest of how he came to New Mexico and got his strange name, but given that we'd have more time on the river together, I could wait for additional explanations. We pulled in under a steep ledge on the east side of the river, our standard practice, as that's where the small towns were. We estimated that we'd traveled about fifty miles, and at that pace, we figured we had four more days on the river before we could start to look for a sharp bend to the shoreline, broken at the tip by a large rock promontory jutting out into the river like an exclamation point, which would point the way to Navajo Joe's village.

When we put in around dawn each day, we'd hide the shell, climb the bank, put on our knitted caps and convivial expressions, then walk into stores to buy water and non-perishable snacks. It was always too early for the newspapers, so we didn't know what had happened at UT since we escaped. We also weren't aware then that an APB had been issued to local law enforcement, including our student ID photos and accurate physical descriptions. Fortunately, we learned later that a bureaucratic snafu from the police in Taos Heights had eliminated a critical paragraph on the fact that we were members of the crew team, which would've suggested some scrutiny of the river by patrol boats. We'd been wise to steal an old wooden boat that'd been mothballed in the crawlspace of the boathouse instead of making off with a newer model, which would've been faster and easier to row but clearly would've tipped off the cops as to our plan of escape.

We'd snuggle up in our blankets next to the shell, usually finding some foliage to divert rain that would also serve as an effective shield from someone who was stumbling by with a bottle in a bag or looking to cast a line for something to eat. We made sure to whisper on the bank, not only to avoid been discovered, but also to keep curious animals at bay. Each night as we silently pushed out, we'd talk, albeit *sotto voce*, a term that Ben Veniste had explained to me when we first went into the tunnel.

Although my anger had abated somewhat, my frustration and disappointment was ever-present, and I pined for the time when I'd have the opportunity to recreate my notebook. I was concerned that each day that the contents were further removed from my memory would result in me not being able to resurrect it, so I defaulted to mnemonic devices—a trick I'd learned when I first got to UT that made preparing for exams easier. Herzl would hear me mumbling, first misinterpreting it as groaning, then recognizing words, he'd quietly inquire, "What?" and when he got no response, would settle into his effortless rhythm, allowing me to practice my patterns.

CHAPTER 13

Well, one male friend, yes,

but don't forget about Mir

Before dawn of the seventh day on the river, stroking rhythmically in the glow of the moon, I caught sight of a group of large stones that appeared to be a map of the constellations we'd see in the wintertime, so I knew that was the foot of a rise on the western edge where a path would lead up to the Navajo village.

I began to shiver. I looked down the river, staring, mute, absorbing the sights and smells, a minute that was both singular and intimate. I could once again see the striated rainbow-like threads of currents that alternately competed with and calmly nestled alongside each other, giving the impression of a race between elements to find out which could claim dominance. It was these river threads that had given me the support to make my way home, free from the chaos, angst, embarrassment, hurt, pain, and loss from which I'd fled.

Only later would I come to recognize that this, too, was a moment of swing.

We put ashore and hoisted the heavy shell onto our shoulders, portaging it to a spot behind a clump of gray saltbushes so it couldn't be seen from the river. Silently, we plodded up the hill, sat down with our backs up against a juniper and waited for light, not wanting to be accosted if we were to walk into the village when it was still dark, where we might be perceived as a threat.

When we could hear activity, we walked into the plaza, where we were greeted by a group of curious children and their passive aggressive dogs, whose tails were wagging as they came close to us, barking but not growling, and would then back up when we bent down. The younger children giggled as if they were spectators watching a new game. I took off my knitted cap, hoping one of the kids would recognize me, although with my bandana, longer hair, and thicker beard, it wasn't too likely. The chattering of the kids and the concomitant barking and baying of the dogs had reached a noise level that got the attention of some adults, who came to see what the hubbub was all about. Out popped Navajo Joe, who approached me with a gesture of warmth: two open almost vertical palms, a signal for me to approach. His palms clamped onto each upper arm and gave a tight squeeze. I smiled, told him how happy I was to see him, and introduced Herzl. He motioned for us to step inside, but because we were aware of how disheveled we were, not having bathed in over a week, I pointed to the garden of white and blue mountain lilacs. He grinned and retrieved a bucket for us, which we took into the juniper forest, having first picked the flowers that would serve as our soap. As we walked to the trees, the adults who'd gathered to find out what the commotion was all about restrained the kids, while the dogs followed us and watched as we washed away a week's worth of grime.

Navajo Joe approached and handed each of us a beautiful shawl, leggings, and moccasins. He broke into a wide grin when he realized that because of our height, the leggings wouldn't cover our calves, which caused the children to point and laugh uproariously when we came back to the plaza.

Later in the morning, we showed Navajo Joe where we'd hidden the shell, and he got the kids to gather more sagebrush to cover it completely. We stayed until sunset, kicking a ball and playing games with the kids, watching impatiently as Navajo Joe and a few of his cronies were bent under the hood of his 1941 Ford flatbed, attempting to determine why it was sputtering and failing to ignite. Just before sunset, we heard the unmistakable whir of an engine starting. We all piled into the tight cabin and headed off to Arroyo Grande. I was relieved that Navajo Joe didn't ask me a single question. No *how come you're here without your father knowing you were coming*? No *why did you row a boat down the Rio Grande from Taos Heights to get here*? No *who is this young man you are with*?

I was both excited and nervous when Arroyo Grande came into view from a small rise as we approached it at a hundred yards from the east. Navajo Joe parked the truck in front of the ancient footbridge that leaped over the now nonexistent arroyo, which in any case couldn't have been too grand—the name likely reflected an aspiration as much as a description. The narrow span had been hewed from Gambel oak, foot-wide planks underpinned by a half dozen boughs lashed together by hemp rope. It croaked with each step, no matter how gingerly we placed our feet. Herzl, however, showed no signs of concern, walking at the same pace as he did on land.

"We should come back a little before noon," I said. "That way you can see the fog carried by the wind over the lake out there in the west. It gets trapped by the warmer air and makes the village look like it's floating in the sky. It takes until mid-day to see the church steeple that's tilted off to the side. People say it looks like it's sad or drunk or spooky."

Once we crossed the footbridge, the outline of the village began to emerge from the light of the full moon. As we got closer, the uniformity of style to the houses became apparent, although each expressed its own flair, the adobe having been washed with a residue of dust. I could tell that Herzl was taking it all in with a sense of wonder. I pointed out the variations of brown, gray, yellow, and red that adorned the houses.

"The colors come from stones cut from the rocks. You can see them all around, especially down there," I said, pointing down to the walls of the dry arroyo bed.

"You get paint from rocks?" he asked.

"It's not paint. They crush them, then they're milled into a powder with water or goat's milk. They mix it up with dyes from flax and safflower seeds, sometimes with red alder barks. My father supervises a lot of this work. You should see him teaching kids how to apply this with a porous wool cloth. I helped with our house. It's fun. Pretty similar to preparing a wall for a fresco. Although the houses have slightly different shades of color, it ends up looking like a blend. From one to the other."

"I have to tell you, Jacobo, it looks like the whole village has been painted by Monet. Are you sure he hadn't come to Arroyo Grande like Gauguin went to Tahiti?"

"Shhh," I said, "it's still a secret."

He cuffed me on the arm.

As we got closer, I pointed out the community house, the cantina, the shops, and the bazaar, still teeming with fruits, vegetables, pottery, cloths of every color and size, handicrafts of wood and string, as well as highly polished stones made into jewelry by older Córdoba women.

"None of this stuff's put away," he said.

"Why would they have to?" I said and immediately realized that by saying it like this, I was implying that my community, with its different rules, standards, and customs, was superior to that of Taos Heights, where locks and keys were a necessity. So I quickly added, "Same as in Navajo Joe's village," which had the effect of portraying Arroyo Grande as less unique.

As we approached the center of the village filled with colorful tents delineating one section of the bazaar from another, Herzl said, "It's like a dragon that's snaking its way around the plaza. You know, kind of make-believe."

It was time to go home.

I opened the front door slowly and saw my older sister Débora who gasped and threw her arms around me, but I could sense that her eyes were fixed on Herzl.

"Madre!" she called out, and as if my mother had been waiting in the kitchen for the express purpose of greeting me, she came with a skip in her step, arms extended, watery eyes, and a grin from ear to ear.

"This is Herzl," I said, "my best friend."

My father appeared, giving me a warm hug with his left arm and pumping Herzl's hand with his right. Nohemi wandered in to find out what was going on, and when she realized I was home, she actually jumped into my arms. We all laughed.

There was no interrogation. I was home and that was that. We were exhausted. I made a bedroll for Herzl, who zonked out shortly after his head hit the rolled-up blanket that served as a pillow.

When we got up, breakfast was being served. Herzl and I recounted what had happened at the UT and on our flight, which proceeded like alternating soliloquies, members of my family asking for more detail on a particular topic that sparked their interest. My father focused on the events when we took over Kettys-Burg Hall, Madre dug gently into my relationship with Mir, my younger sister wanted to know more about the shell and the trip down the river, and my older sister, Débora, offered some comments without making eye contact with Herzl. As I had been with Mir, I suspected she was a bit unsure of herself and didn't want to say anything embarrassing that might cause her to blush and reveal an attraction. I wondered if Herzl received the signals that Débora was sending, which were evident to me, and I now understood how obvious my behavior was to others when I'd been around Mir.

After breakfast, Herzl and I gathered at the center of the plaza, drinking cool lemon-flavored water and exchanging pleasantries with the women who stood behind their tables with their wares. We patted the dogs that sniffed our legs while pretending not to notice the girls who'd look away the second they thought we were glancing at them. When I saw some kids come out of the *eskola*, I took off my knit hat and waved it back and forth, which elicited squeals of delight equivalent in intensity to the starter's pistol that we'd hear on the water at the beginning of a race. All the kids ran full speed directly toward us. We stood our ground, engulfed in a swarm of children, some of whom I recognized but was amazed to see had grown a few inches or were beginning to show signs of puberty. Many called out my name, some rhythmically—Jacobo, Jacobo, Jacobo—and touched me while others were content to circle me, their little hands making contact with my legs as they made their revolutions.

They were ecstatically happy to see me, their huge smiles as wide as the plaza itself. As I strode up to greet them, I received kisses from the girls who looked at Herzl and blushed, some managing a barely audible "hey there" to him, while others mumbled welcome and extended their hands self-consciously, accepting his handshake without meeting his eyes. Some of the younger ones approached Herzl cautiously and politely, bowing or curtsying awkwardly, extending their hands to shake formally with him, then running back to me or their friends, smiling and laughing.

I motioned for Herzl to come with me to the path to the farms out west. That part of the village was at a higher elevation, and the ground was mostly covered with grasses, the trees having been cleared both for timber and planting. Every few minutes, Herzl stopped to look back to get a glance at the town, shrinking in the distance. The fog was beginning to form. He put his hands over his eyes to shield them from the sun, and made remarks about the mountains toward the south, the tall trees in the ravine to the north, and the emerging roofs of the farms in the west.

"I want you to see something, hurry," I said.

"What's the rush?" he asked. "I want to take this all in, savor it."

"It might be gone in a few minutes," I said. "Let's go. Come on."

"What might be gone? Where are we going?"

I didn't respond.

Reluctantly, he picked up his pace, and when he got to the top of a rise, I told him to look to the southwest, his sight pivoting to a position between the mountains and the farmhouses.

"I don't see anything," he said. "What's the big deal?"

"Wait. Any second."

And as if on cue, it formed—a perfectly designed arc, consisting of bands of red, orange, yellow, green, and blue of different widths, a skybridge connecting the lake that was fed from the runoff of the mountains to a point that disappeared into the thick pine forest of the ravine to the north.

"My God, it's extraordinary. It's like a blessing. How often do you see it?" he asked.

"It depends," I said. It was one of those non-answers that doesn't generate a second set of questions.

"It lasts until the mist that's created by sunlight hitting the lake evaporates. It can be seconds or minutes," I said. "You can see it from the plaza, but I wanted you to get close to it, even though there's really not much difference in distance."

"Like when the full moon looks so close a plane could fly to it," he said.

"When I was much younger, I used to come out here with my little sister, and we'd make up rainbow stories. Like how the colors decided to come together and agree on who's on top, or that fish from the lake used it as a way to swim up between the bands and then slide down the other side into the forest where they'd turn into deer and rabbits, or that the birds who flew through it would become the color of the first band they touched. You know, silly stuff that kids don't believe is real, but then again, maybe there's a chance that it is. That kind of thing.

"Nohemi and I tried our hands at telling our rainbow stories right after my father would finish with the Holyman tales. Boy, did he indulge us."

"There's something to be said for growing up in a place like this, where your dreams aren't nightmares, that's for sure," Herzl said.

I could only imagine where this came from.

He ambled over to a mound of Indiangrass and sat like a pasha on a throne. He took it all in.

Maybe he'd tell me.

"You never finished...about your family, when we were on the river," I said. "You left off just before your parents got to Italy."

"Let me think. Right. Did I tell you about their getting on the boat?"

"You did. You said in the middle of the night."

"Okay, so they showed up at my mother's cousin's home on the mainland, near Venice, out of the blue—or black I should say. Now get this this: they stayed in the basement until the Germans were forced out in May of 1945. It's true. Incomprehensible, no?"

"In the basement? Are you serious? My God, you've got to be kidding."

"It was like that for many Jews. They weren't alone."

"There were others with them?"

"No, sorry, that's not what I meant. Nobody else in the basement. Other situations, like that. Everywhere."

"Other places in Italy?"

"All over Europe. People lying under porches for so long they could hardly stand up when they came out. Living in forests, like the pine one over there, only it was filled with people trying to hunt them down. It's nauseating. Heartbreaking. That's why we say 'never forget'."

Nightmare dreams.

He didn't say anything for a while.

His rainbow stories weren't made up.

I wanted to know more.

"I didn't think that Italians hated Jews," I said.

"No more than anyone else. It was beat into them for 2,000 years that we killed Christ. That's at the bottom of it. That's where you start. Then the Germans came along. They dehumanized us. Propaganda. Years of it. It took hold."

"What about your parents' cousins, the ones who lived in the house? Upstairs. *They* were Jewish, no?"

"They pretended to be German Catholics from Austria. They *passed.* You know what that is?"

"Uh-huh, I do," I said.

"They got there right before the start of World War I. They had a pharmacy. I'm sure there had to be people who *suspected* but then looked the other way. You know how it is—they needed drugs and medical advice. Insulin trumps the crucifixion.

"Then you wake up one day, and they're gone. The Germans. It was over," he said.

But the nightmare dreams remained.

Insulin trumps the crucifixion.

He paused and with a smile, said, "I was a celebration baby—*capisce?*"

"Ca-peesh-eh?"

"Sorry, it's simply Italian slang for *do you understand.* I was born in February 1946, nine months after the Germans left."

"And your name?" I asked.

"Oh, that. Well, my parents went back and forth for months with names all beginning with an h, in honor of my paternal grandfather, of blessed memory. But Heinrich—too German, Henri—too affected…*capisce?*"

I nodded yes.

"Herbert and Henry—well, they just didn't like how they sounded."

"But Herzl?"

"What better way to thumb their noses at the defeated Germans than to proudly name their son Herzl! What irony, giving me the last name of the man credited with championing the return of the Jews to their homeland. You see?"

I did.

"So how did your parents come to New Mexico?" I asked, "It seems you know, well, pretty far removed."

"Los Alamos."

"But if your family came here in 1949, what did that have to do with the A-bomb?"

"No, it was his German. He was fluent in so many of the local dialects from different parts of Germany, Austria, and Czechoslovakia. You should hear him mimic the *Schweizerdeutsch* of Zurich. Amazing. What an ear. No kidding. The army found him critical in interrogating German POWs and then someone got the bright idea to ship him to Los Alamos where the Americans had brought so many German scientists. For the H-bomb."

I always had trouble grappling with the idea that our side had rescued the very Germans who'd been using their scientific and engineering expertise for the Nazis, trying to assemble the same kind of bomb that could be used against us. This was hard to fathom. Some called it an act of forgiveness, while others said it was simply a cynical ploy to take advantage when you can. Survival of the fittest, even if those you designate to be fit are only so according to a narrow definition that whitewashes the parts that aren't fit at all.

"The Germans all hated each other, by the way," Herzl continued. "The Lutherans—you know, the ones from the north, Hamburg and Berlin—couldn't stand the Bavarian Catholics, and they all detested the Austrians, thought the German speakers from the east were provincials, rubes, and how the blame game went all around: who was responsible for the Nazis, who was secretly anti-Nazi, who was trying to out-American the Americans. My father found it all nauseating. He was just a translator, but the truth is that he was the instigator of warfare among the various German-speaking scientists. He promoted rumors, stirred up jealousies, ascribed tales that never occurred to those he knew would take offense the most. He *loved* it."

"Kind of a revenge thing, I guess," I said.

"Sure, on a small scale, of course."

"Well, you do what you can, right?" As soon as this came out, I wondered what kind of revenge Myles would plan for me—us—because sure as ever, we'd turned on him.

"They all confided in him. He had their trust. Can you believe it? He was a pseudo-shrink," Herzl said. "They all bared their souls to him, never suspecting that it was this poor *Juden* tailor who was manipulating *them*. And oh, how he loved to wear his Judaism on his sleeve. This Jew, who'd probably not been to synagogue in ten years would leave early on Shabbat and not come in on holidays whose meanings were unknown to him. He played it to the hilt."

He paused for a minute, then said, "Proud Jews, with nothing to hide. Just like Mir."

"What about Mir?"

"She's a Jew, that's all."

I was startled.

"What? She's Indian. Did she tell you she's a Jew?" I asked.

"She didn't have to. I knew. I could sense it."

"What does *that* mean?"

"I'll tell you, but I'm not sure you'll be able to get it," he said.

"Try me."

"Look, it can be how someone approaches a situation or a problem. How we think something through. How we use our body language to communicate."

"Yeah, but none of this is with words."

"Think of it, Jacobo. All those years of being segregated, adapting to the Romans or Spanish or to the kings and dukes of wherever, without giving up our own customs, knowing that at any point in time we might have to pick up our bags on a moment's notice and flee.

Suffering, you know, breeds a mindset we can actually feel, and we can transmit it with the tiniest facial tic or rapid eye movement. Sometimes, a guttural sound is all it takes. It's animal-like, and it can be more potent than words."

"So with Mir..."

"The first time she came into my room—I don't even remember the reason—I saw her through the reflection in the window. She noticed that I was reading one of our texts, and in that fraction of a second, I saw the glint in her eyes. That was it. I knew. I asked her if she was from Yemen. She shook her head and told me she was from Cochin."

"Oh, I get it. On the southwest coast of India; that's why Myles introduced us," I said.

"He thought you both were Indians. Americans, natives."

Serendipitous occurrences, like earthquakes, can have obvious momentous impacts in the short term that really can only be properly measured over time and with perspective, which I've always thought of as the fifth dimension. It's the one that really helps to define us; it provides us with our individuality and allows us to adjust as the angles get sharper or diminish, the distant events themselves remaining stationary, yet somehow changed as we evolve.

This was one of those moments. I'd need some time to let this all sink in.

She's a Jew, I said to myself. Mir's a Jew. She was on the phone when Myles was making his anti-Jewish comments. What was she thinking? Why didn't she say something? Did she instinctively know it was better not to react because the consequences wouldn't lead to a positive outcome? If she'd caused a scene, would that have disrupted the plans for the Free Speech Movement? Or, was her calculation that she'd bear the brunt of Myles' or Claudia's ire, perhaps for not telling them she was a Jew—or worse, that they'd accuse her of hiding behind her Indian-ness and that they were the ones who'd been betrayed. People do that. They turn things on their heads to avoid taking responsibility, or maybe it's just a matter of arrogance. They're never wrong; to admit it once, suggests that it is endemic, a part of their personality and that's something these kinds of folks could never acknowledge. Because they'd turn into Humpty Dumpty.

She's a Jew.

"And you?" he asked.

"Me what?"

"Your story. We all come from somewhere else."

I'd held my tongue for a year and a half and could attest to not having betrayed my father's admonition not to reveal any of our secrets. *La palavra es de plata i la kayades de oro: Speaking is silver, silence is gold.*

It was time.

"I want to show you something," I said. "Come with me to the church."

CHAPTER 14

What I mean is that

I don't have to read it

Herzl gave me a look. I ignored it. We crossed the plaza and opened the front door. The pews were dusty. The shades were pulled down on the tall, narrow windows. The pulpit looked frail and was precariously perched against a pole that couldn't possibly hold the weight of an average man.

"This way," I said, pointing him to a hallway on the side that led to a staircase with a steep decline.

"What's behind that door?" he asked, looking at the landing on the bottom that fronted a narrow doorway.

"A small room where wood is kept to dry. For the fireplaces. We're not going there."

"Where to, then?" he asked.

"Here," I said, stopping halfway down the steps and rapping my knuckles on the wall."

"Ummm, Jacobo, what are you talking about? Is this some kind of a joke?"

I didn't respond. I stretched my right arm up and pushed hard on a small pine panel, which gave way to reveal an opening. My fingers nudged against the back of the opening which elicited a thump; the sound was the disengagement of a rod from a lock. Suddenly, I was reminded of how Ben Veniste opened up the door to the dark tunnel that led to the basement of Kettys-Burg Hall. I had the feeling that what I was about to show Herzl would be as transformative to him as my experience had been.

"Use both hands," I said. "It's heavy. It slides to the left."

Hooking our fingers between the narrow slits that separated the vertical boards, we slid a section of the wall to reveal an opening almost eight feet wide. I stepped through, motioned for him to follow me, then had him help me close the panel back up. We stood on a wide platform from which a dozen steps descended. It was dark.

"Hold onto the rail over here," I said, guiding his hand to the rail on the right. "When we get to the bottom, there's another door and, once inside, there'll be a flashlight. We'll be okay. Better than the kerosene lamps they used to have."

"I can't get over how well this was concealed. Kids can't reach where you pushed, there's no way in the world you could tell that the panels can move, and it's so cool how the bottom of the panel has the same angle as the stairs. Who did this?"

I interpreted this as a question for which I needn't answer.

We stepped down carefully, holding onto the rail, then I opened the unlocked door. I ran my hand along the wall on the right, retrieved a flashlight, and shined it straight ahead.

"Wow. This space. It's much bigger than what you'd imagine," Herzl said. "You've got ten, twelve, fourteen benches on both sides of the aisle," he counted as he walked down the center, "and I bet you could put at least ten people on each bench. Two fifty to three hundred people, for sure."

I swept the arc of light slowly along the wall from right to left to give him a better overall view of the room. The floor had no covering. It was hardpacked dirt.

"What's in the cupboards?" he asked, heading to the ones on the left.

"Go ahead. Open one," I responded.

He did and stood there staring at the contents. Books. Row upon row of books. All with black covers but no marking on the binding or the front and back cover.

"May I touch one? Pull one out?" he asked.

"By all means," I said.

And that's how Herzl found out.

"Oh, my God, my God, I can't believe it," Herzl said as he opened one of the black-covered books and mouthed the first words he saw on the page. He ran his fingers over the tops of other books, pulling out those of different sizes, mumbling, "Of course, yes, yes," and then reproaching himself. "I'm such an idiot, it was all there for me to see. How did I miss it?" And still facing the cupboard. "I actually told you I could *sense* it. *Sense* it, for God's-sake. Embarrassing, embarrassing, embarrassing. Forgive me. What's in here?" he asked, his tone changing rapidly from self-chastisement to inquisitiveness, opening up the next cupboard. It was one of those questions that isn't really a question, more of a warning that some other action is going to be taken even in the absence of permission from a third party. "Well, *that* goes with the territory," he said, holding a *kippa* in one hand and running his fingers across a *tallit*, his voice now taking on the mien of an announcer. He passed his hands over the Shabbat candles and their silver sticks, absentmindedly arranged several *Yartzeit* candles that weren't lined up in a row, allowed his fingers to follow the braids in the *Havdalah* candles, and then, as if on cue, leaned in to sniff the spice boxes, returning to an upright position as he pivoted to face me. "Jacobo, Jacobo, Jacobo," he started, revving up his motor in neutral before to shifting into gear. "It was all there for me to see. What, did I have blinders on?"

"Sometimes what's obvious to one person is practically invisible to another," I said. "I mean, how about me with Mir?"

"You mean that she's in love with you," he said.

I was taken aback. A lightning bolt crackled within me. I wasn't sure I could stand still, and my skin bristled with excitement.

"Uhm, well," I stammered, "I was thinking more in terms that she's a Jew and I had no idea. At all, really."

"Oh, you gave me so many clues," he said, turning the conversation away from Mir. "You left breadcrumbs all over the place. You know, starting with the names. That was an obvious tell. How could I have missed that? I'm no Sherlock Holmes, that's for sure."

"You mean the families?" I said.

"They're names of cities in Europe."

"Wait, you're right, but why are these tells? They're just names," I said.

"Jews weren't allowed to have last names. Until Napoleon. The Enlightenment. You know, around 1800 or so."

I was thinking, it was the same for the slaves here in the south.

"First names only is a way of making them out to be children. Okay, some had Hebrew last names, like Ben something, you know, son of, but the people here in Arroyo Grande took the last names of the cities they came from. So they ended up with Ávila, Córdoba, I can't remember the others..." he said.

"Pontevedre, Girona, Alicante, Lisboa, and Firenze. You're missing one. Mine. Toledano. It's not the name of a city," I said.

"No, no, you're wrong on that one, Jacobo. It's Hebrew for Toledo, in Spain."

They didn't tell us that in *eskola*.

"Hebrew! Now it's so obvious. And let's face it—I can hardly believe I didn't get the *first* names in your family: Jacobo, Aarón, Raquel, Débora, and Nohemi. I know there are lots of evangelical Christians who take names from the Hebrew bible, so I guess I just put it in that category and didn't think twice about it. You know, assuming you were Mexican."

Herzl walked to the far end of the room, his head swiveling up to the ceiling and around to the other side. He pointed to the cupboard at the far end. "The scrolls are in there, I assume. Can I open?"

I nodded.

He opened the doors slowly and saw three scrolls, dressed in their ornamental silver cylindrical cases. He bent down to get a closer look, eyes riveted on the intricate designs etched into the metal. "They're beautiful," he said, "so different from ours, covered in fabrics." As he took a step back, in preparation for closing the doors, he was startled to see three sheets of parchment behind glass on the insides of the doors. "What are these?" he asked. "I've never seen anything on doors to the ark before."

"*Pequeño Atorá*," I said.

He gave me a quizzical look.

"Little Torah. It's a colloquial expression from our community. We just refer to it as *Pequeño*."

"Words taken from the Torah in Ladino?" he asked.

"Ladino, yes, but not from the Five Books. It was created here, by a man named Efraín Valencia. He was the leader. From when they left Constantinople, throughout the wanderings to get here," I said.

I went to close the doors.

"Wait," he implored. "Can you read it to me? I'm really curious."

"I don't have to," I said, then, realizing that he would take that the wrong way, I added quickly, "What I mean is that I don't have to *read* it. We all memorize it. We say it every Saturday night before we go to sleep."

I closed the doors, then told it to him in English, a little slower than how I'd say it in Ladino, wanting to make sure the translation was accurate.

It came to pass that our fate was in God's hands,
and we trusted in the Lord;
He sent us a man who was holy, who enabled us to see
when there was no light;
When all around us there was conflagration, horror,
and death for the faithful;
Yea, though the darkness suffocated us so that the very
act of breathing was conscious;
When apostasy was a destination worse than
incapacitation, disease, or death;
We embarked on a journey fraught with danger
where unknown dragons could slay us;
Where acts of will propelled us when we had no
strength, and our bones were cold;
Where we clutched children and memories of ancestors
alike, never letting go;
Despite the distances, the separations, the
remembrances of lost touches and gazes;
We sup at a table of community bound by hardship
and bordered by skin of no thickness.

We have known deprivations, have endured blood
libels, have been torn asunder;
Yet we gather strength from our passage and pity our
mighty enemies;
Who seek salvation in hollow words and absolution
from transient promises;
While our beliefs never waver, we are obliged to speak
in their tongues;
Mimic their customs, assume their identities, placate
their leaders, renounce our own;

With pain that wracks our core, burns our eyes
and ears, eviscerates our self-esteem;
We cry out for the time when we walk unafraid
through the parted seas;
When goodness, justice, compassion,
and mercy will follow us the rest of our days;
When our children will know of our devastations for
not having lived through them;
And can take pride in our celebrations without fear of
retribution or persecution.

We wandered through deserts and oceans,
mourned generations deprived;
Never forgave those who rejoiced at our misfortune
and celebrated our exodus;
Cast aside false idols, preserved our memories,
sustained faith in the One Who Is;
Took an oath to remember all of our vows,
that their recitation speaks only to the past;
We now bask in our aloneness, free to be who we are,
who we were meant to be;
Helpless and weary no more, we welcome each sunrise
and sunset;
With heartfelt thanks, our secrets preserved in our
everlasting traditions;
We ask the One Who Makes Peace in the high heavens
to make peace for us all;
So that our children's children's children will sit under
their vines and fig trees;
And none shall make them afraid.

CHAPTER 15

She's in love with you

We walked out of the basement of the church. Neither of us said a word. We closed the sliding door in the wall, walked back up the stairs, out the front door, and made our way silently to the bazaar. We stuck our heads under a pump to cool off, cupped our hands to drink, then found a spot in the shade.

"It's poetry and history and prayer all wrapped up in one," Herzl said, referring to the Little Torah. "I'd like you to teach it to me."

"I have a better idea."

"What's that?" he asked.

"I'll ask Débora."

I could see the red rise from his chin to his forehead. He offered a nonchalant "okay" which hid his excitement about as well as I did when I'd see Mir.

After a minute or so of silence, he muttered "of course" when he saw the blue and white knit caps with the number eighteen festooned on a couple of kids. He made a self-berating face when he saw a few men wearing exquisitely carved wooden amulets around their necks—a thick horizontal bar with a bulge on the left and two protruding legs. And he rolled his eyes when he saw strips of multi-colored wood that were placed at an angle affixed to the vertical support beam next to the front door of the cantina and the library across from where we were sitting.

"It was all there, and here," he said, as much to himself as it was directed to me.

I let him come to grips with all of this and then said, "Can I go back to what you said about breadcrumbs? Clues. What did you mean? I thought I did a pretty good job, you know, hiding everything, like my father told me to do."

"Look, you didn't betray anything. Don't worry about that. So, okay, besides the names, you didn't know what stigmata were—what Christian doesn't know that? You used the word *eskola* for school. At first, I just thought it was a colloquial in Spanish, you know, how we Ashkenazi say *shul* for synagogue, but of course, it's got to be Ladino, right?"

"Uh-huh," I said.

"And when I said *eesh* when we were on the bank of the river, you didn't blink, didn't ask me what I was saying. *That* should've been enough for me. My antennae are usually up, but they weren't picking up these signals, that's for sure. I'm a dope."

"To be honest with you, when I took the stone I was using for a pillow and turned it upright, it came second nature to me—my own *Beth El*—I immediately thought I'd blown it, that you noticed."

"Talk about a tell," he said. "Jacobo's pillow, now that's practically *show* and tell."

We both laughed.

"Oh," he continued, "*this* could've been a dead giveaway: you only eat the kinds of food they serve at the café, like eggplant, eggs, hummus, tahini, vegetables, chopped salads. Practically an ad for a menu of what the Sephardim eat in Turkey. Or Morocco."

He was right.

Herzl approached me with open arms, the way grandparents do generally when they approach one of their small ones. I was proud to be enveloped in his warm embrace and reciprocated, hugging him and patting his back. He pulled a few inches away so he could look me in the eye and said, "Since we're practically *mishpucha*, I want to hear a family story," he said.

"Mish what?"

"Yiddish for family. What's it in Ladino?"

"*Familia*, just like Spanish."

"Okay *hermano*, out with it," he said, and sat on a bench opposite me.

I started slowly. "This is what we were taught: A group of families left Spain, by boat, from Valencia, on the east coast. They put ashore near Montpellier."

"How soon after the Edict?" he asked.

"Six, eight weeks. It had to be quick. Queen Isabella was a witch who might change her mind."

"About letting people go," Herzl said.

"Or not. It was get out or be killed."

"The auto-da-fé," he said.

"You got it," I said. "They walked through southern France—it was a place to go through—not a place to stay. It took them a month to get to Genoa. They did it mostly at night."

"Like us, it's safer that way," he said.

"They were going to continue on, walking, to Venice, but by luck, they met a man from Firenze. He was there on his way to Palos on the west coast of Spain. But after meeting the group, he changed his plans. He was rich; he had gold. He took them on a boat to Constantinople. Where they stayed."

"No inquisition."

"*Inkizisyon*," I said in Ladino.

"Your ancestors, what did they do?"

"Traders, innkeepers, money changers. It was a good life," I said.

I knew from *eskola* that this was where east met west. Everything converged in Constantinople. Goods from China and Java and India could be traded for those from the Austro-Hungarian and the Holy Roman Empires. The Silk Road.

"But they left," Herzl declared.

"In 1672. They'd been there for almost two centuries. They thought they'd never leave. Then, out, gone, poof, like that," I said, snapping my fingers.

"Do you know why?" he asked.

"Sabbatai Zevi."

"Oh, of course, the false messiah," he said.

"Takes a whole lot of faith for a messiah to choose conversion over martyrdom," I said, my tone echoing sarcasm mixed with disdain. "And of course, you know what happened."

"I can only imagine, but whatever it was, it was same old, same old for the Jews," he said.

"It brought back that old feeling…"

"*Déjà vu*," Herzl said. "Here we go again."

"Time to move on. What do they say—'time to get out of Dodge'?" I said.

He laughed, leaned over, and tapped a closed fist against my arm. I smiled.

"Can you imagine what was going through their minds? The word *home* didn't have any meaning to them," I said.

"Well, that's why we say, 'Next year in Jerusalem'!" he said.

"Amen," I added. "Anyway, they took off. Short stays here and there, following the map west, always hoping they'd find peace, a place to sink roots. Nothing doing. Eventually, they crossed the Straits."

"Back into Spain," he said.

"This time, only to make their way to Palos, to get on a ship to Mexico, where they stayed for a couple of years. Then you know, the *inkizisyon*..."

"In Mexico," he interrupted, his voice rising into a what could be interpreted as a question.

"Yup," I said.

"That's when they fled north?"

I nodded.

Herzl said, "What amazes me is that the community stayed intact here."

"For two hundred years."

"I mean, you can imagine what it took to create a self-sustaining society for all that time? And no interactions with the rest of the world."

"Until the Navajo came. And I have to tell you that if they were going to have to interact with someone else, it was better that it was this tribe as opposed to some ranchers or farmers or railroad workers," I said.

"But the church. They didn't practice Christianity."

"It was for show. You know, in case someone discovered them. Us."

"What a nightmare to build under it," he said.

"They built the room down there first. Then added the church on top. It was also a shelter, in case they had to hide."

While this conversation was taking place, in the back of my mind, I couldn't stop thinking about what Herzl had said earlier: "She's in love with you." When would I get a chance to see Mir again?

I ached.

CHAPTER 16

The U.S. will never be the same

The handle moved easily although the door was heavier than it appeared to be. There wasn't much light, but that didn't mean it was difficult to see all the men. They were standing in anticipatory poses with friendly expressions. And why not? There was no reason for hostility, it was just going to be a few remarks, some questions and answers, and then it would be over. Easy.

George Townsend approached Myles as soon as the door swung open and thrust his hand forward to shake, while at the same time, he took the liberty of placing his left palm on Myles' shoulder, which had the effect when he twirled around for the cameras of showing the two of them in kind of an intimate position, the chief smiling, Myles stone-faced, a juxtaposition that'd be dissected by all the reporters when they filed their stories.

The police chief was jocular, pumping his hand longer than normal, the better to make sure the cameras caught his conviviality. Claudia had told Myles to make sure that after the plainclothes cop was released, he should make his remaining two demands.

"Remember," she admonished, "since you've got nothing more tangible to give him, you've got to show your superiority."

Myles dismissed her comment with the flick of a hand, especially hurtful in that this gesture had been done with other students around. He'd humiliated her again. She could barely contain her anger, putting the affronts by Myles behind an expressionless façade that would mask her feelings. Myles had the ability to enable her to believe that he was taking her advice, but then could turn on her quickly, the same way their sex always seemed to end with a violent physical and verbal confrontation. It was then that she realized he was going to do something he'd cooked up himself, in public, with cameras ready for pictures, microphones anticipating voices, American eyes and ears glued to this heretofore unknown place to witness his day in the sun.

She wanted to scream at him, to all the people in front of the building, to show them what a true revolutionary looked like. In her imagination she'd pirouette in dramatic fashion, turn her back on the crowd, thrust her hand in the air with the middle finger raised defiantly, and step back inside the door, locking it and Myles out of her life.

He disengaged from Chief Townsend. The plainclothes cop was released. Myles whispered in the chief's ear. A fireman came running to assist the cop into an ambulance that roared off with the siren on.

Myles waited for the last sounds of the siren to fade, then grasped the microphone with his right hand more reverentially than he had taken the chief's hand. He used his left hand to pull out a sheet of paper from the right breast pocket of his jacket and positioned it slightly in front of the microphone. Without introducing himself or making any introductory remarks, he read the following in a measured, yet forceful manner:

> "a confluence of events has led to a moment that in the future will be either cherished or looked upon with great shame. we are faced with

the decision of choosing between honoring the grand principles upon which this nation was founded or betraying that cause to serve self-interest above national concern. the consequences are significant.

"for the last twenty years, we have been wracked by a series of events that have pitted those without financial, social, or political power against a privileged elite, unwilling to share the fantasies of the American dream. we have endured strikes; blacklists; false accusations of disloyalty; employment, housing, voting, and school discrimination; civil disobedience and unrest; assassination; police action; war; economic imperialism; and government interference in private matters of sovereign foreign governments.

"today, a black man cannot attempt to sit at a lunch counter, enter a university, join a union, secure a mortgage, and plan for a future. if he pulls on the door to opportunity, he finds it locked and realizes that he will never have the right key to open it. yet also today, we select men of all colors to put on a uniform, swear allegiance to the Constitution, and then send them overseas to kill and be killed, in the name of God and country.

"now, we are denied our rights to petition and free speech to protest against these evils and to restore our liberties. this, we cannot abide. we open our arms and hearts to all those gathered here to join together to reaffirm commitments to vows of life, liberty, and the pursuit of happiness—with perseverance, honor, and dignity."

There was silence when he finished, possibly because no one was quite sure it had ended. Myles turned in a military about-face and marched squarely back through the open door to Kettys-Burg Hall.

Hardly anyone paid much attention to the young woman who ran at full force to the campus radio station where they transcribed Myles' speech from her tape recorder. Breathlessly, Mir told everyone she'd be back in a few minutes, ran to the bookstore darkroom where she developed the pictures she'd taken of Myles, the chief, the plainclothes cop with the fireman, the ring of cops, the spectators, the kids hanging out of windows of the administration building waving Free Speech banners, and Claudia leaning up against the front door. By the time she got back to the radio station, someone told her that Myles' speech had been exactly 272 words, and they seemed overcome with joy.

"I don't get it," she said quizzically. "What's the big deal?"

"Lincoln," someone said brushing by her to get on the air.

"Lincoln what?" she asked. "What's going on?"

The young man with the speech in his hand whirled around and said, "The Gettysburg Address, it was 272 words. It changed a nation."

"And?" Mir interrupted anxiously.

Striding to the microphone that was not yet turned on, he said, "Mir, that was a hundred and one years ago to the day. November 19. Now we have Myles and The *Kettys*-Burg Address. The U.S. will never be the same."

CHAPTER 17

Triumphs and downfalls,

celebrations and losses

Mir made her exit from the radio station, went back to her room, collapsed in exhaustion, and then meandered over to Ben Veniste's café to have a light supper. As soon as it was dark, Ben Veniste handed her a flashlight and had the young Mexican men load the bikes with food and escort her the back way to Blueberry Creek, where she could go down the embankment, slip between the Spruce trees and disappear into the tunnel that would take her to Kettys-Burg Hall with the provisions.

The phone had been ringing non-stop in the president's office for most of the day. Myles enjoyed his renown by frequently not answering it, listening constantly to the news on the transistor radio, hearing his name mentioned frequently along with 'The Kettys-Burg Address.' He knew full well that this moment would pass, whispering to Claudia cynically that his notoriety would last for only a short time, he noted in that special way people have of deliberately downplaying an event or circumstance about themselves, which is intended to elicit a fawning response in opposition from an acolyte. Claudia could bask in his glory since she'd kept her feelings to herself. By the late afternoon, everyone in the building had become hungry, the psychic fuel that had sustained them through the night and into the day had been consumed, and a ravenous, post-cathartic craving for sweets and drinks had taken hold. Mir's appearance was, therefore, greeted with an aggressiveness that jolted her as hands grabbed indiscriminately for the goods she'd brought with her.

In my absence, she decided to be the scribe—to interview Myles and Claudia to get all the details from them, first-hand, which she could add to my notebook at the appropriate time. She made her way first to see Myles, to take some shots, and to record his thoughts. She knew that no other photographer or reporter would be inside, so her unique position would auger well for her future portfolio that she could show to prospective newspapers, radio, or TV stations. Myles was eager to see her, greeting her with both a broad smile and a hug that not only went on too long but also she felt as if he were pushing against her back such that her breasts were rubbing up and down his chest. She pulled back without saying anything about it. Despite being uncomfortable, she proceeded as if nothing were troubling, asking him if she could record him, telling him it was a great opportunity for him to be heard as the leader of the movement. She played the vanity card as well as Herzl rowed an oar.

She set her tape recorder on the desk and flitted around the room taking photos of him and the others from every angle. She ignored those who seemed to pose for her, and as time went on, the others appeared to relax, which made everyone less self-conscious and resulted in some truly insightful shots that would become part of her proprietary oeuvre. Mir was most interested in The Kettys-Burg Address. How did he come up with the idea of it? When did he compose it? Did he practice making it? Was he nervous when he was in front of the microphone delivering it? Had he anticipated the reaction to it? What was he planning for an encore? His answers were thoughtful, and he had the rapt attention of the others in the room, including Claudia when he responded.

"I guess subconsciously I've been thinking about it since we were outside, before we even thought of storming the administrative building. Every undertaking that's on the cusp of big changes needs something to sustain itself beyond the moment, something that will resonate with people who weren't there, kind of like 'Taxation without representation,' or 'Give me liberty or give me death.' I mean, most Americans can't recite the actions that led up to the start of the Revolutionary War, but they remember those slogans."

It was as if Myles were back at his apartment, surrounded by toadies desperate to have some of his fairy dust sprinkled upon them.

"But they do recall the catchphrases and the descriptions of events. Honestly, the person who came up with the idea of calling the dumping of tea into the harbor 'The Boston Tea Party' was a genius. In four words, a rather unremarkable stunt—let's face it, that's what it was—got transformed into something that could be passed along and down to everyone, in words and images, without regard to their level of education or their knowledge of the issues.

"Words matter. Symbols matter. So yeah, when I said, 'For the last twenty years, we have been wracked by a series of events that have pitted those without financial, social, or political power against a privileged elite, unwilling to share the fantasies of the American dream,' I had a feeling that the press would jump on this, that people would read or hear it on the radio and be able to come to grips with the fact that this—what we're doing here—isn't really about taking over a building or defying the police, it's about the right to say those things that've been bottled up for so long. That it's okay to make these things part of the national conversation, which is the only way politicians will get off their duffs and start to right some wrongs."

The room erupted into spontaneous applause. Myles neither blushed nor acknowledged the tribute. He continued even before the clapping died down, eager to answer Mir's other questions.

"When did I write it? First, in my head, last night, when everyone else was sleeping. Then I wrote it down, several drafts, by the way. I was making changes into the wee hours of the morning. And yes, I'm not embarrassed to say I practiced it, whispering it. Once, when I was in the men's room after taking a leak, I tried it from memory in the mirror. But I was so tired, I decided it'd be better if I read it so as not to screw it up."

He paused and then resumed when no one made a move or started to speak.

"No, I wasn't nervous. I mean, I wasn't up against a group like a doctoral dissertation committee…"

That caused some nervous laughter, perhaps a few thinking about how their participation in the takeover would affect them when it came time to resume their normal lives as students seeking degrees.

"Did I anticipate the reaction to it? Maybe. Somewhat. It's difficult to say. I did expect a certain reaction in some circles, here and at other campuses. I figured it'd be in the evening news, locally anyway, but wasn't sure it'd make it into *The Huntley–Brinkley Report*.

"You asked about an encore. Well, not today…"

Which got a big laugh, the kind that's exaggerated, as when back-scratchers yuk it up to bigwigs to curry favor.

Mir was so astounded by all of this that when she wrote it down later, she included a note to tell me to draw an image of a man staring into a mirror that lacked a reflection.

He got up from the seat behind the desk while the laughter still lingered in the air, wordless encomiums warming him as he made his exit. The others filtered out, Claudia leading the pack, to grab some food, go to the bathroom, or catch a few winks. Mir was alone. She looked around the room to see if there were any more shots that'd be interesting—for posterity she mused—and her eye caught the piece of paper that contained the speech peeking out of Myles' jacket pocket like a newborn kangaroo peering out of her mother's pouch for the first time. His tweed jacket was draped around the president's chair, and she gave a soft laugh of recognition as she had the image of the expression that someone was an empty suit. She snapped the picture and then decided to remove the paper and put it on the ink blotter, as if she were recreating the scene in which Myles wrote out The Kettys-Burg Address the night before.

Mir bent over the piece of paper for a full minute, her eyes taking in each paragraph, seeing the slant of the letters, the spacing between the words, the punctuation, the pre-printed lines on the page, the perforations on the left. She felt lightheaded and had to brace herself on the desk with her right hand. She put the piece of paper back in Myles' jacket pocket and had a momentary feeling of vertigo. She stood perfectly still for a few seconds, then lay down on the sofa. She wasn't okay. Her pulse raced, her head hurt, her fingers trembled. She buried herself deeper into the sofa and pulled a decorative throw blanket over her to ward off the chills. She couldn't get the images of the paper on which The Kettys-Burg Address had been written out of her mind. Her frustration became greater than her disconsolate feelings after an hour. She willed herself to stand, planted her feet squarely on the ground, took a few deep breaths, and used the arm of the sofa and then the wall to rise without feeling nauseous. She fumbled in her purse for the flashlight that Ben Veniste had given her and slowly walked down the hall into the basement, through the tunnel, out onto Blueberry Creek, and made her way to the café.

She burst through the backdoor, almost clipping one of the young men working in the kitchen, then approached Ben Veniste without salutation, telling him about her conversation with Myles and The Kettys-Burg Address.

"It's all anyone's talking about, Myles' speech," he said.

"You mean Jacobo's speech," she insisted.

"What? I don't understand. It was Myles. I saw it on the news. What are you talking about?"

"He ripped it out of Jacobo's notebook. He must've found the notebook, leafed through it, and when he came to that page, realized that it was something brilliant, so he tore it out along the perforations. I'm telling you, that's what he did, he didn't write it."

"Mir, how do you know? How can you be so sure?"

"Because of the handwriting. I saw the speech. It was in Jacobo's handwriting. I've been through that notebook. I know how he writes, how he angles his letters, how he leaves too much space after sentences, how there's no capitalization at the start of his sentences. Those were his words, not Myles'. God, I'm so angry."

"Do you have a copy? Did you take photos of it?"

"How stupid, stupid, stupid of me. I take pictures of everything, the most inconsequential things, all the time, but I was in such a state of shock, the very time I should've taken one, I didn't. I was concentrating on remembering it, everything about it and then, well, I guess I didn't want to be caught so I instinctively rushed to put it back. It's killing me."

He knew not to ask the question most adults do when they challenge a younger person, so there was no *You're sure, aren't you*?

"We should get word to Jacobo. That's the least we can do," she said.

"How? He and Herzl have been gone for a whole day. Who knows where they are?"

Mir knew she couldn't confront Myles or go through a backdoor route via Claudia with her finding, first because he'd deny it in the most intimidating way, lash out at her for insinuating this slanderous insult, and brand her a traitor to the cause. Second, because Claudia would tell Mir publicly in a most venomous fashion that she was a liar and a slut who'd defend the now missing Jacobo at any cost. And third, well, because the damage was already done. Myles was being lionized in the papers and being interviewed on the radio as the author of The

Kettys-Burg Address, a most powerful social and political statement that had caught the public's attention. It was instantly accepted as the bookend to Dr. King's "I Have a Dream" speech in front of the Washington Monument in 1963. The movement had been given a national imprimatur, and she knew that it wasn't going to be challenged by a *girl* from India—a dark-skinned foreigner, something that would be seized upon by many as a means to isolate and delegitimize her—and to confer outsider status on her. She knew, too, that once the spotlight was trained on her, that being a Jew would somehow be uncovered, and that it would be added to an indictment which was as good as a guilty verdict in the court of public opinion.

She was at Ben Veniste's café the next morning as early as the young Mexican men who worked in the kitchen. She asked if he'd heard from Jacobo and Herzl and could see by Ben Veniste's expression that the answer was no. She waited for five increasingly restless days, then, the morning of the sixth, still getting a headshake from Ben Veniste, she asked, "Can I have the keys to the truck?" She nodded in the direction of the produce truck that was used every morning to pick up provisions for the restaurant from the farmers' market in Oak Land. "I have to get to Jacobo." When he winced, she realized that the truck was essential to his business and chastised herself for being so thoughtless. "The old Nash Rambler?" she offered in the way that many young women do by lifting their voices near the end of a string of words that can turn a non-sentence into a question in a most charming and convincing way.

"Do you have a license? Do you even know how to drive?" he asked.

"Yes and yes," she replied. "Really, I did go to school here," she responded in a most solicitous way, as if to counterbalance how she might have come across when she more or less demanded the keys to the truck.

Mir's parents emigrated from India in 1948 following the Partition, worried that their hitherto peaceful lives in the tiny community of

Jews in Cochin would be changed forever after watching the trauma that overtook the country as it split into two separate religiously antagonistic nations. Her father had told her that he had pictures, horrible images of violence: rampages, murders, burnings, rapes. He wanted to share them, but couldn't. Mir didn't realize until she was older that they were sealed within him, to be recalled, but unable to be distributed to anyone else.

"His inability to show me was the reason I became a photographer," she told me later. "To make a record. So no one can say that something didn't happen. They do that, you know," she said.

Desperate to leave and desirous of going to a country where they could use their fluency in English, her father sent telegrams to medical schools and hospitals in major American cities, offering his services as a pharmacist but received no positive responses until he heard from a Dr. Benjamin Tudela from a well-known New York medical school, who was intrigued to read the telegram from a man in India who possessed the same name. Dr. Tudela provided him with the contact information for his cousin, a physician in the U.S. Army who was on the staff of the Veterans Administration Hospital in Albuquerque, New Mexico, a city and state that were unknown to Mir's parents. Benjamin Tudela, Mir's father, was eventually offered a position in the hospital pharmacy and Ruth Tudela, her mother, was able to secure a part-time clerical job in the administrative department. Mir attended Highland High School where she took a course in driver's education, which came in handy when she opened the door to the old Nash Rambler that Ben Veniste parked behind the restaurant and saw that it was a standard shift.

Ben Veniste packed a box of food for Mir, all the while giving her instructions on how to find Navajo Joe's village. "Look for an old bridge just below Socorro. Cross it to get to the west side of the river and head south. In a few miles, you'll see what looks like a wide gravel path on the right going up to nowhere. Turn there. It leads directly to the village. Navajo Joe will take you either to The Trading Post, where Jacobo's father works, or if you get there at night, directly to Arroyo Grande. And oh, by the way," he added, leaning in near the window on the driver's side, "ask for Joseph Deschene, that's Navajo Joe's name."

She thanked him profusely and drove off, watching him wave his cane in the rearview mirror, a heartwarming semaphore that spurred her on. She headed south on Route 66. Enthusiasm soothed her jangled nerves…until it didn't, causing her to question her sensibilities. Was she overreacting? What was driving her? A motivation to assist Jacobo in righting a wrong? A desire to be reunited with him at the expense of leaving school? A curiosity about his home? A combination of all three? She mulled these over as assiduously as her father would study the labels of drugs and the literature about drug interactions, always making sure that there'd be no mistake related to any patient. "If you are not sure, you could be doing things that are wrong and that can have tragic unintended and unforeseen consequences," her father would say. "So make it your business to be certain of your actions from both your perspective as well as those that are affected by your decisions." Such good life advice. Oh, how she wished her father were with her now. It wasn't too late to turn back. She could return to Taos Heights, park the Nash Rambler at the back of the café, and wait for news of Jacobo.

While all this was swirling around in her head, she was driving relentlessly south, an unconscious decision having already been made. She proceeded carefully, neither wanting to get a traffic ticket nor going so far south that she'd miss the cut off to the bridge. All of a sudden, it occurred to her that if her parents were to call the phone in her dormitory and someone were to say that she was missing, it would cause an unnecessary panic, so she stopped at a gas station phone booth, called home, and told her parents that she was on a journalism class-sponsored trip to visit newsrooms throughout the state.

On the afternoon of the second day on the road, she saw the rickety old bridge over the river that Ben Veniste had told her to take. She turned south and proceeded so slowly that several drivers pulled alongside of her and asked if she had engine trouble. She was relieved when she saw the rutted gravel road. The Nash Rambler had difficulty holding traction on it, causing the car to slip and requiring her to be more conscious of when to downshift to a lower gear. She began to talk to the car as if her commands and laments would be enough to wrangle the last bit of thrust in a straight line to get her to where she needed to go. After a few anxious moments, she was on level ground and wended her way into the middle of the Indian village that looked just as Ben Veniste had described it to her.

Friendly children and barking dogs surrounded the car. As she was bending down to pat the dogs, she reached into her pocket to fish out a picture of Jacobo—the one that she'd taken the day when he was observing the action of the crowds on the Worthington Strip. She approached a man who was resting his feet on a wooden rail and asked if he were Mr. Deschene.

"Ah, you want Joseph," he said, then got up, went inside and came out with a man who looked exactly the way Jacobo had drawn him.

"My name is Mir Tudela, Mr. Deschene, and I'm a friend of Jacobo Toledano, from the UT. I drove here from Taos Heights and am wondering if you can show me how I can get to Arroyo Grande." She gave him the photo of Jacobo as if she were an attorney providing *bona fides* that her request was legitimate.

"Do you want some water?" he said.

"Yes, please," she said, thinking she should have asked him for a pitcher before he disappeared into the building, as her head and neck were competing with her throat for the attention of cool water.

He came back out with a wooden bucket and a ladle. She drank from it as if she were a horse tied up to a rail, then drenched her face, hair, and neck with the cold water. The children laughed as she poured it over her head, making a funny dance as it struck her overheated skin. The kids howled in delight. She took the bucket and pretended to run after a few of them as if she were going to pour water over their heads, retreating into their world, a girl without pretense, letting her anxieties and worries evaporate in the still, hot, dry air for a few precious moments. She put the bucket down and placed her fists against the sides of her head, extending her index fingers, hunching over as she ran after the kids like a makeshift bull would charge matadors or rodeo clowns.

Later, Navajo Joe would tell me that watching her play with the kids without any airs made it easy for him to make the decision that he'd take her to Arroyo Grande.

Later, Ben Veniste would tell me about his conversation with Mir.

Later, when she showed up at my house, she relayed all of what had transpired back at the UT, which ultimately led to triumphs and downfalls, celebrations, and losses.

It was then that she'd tell me that she thought it was strange that Ben Veniste knew Navajo Joe's real name.

CHAPTER 18

I don't believe

in long good-byes

Herzl and I were out back of my house when we heard Madre shout out, "*Mia dio*!" We got up and dashed into the kitchen to see Navajo Joe with Mir. I was flabbergasted that Mir was in Arroyo Grande. I couldn't imagine the circumstances that brought her. I waited for Madre to stop hugging her, a genuine expression of warmth and hospitality that derived from my stories about her, having left no doubt as to my feelings. When Mir caught sight of me over Madre's shoulder, she waited a few seconds before gently disengaging, then unabashedly skipped to me, burying her head in my chest, which must've brought back memories of Madre in a similar position with my father, as the height differential was almost exactly the same.

Madre's large, oval-shaped dark brown eyes overwhelmed her face, drawing attention away from her nose, which pointed to delicate, thin lips that could expand in an instant to open wider than what one could possibly conceive. A caress, a compliment, a joke, or a moment of pride would prompt her lips to open in such a way as to create a crease that seemed to connect to her ears, a sketch of which I'd drawn many times to illustrate her radiant smile.

In expedited fashion, Mir recounted her journey. She showed us Polaroids of her playing with the kids at Navajo Joe's village and mimicked her pretending to be a charging bull. Madre and my sisters were enchanted.

"The three of you," Madre said with false annoyance when Mir was finished, looking at Herzl, Mir, and me, trying as best she could to suppress her excitement, "go outside. I haven't finished preparing dinner. Débora, Nohemi," she called out to my sisters as if they were anywhere but right next to her, "set the table and then come here. We have work to do."

As soon as we were beyond earshot of my house, I looked at Mir. "Herzl told me you're a Jew."

Without allowing for a second to pass after the word Jew came out, Herzl jumped in and said, "Mir, you're not going to believe this, but Jacobo's one too. I'm not kidding."

At the same time she moved her head back a few inches, she extended her arm to touch my shoulder and said rapidly, "Are you serious? What are you, a converso? Is that what this village is all about? I can't believe this. No, no, I don't think you're lying. That's not what I mean. Really? Wow!"

"No," I said, smiling, nodding, and placing my hand on top of hers. "Not conversos. No one here is pretending to be Catholic by day and Jew by night. We're practicing Jews, twenty-four hours a day. We just don't tell the world. Anything. Nothing about who we are."

"By living apart, they live better with everyone else," Herzl interjected.

"So everyone assumes you're Catholic because of your Mexican name?" she asked.

"Or because we're Indian," I said, cueing her to remember when Myles rounded me up when I was wearing a Navajo shawl.

We laughed.

"And also, who'd think there are Jews in a remote village west of the river," Herzl said. "It's so unlike what people think and know about Jews."

Mir nodded her head a bit side to side, looked at Herzl, and said, "I don't know about that. Who *wouldn't* think that a six foot four, red-headed, gray-eyed, Spanish-speaking Indian who looks like a wolf from southwest New Mexico isn't Jewish!" She gave me a hug and kissed me in the neck. I shuddered.

"You never told me," she mock scolded. "I can't believe it. I just can't believe it. I mean I do, believe you, that you're a Jew, it's just so, ah, ummmm, unexpected. This is so wonderful. It makes it so much easier," she said and pirouetted around both of us, almost losing her balance and reaching out to me to steady her.

I clapped. Herzl joined in.

"You have to know that I didn't tell Herzl about me until he got here."

"How come? The two of you are so close," she said.

"You have to understand that we've kept this all under wraps for so long, and it's been good for us."

"For once, an ancient Jewish story that's not built on modern tragedy," Herzl said.

We all took a breather for a bit. Just then, Madre rapped a couple of metal kitchen utensils half a dozen times, the signal to us to come back in. When Mir went to wash up, I whispered to Madre and my sisters that Mir was a Jew. Nohemi pointed at me and giggled, Débora buried her head into my shoulder, and Madre put her hand over her mouth, then fluttered to tell my father.

My sisters flocked around this exotic bird as if she'd let them in on the secret of how she acquired her gorgeous plumage. They couldn't stop asking her questions, one after the other. Her responses triggered questions and comments, the conversation turning into a relay event in which the baton was continually passed. Madre told them at one point to slow down, Mir had to eat, but this had no effect on them.

We had a festive dinner that Saturday night, the evening filled with rollicking stories about me, designed to give more ammunition to Mir that she could use in the future to shoot back to me, as well as countless questions about India, how she came to New Mexico, and how we were introduced. That I was the pretend Indian set up with a real Indian but not an American Indian was a tale that was going to be passed on and recounted over the years.

Just after the sun set, Madre got up, looked around the table, made sure to catch Mir and Herzl's eyes, and said, "Now it's time for us to say goodbye to Shabbat!" She got up to retrieve the *Havdalah* candles and the spice box. We all said the blessings, sang *Eliyahu Hanavi*, and ended with *Shavua tov's*! all around. I found myself staring at Mir. I noticed that Débora was sneaking glances at Herzl.

Madre excitedly clapped her hands above her head, the signal that the formalities were over and started to clear the table. She put her arm around Mir's shoulder, gave it a light squeeze, and said softly, "Raquel," having realized that she'd never formally introduced herself by her proper name. Mir beamed and said, "Miriam." All along, I'd assumed that her name was Hindi.

Débora and Herzl slipped out back to sit in the big chairs. Mir and I went out the front door and walked in the direction of the plaza.

"What happened after Herzl and I left? Did Myles and the others stay in the building? Did the cops invade it? Did Myles strike a deal? Is it over?"

"Yes and no."

"What do you mean?" I asked.

"Myles made a speech; honestly, a great one that made headlines all over the country. It was short but so effective that the cops pulled back, the students left the building, there were no prosecutions, no recriminations."

"There must've been a deal," I said.

"There was. Myles, Claudia, and the rest of the students were allowed to set up tables with pamphlets anywhere in Taos Heights as long as they didn't harass anyone or block access to stores. The administration took no action against any of the students. The chief, Townsend, was given a letter of commendation from the Taos Heights Council for showing restraint. I guess that was part of the arrangement all around. Something in it for everyone."

"Wow," I remarked. "It seems as if everyone opted for civility. That's a surprise."

She continued. "No kidding. Hostility wasn't going to lead to anything but an ugly confrontation and a hardening of opposing views, solving nothing. Myles even remarked in an interview that this was *civil* disobedience, and he emphasized the dual meanings of the word civil. There was a lot of newspaper coverage, and a few of my pictures were picked up by the AP and appeared in the largest papers, including the *Albuquerque Tribune, The New York Times,* and *The Washington Post.*"

"That's terrific. Amazing. I'm so proud of you. So what's the *no* part? You said yes and no when I asked if it was over."

"Townsend knows about the notebook. He still wants it. He knows it paints unflattering portraits of his cops. He's willing to make a deal. If you give it back, he'll speak to the DA to drop charges, and then you can come back to school," she said.

"Drop what charges? What did I do?" I was becoming hostile.

"You stole the shell."

"We can bring that back. Put it in Navajo Joe's flatbed. No big deal. What's more important is that I lost the notebook—for real—so they're never going to get it back, which means what, I'll have to remain a fugitive? Well, if I have to hide out, I can do it in Navajo Joe's village, they'll never find me."

"You lost it?"

"Un-huh. On the trip with Herzl. I fell asleep, on a slide in a playground. I was so tired, all that rowing at night. I was exhausted and someone, perhaps a kid playing in a nearby park, I really don't know, took my knapsack and everything I had inside. My clothes, food, and my notebook, gone. Kaput, as Herzl would say. The only thing I salvaged was one page of the notebook that I'd ripped out and put in my pocket, but it had nothing to do with what was going on, so I couldn't trade that for my freedom."

By this time, we'd made our way to the plaza and were sitting on a stone wall. She leaned her head into my shoulder.

"There's one more thing. And it *is* a big deal. I mentioned that Myles made a great speech. Here it is."

She unfolded a page of a newspaper that had a picture of Myles on it and underneath it had a couple of paragraphs, indented and in quotes. She handed it to me. "Read it," she said softly.

I really wasn't in the mood but didn't want to insult her, so I took it and began to read it out loud. I didn't need more than the first four words, 'A confluence of events…' to know that this was what I wrote on my last night in Kettys-Burg Hall, the start of a speech that I penned when I was practically in a daze, so dreamily that when I finished it I thought at first that it'd been Myles who'd been reading it to me. I quickly scanned the rest of it and recognized every word. I was astonished—furious that Myles had taken ownership of it, that the press had labeled it the Kettys-Burg Address, and that this was the impetus for the stand-down and the resulting accommodation that'd been reached.

"You know I wrote this," I said agitatedly, bolting up and walking about.

She nodded.

"How'd he get it?" I practically shouted. I was livid. And jealous.

"It was in your notebook. There were times you left it lying around. He must've gone through it, probably innocently enough. It's obvious that when he came to the page with these words on it, he ripped it out. Look, when he realized that you'd taken off, he knew he could claim ownership of it, there was no other copy. All you could offer would be a weak protest that'd be perceived by everyone else as preposterous. Who are you and who's Myles? Let's face it, he recognized the position he was in, the power of these words, and his ability to present them in a dramatic way that would benefit him."

I remembered:

You know, it's all about Myles, mark my words.

I wouldn't worry about it. It's never been about what it seemed to be.

Myles has something in mind—something big, and attention-getting. We'll see.

Did it ever occur to you that, well, he cribbed a lot of what he said from those papers and books.

Sometimes the king does something that his subjects don't fully appreciate until it's too late.

It all came chillingly back to me. If I were to have drawn a picture of myself at this point, it would've shown me with clenched teeth, cinched eyes, and a bitterly twisted mouth, red cheeks ablaze in anger, body in motion leaning forward, ready to seek revenge.

From ten yards away, I whirled around and asked her, "How'd you know I wrote it?"

"I lifted it out of Myles' jacket when he left the room. I could see that it was your handwriting. You don't start sentences with capitals. You have a slant to your letters, and you leave extra spaces between words."

She was right.

"But beyond penmanship, Jacobo," she said in the most tender way, "I know the way you think, the way you hold yourself, how you speak, what's going on in your head, all the good stuff and, well, the little things too. You know, how you double knot your shoelaces, rarely tuck your shirt in, those kinds of things."

What I didn't say to her was that my knowledge of her was reciprocal. I knew when she was going to take her right hand and sweep her hair behind her ear signaling disapproval. I knew how she looked at me differently than when she met the gaze of another boy. I knew that when she spoke rapidly that this was a sign of her self-confidence. And I knew that when she brushed against me or touched my hand, that these were not accidental occurrences. I started to calm down, resigned to my fate.

I reached into the back pocket of my pantaloons and held out my folded piece of paper.

"What's this?" she asked.

"Open it," I said gently.

She took it from me, unfolded it and let out a gasp.

"It's me!" she exclaimed, "Just like me! You caught me in one of my pensive moods. I can't believe how good this is."

"I did this the last night at Kettys-Burg Hall, right after I wrote the now *famous* speech," I said sarcastically. "I ripped it out because I didn't want, well, to be embarrassed if the notebook got into the wrong hands, you know? It's so personal. I'm glad you like it. It's the only thing I salvaged from it."

Mir was examining it intently; she brought it up directly in front of her eyes. She scanned each section as if she were reading a book, line by line, top to bottom, from left to right. She looked at me and then looked back at the pencil-drawn image.

"Jacobo," she said, still staring at the page. "Look here. Come close. Do you see what I see?"

"No, what?"

"Don't look at my image. Here," she pointed to a part of the page to the left and above her hair. "You see these marks?"

I leaned closer to the page and squinted.

"Yes, there's something. I'm not sure what they are. They're faint. It's hard to make out, maybe an imperfection in the paper."

"Look at this," she ordered. "You can see characters, maybe letters. Yes, they're letters, from impressions. See? About two inches in from the left, near the top. It's an 'h,' then an 'a,' and an 's,' then a small space, and it starts up again with an 'l,' at least I think it's an 'l,' and here, an 'e,' and what may be a 'd.' Can you see this?"

Barely, but I wondered if I was agreeing just to curry favor with her.

"And here, lower down," she pointed to a section in the middle of the page, "there's an impression of a 'c' and an 'i' and perhaps a 'v' and another 'i.' Wait oh, I can't see any more on this line, my hair is obscuring the marks. They're words, Jacobo, words, and they've been made by impressions from your writing on the previous page."

I stared intently at the page, realizing that when I'd looked at it countless times since I left UT, I was fixated on Mir's face, not the spaces around it.

"Maybe there's a 'has' and a 'led.' What do you make of 'civi'?" I asked, trying to be helpful.

She didn't answer. Instead, she grabbed the newspaper clipping in her left hand and put it next to the pencil drawing in her right and shot up into a standing position. "Jacobo, I can't believe it, it's the speech, the Kettys-Burg address! See, the 'has led' on the first line and the 'civi' represents the first four letters of 'civil', what you wrote in the second paragraph."

I'd used a ball point pen when I wrote the speech and had pressed down hard so that the impressions were embedded onto the next page. It was dark when I'd drawn Mir's picture. There was no way I'd have seen the marks from the previous page.

"My God, Jacobo, look what we have!—*proof* that Myles used your words. We've got the goods on him." With that, she circled her arms around my neck, still holding the two pieces of paper, and gave me a kiss on my lips that I'd later say went on for minutes, probably because the sensation stayed with me for the whole evening.

"Jacobo, give me the page. I'm going to put this in the right hands. I've got ins now at the top papers. They've all carried my photos. They can introduce me to the right people."

Being riled up about Myles, it seemed as if this were the right time to talk to her about his anti-Semitic remarks.

"Okay, but before you go off running into the night, I've got to ask you something."

"About the speech?"

"No, something else to do with Myles. Do you remember the call to you, the one where he made some really nasty remarks about Jews?" I asked.

"How could I not," she said. "He's an anti-Semite. I hear things even when people don't speak them."

I wondered if I'd ever get a sixth sense.

"I was concerned that you'd pass it off, you know, like 'that's just how some people talk, they really don't mean it' kind of thing," I said.

"Give me more credit, Jacobo."

"You didn't say anything, that's all."

"What good would it've done? You think he would've been embarrassed if I pointed out his bigotry? That's not how his kind think. The best I could've hoped for is him saying something like, 'it was a joke,' or 'I'm only kidding.' And you know what? The minute I would've said something, I would've been shut out from him, Claudia, and the rest of them in Kettys-Burg Hall. I would've been Kryptonite, never allowed back in. They would've gotten someone else to take pictures. I would've been the crazy Indian—or worse yet, the Jew-lover." She paused, came right up to me, and said, "Which I am, of course," and lightly bit my ear.

She was a hundred percent right.

"Was this a surprise to *you*? About his view of Jews?" she asked.

"He'd said a few things, kind of mild that I didn't pay too much attention to. You know, like someone at the bookstore who asked about a discount for a large purchase. He told me that the guy had tried to Jew him down," I said.

"So in the bigot's dictionary the word Jew is also a verb."

"I'm not going to worry about that until it makes Webster's," I said.

Mir managed a weak smile and spit out, "What a bastard."

"Let's go home and relax out back with Débora and Herzl."

The four of us sat quietly, listening to the transistor radio for news of the day, rotating English and Spanish stations when a commercial came on. Shortly before midnight, when Herzl and Débora were half asleep, I caught the end of a flash that mentioned that Myles would be appearing on a television show in Albuquerque in two weeks, to be interviewed by David Sussman, a renowned host who broadcast his show from the place where the news originated, made famous by his tag line, 'National news, locally.'

"Did you hear that?" I asked Mir.

She nodded. "I've got to do something," she said, eliding from a semi-stupor to whirlwind practically instantaneously.

"Like what? What can you do about it?

"I don't know. I'll figure it out. I've got to go," and she got up as if she were going to leave Arroyo Grande that very moment.

As she was pacing around the yard, I told her about the *Pequeño*.

"Will you say it tonight, now, before we go to sleep?" she asked.

I mouthed *Pequeño* to my sister and together, we recited our community's prayer, first in Ladino, then in English. We were ready for whatever was going to happen.

Mir and Herzl left the next morning. She kissed me on the lips and said, "I don't believe in long goodbyes. Herzl, let's go." My sister mirrored Mir's way by giving Herzl a kiss on his lips then waving him off with both hands.

My father drove them to Navajo Joe's village, where Mir would pick up the Nash Rambler and go back to Taos Heights.

I stood next to my sister, our arms around each other's waist. We didn't say a word, each of us was wondering when we'd see them again.

CHAPTER 19

They give you a last name

on the reservation, Tonto?

For the next three days, I kept the transistor radio in my pocket, practically listening to it nonstop. I'd go to The Trading Post and sit near the phone, waiting for the call from Mir to give me an update on what she was doing. I was fidgety and uncharacteristically moody. I was seething inside. On the morning of the fourth day, having heard nothing from Mir, I told my parents that I was going to return to the UT to plead my case for reinstatement. Since they had few facts about the circumstances in which I fled in the dead of night, they had no reason to suspect that this wasn't actually my plan. I made a bedroll stuffed with a few shirts, pants, and underwear, tucked some personal items into the pockets of the pants, sequestered the transistor radio within my underwear, and slid the copper-encased mirror down the inside of my thick sock on my right foot. I wasn't going to take the chance of losing prized possessions a second time. I wore a hat with a wide brim to keep the sun from beating down on my head and neck.

My scheme was simple. I'd get a lift to Navajo Joe's village and then either grab a ride with someone who was heading north or make my way across the rickety old bridge that spanned the Rio Grande and hitchhike to Albuquerque where I'd find out where the interview with Myles was going to take place.

I was motivated by resentment against Myles. My admiration for his striving to bring about change was acknowledged. Nevertheless, I could separate that aspect from the self-aggrandizing act that he was performing on a national stage. It wasn't that I wanted to substitute for him, to be the understudy that gets his turn to take the lead role when the star gets sick. If Myles had gone to the microphone in front of Kettys-Burg Hall and told the crowd that he was going to read a speech that had been written by one of the occupants of the building, it would've been okay with me even if my name hadn't been mentioned. It was his usurping of my words and claim that he'd penned them that had me thinking that this was one more incident in which a Jew didn't get a fair shake.

Herzl's influence on me had taken hold.

Navajo Joe was delighted to see me and gave me another shawl that I could use at night when it got cold. I walked behind the village where Herzl and I had hidden the shell; it was undisturbed. I found out that no one was driving north from the village, but I could get a lift from one of Navajo Joe's friends who'd drive me across the old rickety bridge that spanned the Rio Grande and let me off as he turned south toward El Paso.

I'd never hitchhiked before and was easily frustrated when a car would pass by with the driver looking straight ahead as if I were invisible. Only later would I realize that the Indian shawl, the long straggly beard, and the floppy hat were a signal to most drivers that I wasn't a desirable passenger. Despite being more than two hundred miles away from my destination, I began to walk, an automatic impulse that somehow dupes the mind into thinking that you're actually satisfactorily performing the task you intended to complete. After an hour, an old pickup truck driven by an Indian slowed down. He motioned for me to get in when it came to a full stop. He offered me piñon nuts, grapes, and conversation, all of which I enjoyed. After a couple of hours, he stopped at a dirt road that turned east and bid me farewell. I thanked him profusely, waving to him as he honked and made the right-hand turn.

I was offered two other rides that day, both of only a few miles duration, but they kept me moving in the right direction. In the early evening, I stopped at a roadside stand and had a dinner consisting of corn, beans, and squash, washed down by greenthread tea sweetened with honey. As it got dark, I looked for a place to bed down for the night. A mile or so north of the roadside stand there was a clump of tall Indiangrass, which I could knead into a soft cushion on which I could place my bedroll. I lay down under my shawl, put my hat over one side of my face, and drifted off.

When I saw the bright light, I assumed I'd overslept and was angry that I'd lost precious time. Then the bright light disappeared, so I thought I'd been dreaming. Suddenly, a man's voice commanded me to get up, and as I leaned against an elbow, I could see the bulk of a police officer, baton in hand, listing back and forth a bit, alternately blocking and allowing the headlight on his cruiser to shine on me.

"Up, up you go, chief," he barked. "Really tied on one last night, huh?" he continued, keeping his hand on his billy club. "Can you stand, kemosabe? You speakity Inge, my young friend? What reservation you from, tell me."

I scrambled up, offered a good morning that was reciprocated by a demand for me to show some identification. I didn't have anything to give to him. He asked me my name and where I lived.

"Jacobo," I answered. "I'm a student at the UT in Taos Heights."

That was a mistake.

He told me to pick up my bedroll and hand it to him. He went through every crevice, found nothing but clothes and some personal items and heaved them through the open window into the back seat. He told me to turn my pockets inside out. I was thankful that I'd hidden the transistor radio and the copper-based mirror. He told me to grab my hat and get in the car. As I started to open the front passenger-side door, he slammed me hard against the side of the car, causing me to lose my breath, which distracted me from the stinging pain from where my head smashed against the roof.

"Wiseass," was all he said as he grabbed my right arm with his right hand, used his left to open the rear door, and both shoved and kicked me into the back seat. He locked both back doors, slid into the driver's seat, and picked up the microphone.

COP: Louis, car three, code six, go ahead.

DISPATCHER: Louis, car three, code six, go ahead.

COP: On 85, west of Jarales, go ahead.

DISPATCHER: Go ahead.

COP: Male, eighteen to twenty, Injun, tall, red hair, beard, says UT, no ID, possibly drunk, go ahead.

SILENCE (FIFTEEN SECONDS).

COP: Dispatch, name is Jacobo, go ahead.

DISPATCH: Last name? Go ahead.

COP (TO ME): They give you a last name on the reservation, Tonto?

ME: Toledano.

COP: (to me) What's that, Toledo? You're named for a city in Ohio? Ha ha! You got a brother named Cleveland?

ME: practically under my breath: Toledano, not Toledo.

COP: (to me) What're you, a wop? A dago Indian? Huh? Toll what?

ME: (slowly, phonetically) Toll—a—dan—oh.

COP: Tolla—dano.

ME: (Nodded affirmatively as he caught my eyes.)

COP: (to dispatch, mocking me) Tolla—dano. Go ahead.

SILENCE (THIRTY SECONDS).

DISPATCH: Outstanding w, from Taos Heights, theft, go ahead.

COP: Copy, call ahead to Los Chavez, ten-four.

CHAPTER 20

It's the American thing to do

The jail in Los Chavez wasn't so bad. They'd taken a gas station abandoned after the Interstate system paved over the future of rural America and set it up as a holding pen for up to a dozen men. Ancient army cots were spaced every few feet where the bays once held up the manifestations of local pride. The desk sergeant sat on the other side of the counter where they used to ring you up and dispense road maps, gumballs, and cigarette packs. Each of us was provided with a drawer, one that fit under our cots and held our clothes and those few bathroom accoutrements we were allowed to have—a toothbrush, paste, comb, brush, some hair cream, and a bar of soap but no razor, so I watched each day as the faces of my cellmates disappeared, which allowed me to determine the amount of time someone had been there, a method as accurate as studying tree rings.

We were lucky that the southern and western sides of the building were shaded by large Chisos red oaks, planted as part of a Civilian

Conservation Corps program in the thirties that included tables and chairs hewn from white fir, offered as enticements for travelers to rest after gassing up before continuing on in search of work. The shade made our lives tolerable, as we had only two barred-over windows and a slowly rotating ceiling fan; the east-facing, roll-up garage doors had been nailed shut, effectively preventing breezes from reaching us.

At first, neither the transistor radio I'd tucked into my underwear nor the bruise covered by my long hair was noticed by anyone else. Late on the night I was arrested, when everyone was asleep, I snuck my hand down, retrieved the radio, turned it on very softly, and placed it under my right ear. I tuned into the David Sussman show. Mir was telling him about the notebook when Myles burst in screaming "Whore, slut, nympho, kike, yid, Christ killer!" in a mantra, which upset Ben Veniste, who threatened to slice him up with a paring knife as he chased him around the set swinging his cane, then threw mushrooms at him while my father and Madre sat holding hands, dabbing at tears as Herzl and Débora exchanged wedding vows. Strapped to his chair, the plainclothes cop spit at Claudia, who walked around with her top off, reading passages from the Communist Manifesto, giving everyone the finger. I was sitting side-by-side next to Chief Townsend, pulling up on my controls, delivering my 272-word speech over and over again, exasperated watching him holding his fingers in his ears, pushing down on his controls with his extended belly. Finally, David Sussman paddled around the set splashing wildly, approached Myles, used the oar as a club, thrust it toward his face, missed him but toppled the long ash from his cigarette that then fell to the seat of the canvas chair and ignited it, which caused the sprinklers to drench all of us. We ran to the exit, down the stairs, out the tunnel, and made our escape up Blueberry Creek, where we sat in a circle watching the rainbow that came up out of the lake in Arroyo Grande and descended into the forest.

The second time was the same, except that Navajo Joe entered with Nohemi wrapped up in one of his colorful shawls, her frightened uuuuuuuuuums causing him to trip over the cat repeatedly.

The third time, when everyone spoke, you couldn't hear their words. They appeared in speech balloons suspended over their heads.

I think this was just before I awoke.

I got up quickly, dressed quietly, and waited for the desk sergeant to arrive.

I could hardly contain myself.

I was ready to write again.

They allowed me to call the pay phone at The Trading Post. I told my father where I was and not to worry, that it was all going to work out well, and pushed back against his wanting to come immediately to visit. I suggested that he come in a week or so, which is when I imagined I'd be finished with my plan.

I positioned myself directly in front of the sergeant, pointed to the ancient typewriter sitting under a cover of dust on the side of the desk, and asked him if I could use it. As both the typewriter and I were within his field of vision, his eyes darted from me to it and back several times, without moving his head. He spoke in a gruff voice.

"It's not a weapon, kid, if that's what you're thinking."

"I want to *write*, sergeant," I said, nodding my head a bit, slightly pursing my lips, and opening my palms, a non-verbal set of techniques that I'd learned at the UT that showed exasperation without being insulting.

He stared at me intently. "It doesn't work good, you know, the ribbon gets stuck in the thingy, and your fingers'll get ink all over them," he replied in a tone that clearly signaled he was now not going to be confrontational.

"That's okay," I said cheerfully. "It'll be better than writing in longhand."

He pretended to be miffed that he had to suspend setting up a Monopoly game board, and made a big show of handing the typewriter over to me, disparagingly calling out to a mythic audience that he was being generous to the *college boy*. He may have said "college spic." At least that's what the other inmates said, but I focused on the word "college" instead and strutted back to the community table inside the cell lugging my prized relic like a boxing champ caressing a title belt, feeling proud that I'd attended the UT, even if for only a year and a half.

My cellmates ranged in age from late teens to mid-forties, almost all with hedgerow black hair and eight-ball eyes, tobacco-stained teeth, and sepia skin that appeared to change color depending on the intensity of the light. They were generally of average height and eyed me up and down my 6'4" frame, speaking to the others using the third person invisible when I first entered the cell, not self-conscious to point to my long red hair, thick multi-colored beard, and marble gray eyes.

I'd been picked up for vagrancy, the state trooper not realizing the value of his catch until he called in to the dispatch officer who told the trooper that my description matched the warrant that was on an APB, the printed output from a teletype machine that provided updates of people on the run.

For the most part, my cellmates were in for disturbing the peace, loitering, driving without a license, public intoxication, and not understanding the arresting officer. Nothing really untoward, and their time inside was usually short before being brought in front of the judge in the town down the road. They were customarily sentenced to time already served. Once or twice, a former inmate would trudge through the door again, sheepishly acknowledge my presence with a shy wave and smile, then indicate what went on in court and why he was back. Invariably, a returnee would ask, eyes widened, if I was writing about him or life in jail, eager to play even a small role in a play he'd never get to see. I'd placate him. "Perhaps," I'd say, pursing my lips, clenching my jaw and making the slightly repeated vertical nod, which allowed him to infer that yes, he might live on in another world beyond the barrio. Only many years later did I recognize that this glimmer of hope revealed the futility of his life, and I wished that I had, indeed, written a piece about this one or that one or all of them, but that was something that didn't occur to me then, fixated as I was on telling *my* story.

None of the folks I was locked up with could figure out why I was there.

"You in for *not* giving something that was *yours* to someone who *asked* for it?" would be repeated in similar fashion by each new inmate, which was usually followed by a declarative sentence in which my name and *demente* or *loca* both appeared. "This is America," someone would invariably blurt out, barely suppressing the guffaw at the absurdity of my situation, then would pretend to ask for something someone else was holding, having that other person refuse, and then hearing shouts in Spanish of, "Sergeant! Lock him up more! He won't give me what's his!" This was the prelude to uproarious, infectious hilarity, in which I willingly joined.

Unlike the others incarcerated with me, I had an out similar to the Monopoly get-out-of-jail-free game card the desk sergeant waved at me that depicted the prisoner in horizontal stripes getting the boot from the not-to-be-seen judge. All I had to do was accede to the DA's request to turn over the notebook, and I could walk out. A free man. If I didn't, well, I had two choices: stand trial for an act that really wasn't a crime but where a group of twelve people culled from the lists those most anxious about the fraying of the social fabric could be persuaded otherwise by a zealous prosecutor in cahoots with the local press. After all, this was an era when violent student protests and other acts of civil disobedience colored the minds of potential jurists. Or, instead, agree to be escorted from the jail to the U.S. Army induction center in downtown Albuquerque, where I would raise my right hand

and "...solemnly swear that I will support and defend the Constitution of the United States against all enemies, foreign and domestic; that I will bear true faith and allegiance to the same; and that I will obey the orders of the President of the United States and the orders of the officers appointed over me, according to regulations and the Uniform Code of Military Justice. So help me God."

I didn't have a third option of returning to the UT. The cops told me that I'd been suspended for a period of two years, conveniently consistent with a term of military service. I'd pretty much decided to hook up with Uncle Sam, my public defender having told me that the odds weren't good for an acquittal for someone like me. In the absence of my voluntarily giving the notebook to the authorities, they wanted to inflict a punishment on me that they assumed I'd avoid at all costs, thereby delivering to them what they needed. I told the public defender that I didn't have the notebook, that I'd lost it, plain and simple. No one believed me, and I became the DA's favorite bête noire, hence their "either/or" deal that they assumed I'd turn down and ultimately give them what they demanded.

I wanted to recreate the notebook, yet it'd be a fruitless exercise unless I had a way to decide how to smuggle the new version out. Hiding it in my underwear wasn't going to work, there was no guarantee I'd get it back if I gave it to one of my cellmates, and I knew that a judge would look at a new version as a fake—which the prosecutors would confiscate anyway—and certainly not as exculpatory. Although the original would've gotten me released, I knew if I still had it, I wouldn't give it up, couldn't give it up, as it would never see the light of day. At least with a second version, I'd have a record, and who knew, there might be a way it could yield a benefit at some time in the future.

I called out to the desk sergeant.

"I'd like to play this Monopoly game you're so fond of," I said.

"Ah, my young friend, you want the *card*, is it?" he asked, referring to the get-out-of-jail free card, in the manner that an adult deceives a child with an affectionate voice into believing that a reward is on the way.

"No sir, the game itself. I'd like to learn and so would the other guys," I said respectfully, which would have morphed into unctuousness, if necessary, to get what I wanted.

He handed over the box cheerfully, mentioned that it was in English, and I told him I'd translate for the others. More than that, I told him, "I'll write down in Spanish all the instructions printed on the inside cover of the top, and I'll create a booklet with drawings of all of the cards and explanations as to what they mean."

"That's great, Jake," he said, addressing me with a nickname, which strangers have a penchant for doing—an offhand gesture intended to create a brief, false moment of intimacy. "Once you decide to leave, your friends will be able to learn how to get rich," he chortled, having accented *friends* in a disparaging way to distinguish me from my cellmates.

I tackled what I told the desk sergeant I'd do, creating a multipage document that went into great detail, much more than was necessary. It looked like a term paper for school that included footnotes as well. To master the Monopoly game, translate the rules, provide examples of strategy, and spell out circumstances so explicit it would avoid disputes—all the while writing in Spanish—took longer than I'd originally anticipated. It was made more difficult by the constant rethreading of the ribbon and letter degradation due to overuse. But to be honest, I enjoyed the project. It kept me busy, and I was sure I was doing something that would be of benefit to these and other inmates in the future. When I finished this part of my plan, I then began work on recreating my notebook under the guise of now redoing the set of Monopoly rules in Ladino.

I worked feverishly, straight-backed, fingers pressing keys, hitting the carriage return, feeding paper, correcting for typos, writing down everything that'd happened, recalling images of whole pages of the notebook that recorded the jumble of characters, conversations, observations, places, and events that'd converged with a cataclysmic force over such a short period of time that I was sure a diamond would emerge from the effects of the compression.

I worked nonstop for a few days because I had so much to remember, and it needed to be set down in the order in which the events occurred. I had to be sure that I wasn't missing details that were critical to understanding the context of what happened, who was responsible, who was involved, what their motivations were, and who'd planned to do what to aggravate or settle the conflict. What vexed me more than the reportage was the recreation of the sketches of the people and scenes that originally had included balloon-like speech bubbles as if it were a comic book. I must confess that, with the addition of time, my sketches were more sophisticated and nuanced, and although I took a few liberties with some of the quotes, in no case did I change the substance.

When I was finished, I could honestly say that my handiwork was not a fake. It was, for all intents and purposes, a recreation of the original, by the same witness and in the same time period, so as not to be jaded by distant memories or an attempt to portray what had occurred in a more favorable light to the writer.

I put the version of the Monopoly rules I created in Spanish together with my new notebook and on the top of the first page, in all capital letters, I wrote MONOPOLY: JUEGO, Spanish for "game." The whole thing was, I knew, wretched excess, but it was a critical part of my plan, as I then created a second cover page on which I wrote MONOPOLY: DJUGO, Ladino for "game" and put it in front of the replica of my notebook. When I was finished with all of this, I called out to the desk sergeant and told him I was ready to speak to the DA, and he called to arrange the meeting that would ultimately lead to the army recruiting station in Albuquerque.

I phoned The Trading Post and told my father that he could visit. After lunch, he walked in along with Madre, Débora, Nohemi, and Navajo Joe. The desk sergeant allowed me out of the cell to greet them after having noticed the Silver Star dangling from the chain around Navajo Joe's neck. He approached Navajo Joe and saluted. It was reciprocated.

"I was a jarhead," the desk sergeant said.

"Me too," said Navajo Joe, both men still keeping their right hands above their right eyebrows.

"Fifth Division, Iwo Jima, twenty sixth regiment," said the desk sergeant.

"Twenty eighth," said Navajo Joe.

They grasped each other's forearms. Then the desk sergeant rolled up his left sleeve to reveal a jagged scar running about six inches up to his elbow.

"I didn't even know I'd been hit," he said. "I heard the grenade and felt the waves. What do they call that?"

"Concussion." I said.

"Yeah, I was dizzy and all, but so what? Big deal, I thought. Then I bent down to help a buddy who'd been shot bad. 'Holy cow,' I yelled when I saw his guts spilling out of his body. I almost puked. My wound? If that was going to be the worst of it, I was going to make out like a bandit.

"You? The Star?"

"I got it in the..." Navajo Joe turned to me and whispered, "Jacobo, how do you say ass in front of women?"

"Derrière," I said out loud, and we all laughed.

"I'd crawled to where a buddy was lying right in front of the Japs. He was in bad shape. I used his Johnny gun until the boxes were empty. I think I went through three. My hands were shaking so bad. I guess I got 'em good, you know, nothing was coming at me, so I took the strap off my canteen, made a tourniquet, lifted him up, then put him on my back. It was quite a load. I was all bent over and got back to the sandbags on the beach where the medics took him. Then, bang! I got hit. Sniper, from the trees."

We'd never heard this story before. In fact, we hadn't known that the pendant was a medal for bravery. All this time.

"Heh, heh," the desk sergeant said good-naturedly. "When I saw it, and you being an Indian and all, I thought, 'Hey, this guy's a code talker!'"

"Ah, *Diné Bizaad yee*," Navajo Joe said, code talker in Navajo.

Only later did I realize that the desk sergeant was likely implying that Navajo Joe got the award for being a code talker, not for his bravery in saving the life of a fellow marine at risk to his own.

I gave my family the abbreviated version of what was going to happen, in Ladino, so there was no concern about retreating into a corner for privacy. Then it was time for them to go. I told my father to get in touch with Mir and to give her the score.

"I'll call Ben Veniste," he said, and immediately I felt better.

I hugged and kissed each member of my family. Then Navajo Joe came up close to me, and with a straight face said, "Don't get hit in the ass!" I saluted. He saluted back. I gave him the version of my notebook written in Ladino and told him to hide it in his house. He slipped it into the bag he was carrying without asking me what it was.

Later that afternoon, I said goodbye to my cellmates. I heard the sound of the dice and expected them to be arguing about hotels on Park Place or houses on Tennessee Avenue but instead found them crowded into the corner, playing street craps. The Monopoly game rested on the table, my instruction book in Spanish still tucked inside the top cover. A few turned, smiled, and waved, but I was never sure if this reflected good wishes for me getting out or for them having a winning roll.

I supposed the desk sergeant and the other cops suspected that my fidgeting was related to a concern that I was eventually headed to Vietnam. This wasn't the case at all. I knew that Myles was going to be interviewed on the David Sussman Show within a few days, and I wasn't going to find out about that at boot camp. I had to find a way to get in touch with Mir, which would have the salutary benefit of hearing her voice.

The two cops who drove me were surprised that I'd opted for the army as opposed to staying in jail. "I thought guys like you," by that he meant young, with long hair, and who'd been busted for activities associated with a headline-grabbing student takeover of the UT administrative building, "were against, you know, the government."

"Yeah, like all of you were protesting ROTC and the war." This was said by the other one as a declaratory statement, but it really was in the guise of a question hoping for an answer in the form of an explanation.

"It's the American thing to do," I responded nonchalantly. This apparently satisfied them, as they assumed I was referring to the patriotic duty of undertaking national service. They then animatedly joined the conversation, informing me of their own experiences, one in the Marines and the other in the Air Force. Not wanting to disturb the peace, I let them banter, occasionally adding an "uh-huh," or "oh, that's interesting" and refraining from telling them the true interpretation of my rejoinder to them: that Americans have rights of privacy, property, and speech, and that to retain those rights was as American as apple pie… or as a *burék* washed down with cool lemon water.

CHAPTER 21

You people,

you ought to be ashamed

of yourselves

Sitting in the cramped greenroom of KNME in Albuquerque, Myles was treated like a potentate by the two young production assistants who gushed each time he thanked them for a glass of water or acknowledged their popping in with bright smiles and letting him know how many minutes to airtime, his cue to get up and move to the canvas-backed director's chair on the set opposite David Sussman. A low oval table was configured with pitchers of water and coffee, cups and saucers, glasses, a basket of rolls, lighters and ashtrays. The stage was bare: you could see a ladder and a camera, props that were there to give the impression that the guest had just dropped in for a casual chat and happened to catch the host in a moment by himself. Two spotlights hovered over the host and the guest with the rest of the stage in deep shadow. Sussman didn't acknowledge his guest until the switch was thrown and the show went live, something that caught most guests unaware and ill-prepared for the introduction or first question. Because there was no script and no blocks (the show wasn't called *Open Ended* for nothing), it was a disquieting situation for a guest who wouldn't be able to judge either a beginning, a middle, or an ending, so he or she was at the mercy of the host who could set a trap and then choke off a response with the guest left hanging.

Claudia had told Myles that it was best if he hijacked the conversation early on, spoke rapidly, and talked over the host, making sure he got his points across quickly and vociferously. She reminded him that this might be his only chance in front of a live, national audience of literati—when he could sustain his fame beyond the dreaded time limit of the show's hour.

So, when he was asked to comment on the impact of the Free Speech Movement on America, he launched into what could only be described as a set piece—similar to what politicians call their stump speech—and what others might call a harangue. He went through the chronicle of what'd occurred at UT in excruciating detail, building to a crescendo that would hopefully prompt Sussman to get to the Kettys-Burg Address—his pièce de résistance, his gift to the history books that would enshrine him forever alongside such luminaries as Samuel Gompers, John L. Lewis, Susan B. Anthony, and Martin Luther King, Jr. But much as a Supreme Court Justice interrupts an attorney making an oral argument with no regard for the status of his or her brief, Sussman sliced through the loaf of a pretentious moot court presentation and, talking over Myles' words, asked, "How have you served your country?"

Myles was caught off guard and tried to dissemble by attempting to finish his monologue and to frame his service through leadership that would assist in changing America for the good. Sussman would have no part of it. He leaned in, the camera catching a reflection of an overhead light on his wavy, tightly kinked grayish-black hair, giving him an unintended halo effect as he flicked his filtered cigarette into an ashtray, an exclamation point to emphasize that he wanted a direct answer.

"Peace Corps?" he asked. Myles shook his head side to side.

"VISTA?" he inquired, using the acronym for Volunteers in Service to America. Myles again shook his head negatively.

"I have to presume 'no' to the army, the national guard, and the reserves, yes?"

Myles now gave no head motion.

Sussman persisted. "A bill for the National Teacher Corps is going through Congress right now. Is that something you—with your academic credentials—would be interested in pursuing? Or perhaps Sargent Shriver's other big program, you know, the Job Corps—a program for which you and your comrades could make a big impact, don't you think?"

It suddenly dawned on Myles that the invitation to appear on the show wasn't a coronation. Instead, it was theater. A chance for Sussman to create some sort of news or controversy and to get ratings and to raise his own profile, much in the way his interviews with Nikita Khrushchev and Jerry Lewis had attracted gigantic Nielsen ratings and put Sussman into the vernacular of the national conversation. It was quite a coup for the former press agent/talent agent/producer turned member of the cognoscenti.

Myles squirmed in his now uncomfortable seat, trying to shift his body to appear to be relaxed while, at the same time, making sure his squirming wouldn't collapse his flimsy chair, only to have him fall ignominiously onto the uncarpeted floor. He was flummoxed, outwitted by Sussman in a manner similar to what he'd done to George Townsend. He needed to regain the upper hand. He began a monologue of his exploits in voter registration campaigns and in the south and went on seamlessly to tell of integrating restaurants, hotels, trains and gave accounts of getting establishments to take down their *Whites Only* or *Colored* signs. He told of trying to persuade unions to expand into the public service sector, a burgeoning labor pool that was disproportionately staffed by men and women of color. He ended with a declaration that some have said was haughty, but others felt was simply a generational pushback to an ill-informed question from Sussman: "*That's* how I've served my country, *sir*." It was the addition of the word "sir," of course, that those who read a transcript of the show felt was a wonderful show of respect. While those who watched the kinescope later would describe the nearly hissed word as the most trendsetting element of the exchange: the "sir" delivered as an intentional faux show of conversational decency that was, in reality, an upbraiding that soon made its way into the common vernacular in a debate or an interview.

David Sussman appeared not to take offence. Leaning backward, he took an overlong drag of his cigarette, then came forward and exhaled, the smoke acting as a theatrical prop to his question, carrying his words directly into his guest's face, a slap that was seen by hundreds of thousands and read about by millions the next day: "So tell me, Myles, do you serve your country by being a plagiarist?" Before Myles could parry this thrust, Sussman followed it up quickly by saying, "I'm referring, certainly, to the so-called Kettys-Burg Address." He stopped abruptly, stared at Myles like any good attorney would in a deposition, making no sounds, keeping his body motionless, watching the dead airtime seep into Myles' lungs, hearing nothing but silence from the people on the set. Myles sat ramrod straight for a few uncomfortable seconds, then uncoiled as he stood up, ripped off his lavalier mike, approached David Sussman the way a boxer tries to intimidate his opponent at a weigh-in and spat out, "You people, you ought to be ashamed of yourselves. I may not be Superman, but I'm fighting for truth, justice, and the American way while you sit there smugly with your cigarettes and foul, baseless accusations. How dare you!"

It was riveting.

The Worker made a headline out of "How Dare You!" with a cartoon of Myles as Émile Zola stabbing his finger into the chest of a fat cat, labeled "Moneyed Interests." *The Forward* fixated on Myles' "You people," labeling it as anti-Semitic coin of the realm. *The New York Times* took a different kind of umbrage, interpreting this two-word accusation as a jibe against the press, not directed toward Jews. Joe Pyne on TV and Barry Gray on radio couldn't get enough of this exchange and used it to incite conflict (Pyne) and a brokered exchange of views (Gray).

It shattered the record audience for the Khrushchev interview and sent the comet of Myles' public life into orbit around Pluto.

CHAPTER 22

I'm a member of the tribe,

for God's sake

I called Ben Veniste from boot camp at Fort Ord near Monterey.

"I've got only a few minutes at the pay phone, so do you know what happened? I mean with Myles and the David Sussman Show. I'm dying to find out."

"Mir told me she got in touch with an AP reporter who'd used her photos to illustrate his stories of what was going on here," he said. "He opened doors for her. Arranged calls with friends at *The New York Times*, *the San Francisco Chronicle*, *The Washington Post* and *The Boston Globe*. Nothing. They wouldn't bite."

"How come? It's such a huge story. Plagiarism, a phony speech. You think they'd be all over it." I was angry. Myles had gotten away with it.

"Jacobo, if she spilled the beans, there'd be no guarantee that a reporter wouldn't steal it for his own. They don't call it a scoop for no reason. She wouldn't reveal her proof, so no one was willing to trust her."

What a world we were living in: someone had stolen a speech, and it was likely that a reporter would claim the story as his own. Was I the only one in this mess who had principles? Maybe I was just a sap.

"No one was going to listen to a nineteen-year-old girl with a strange name, a foreigner with a faint, undiscernible accent from a university in New Mexico, period. She was so dejected. I'd never seen her like this. When she finished telling me her tale of woe, she gave this really sad sigh that she couldn't even get a call back from a lowly production assistant named Shuky Goldman from the David Sussman Show. I asked her immediately to give me this guy Shuky's number, and by the end of the day, everything was set."

"What do you mean, everything was set. What's set? I don't understand," I said.

"The plans to fly Mr. Sussman to Albuquerque to set up the interview with Myles."

"What? Wait a minute. Is this a joke? You called this production assistant and like *that*, everything's all set?" I was mystified as to how this all came about.

"Jacobo, you have to understand how the world works. At any rate, how the Jewish world works. I could tell you about a street in New York City where a jewelry store owner can make a $100,000 gem deal with a wholesaler—you know what that is?—never mind, we don't have enough time—on a handshake. That's it. No paperwork, no banks, no signatures, no lawyers, no insurance, nothing. Shake. My word, your word, that's it."

To be candid, I had no idea what he was talking about, at that time never having heard of the diamond district in Manhattan that was dominated by Jews. And I certainly couldn't make the connection to Shuky Goldman.

"Look, Jacobo, I asked this Shuky guy where he *davened*. He told me. I mentioned to him that I knew the rabbi at his shul and how impressed I was when I'd studied with him on a visit to his synagogue in Brooklyn."

It was as if Ben Veniste were speaking in Navajo. The guys behind me on line were starting to get agitated, cursing, making crude comments, and rapidly vibrating their palms against their lips to accentuate a woo-woo-woo-woo-woo sound designed to get me off the phone.

Exasperated, Ben Veniste said, "Shuky's a Jew, Jacobo. I gave him my word, as a Jew. I told him that I could prove the plagiarism, and that's all he needed to hear."

To say that I was dumbfounded was an understatement.

"Look, I'm astounded that you were able to pull this off and really, really happy about it. And, I have to say, that it was unbelievably clever of you to tell this guy that you were a Jew and all and that you went out on a limb for Mir. For us. I mean for everybody. The only thing I can say is thank you, really," I said.

As I was saying this, I heard a lot of commotion on his end of the phone, which I realized when I finished was his cane being whacked against any wooden or metal object within reach, an attempt to gain my attention.

"Jacobo, Jacobo, listen to me," he thundered. "I'm a member of the tribe, for God's sake, just like you. There's no favor I wouldn't do for a fellow Jew in distress. The important thing is that Myles had to be exposed for who he really is. I'll give you the details when you don't have a bunch of hooligans yelling at you to hang up. Call me back," he said, and the line went dead.

I had so much to process. I hung up and walked away from the pay phone. I was in a daze. How was it possible that I didn't know that Ben Veniste was a Jew? That Mir was a Jew? That I only knew that Herzl was a Jew because he told me so. I'd picked up so many current colloquialisms, was *au courant* with contemporary customs and sayings, was as up-to-date on history and literature as any college student, yet I didn't know who was a Jew and who wasn't.

Although, to be fair, I quickly realized that no one knew I was a Jew unless I told them. I let Herzl see it only when we were back in Arroyo

Grande. Herzl told Mir about me. No one else at the UT knew, certainly neither Myles nor Claudia. What was it that Ben Veniste said? *I'm a member of the tribe, for God's sake, just like you.*

Three things popped up at practically the same time.

How did *he* know I was a Jew? I'd never said anything to him.

Would Ben Veniste have undertaken his assistance because it was the right thing to do even if he weren't a Jew? I was inclined to think *yes,* but in truth I didn't know.

Some Jews were named Ben something, son of.

That's what Herzl had told me.

I knew about the bens and the begats from studying Torah. Yet I'd assumed that Ben was his first name and Veniste his last. I had to check this out. I hovered near the pay phone, and when the last of the GIs had hung up, I dialed 4-1-1.

"Operator, can you give me the number for Ben Veniste, that's V-e-n-i-s-t-e in Taos Heights, in New Mexico."

After a while when I thought that she could hear my rapid heartbeat, she said. "I don't have anyone by that name."

"Um, okay, how about under B for the last name Benveniste," I said. "Just add a B-e-n to Veniste."

After a few seconds, she said, "I have a Ricardo Benveniste."

"What's the address?" I asked.

"2128 Cambridge Street."

That was the address of the café, and I knew that Ben lived above it. What do I call him now? Still Ben? Ricardo? He was Ricardo, son of Veniste. It struck me then that as my father was saying goodbye to me when he dropped me off at UT, he didn't just *say* goodbye to Ben Veniste at the café—he gave him a *hug*. I needed to ask Ben Veniste about this. When I did have that conversation, it was the same time I found out that he'd neither heard of the rabbi or the synagogue where Shuky Goldman prayed nor had he ever been to Brooklyn.

CHAPTER 23

There were pictures

of the men

with their families

Each Sunday during the eight weeks of basic training, I'd call Mir, and by the third week when I told her how much I missed her, she responded with, "I love you too." In the last week, I was selected to train to be a combat medic. On what basis, I have absolutely no idea. Perhaps it was that I'd spent a year and a half in college or maybe it was just related to the fact that I'd never held a gun before. This required me to spend sixteen more weeks at Fort Sam Houston, in San Antonio, Texas. In December, I received my orders indicating I was going to Vietnam. As it was over the holiday season, Mir arranged to fly to Sacramento, then took the bus to Travis Air Force Base in Fairfield, where she met me for the one day I had before getting on a C141 to fly to Honolulu, refueling in Guam, then on to Danang.

We kidded about eloping or me going AWOL, which, in retrospect, was our way of shedding nervous energy. The unspoken was that I might never return. At the end of 1965, there were more than 180,000 soldiers in Vietnam almost 2,000 men had been killed in action. It was something we didn't talk about directly. We referred to it as 'the odds,' and by keeping it as a percentage, any discussions with Mir or my buddies could be characterized as conceptual, something we do when we don't want to confront the inevitable head on.

What I'd been exposed to in nearly six months of training at two bases was incomprehensible to me. The American war machine—in men and materiel—was of such magnitude that I couldn't imagine the resources necessary to create and maintain it. I was a member of the Third Platoon, Charlie Company, Fifth Battalion, Five hundred and third Infantry of the One hundred seventy third Airborne Brigade. Hank was the other medic in the platoon, and we were paired up for nine months before he was sent to another unit. Every night, we wrote down on a slip of paper what each of us thought the odds were of us making it back home, which was heavily influenced by the events of the day. We agreed to destroy the piece of paper when we shipped out. I told him I would, but I didn't. I've kept that one piece of paper with 270 numbers in order, folded over four times, where it's tucked into my wallet. After I got back to the States, every time I heard about the death of one of the members of my Company, whether in combat, from in-theater contracted disease, or by suicide, I took the sheet of paper out, said *Kaddish,* and tried to recollect something—a conversation, an act, a facial expression, a pose—anything to remember the fallen comrade.

Around the end of year holidays, the president called for a halt to the bombing of the north. In Washington, there was hope that this could lead to an extended truce or even a peace conference. We knew better.

Hank and I would follow behind the tanks and armored personnel carriers over rough terrain and scramble out of our unprotected Jeep when we got the radio signal to enter the combat zone and minister to the wounded who needed our attention. Hank and I'd been issued handguns, but neither of us could imagine a set of circumstances in which we'd ever have to use them. We wore our gear at all times so that when we got the message, we were completely prepared to get into action as quickly as possible. Seconds lost could be the difference between life and death. For the most part, as we raced to where an NCO was pointing, we'd see a body on the ground, surrounded by soldiers, some cradling a head, some applying compression to a wound, others using a knife to cut off a piece of clothing or a boot. They were always screaming at us to go faster, which was difficult because of the weight from the packs on our backs and what we were carrying in our arms as well. We weren't helped by the hunched over position we were forced to assume, as VC or NVA snipers would try to pick us off—soft targets who wouldn't be responding in kind. Once inside the perimeter, our gear would be unloaded swiftly while we assessed the situation carefully and made triage decisions that still haunt me today. Our job was to do whatever we could, such that when a GI was evacuated to a base to be worked over by a team of physicians, he'd have the best chance of survival and recovery.

For all except for the most superficial of wounds, we had to apply compression to stem the loss of blood and to clean them as best we could—no easy job, given the debris in the air from dirt, foliage, and fumes that flew all around us from bullets, tracks, tires, exhausts, and discharges. We'd apply an antiseptic to an arm and hook up an IV with glucose or saline, making sure that one of the soldiers was holding the bag up. If the wounded man was conscious, we'd give him a pain pill to swallow or chew. When the wound was gruesome, as in the case where an arm or a leg had been blown off by a mortar or land mine, we had to apply a tourniquet quickly and efficiently. Many times, our jobs were made more difficult because of a patient so far gone that he couldn't cooperate to tell us what hurt most, and frequently we had to deal with interference from unwounded soldiers getting in our way. The most difficult part of our jobs was the declaration or call—a decision that could cause such intense anger among the fallen soldier's comrades that it was almost impossible for them to place the deceased soldier in a body bag. This could prevent us from moving on to the next downed GI, where we'd be screamed at by *his* comrades for us to deal with the living and forget about the dead. More than once, we witnessed confrontations between a group unable to cope with a death and another desperately trying to prevent one.

Death was all around us in the combat zone: the helicopter rides back to the base, the hospitals, the field barracks, the places where we'd meet with the chaplains, and in the letters or telegrams that were sent to the families of the fallen. And it wasn't just American or allied forces' deaths. We were witnesses to it each time we entered a village and saw the burned-out huts, observed the freshly dug graves, and received the hard stares from those who'd never heard of Vietnamization, didn't care about ideology, and knew nothing of the domino theory. We were the agents of death. It was that simple.

In our hearts, we were the good guys—the ones who'd hop off the Jeep to give medical care to a bleeding Vietnamese kid, but it became clear to us after a short period of time that some bandages and antiseptic lotions were no salve to a village that'd go on in its ancient ways regardless of whether it was under the influence of the North Vietnamese, the VC, or the Americans. "Holding the line against the reds" was an abstraction created by politicians 9,000 miles away, and within a few weeks of our being in-country, it had no meaning to most of us either.

I was one of the few who had some college. Most of the grunts were fresh out of high school and had fathers who fought in World War II. At both Fort Ord and Fort Sam Houston, they were generally gung-ho: supportive of the war effort and eager to get to Vietnam. One would notice a change in that attitude relatively quickly, brought on as much by the oppressive heat and humidity, the torrential rains, the insect swarms, and the diseases that affected a large percentage of the troops. Malaria, dysentery, black syphilis (better known as Saigon Rose), and hepatitis C were the main culprits, although we treated many GIs for head lice, crabs, and athlete's foot. We had to beg to get more tetanus shots when we first got there.

Once we were in the jungle, we were confronted with soldiers who had trouble breathing from the intake of napalm, white phosphorus from tracers and smoke grenades, and unaccustomed odors from stagnant water and dead animals. Our own bodies reeked of not having bathed, and we spent inordinate amounts of time burning leeches off the men with cigarettes, warning them not to pull them off as this would strip their skin and likely lead to an infection. While omnipresent snakes initially caused undue panic, we got used to them and, in a way, looking down at each step turned out to be to our advantage, as it allowed us to avoid many booby traps. In general, we could deal with the crude made-in-jungle constructions, but what caused dread and great trauma were the pressure traps—sophisticated devices that would blow only when your foot stepped *off* of one. Trying to save a life in the jungle from a soldier who'd been blown up by one of these traps was almost impossible. And, given our credo of not leaving anyone behind, Hank and I had, on more than one occasion, carried a soldier back over long distances through bogs, where heavy growth required us to use machetes, all the while avoiding rats that seemed to trail us with great efficiency. And we were always wary of tigers, which fortunately, we never encountered.

Disillusion set in on most of us within a few weeks of being away from the base. It affected the gung-ho guys the worst, the fall from the height of supreme confidence in the U.S. mission into the abyss of despair was swift and calamitous. The most obvious manifestations of this behavior were pot smoking, excessive drinking, sex with local women who may or may not have been agents of the VC, the indiscriminate use of firearms without provocation, and hostility toward the commissioned officers, who seemed to understand that decorations were the key to advancement, so they pushed the grunts into missions that may not've been for any utility other than to collect ribbons.

Hank suggested that we create what he named the clam patrol—consisting of just us—a twosome that vowed to retreat into our shells to avoid the problems with the out-of-control everyday soldiers as well as the commissioned officers. Since we were the first line of defense against wounds and disease, we were generally left alone.

My only knowledge of the war had been garnered through observations of the student protesters, who'd wave American flags with the hammer and sickle placed over the stars or who'd sewn a peace symbol or the numbers 666 over the stars. Those who didn't carry flags would greet others by holding their index and middle finger up to form a V, with the thumb holding down the other two fingers, a kind of non-military salute that, if reciprocated, was a sign of agreement against having American troops in Vietnam and against war in general. I admired their passion, but my view of the "make peace, not war" position was heavily influenced by Herzl's illustrations of the naïveté of this outlook by pointing out circumstances—such as World War II—in which there was no alternative to war. Hank and I were there to perform a highly critical job, and we'd do everything possible to carry it out without compromise. We were, of course, aghast at the arbitrary shooting of civilians and the blanketing of fields with napalm but felt that if the U.S. could push the NVA invaders back to the north, the VC guerilla war would fizzle and the country could return to some semblance of normalcy, which meant we could go home.

Hank was an ethnic Catholic from Chicago who'd been drafted right after his high school graduation. Although he was only a couple of inches shorter than I, he was universally described as big, while people characterized me as tall—the difference being that he weighed close to seventy pounds more than I did and had the physique of a heavyweight wrestler as opposed to my shape as a rower. We kidded each other that he would've sunk a shell, and I would've been pinned to a mat in seconds. He had massive shoulders and legs. His uniform had been altered by a Vietnamese woman who lived near the base. We could get almost anything we wanted from her for U.S. currency at half the price we could buy it from the PX, where, we were sure, things had been stolen from in the first place. We spent two week's pay for boots that this woman made that left the imprint of sandals typically worn by the VCs walking in the opposite direction.

It was this same woman who taught me some Vietnamese, including one word which I never thought I'd use.

When Hank was first introduced to me by our platoon leader, he assumed that I was Mexican—not surprising given my surname. He extended his huge hand to shake and greeted me with a friendly "*¿Hola, como estas?*" which, it turned out, was practically the complete range of his knowledge of Spanish, something I quickly discerned when I responded by launching into a full conversation that was reciprocated by a blank stare and hands held out in front of him as if to say, stop! He laughed uproariously at his own jokes and instinctively would give me a slap on the back or a jab to my triceps, his playful way of making a connection that took some getting used to.

On July 4, 1966, our platoon had orders to get to a village south of Pleiku, which was at the apex of a triangle midway between Danang and Cam Ranh Bay. We were airlifted in Huey choppers to a site on the east side of a river over which the engineers had just finished constructing a thirty-foot long log bridge. We crossed over, stepping on the innermost two logs and keeping our heads down. Ahead on a rise, we could see the village, at the top of what looked like manicured rows of farmland encircling the huts like rings. Up we went, splayed out over a hundred yards, cautiously climbing while constantly looking from side to side. Hank and I even had our Colt .45s out. We were to interrogate the villagers to find out if any VC were in the area and then to take a position on a ridge that overlooked the town to the east and a river to the west. There were only old men, young children, women, and animals in the village, and our interpreter told us that, while some VC apparently came at night, the place was too remote and insignificant for them to stage an attack from there. We dug in to spend the night. The ground was soft, so we could dig our foxholes relatively quickly and found plenty of fronds and other foliage to lie down on. Lookouts climbed nearby trees and rotated every two hours. No one had night vision goggles so we listened for the sounds of multiple voices, mechanized equipment, boats on the river, or animals. The VC had learned to hide among water buffaloes, cows, goats, and pigs that they'd shepherd by crouching among them, making it appear that this was simply part of the ebb and flow of village life, until it was too late, when they'd pop up and begin to attack an unsuspecting village, army post, or patrol.

A little past midnight, Hank and I were tapped to climb trees to be lookouts. In some ways, it was better than being on the ground, as we could straddle large branches and hook our legs around smaller ones, then lean against the trunk. The foliage was thick, so every few minutes we'd have to extend our arms to peer outside the canopy. There was nothing to see, but it felt as if we were contributing to the safety of the platoon. There was absolute quiet. It was peaceful. There was no rain. We were relaxed.

The sounds of gunshots were magnified by bullets ricocheting off of trees and the metal equipment that was lying on the ground. VC camouflaged with jungle vegetation were running below us, shooting AK-47s and Chinese assault rifles indiscriminately. They sprang up in front of GIs who in most cases never even had a chance to pick up their guns. It was all over in less than a minute.

Their screams coupled with the agonies of our men dying haunt me to this very day.

The VC made their exit quickly, and within a few seconds, we couldn't hear them anymore. I shinnied down first, then Hank. We checked each body. Some had been wounded and then executed with a single shot to the head. No one was alive.

I threw up. I was shaking uncontrollably. So much sweat came out of every pore that it felt as if I'd been submerged in the river. I was nauseous. Bile came up into my mouth. As soon as I spit, an equal amount replaced it. I was woozy. Hank thought I'd suffered a gunshot wound and was checking me for blood and a gash in my clothing from a bullet. I couldn't control my breathing. He ran to his gear to get a paper bag and held it against my mouth, encouraging me to breathe slowly. I had to take my helmet off in order to rub my hands over my scalp, which felt hot to the touch. I could hear the rhythmic beating drum that'd replaced my brain. I was concerned that I was in a medical state of shock for which neither of us had the requisite equipment or skills to handle. Selfishly, I didn't think of how all of this was impacting Hank. He assured me he was okay, but I couldn't tell if he was just trying to protect me so I wouldn't go any more off the deep end.

His calm demeanor and leadership traits allowed him to provide the treatments that saved my life. I've never gone a day without thinking of him under these most trying circumstances, and I expressed my admiration and thanks to him on numerous occasions.

After a half an hour, I began to feel a little better. His eyes and hands asked me if I was in a position to get up and leave. Hank mouthed not to use the radio in case the VC were lingering not too far away. I wondered if the villagers were VC and had gotten the word to the guerillas in the jungle about how many we were and where we had bunked down for the night. But even if we were to go to the village at first light to find out, the interpreter was also dead, so there was no good that could have come of it.

We thought we'd start to make our way to a place far enough from the village and the jungle where we couldn't be heard when we used the radio. But the very act of finding such a place would leave us exposed. It could be a suicide mission. We opted to stay in the jungle and to make our way around the village to get back to the river where the engineers had created the log bridge, near where the Huey had left us. It was a known landing area that could be described accurately. But how to get there?

We headed south, assuming that at some point past the fields, the jungle would connect to the river. We could hear some rustling that scared us enough to stop in our tracks. We froze but couldn't see anything in the darkness. After a few tense moments, we realized it was the sounds of birds and lizards, or perhaps rats, following our smell. When the brush was thick, we crawled on all fours, preferring not to use the machetes that we'd picked up from the fallen soldiers, as this would've made too much noise. We'd also grabbed two M-16s and multiple magazines that we stuffed into our medical bags. We moved ever so slowly, were careful with each step, doing our best to avoid even cracking a tiny branch, stifling coughs, never talking, only nodding and pointing. I thought that my heartbeat could be heard for miles and several times put my right hand over it, as if to give it a warning to shut up and not give us away. After a few hundred yards, Hank stopped, took off his shoulder bag, and reached in to get the special shoes that had soles that made impressions like Vietnamese sandals aligned back to front. I couldn't believe that I'd forgotten about them and did the same. Neither of us were convinced that the track would fool an experienced scout, but it gave us an emotional lift at a time when we could really use one.

Far enough inside the jungle, but close enough to see out, we skirted the rice paddies that seemed to spread out endlessly as the night wore on. The ground turned into a bog that made walking difficult, especially since we were now weighed down with a gun, ammo, and a machete in addition to our regular gear. We needed to rest and saw the perfect opportunity; the remains of a rubber tree plantation that started at the top of a seven- or eight-foot rise would give us cover. Sticky sap was ever-present on the bark and had accumulated in pools on the ground. It was doubtful that any VC would want to bivouac in such a rotted place. The trees had been planted in neat rows, yet they were now almost totally overtaken by the fast-growing plants of the jungle.

Leaning back against the incline, we kept our helmets on and never took our hands off our guns, just in case. After a few minutes, I leaned close to Hank's ear and, in a barely audible voice, asked, "What? What did you say?" At that instant, we both realized there were people on the other side of the embankment, and we knew what that meant. Hank raised his M-16 and motioned to the side, meaning that he thought we should go around the berm, but I shook my head, concerned that we'd be spotted and would lose the advantage of surprise. He raised his head in the direction of the top of the berm giving me a shake. I agreed with that. They'd hear us if we were to crawl up. An alternative was to sit tight and do nothing. I quickly dismissed that option, as we would be sitting ducks if the VC had an inkling we were here.

My mind raced, and for reasons I can't readily explain, it settled on one of the Vietnamese words that the woman who sold us the shoes said, always with a laugh. It spawned an idea. I motioned to Hank that he should stand and cup his arms together tightly to make a footrest for me. When he did, I placed one foot in his hands, then the other, grabbed hold of his neck, and as he raised his hands, hoisted myself first onto his massive shoulders, then placed my hands on his helmet, and started to stand straight up with my boots against either side of his head. Hank bent each elbow up and steadied my legs with his powerful hands. His feet were planted as firmly in the ground as the rubber trees—there was no wavering, no trembling, no huffing and puffing. When I was at full height, my eyes were eleven feet off the ground, high enough to see a group of VC on the other side of the berm, lazily resting, their guns on the ground. I aimed my M-16 and pulled the trigger, screaming "*giết chiết, giết chết*" at the top of my lungs, over and over, the twenty rounds hitting their targets. As soon as the magazine was empty, I dropped the gun and fired my Colt .45 eight times. The only sounds we heard were the squawks of birds taking flight. There was no moaning. Hank grabbed my arm as I bent down, and he lowered me to the ground. We ran up the berm with no hesitation now, Hank's M-16 ready to fire. But there was no need. All seven were dead. We checked each for signs of life and refrained from putting bullets into their heads. We rifled through their clothes and pulled papers that we stuffed into our bags. Then we both puked. The air reeked of gunshot, rubber, vomit, and our stink. After an arduous trudge through the rubber plantation, we came upon a totally unexpected sight near its southern edge: a U.S. Marine patrol coming from a chopper to whom Hank called out frantically, waving his arms: "Dodgers in seven over the Twins, Koufax MVP," an assurance to the leathernecks in the first faint light of dawn that the guys running toward them from the strand of rubber trees were friendlies and not VC.

When we reached the Marines, Hank asked me what I'd shouted out as I started firing. I told him it was Vietnamese for kill, pronounced *zit-jyet*. He repeated it over and over.

"How did you come up with that and the idea of standing on my shoulders? If any of them had looked up and seen a gigantic person with an M-16 hollering his lungs out, they would've been scared to death, no need for you to fire," he said with a huge grin.

"The Holyman," I replied.

"What? Who? A holyman?"

"The golem," I said.

"I don't understand. A Mexican thing?"

"It's hard to explain." And with that, he gave up and cuffed me playfully on my shoulder.

Back at our base, we were debriefed by information officers and turned over what we'd taken from the bodies of the VC, noticing for the first time that among the various papers, there were pictures of the men with their families.

CHAPTER 24

Reminiscences of his bravery,

comradeship, and support

As it turned out, Hank suffered a traumatic injury shortly after he left our unit; by chance, his hospitalization landed him at the VA in Albuquerque, so I was able to visit him after I returned home in 1967. His PTSD was exacerbated by the lingering effects of a drug overdose, both of which the doctors attributed to him witnessing a massacre that came about after a crew of our tunnel rats suffered gruesome deaths near Duc Pho, south of Da Nang on the coast. He wouldn't go into any details but not because he couldn't remember. Rather, it was the opposite: these events were seared into his memory, playing in an endless loop with a voiceover that screamed damnation for him, a burden so severe that he longed for death as a sacrifice worthy of redemption. My visits provided little comfort and became less frequent. After a while, I realized that he didn't know who I was. It was heartbreaking. Mir thought it best if I recreated conversations with

Hank that provided me with reminiscences of his bravery, comradeship, and support.

That's precisely what I talked about at his funeral.

LATER, STANDING UNDERNEATH the chuppah with Mir, the rabbi made sure everyone knew that the empty space between my father and Benjamin Tudela had been reserved for Private First Class Hank Banaszek, of blessed memory.

CHAPTER 25

I'm not going

to break the news

about Herzl

May 16, 1967
Dear Jacobo,

I can't wait to see you. Two weeks. The odds are 100%. Herzl called yesterday from Philadelphia. I wish I could photograph this 20th century Thomas Eakins rowing for Penn on the Schuylkill. I practically had to pry it out of him that he won the single sculls again. Pretty amazing. Maybe he'll get to be on the cover of their yearbook too. They want him for the Olympics next year in Mexico City. He's really agitated about what's going on in Israel. Says he's probably going there. Soon. Did you hear the UN peacekeepers were just expelled and access to the Red Sea has been blockaded? I just can't imagine being invaded. There are so few Jews and so many Arabs. I'm planning on being at Fort Ord on the 1st. I bought the old Nash Rambler from Ben Veniste for a hundred and fifty bucks. It sounds cheap, doesn't it? Do you think he did me a favor? My Sunday calls with your sister are the highlight of my week. I'm not going to break the news about Herzl, that's for sure. I've got all my photos categorized, along with notes. I can't wait to see you!

Mia amor,
Mir

CHAPTER 26

You don't have to spell it out

After Hank's funeral, Mir and I drove to Taos Heights; we were to meet Ben Veniste at the café. This was the first time I'd been back in the UT environs since Herzl and I left that night more than two years earlier to row down the river. As soon as I got out of the car, I was accosted by a group of students whose screams within a few feet of me caught me unaware. My body instantly recoiled from them against the driver's side window, and I could hear Mir shouting as she opened the passenger side door. I yelled at her to get back in the car. One of the students spit in my direction, but I ducked and it splattered against the rear window. The person closest to me whacked me in the shin, and when I reacted by turning my body away, I was punched on the opposite side. The pain from both blows was significant, but my boot camp training kicked in automatically, and I punched back fiercely.

In retrospect, I could deconstruct the individual words from the cacophony that had erupted from the five young men and one woman. Some of the things I can recall include:

"Hey, hey, Bill, how many babies did you kill!"

"Ho Ho Ho Chi Minh, Ho Chi Minh is going to win!"

"Warmonger!"

"Fascist dog!"

"Hell no, I won't go!"

What bothered me more than the spitting, the blows, the vile words, and the rage expressed in contorted faces, was the group bravado that provided the comfort which enabled them to confront me. I knew that had any of them been alone, this altercation would never have happened. In an ironic way, it reminded me of how the guys in my squad would become more emboldened—hence trigger happy and indiscriminate when firing their guns—when they entered a village as part of a whole platoon.

Group dynamics play such an underreported part in how we behave.

Mir stayed on the other side of the car, stopped in her tracks when several of the students screamed "whore!" and "slut!" and "camp tramp!" with such vehemence that the echoes of these epithets seemed to have the effect of pushing her down out of sight. Then instincts overcame fear. She frantically fumbled with her pocketbook zipper to unearth a small camera. She rose slowly, peered through the bottom of the window, and with unsteady fingers, was able to take a whole roll of film, *snap, snap, snap*, many of which, she found out later to her dismay, were not of the quality for which she was known. That night, she watched them emerge on the paper in the pans of the camera room in the basement of the bookstore, exasperated at seeing shots of the insides of the car and even of the door and window. Nevertheless, she did manage to capture photos of all of the students, with the caveat that some were blurry and others were side or back views of their heads.

Unseen and unheard by the students, Ben Veniste came limping from the café, stopped behind the group accosting us, lifted his cane high in the air, and walloped it with such force against the calf of the student in the furthermost part of the group from me that the victim's hideous shriek had the effect of immediately silencing the others, who turned to see what'd happened. Standing in front of them was a lame, older man, who reminded me of a whirling dervish, especially since his loose-fitting shirt billowed in the air as he went after each of the other students, albeit more with bluster than with blunt force, once he realized that the assault on me and Mir was essentially over.

"Next time, take your uniform off when you come to the campus," he said as forcefully as a drill sergeant. "Let's go," he commanded, and Mir and I stepped in front of him in order to have some protection should there be another attack from behind.

We hustled to a table unseen from the street. I spotted the two young Mexican kitchen helpers, so I went over to them and asked if they remembered me. Their faces lit up. One started to howl like a wolf while the other simply called out *lobo rojo*! We shook hands, then I gave the one closest to me a knuckle sandwich. He pretended to be hurt and made the stance like a boxer. Ben Veniste and Mir clapped at this spontaneous performance. Coming with a minute of the fracas outside, it reflected the yin and yang of my life, something I'd be more attuned to as I got older.

While this took the edge off, I was still jumpy. I went to the restroom to splash cold water on my face and to give some extra time for my heart rate to come back to normal. I looked into the mirror and remarked to the person in the soldier's uniform that I was as discombobulated as I was at any time in Vietnam. I tried to talk myself out of this predicament.

It took fifteen or twenty minutes to get back to a semblance of normality, during which we tried to understand what'd just happened—not by replaying a blow-by-blow description of the events that had occurred outside but rather by way of coming to terms with how the war was affecting behavior and changing norms.

I then changed the subject. Enough was enough.

In Vietnam, I'd written a letter to Ben Veniste, asking him questions that'd been on my mind ever since we met, but he'd demurred, preferring to speak to me in person. It was now time. With shared tapas plates in front of us, I started by asking him how he knew my father.

He placed his cane underneath his seat and said, "We met right after the War, by accident. Well, that sure is a double-entendre. See, what I mean is that I parked my car—you think the Nash Rambler is a jalopy?" he said looking at Mir. "It was a '29 Model A sedan. Right at the front of The Trading Post," he said, looking at me. "I was on my way back from Alamagordo. The way some folks are with UFOs?" he said, "I was that way with The Bomb. I had to go see where they tested it. Anyway, on the way back, I pulled into The Trading Post, and that's where I met your father."

"Okay," I said, "that's a start."

"Well, here's the finish. I got sideswiped by another car when I was loading some stuff I bought. You know the rear doors on the Model A open opposite to how they do it now? So, I couldn't see a thing and then *boom*, the lights went out, my left leg was smashed into the door jamb. I must've really screamed because your father burst through the front door so fast that he could still see the other car speeding off. He yelled for his friend Joe..."

"Joe Deschene?" I asked.

"That's the one. Same guy. They lifted me into Joe's pickup and drove like the dickens to the clinic in Socorro. I don't know how they did it without going crazy, me moaning and cursing in the back, screaming when they went over a bump or a pothole. They did what they could. Stopped the bleeding, gave me morphine, thank God, taped a splint—boy that hurt I can tell you—and then sent me off to Albuquerque in an ambulance. In a stupor. I was high, if you get my meaning. They took good care of me there, the surgeons and the nurses, but with so many breaks in the leg—and my hip got it too—I really didn't have a chance to recover fully. So here I am; it is what it is. I make do. I will be what I will be."

His disability had seemed to be such a natural part of him that I'd glossed over it, never having stopped to think about how it had affected him, emotionally as well as physically.

We do that, don't we?

I was ashamed of myself.

"And my father?" I asked in a subdued manner, as if to begin to show compassion to Ben's situation. Or was it contrition for my not having recognized it previously?

"Oh, your father came to the hospital. You know, to see how I was doing. He burst in with a smile, a book, and a newspaper. We talked and talked and talked, all day, about everything. He made it bearable. When visiting hours were over, he got up to leave, to get back to Arroyo Grande, and I asked him to say a prayer for me. I mean, I was hoping someone would, not having a wife or kids."

"I wish I could've been there, to say a prayer for you," Mir said.

He looked at me, nodded toward Mir, and said, "This one's special."

I squeezed her hand.

Ben Veniste continued, "I didn't know what to expect. You know, with regard to the prayer. What your father was going to say. And I didn't care who he was going to pray to. It was for me and that was good enough. He dragged the chair he was sitting in over to the side of the bed. He looked directly at me and mumbled something that sounded like the *Mi Shebeirach*. I knew my bones hurt, but I was wondering if my ears were damaged too. Here's this big guy with flaming red hair—if you told me he was a Viking I would've believed it. The *Mi Shebeirach*! You could've floored me, I'm telling you, that this guy was saying the Hebrew prayer for healing. Well, I was pretty much floored anyway, but you know what I mean."

That's how he'd known I was a Jew.

"I can just imagine. What did you think? What did you do?" Mir asked.

"I said it along with him, by God, and he just about plopped over."

"I wish I could've been there, to see it, the expressions on both of your faces. Actually, I wish I could've taken pictures," Mir said.

"And you stayed in touch," I said, remembering the hug.

"Mostly by letter, sometimes by phone. But every couple of years or so, we meet in Santa Fe or Albuquerque, usually if your father's buying something for the store. I knew, Jacobo, that you were coming to the UT. Your father didn't have to ask for me to be *in loco parentis*. It was just something I wanted to do for him. Keep an eye out, that sort of thing."

"Thank you," I said. "Really. I mean, think of all the things you did for me, for us: getting me into Kettys-Burg Hall; providing us with the food to sustain ourselves there. Coming up with the plan of escape."

"And letting me have the car," Mir added.

"Don't forget giving me a head's up about Myles." I added. "Even besides these things, just coming to the café, it was something like home. Away from home."

Mir leaned over and gave him a kiss on the cheek. I expected Ben Veniste to tap his cane in acknowledgement. Instead, he looked at both of us as if we were his children, which suggested that no spoken words were necessary among family members.

"In any of his visits, did my father ever tell you about us? The history?" I wanted to know.

"Not at first. And I don't blame him. After all, I was a stranger. It took time. We had to get to know each other better. To build some trust. Then one day, he asked me where *my* family came from. Which part of Spain. Because of the name. And how we got here. New Mexico. It was different from your families."

"How so?" I asked. "I assume your ancestors came through Mexico, like ours did."

"We came directly from Spain. We didn't leave in 1492. We were there for hundreds of years."

"I didn't think Jews were allowed to stay, and besides, why would they want to?" Mir said.

"You could stay if you became Catholic. Converted," Ben Veniste said. "*Conversos*."

"I find it incomprehensible," I said, "to *pretend*, to go to church and everything but stay as Jews. I can't believe how people could do this, pass it down, and continue for hundreds of years."

"Especially with the inquisition," Mir said.

Inkizisyon, I said to myself, shuddering as I pictured it happening to me.

"It must have been schizophrenic," I said.

"Right-o," Ben Veniste said. "At a certain point, it becomes too difficult to keep it up. You know, the illusion. And the fear that goes along with it. That you'll be found out. And then what? I don't have to tell you. They had to get out. Look, all I can say is that I thank God and my grandparents that I didn't have to go through this. I'm just a Spanish immigrant. And a good old American Jew."

When dinner was over, we hugged Ben Veniste and took our leave.

Mir and I walked back to her small apartment, holding hands, not saying much. Her rooms were in a state of semi-disarray. Books strewn about along with cardboard boxes next to piles of clothes and personal effects. She's just obtained a master's degree in fine arts, and her lease coincided with the end of the school year—she had to be out by the end of the week.

"Listen," she said, "first thing tomorrow morning I'm going to take the photos from the altercation with the students at the car and bring them to the UT newspaper. This is something they've got to publish. I want to give them the whole story, not just the pictures. Let's sit over here," she said, clearing debris off of the small table next to the tiny kitchen. I helped her write it out; within two hours, it was neatly typed and ready to be published alongside the photos.

It was a satisfactory moment that brought back the times we worked together more than two years earlier during the siege of Kettys-Burg Hall.

I spent the next morning tidying up while Mir developed the pictures at the student newspaper office. When she came back in the middle of the afternoon, she uncharacteristically slammed the door, threw her bag onto the sofa and hissed, "Bastards!"

"What? Who? Are you all right?" I asked, jumping up from the kitchen chair and approaching her, assuming that she'd been accosted or threatened, perhaps by the same students who'd gone after me the day before.

"The sons of bitches at the newspaper wouldn't take our story. Won't print the photos, nothing to do with what we went through. Real pricks!"

I kept my distance as she paced around the living area, carrying on a conversation as much with herself as with me.

"'It's a false narrative' the editor said to me. Can you believe that?" she asked rhetorically. "'We don't glorify baby killers,' he said. Then, I thought my ears were on fire when he added, 'I'm surprised he didn't take out a gun and shoot the kids.' He meant you, Jacobo. 'We were attacked, unprovoked,' I told him, 'spat upon, hit, punched.' He said, 'Fascists don't get coverage; take your stuff and go.'"

"What's happening?" was all I could say. "How did things change? Just two years ago…" I trailed off. Then I added, "Maybe it's the war. It's driving people crazy."

"It's more than that, Jacobo. About the only thing that hasn't changed in the two years that you've been away is that gas is still at thirty cents a gallon. African Americans have kicked whites out of the Civil Rights Movement. Raised fists. Black power. *Crime in the streets* is the slogan of the day, and you know what that means. The guy who said, 'segregation now, segregation tomorrow, segregation forever' is going to run for president. *President.* Can you believe someone so unqualified is going to run? He's going to get a lot of white votes by the way. It's deplorable. And now, of course, an anti-Semite can hide behind the curtain of anti-Zionism and not be accused of being a bigot. Around here? *Don't trust anyone over thirty* is repeated as if it's the new Pledge of Allegiance. Soldiers are murderers. Hello yesterday. And who do you think is going to get blamed when the USS America goes down for the third time? Take a guess."

"You don't have to spell it out," I said wearily.

"Say it, Jacobo. When you hear it yourself, that's when you can start to believe it."

"I know, I know. People like you, me, Herzl, Ben Veniste."

"Look, I'm not Chicken Little, not saying the sky is falling, but I'm going to add *now* to the end of it. It's not falling *now*."

"You mean yet," I said.

We were silent, Mir was now slumped in the sofa. I went back to the kitchen chair.

"Maybe we could ride it out in Arroyo Grande," I said to lighten up the mood. "It technically doesn't exist, you know. They'd never find us."

She made a face.

"Fight or flight," I said.

"How do we know which to choose?" she asked.

"Well," I said with a hint of a mile, "it isn't flight or fight. I think it's in this order for a reason. I'll try fighting first. And I won't have to put on my uniform."

CHAPTER 27

Recognized

but not approached

It sounded good when I said it. What did it mean? How do you fight when you're just one person? Two, counting Mir. What arrows did we have in our quivers? Going up against the guy at the student newspaper to argue a case was as foolhardy as the Medieval disputations between Jews and Catholics—usually converted Jews—set up by popes and kings to prove the superiority of Christianity and the illegitimacy of Judaism. To say the goose was cooked for the Jews was an understatement, and it certainly wasn't going to work in the campus environment of 1967.

Mao said political power grows out of the barrel of a gun. That's okay if you have a half a billion people following in lockstep. We'd seen the devastating effect of a gun with Medgar Evers and JFK and were hoping that kind of thing wasn't going to happen in the future. I'd killed VC in Vietnam.

But what works in the absence of guns?

I was stymied, waiting for Mir to return with her deposit from the landlord.

"We have to think of something," I said perfunctorily when she walked in.

"Myles won a contest with a police chief, albeit using a plagiarized speech. David Sussman started and finished a word fight over the airwaves," she said.

"I just don't see what we could do."

Mir wouldn't buy into my dejected tone.

"We could do something as a team," she said hopefully.

"Like Laurel and Hardy or Abbott and Costello," I replied snottily, feeling low about the prospects of actually making a difference.

"Well, how about Eleanor and Franklin Roosevelt instead?" she said.

"To the manor born we're not," I said, my melancholia on display.

"How about pens and photos together being mightier than the sword? A new genre," she said.

My nod was in concert with my head making a semicircular rotation, along with an exaggerated eye roll.

"Look, mister pouty, I was thinking of James Agee and Walker Evans. It makes sense, you know, especially with one of us being a writer and the other a photographer. Let us now praise *in*famous men," she said.

I went from low to high as quickly as a switch turns on a light. Even before we moved to the sofa and got comfy with some pillows, I apologized profusely for my childish behavior, and she accepted it by giving me a kiss.

It was the right time to talk to her about how I'd misled her and the others about my wound, more than two years earlier.

"Listen, I have to tell you something."

"Sure. What's up, buddy boy?"

"It's about glass houses and throwing stones."

"Don't be so cryptic," she said, arranging photos on the table.

"The bandana."

"The ban*dana*!" she exclaimed. "What are you talking about? *Your* bandana of all things?"

"Yeah, well, it's not really about the bandana as much as it's about how it covered up the wound."

"What's there to tell?"

"Well, I fell down the fire escape on the building at the corner of Broadway and Worthington. It collapsed. While I was on it."

"Oh my God. Was this before or after you got hit by the cop?"

"See, that's what I want to tell you. Confession: there was no cop. Well, there was a cop, but I didn't get hit by him."

She turned to stare at me intently.

"Remember the cop who stopped us when we were on the way from your dorm to get pictures developed? And he had a short conversation with me? You asked what was *that* all about? Well, when the fire escape broke free from the building, I was on it. I was coming down from the roof where I'd been observing the goings-on in the streets. My head slammed into the ground, and my foot was caught between steps. I couldn't free myself. That's when a guy came over—a real muscular guy, but still I don't know how he managed to spread the metal steps. Anyway, he freed my foot, helped me up, took me across the street to a luncheonette, got some ice, put it against the wound, and wrapped a dishtowel around it in the shape of a bandana. He was just some guy in chinos and a blue shirt. A good Samaritan. But I realized when he walked away, that he must've been one of the cops I'd observed when I was up on the roof who'd shed his uniform to pretend that he was just an ordinary person. He left me to go plunge into the crowd. He was one of the cops who started the riot. Or at least made it worse. And when I saw him that night when you and I were walking to the photo lab, he and I recognized each other."

"You couldn't just tell us? You had to make us believe that you'd been in the midst of it all? So we'd think of you as what, a *hero*?"

I shook my head.

"I hadn't planned to say anything. At all. It's just that once that split second came and went without me setting the record straight, I got locked in. I thought it'd be worse to correct myself—to then be called a hypocrite—than to simply not say anything. I never actually told anyone I'd been part of the fight, although I know that's not an excuse."

"All this time," she said. "Who else knows? Everyone but me?"

"You're the first I've told," I said.

"Is there anything else you need to unload on me? Might as well do it now."

"No. Nothing."

"The story of you and Hank with the Holyman?"

"All true. One hundred percent."

"Of how you met me at Myles' place?"

"Just the way it happened."

"Of how you lost your notebook and then recreated it in jail?"

"Not a word of fiction."

"Of how you were arrested?"

"Just the way I told it."

"Of Navajo Joe and the sergeant being in the War and both getting shot?"

"Yup."

"Of how Herzl discovered that you were a Jew?"

"Same."

"Am I missing anything? Any small thing?"

"No, nothing, nothing at all."

"Even the mailman story?"

With that she approached me and started to smile. And I did too. The mailman who I thought was a cop and how Herzl and I must've looked to him. It made us both laugh.

"Oh, Jacobo, if I didn't love you so much, I'd grab a dishtowel and slap your forehead. Hard. I'd leave a mark as bad as your wound. Listen to me. I'm not going to say this another time: don't you ever, *ever* lie to me again. I don't want to hear a little lie, a white lie, a lie of omission. Don't even think about an exaggeration, forget about stretching the truth. Got that?"

"I do, yes. I'm sorry, really sorry."

"You've got to face the music with Ben Veniste and Herzl."

"I will."

She moved to the kitchen table, opened up a box of photos that she'd taken at the UT during the street confrontations and the take-over of the administration building, and pulled out a copy of the pages that I'd typed and sketched in jail more than two years earlier—the ones I'd given to Navajo Joe the day I left to go into the army. My father had translated them for her when I was in Vietnam. She spread out the pages and the photos, along with some new shots that she'd taken, including those of Blueberry Creek, the tunnel under Kettys-Burg Hall, Ben Veniste at his café, the bicycles that we used to carry food to the students who'd occupied the administration building, the young Mexican men from the café who assisted us, the open window through which Herzl made his escape, the darkroom at the bookstore, the campus radio station and newspaper office, the boathouse, the old wooden shell—that had been returned—the embankments along the Rio Grande, the park where I lost the notebook, the side of the road where I was arrested, the jail where I was locked up, me at Travis Air Force Base, and me with Hank at the VA Hospital in Albuquerque.

She also had a copy of the article that was published in *Life Magazine* in 1965 under her byline. We began that night to work on assembling these photos and my notebook into a linear sequence of events that would capture the activities at the UT with perspective and nuance. We agreed that once we were confident that we had an important story to tell in a way that would be understandable to those who weren't there, we'd present this to publishers who might be intrigued by the idea of this personal inside history.

Intrigued as I was by these memories, I was fascinated by the recent pictures Mir had taken of Chief Townsend as a candidate for mayor of Taos Heights. He stood in front of an enormous American flag banner, caught with a snarl and a bit of spittle, while speaking into a microphone in front of a crowd that didn't include a single person under fifty. Unbeknownst to Claudia, Mir had caught her upbraiding a cowering younger student at a rally, presumably for some infraction of a rule that she'd more than likely never issued. And, too, there were shots of Myles—at the bookstore, then walking home by himself, tweed jacket slung over his shoulder, cigarette dangling with long ash from his lips as he strolled on the Worthington Strip, recognized but not approached. He appeared to be living in his own world, which I characterized as a place where doubts weren't tolerated, self-reflection was outside the law, and third-party admonitions were inaudible. These were all the elements necessary for a self-aggrandizing one-time leader to use to try to claw back into the public sphere under the guise of having been wronged and seeking recompense. Victimhood, I said to myself, can be a dangerous platform that one person might see as a ledge and another as a springboard.

The next day, I went to the café and apologized to Ben Veniste. When I was finished, he said simply, "Youthful indiscretion," then motioned for me to approach him. He hugged me, tapped his cane gently against my leg, the signal to disengage.

He stood up and told me to come with him to the counter, where he pulled a piece of paper out of a pile and told me to read it.

"It's a telegram from Herzl."

רשות הדואר

TELEGRAM מברק برقية

❑ בארץ في البلاد ❑ לחו"ל للخارج ❑ לאניה للسفينة

❑ במעבר بالواسطة
❑ נכנס الوارد

תאריך משלוח تاريخ الإرسال	שעה الساعة	מספר מלים عدد الكلمات	מסי מלים לתשלום عدد الكلمات للدفع	הסכום	המבלغ שייח شاقل جديد	הוראות שירות تعليمات الخدمة

חותמת יחידת הדואר ختم فرع البريد

מספר מקורי الرقم الاصلي

שודר בשעה ابرقت في الساعة

בידי من قبل

מסי סודר رقم التسلسل | אל الى

ADDRESSEE تفاصيل المرسل اليه (برقية للخارج - سجل باللغة الاجنبية) **פרטי הנמען** (במברק לחו"ל רשום בלועזית)

NAME RICARDO BENVENISTE השם الاسم

STREET & NO. 2128 CAMBRIDGE STREET רחוב ומסי בית الشارع ورقم البيت

LOCALITY TAOS HEIGHTS, NEW MEXICO יישוב البلدة

COUNTRY UNITED STATES OF AMERICA ארץ היעד البلاد المقصودة

TEXT: התוכן: المضمون:

JUNE 16, 1967

SHALOM, RICARDO. I'M OK. NOTHING TO WORRY ABOUT. WAS WITH AN UGDAH AT ABU AGEILA. CAN'T SAY MORE. IF ONLY IAF HAD EXISTED TO BOMB THE RAILS. NEVER AGAIN. GOING TO THE GOLAN. A NEW KIBBUTZ. WILL TEACH ENGLISH AND TRY TO GET RID OF MY AMERICAN ACCENT. BE HOME DEC 26 FOR 1ST NIGHT. HAVE HANUKIAH, WILL TRAVEL. JEWISH PALADIN. SHARE WITH MIR AND JACOBO. SEND LOVE AND KISSES TO DEBORA. HERZL.

פרטי השולח (לא לשידור)
تفاصيل المرسل (ليست للارسال)
SENDER'S PARTICULARS
(NOT TO BE TRANSMITTED)

שם الاسم NAME: HERZL SCHNEIDER

מען العنوان ADR.: 4 BEIT LEKHAM ST. BE'ER SHEVA

טלפון هاتف TEL.: 057-273976

חתימה التوقيع SIGN.: Herzl Schneider

ר"ח (1/95)

426-05 במקום 748-0092

ראה מעבר לדף תנאי חלוקת המברקים ביישובים השונים

من الخلف تجد تفاصيل عن توزيع البرقيات في القرى المختلفة

CHAPTER 28

Tell me with whom you go,

and I'll tell you who you are

We finished four months later. Then came the hard part: we didn't know how to get it published. We'd been so engrossed in the *what* that we spent no time on the *how.* Mir called the assistant editor who'd helped her at *Life Magazine*, but this woman had no relationships in the world of book publishing. We thought about sending a summary of the book along with the first chapter over the transom to publishers in New York, but without an introduction from a previously published author or a celebrity, we realized that our submission would be placed into a slush pile, never to be read. We lamented our woes at dinner with Ben Veniste at the café.

He listened intently and then said, "I'm going to call Shuky Goldman from the David Sussman Show."

"What are you going to tell him?" I asked. "It's only a manuscript, and we're nobodies."

"I'm going to say that the 'nobodies' who got Sussman the third-highest ever Nielsen rating with the interview with Myles in 1965 have written a book with some revelations about what *really* happened during the Free Speech Movement. Behind-the-scenes stuff. I'll tell him that one of them is the photographer who got all the pictures of what was going on, and the other is the guy who took the notes from inside of Kettys-Burg Hall and actually wrote the speech that Myles gave. My pitch to Shuky is really simple: ask David Sussman to make an introduction for the two of you to his book agent. I mean, come on, he owes me one, don't you think? Oh, and I'm going to get it in there that the two of you are Jews."

Needless to say, we were elated. We toasted with glasses of sangria. We got a little loopy. He tapped his cane lightly on the floor next to his chair, something he'd do instead of clapping.

It turned out he was right. It took a few months, but after Sussman's agent read the summary and the first chapter, she wanted the whole manuscript.

Herzl returned from Israel the day after Christmas, exhilarated yet fatigued. I noticed he didn't want to shake, preferring instead to drape his arm over a shoulder. His fist remained clenched. When I asked him about it privately, he opened it up slowly to reveal it was puffy with a streak of yellow and black, roughly parallel to where some stitch marks were still visible.

"It hurts," he said.

"I'm pretty sure it's infected," I said. "You've got to have it looked at, pronto."

"It was all right at first," he said. "They stitched me up in the field. Got cut removing shells from boxes. A nail. Scraped. I thought over time it'd be okay."

"Listen," I said, "I don't want to cause you any more pain, but I have something to tell you."

I came clean on *my* wound.

He listened intently. I told him of my conversations with Mir and Ben Veniste.

This is what he said: "Look, Jacobo, on the scale of things, it's pretty minor. Putting ourselves in a better light is what we do. Intentionally or not. Everyone does. Sometimes proactively, other times, well, we can't account for the *why* we do it, we just know *that* we've done it. It's the self-awareness that counts, regardless of when you see the light. Sooner is better, but later is acceptable; it's at least an acknowledgment of a wrong. Should you feel guilty? My guess is that's why you're telling me."

"Guilt, sure, but it's really shame. And remorse."

"Think of it this way," he said, "you're way ahead on the atonement schedule. You've repented ahead of time."

That made me feel better.

"Now let's get my hand fixed, okay?" he said.

"I'll get Mir to call her father."

She arranged for Herzl to drive to Albuquerque that night, where he was met by Benjamin Tudela, who walked him into the emergency room at the hospital to have his wound cleaned, debrided, treated with an antibiotic, and bandaged.

The next morning, Herzl drove south to Arroyo Grande, stayed for a few days, then returned to Taos Heights with Débora, a bandage on his hand and a sparkle in his eye. This, despite knowing he wouldn't be able to train for rowing for months, putting an end to his hopes of competing in Mexico City. He never complained about it.

We celebrated the four of us being together at the café. We drank coffee and shared *buréks*, Madre having given the recipe to Débora to bring to Ben Veniste. Then, Herzl mentioned that he had a couple of things to tell us.

"About Israel?" Mir asked.

"The first thing, yes."

"Is it a victory lap?" I asked, knowing how excited he was about the outcome of the Six-Day War.

He pulled a slip of paper out of his pocket. "This came to me in a dream," he said. "When I woke up, freezing my *tush* off in a tent in the Golan after midnight, I immediately wrote it down so I wouldn't forget it. Sometimes, you know, you say or hear something so clearly when you're out of it, but then when you wake up, you've either forgotten it completely or it all comes out in a jumble, and you wrack your brains trying to figure out what was it that so got your attention. Anyway, here it is."

He read the following: *Israel is a state that's bordered by threats and built upon a foundation of texts. Remove the former, and it'll fulfill its mission to be the light unto all the nations. Remove the latter, and it'll become a country like any other.*

I was struck by its elegance and simplicity. This was Herzl to the core. In a flash, I could tell what was coming. So I just came out with it: "Are you going to make *aliyah*?" I asked.

"Well, I'm not going to give up citizenship, if that's what you're asking. How long we'll be there, I just can't say." The *we* was a dead giveaway that my sister was going with him.

We toasted the two of them and asked some questions about what Herzl had done when he was there; he was evasive, giving little more than what he'd written in the telegram. Neither Mir nor I ever bought the hurt-my-hand-when-a-nail-scraped-it-moving-a-box story. However, we didn't push.

Mir said, "You said you had several things to say."

"I wasn't sure I was going to bring it up, but I think I should. I ran into Myles yesterday."

We were all shocked.

"Oh my God, really? Did he say anything to you? You to him?" Mir asked.

"I turned a corner on Vista—how appropriate, huh—and bumped into him. He cut the corner too close. He wasn't looking up and didn't know it was me. He said 'Excuse me, sorry.' At first, I didn't realize it was Myles and said, 'No problem.' Then, seeing who it was and trying to be conciliatory, I said, 'It was bound to happen.' You know, running into him at some point. He stared at me. I don't know why I didn't mosey along. I had nothing more to say to him, but it was as if I were stuck in cement, waiting for him to say something. It was really bizarre."

"Did he? Say anything?" I asked.

"You're not going to believe this. What he said was, 'Ah, the return of the wandering Jew.'"

"First off, it's more than bizarre," Mir said quickly. "It's anti-Semitic. So like Myles. The 'wandering' thing. Do you think he meant returning from when you went out the window?"

"My guess is that it had to do with coming back from Israel," I said. "No doubt he was keeping tabs on you, I'm sure."

"Yeah, you're probably right. But what gets me is that it came out as if he'd been planning it, waiting for a time he'd run into me," Herzl said.

"He's an actor," Mir said. "He remembers his lines."

"*T'shuva* for you but no *t'shuva* for him," Débora said. "For you," she looked at Herzl, "it's all about returning from Israel, but," her head turning to me, "for Myles, there's no repentance until he asks forgiveness from you." Her short declaratory statement had captured the double meaning of the word so well that we had nothing to add.

There was no chance that Myles was going to ask for forgiveness. Despite the revelations about his sexual proclivities, anti-Semitism, plagiarism, and hypocrisy vis-à-vis free speech, he wasn't shamed in the least. He dropped out of the doctoral program, citing its bourgeois nature. In an interview with an underground paper, he actually quoted the Groucho Marx line, "I don't want to belong to any club that would accept me as one of its members" in response to why he wasn't going to pursue an academic career. When it was pointed out that it was ironic that he was parroting a line made famous by a Jew, he denied ever making that statement, notwithstanding the fact that the student reporter had a tape of what Myles had said.

The former leader of the Free Speech Movement channeled his considerable energy into coordinating activities among fringe groups, whose missions and tactics might have differed, but whose commitment to publicizing the role of an international Zionist conspiracy to control the world was a unifying force. Myles could cite his own experience as proof, railing against Herzl's treachery, Mir's deceit, Ben Veniste's complicity, Sussman's collusion, and my inauthentic claims of authorship. "It was a planned coordinated conspiracy," he said when interviewed on the campus radio station, "to create this preposterous lie that a barely literate Jew who assumed an Indian persona to generate sympathy wrote the Kettys-Burg Address." He didn't stop there, going on to call both Herzl and me war criminals, and to accuse Claudia of being a lesbian and a Jew lover.

THE FOUR OF us got up to go. As my sister placed her arms around Herzl's neck, she said, "*Dime kon ken vas, te dire ke sosh—Tell me with whom you go, and I'll tell you who you are.*"

CHAPTER 29

It's not time

On the last day of the year, I got a call from David Sussman's agent.

"Happy New Year," I said to Mir, walking into the living room. "Sit tight, I've got news for you. Great news. Are you ready?"

"About tonight?"

"No, no. Listen, the agent called. She wants us to negotiate a contract and work on a few revisions of what she's calling *Kettys-Burg and the Address*."

Mir bolted off the sofa and jumped into my arms—the way Nohemi used to do.

"When do they want to publish it?" she asked, her head dropping backwards, her smile incandescent.

"November 19, 1968, the 105th anniversary of Lincoln's speech."

She slid down and landed both feet on top of mine, keeping her arms around my neck; we danced as one, around the furniture, laughing and kissing.

Giddy, we collapsed onto the sofa and let it all sink in. After a few minutes, Mir stood up and looked down at me.

"Okay, I have some news too," she said.

"It can't be any better than this, but go ahead, I'm game."

She waited a few seconds, switched to her serious face, and said, "I think it's good. Yes, I know it is."

"Okay, out with it," I said.

"The test results came back. I'm not pregnant. I'm relieved," she said. "It's not time."

We celebrated both things that New Year's Eve.

CHAPTER 30

Mir stole the show

At the start of the publicity tour, we were booked on the David Sussman Show in January of 1969., again in Albuquerque. Our excitement was offset by nervousness over his *modus operandi*, which was on display when he'd interviewed Myles in 1965. Ben Veniste had just come back from what he told us was his first vacation in years. He was in especially good spirits and eager to assist us when we asked him to impersonate David Sussman, even so far as pretending to smoke. We had him not only asking edgy questions that we composed ourselves but also gave him the opportunity to lean in and extemporaneously probe with something we hadn't thought of—and to do so in a sneering way—to best acclimate us to what really could be in store when the lights went down and the mic went on. We did this several times. It was wearying. We worried it might even have the opposite effect, as if we'd overstudied for an exam, walked into the room, and got a blue book whose blank pages reflected just how little we knew about the course for that semester.

But we did our homework. We spent endless hours in the library going over microfilms of newspapers that carried the stories of the Freedom Summer. We scanned articles for the anecdotes that Myles had recounted at his apartment and searched for mentions of his name in Alabama and Mississippi police reports. We interviewed UT professors of American history and borrowed copies of scholarly journals that chronicled the emergence of the Freedom Rides and read them seeking passages that sounded like Myles' soliloquies. We amassed a pretty good-sized file to be able to say there was a pattern of Myles' spoken and written words appearing to be said and penned first by others. Legally not a crime, but enough to generate decidedly unfavorable headlines in newspapers and broadcasts. And it certainly added context to the earlier plagiarism issue.

We rounded up the names of female students from the manager of the bookstore where Myles worked and requested interviews of their relationships with him, promising to keep their names confidential. We were only able to get a few to cooperate, but in a variety of ways, they told stories that fit a pattern of aggressive behavior that occasionally turned forceful; we didn't find a single association that turned out well. Some denied knowing him, others were no longer in the city, and a couple were hesitant to reveal anything that would bring back unpleasant intimate encounters, especially since they'd never told anyone about their personal interactions with him. And we did have Mir's account of Myles pressing her breasts against his chest in a romantic fashion. Yet, had we been lawyers looking to present a case, we wouldn't have had all the goods to go to the DA to get an indictment, and we weren't sure that we'd ever have enough to enable people to see this as a legitimate matter and not simply as salacious material to garner headlines. So, while it was *something*, it wasn't enough. What we needed was for Claudia to come forth.

On the issue of anti-Semitism, we had first-person observations, corroborated by my notes taken on a contemporaneous basis. Most important, however, was Mir's reminder that the police had tapped the phones at Kettys-Burg Hall. She went to the police department, never revealing her true mission, and told them that she was writing a graduate paper on anti-Semitism and wondered if anyone there could recall student leaders making negative comments about Jews to the cops during the takeover of Kettys-Burg Hall. She never mentioned Myles by name. Cleverly, she didn't reveal that we were aware of the phone taps. She said that she'd sign a document not to reveal names. She not only got them to talk—and tell her about Myles' comments—one of them casually mentioned that there were tapes of his calls with the police during the free speech takeover of the administration building. As she listened to them and surreptitiously created a copy of the tapes by using the small recorder she kept in her pocketbook, she knew she had the goods on Myles. But what she found extraordinary was a comment that Myles made to the chief near the end of the siege of Kettys-Burg Hall. Speaking to him about Claudia, Myles said, "She's just a tramp who wants to hump her way to the top of the Movement. At least if she was any good."

This was what they call 'the smoking gun.'

Mir tracked Claudia down under the pretense of shooting a pictorial spread on what happened to the leaders of the Free Speech Movement for *Life Magazine*. Claudia was hesitant to meet up with Mir at first, but my wife's persistence fed into Claudia's vanity. After listening to the tape, Claudia penned a scathing letter to the editor of the *Albuquerque Tribune* that received an enormous amount of attention:

WHAT DOESN'T MAKE THE HEADLINES

I read the report in Sunday's newspaper that Mir Tudela and Jacobo Toledano would be appearing on the David Sussman program this coming Thursday at 8 p.m. to discuss their recent book *Kettys-Burg and the Address.* As I was a key participant in the takeover of the aforementioned administration building at the University of Taos in the fall of 1964, I thought it would be appropriate for me to weigh in on a particular activity during the so-called Free Speech Movement, inasmuch as I was not invited to participate in the TV show alongside Tudela and Toledano.

What made the headlines of the *Tribune* and other papers across the country was that the student takeover ended peacefully after a speech–*The Address*–was delivered by graduate student Myles Bradford III. It defused a confrontation before it became violent and spun out of control. Subsequently, we found out that Bradford had plagiarized the speech. It will be reported on Sussman's show that it was Toledano himself who wrote the speech and that Tudela and Toledano's book provides incontrovertible visual proof of the theft.

What hasn't been publicized is that the "sexual revolution" that was—and still is—taking place on college campuses (some people call it the 'era of free love') isn't marked exclusively by equality in the relationships between young men and women. How do I know this? I, myself, was a victim, taken advantage of inside Kettys-Burg Hall by a predator, who used me for gratification and then—like nothing has changed—engaged in 'locker room talk' with others, painting me as a person without morals. All of this was captured on tape and will be discussed on Sussman's show. I'm not embarrassed by any of my behavior. I wonder if the predator will be after he hears his own voice. Stay tuned.

Claudia Novak
Santa Fe

Although Claudia spilled the beans on our closely guarded secret that I was the author of *The Address* and gave a jab at us for not being invited onto the show, her letter was picked up by the AP and reported across the country, which helped build the buzz before our appearance later that week.

We were alternately confident and nervous as the date for our appearance on the David Sussman program approached.

Sussman started by asking Mir to tell the audience about her background.

"I'm from India," she said. "I came with my parents right after the war that separated Pakistan from India in 1948. They felt that no matter who won, we'd lose."

"Why is that?" Sussman asked.

"Because we're Jews. It always seems to work out that way."

"From the Bene Israel community?" he asked. "The people who some scholars think are one of the Lost Tribes," he offered for the audience who may not have known of his reference to this group of Jews.

"No, we were from Cochin, on the coast. Our ancestors came after theirs. Now, both of the communities are much smaller."

"Many have gone to Israel," he said. "But your parents chose America."

"We spoke English. It'd be easier to assimilate," Mir said.

"You speak Hindi, I presume," he said.

Mir nodded, forgetting momentarily that answering in words on television has more impact than head tics or hand motions.

For the next fifteen or twenty minutes it was as if we'd written the script. Sussman quoted passages from Karlstein's book and Claudia's letter to the editor. He played the tape. Sometimes his questions on Myles' fraudulent writings, vile treatment of women, and anti-Semitism were more statements with conclusions than interrogatories, which made it easy for us to comment.

After what appeared to be his last comment on Myles, he pivoted to me.

"And you, Jacobo? Can you tell us about your background?" he asked.

Once he got our histories out of the way, he could get to the book, which was on the coffee table between us. I had a riff that would get us out of biography mode and into a discussion of the book within less than a minute. I was pumped up.

"I was born here in New Mexico, in a little town a couple of hundred miles to the southwest. Arroyo Grande. About a thousand people."

"What languages do *you* speak?" he asked.

"Other than English, primarily Spanish," I responded.

"Primarily?"

"I do speak another one. At home. It's a little like Spanish. Some of the words are the same, but it's not as close as Italian is with Spanish."

"Ladino," he said.

"Yes." I was impressed that he'd figured it out.

"The language of the Jews who were kicked out of Spain in 1492."

"Uh-huh, correct," I said.

"Who pretended to be Catholics but were secretly Jews."

"There are some like that, but not us. We're just Jews."

"Who have a church in the middle of your village but no outward signs of a synagogue. Sounds like pretending to me. Can you explain that?" he said.

I couldn't figure out how he was aware of this and why he was on this tack. I had the dark thought that this was going to be Myles redux.

"My ancestors came in 1677 when this area was still part of Mexico and the Inquisition was in full bloom. It gave them cover in case they were discovered."

"I understand that you're a good storyteller," he said.

"If that's a compliment to Mir and me on our book, thank you," I said, noticing Mir's smile at my rejoinder.

"That may be, but what I'm getting at is stories from Arroyo Grande. From your father."

How would he know about them?

"We didn't have home movies. No TV. And radio came on only very late at night. Batteries. We didn't have electricity. So they'd tell stories to me and my sisters after dinner on Friday nights. You could think of this as part of our entertainment."

"About a made-up man, as tall as two, someone like Superman, I presume," he said.

And about this?

"You could think of it that way, yes," I said.

I had no clue where this was going.

"He'd come to the aid of children in trouble, fighting off enemies, killing them," he said.

"Sometimes, sure."

"You called him the Holyman, didn't you?"

"Yes."

"Murdering is holy—was that the message of these stories?" he asked, staring at me intently. Although the air conditioning was on high for the lights and the cameras, I began to feel warm.

"They're stories. Fables. Tall tales."

"What did you take away from them?" he asked.

"I don't know what you mean."

"Were they just stories or something you could use as a blueprint to act on in the future?" he said.

"They were like what other kids hear as ghost stories. Nothing more."

"So you never thought of yourself as the Holyman?" he said.

"That's ridiculous," I said, realizing I had to make sure my annoyance did not come out.

"Is it?" he asked as he reached down to pull out a piece of paper from a file on the coffee table. "I have here a statement from a member of the First battalion, Third Marines, from May 14, 1966, in which he states that he was told by a medic named Hank Banaszek that you killed seven innocent Vietnamese men working in a rubber plantation, surprising them as they sat eating lunch while you were pretending to be the Holyman."

"This is absurd," I said, on the verge of losing my cool.

"Are you calling..." he scanned the piece of paper, "Lance Corporal Weaver a liar?"

I took a deep breath and made sure my words were measured, delivered in a straight-forward manner. I looked him squarely in the eye.

"That name's not familiar. I honestly don't know who he is or what he thought he heard from Hank. Or when. Unfortunately, Hank died," I said, ignoring the trap of responding to his question about whether I thought this Marine was a liar. Let's face it. If I said he was, there'd be a confrontation that could easily turn ugly. If I said he wasn't, then I was admitting his version of the facts. This might've been the first time I hadn't given a direct answer to a question, a sign of comprehension of how and when to maneuver through conversations—a trait that should be taught as early as one learns the declensions of words. If only.

"How convenient," Sussman said sarcastically.

I knew I couldn't make a scene the way Myles did, which ended with him living a life of ignominy. This was theater, and I was in the role of an improv performer, up against someone who had a script. However, I couldn't let my disadvantage be an excuse for getting a bad review.

"I want to tell you what happened, Mr. Sussman, in Vietnam," I said, respectfully, ignoring the audience as I watched the cameraman come in closer to me so that the frame could reveal an intimacy between me and the hundreds of thousands of people watching from home.

I gave him the account of how the VC had ambushed our platoon and killed everyone except Hank and me who were perched in the trees. How we walked and crawled through the jungle, trying to find the way back to our lines. I went into detail of our realization that the VC who attacked us were on the other side of the berm in the rubber plantation and got up to demonstrate my climbing onto Hank's shoulders with the M-16 and Colt .45, which gave me the vantage point to see them clearly and to shoot them. I didn't leave out saying *zit-jyet* in Vietnamese or of telling Hank I got the idea from the Holyman stories.

"Let me add this," I said calmly, "I'd do it again in a heartbeat. My guess, with all due respect to Corporal Weaver, is that he fell victim to the kind of game little kids play when they sit in a circle and someone starts by whispering something into the ear of the kid sitting next to him and asks him to pass it on. By the time it finally gets back to the one who started it all, it's like night and day from what he originally whispered.

"You have to understand," I said, "with all the chopper noise—unless you've been in a Huey you can't comprehend it—plus the pilot practically screaming into the radio, Marines firing indiscriminately into the trees to make sure we could take off safely, and the excitement of Hank telling him what happened, he got mixed up, that's all. And you know what? It's war. It's insanity. It's a different reality.

"I'd say this to Corporal Weaver if he were standing right here: you said what you thought you heard. I buy that. It's okay. I don't hold a grudge."

David Sussman bent down to grab the book, then lifted his head, clearly a signal for the camera directly opposite to focus on him, and said, "We'll be back in sixty seconds. Stay put to hear all about '*Kettys-Burg and the Address*'." He held the pose for another second until he got the signal from the cameraman that he was off the air.

"You want to sell books. I need to sell ads," Sussman said to me in a businesslike manner, "and this is the way I get ratings." He then offered me an olive branch by saying, "You're as cool as a cucumber, young man."

The three of us sat in silence until Sussman got the thumbs up from the director. My mind was racing as to how he knew about the Holyman and the events in Vietnam with Hank.

"We're back," he said, "with Mir Tudela and Jacobo Toledano, who co-authored the firsthand account of the events surrounding the Free

Speech Movement at the UT here in New Mexico in the fall of nineteen sixty-four. Let me tell you what someone else has written about what these two students experienced." He opened the book and read from the preface:

> "In this book, you'll find the kinds of insights that '*we the people*' hunger for, but are typically denied until documents are declassified thirty or more years later. But with this riveting up-to-the minute chronicle of the movement that jump-started the national conversation on speech, we have the opportunity to get behind-the-scenes to see and read about what went on before the shadow of history plunges us into darkness, when memories fade and fictions become fact.
>
> "This is not merely a chronology of the events at the University of Taos that spawned the Free Speech Movement—that can be understood by reading the pages of newspapers and listening to tapes of news broadcasts that reported on the comings and goings of those days. Instead, the authors have allowed us to understand the subtleties and complexities of an earthquake that rattled the land, shifting the tectonic plates of our society and enabling us to see how the clash between nobility and narcissism didn't end with the French Revolution.
>
> "As *au courant* participants and not just *voyeurs* from a later date, Tudela and Toledano eschew a particular political orientation and instead offer us the opportunity to assess how social actions originate and why they can go off track, oftentimes under the direction of eccentric, narcissistic, or bigoted self-appointed leaders. It's something we need to keep in mind the next time we're inclined to jump on a change train before we know more about the conductor."

"That's from Hayes Jackson, winner of the Pulitzer Prize for his seminal reporting on the deaths of Michael Schwerner, Andrew Goodman, and James Chaney in Neshoba County, Mississippi, in June of 1964," David Sussman said to his national audience.

He began the second part of the interview by referencing photographs from the book that were projected onto a screen at the side of the studio, where a camera could show them to the American people. Despite the fact that I'd been a witness, I was captivated by Mir's exquisitely shot color pictures, spread to life-sized dimensions, practically enabling anyone to insert him or herself into the history, much as Walter Cronkite did on the CBS show *You Are There* in the nineteen fifties.

Sussman used the photos as props to ask us questions, doing so in a way to illustrate the larger issues and not resorting to the snarkiness of the first part of the show. He'd done his homework, and I had to give him credit. But Mir stole the show. She was able to transport us back to the UT and give context as well as content. Her explanations were succinct. She had the answer to every one of his questions no matter how obscure the reference. She knew instinctively when to make eye contact with Sussman and when to switch to the people watching. The camera ate her up.

At the very end, he acknowledged Myles' appearance on the show four years earlier and gave assurances, unprompted by us, that the portrait that we'd painted of him hadn't been tinged with *schadenfreude* by dint of our writing of his anti-Semitic remarks or his inappropriate touching of Mir.

With that, he made his customary leave, turning abruptly and walking away, the stage fading to black when he exited stage right.

CHAPTER 31

So do something about it

Early the next morning, I put in a call to the pay phone at The Trading Post. My father got on the line. I gave him a download of what'd happened on the David Sussman Show. Then I asked him point blank: "Do you have any idea how he would've known about Arroyo Grande? The church? The stories? The Holyman? Ladino?"

"What does he look like?" my father asked.

"Why?"

"If you describe him, I might recall his being here."

"You mean at The Trading Post."

"Yes."

I did my best.

"I can't recall anyone who looked like that. But even if I don't have the right picture in my mind, I'd never speak to a stranger about these things."

I was stumped. I didn't know what more I could ask.

Then my father said, "A few weeks ago, I did say a few things to Ricardo."

"Ben Veniste? He calls you and you open up about the Holyman? Or the church?"

"He was here," my father said. "He drove down. He stayed a few days with us. It would've been rude not to tell him some things. I didn't see any harm. He's one of us, and he's been so kind to you. It was an honor to have him here. He was delighted to learn about us."

It wasn't difficult to put it all together. I was sure Ben Veniste thought he was doing us a favor by speaking to Shuky Goldman and giving him some background on me to assist David Sussman in preparing for the interview. Knowing Sussman, he had someone on his staff do some research, and one thing led to another—that's how it goes—and he ended up with Corporal Weaver's account of what happened in Vietnam.

"Personal history isn't private anymore," is what Mir said when I got off the phone.

"What concerns me is that someone with an agenda who tuned into the show will be fixated on Arroyo Grande and not in a good way. They could write something as pernicious as *The Protocols*. It'd be the end of Arroyo Grande as we know it."

"So do something about it," she said.

"Like what? I can't stop anyone from finding the place. You don't need a visa to get in. Or to talk to people."

"Write it yourself, Jacobo. Take it on. I'll help you."

I heard Herzl's words ricocheting in my brain: *If there's anything we Jews have learned in the last twenty years—why it hadn't been already pounded into our pious anemic brains for the 2000 years prior to that I'll never know—is to set our own course and not to depend on others for anything.*

CHAPTER 32

Ladinglish

My wife did indeed provide assistance, not only by taking beautiful photos but also by editing all the drafts and working with our agent to get the galleys into the hands of those who could write blurbs and reviews for it. We'd worked closely with the ten members of the *konsilyo* to ensure accuracy of, and sensitivity to, ancestors and historical events. We stayed in Arroyo Grande, where we worked on the book at the cantina, and held court when friends and relatives would stop by to inquire how it was going but who, in reality, wanted to peek over our shoulders to catch a glimpse of a photo of or paragraph about them. They were solicitous to us in an attempt to get us to write favorable things about them. It reminded me of how my cellmates were eager to know if they were included in what I'd been writing. We did our best to ensure that we incorporated information from the histories of each of the Ávila, Córdoba, Pontevedre, Girona, Alicante, Lisboa and Firenze families.

The book was published in September 1972 under the title *Hiding in Plain Site*. We held a celebration event in the plaza. Herzl and Débora drove down from Taos Heights with Ben Veniste, whose health had been failing for over a year. His cane had been replaced by a walker, and a stairlift had been installed for him at the café, as he could no longer negotiate steps.

Several hundred people gathered in the plaza right before sunset to hear Mir and me give short speeches. After the *Havdalah* service and the *oneg*, Mir and I signed copies of the book donated by our publisher. Mir and I made our way through the crowd, stopping to speak with well-wishing friends and acquaintances. For the most part, I spoke Ladino, which Mir understood, although she was hesitant to speak it, preferring instead to use what we referred to jokingly as Ladinglish.

It was, by any standard, a magical evening topped off by what I overheard my father say to Madre when he thought I was out of earshot as we were making our way back to my parents' house: "*Bendicha tripa de madre ke tal ijo partio*"—*Blessed be the belly of the mother who has given birth to such a son.*

It was the most wonderful compliment to me. I shared it with Mir by placing my hand on her extended abdomen, feeling the little boy's kicks that were becoming more frequent and forceful as we approached her end-of-the-year due date.

"It's good to be in *tierra mana leche i miel*—the land of milk and honey," I said quietly to Mir, who responded by giving me a kiss.

CHAPTER 33

A tribute of sorts

Mir and I visited Ben Veniste at the Hospital in Albuquerque, where he'd been taken after collapsing on the street outside the café, congestive heart failure having reduced him to short breaths and long pauses between words. Mir sat on the edge of the bed, alternately rubbing his hand and gently patting his forehead and neck with a cool, damp cloth. His thank yous were barely audible, unnecessary but heartfelt. For the most part, his eyes were closed, yet we knew that he was seeing us in earlier times through anecdotes and reminiscences.

He was alternating between sleep and wakefulness. His breaths were shallow. We saw his tongue try to lick his lips. Mir held a glass and lifted the straw. It was an effort for him to draw a small sip into his mouth. We didn't know if he had the strength to swallow. His eyes fluttered. He moved the fingers on his left hand slightly, in a manner that signaled he wanted us to come closer. We hovered over him, self-conscious that our tears would fall on his face, so we held tissues in our hands. Suddenly, he seemed to gather a bit of strength and made a concerted effort to turn his head toward us and smile.

"Ka...," he whispered with difficulty. I looked at Mir. She didn't understand either. She bent her head down close to him and asked him what it was that he'd said.

"Ka...kad..." came out in a barely discernible exhale.

"What do you think?" I said softly to Mir. "Is he asking for something?"

"It may be that he's talking in his sleep. A dream perhaps, or to someone else. Maybe it's not meant for us."

He motioned again with the tips of his fingers on one hand, so I placed my right ear directly in front of his lips as Mir asked him again to say it one more time while holding his other hand.

"Yis..." I repeated to Mir, shaking my head from side to side.

A few seconds later, he was gone.

Immediately after leaving his room, I returned, picked up his cane, thumped it quietly a few times on the floor, then took it with me as I walked down the corridor.

I couldn't stop thinking about Ben Veniste's last sounds—I couldn't even swear that they were words. I repeated them over and over, using different inflections and stressing different syllables to see if these tricks would help.

As soon as I signed the papers necessary to have his body taken to the funeral home, I had a revelation. Turning to Mir, I said, "*Kaddish.*"

"What are you talking about?" she asked.

"Ben's sounds. He was saying *Kaddish*. He wants us to say *Kaddish* for him. Now and forever."

We buried him in the cemetery at Arroyo Grande.

Madre, my father, Nohemi, Débora, Herzl, Mir, and I stood silently after we said *Kaddish*. One by one, we shoveled dirt onto the coffin. The six of them started to walk back to the village. I told them I'd be along in a few minutes.

I took a small spiral notebook and pencil out of my pocket. I sketched Ben's face and the gravesite, then wrote the following:

I sit here on the edge of a hill running the reel of my life in microsecond bursts, images of people, events, places, conversations… yet each one distinguishable, memorable, interchangeably eliciting pleasure and sadness.

I grab my shoulders and am comforted by the warmth of the blanket that Ben Veniste threw around me without thought of recompense.

I smile remembering the countless enjoyable interactions with a Native American and thank him for his service.

Joyous intimacies overwhelm me as I watch the woman who inspired me to write and illustrate a living will of a strange people, walk slowly down to the plaza.

I feel the unconditional love from my parents and sisters, evident as their outstretched hands that steady my wife as they take baby steps to ensure that she doesn't fall.

I revel in the pride of kinship with someone burdened with a name that could've crushed a lesser person yet whose exploits have validated his parents' conceit. I stand next to him even when we are thousands of miles apart.

I hustled down the hill to catch up with my wife.

"What were you writing up there?" she asked.

"A tribute, of sorts, to Ben Veniste, Navajo Joe, and all of you," I said.

"I've got one too," she said.

Expecting her to reach into her pocket to pull out a piece of paper, she turned to me, placed my hand on her belly, and said, "Let's name him Ricardo."

CHAPTER 34

You can't just

order up inspiration

like summoning an elevator

After the book was published, we decided we wouldn't start any new assignments during 1973, preferring to spend time with baby Ricardo. That year marked the end of the active American military role in Vietnam as well as the Yom Kippur War in the Middle East, yet we couldn't describe our 1974 world as peaceful. The IRA opened up a bombing campaign in Britain, Turkey invaded Cyprus, and India detonated a nuclear bomb, just to name a few headline-grabbing events. There was a recession stemming from the Arab oil embargo, and we witnessed the first resignation of a U.S. president. All of which contributed to an unanticipated general malaise, which was manifested in reactions to the excesses of the previous decade, an outcome that seemed impossible to accept from those who'd lived through the horrors, then triumphs, of World War II and the landing on the moon.

We began to take on freelance assignments for newspapers and journals but didn't find them satisfying. Then we were asked to be scholars-in-residence at universities which had created retrospectives on the Free Speech Movement. (The irony of me teaching at a university without a degree wasn't lost on us.) We led a nomadic existence, decamping at schools for a semester, offering classes, seminars, lectures for the public, and hosting debates where we acted as moderators for discussions between activists on the Left and Right, who offered competing visions of the American future and assigned blame to the other side for all the seemingly intractable issues of the day.

Frequently, we invited Helen Karlstein, whose book had suggested that nightmares were encroaching on the American dream and that they coincided with a surge in anti-Semitism, surfacing on the campus, in the board room, in Holocaust denial documents, and in the foreign policy establishment, sometimes masquerading as anti-Zionism. Our discussions on stage devolved into a preface for the Q&A encore session that became increasingly hostile as rival audience groups strove to drown out an opposing view in increasingly vile and threatening ways. Physical confrontations became everyday occurrences.

At the end of what turned out to be our last presentation with Helen Karlstein, Mir made the following comments to her after the audience had cleared out:

"We can't stop either the Right or the Left from saying obviously false things? From stirring up a pot that might lead to someone being assaulted?"

"No. You of all people should know this," Helen Karlstein replied. "From your days involved with the Free Speech Movement. About the only thing these folks can't do is yell fire in a crowded theater. Or libel. Or defame. Otherwise, it's free speech, no matter how wrong, odious, or that it could be the fuse that lights a flame that kills someone. You want to stop them from doing this? Go to Congress. After all, the First Amendment starts by saying 'Congress shall make *no* law.' So if you want to do something, start a new group, get your representatives to make a *new* law."

Mir replied, "You'd think it'd be *against* the law to make these kinds of statements, which are recorded, played on the radio and TV, and written up in newspapers. Much of it is just dishonest and can lead to harm."

"Tell that to the judge," Helen Karlstein said. "Then watch the defense counsel eviscerate you by quoting the First Amendment."

After nearly four years, we were exhausted and disenchanted. We deflected other requests to appear on college campuses and moved back to Arroyo Grande.

Ester was born at the end of 1977, the "E" in honor of Efraín Valencia, the leader of the group that trekked to our remote village in 1677. Her naming ceremony was conducted in the synagogue in the basement of the church in Arroyo Grande, seven years to the day after Débora and Herzl were married there.

It was a double celebration.

Herzl had been the subject of a short documentary titled: "*The REAL Answer to the Jewish Question*" that came out shortly before Ester arrived. The opening montage was arresting: as the camera honed in on empty fields, the ocean devoid of ships, the sky clear except for a few clouds, and streets with no cars or pedestrian traffic, it settled on a close-up of a gangly, bushy-bearded, thirty-four-year-old man with long black hair pulled into a bun in the back, who stared at you with such intensity it made you uncomfortable, despite the fact that you knew he couldn't see you. The starkness of it all was brought to the fore by it being in black and white, as if to emphasize that what was coming had no nuances; it was going to affect you one way or the other. The camera swung around his back to see a group of about a hundred Jews, young and old, standing and sitting in front of him. Until Herzl spoke, you were struck by the fact that there'd been no sound. As his lips moved, the people vanished in an instant, and you heard the first words that he said: "Even if all the Jews were to disappear, there'd be no less stink of anti-Semitism. It would continue to permeate the world, forever."

The film became a sensation at synagogues, JCCs, Hillels, and selected art houses. Reviews depended upon the orientation of the reviewer. It was the subject of heated newspaper articles and radio call-in shows, all of which prompted Herzl to create RAJ?, staffed by a group of Ashkenazi, Sephardi, Mizrahi, African, Caribbean, and Asian Jews, whose mission was to combat anti-Semites.

Whenever. Wherever. However.

I FOUND MYSELF in the unusual position of not being able to write. I started a biography of Ben Veniste but abandoned it over the paucity of information I could find about his early life and that of the history of his family. I did manage to put together enough for an article which was published in a Taos Heights newspaper. It generated a lot of reader letters to the editor from former students who'd spent countless hours at the café. They shared their fond memories of him, several indicating that they'd been thumped by his cane over some minor infraction of restaurant etiquette.

After the New Mexico State Penitentiary riot on February 3, 1980, in which thirty-three prisoners died, I had an idea to write about my incarceration in 1965 when no one suffered anything more than boredom, as if my light-hearted rendition of how we spent our time would be an antidote to the headlines about the grisly prison murders. I went back to the Los Chavez jail, hoping to find the same desk sergeant and to track down the ancient typewriter with the ribbon that got stuck. But the idea was better than the reality. The desk sergeant was new, the typewriter was nowhere to be found, and there were no records of my cellmates, thereby truncating any stories about them to my recollections from a short period of being cooped up together.

Dejected, I went back to Arroyo Grande. Mir got me up early the next morning, and I was surprised to see Madre in our kitchen with the kids.

"Go," she said to me. "Go with your wife."

"Go where?" I said, my mind racing through a virtual appointment book of things I must've forgotten.

"Come on," Mir said, "we're going to get you some inspiration."

I reluctantly followed her, traipsing behind, an indication of displeasure by not walking beside her.

"You can't just order up inspiration like summoning an elevator," I said a bit testily. "And where are we going, anyway—to the inspiration store? I don't think it opens up again until next year."

Mir didn't take the bait. I grumbled a bit more as we passed through the plaza and set out on one of the trails out west. The sun was rising. When we got to the top of a rise, Mir turned to me and said, "Sit. There. On that boulder. And don't say anything."

Chastened as if I were a little boy, I looked at my wife and was about to apologize for my surly behavior when I noticed a magnificent rainbow that'd emerged in the west.

"Pretend it's twenty-five years ago. I'm Nohemi. Make up a story. A good one," she ordered, lowering herself onto a mound of Indiangrass a few feet away. "Hurry up," she said, "before it goes away."

My first reaction was to be defensive, to say that you can't simply order someone to come up with something creative, whether it be a joke, a pronouncement, or a piece of fiction. *Life doesn't work that way*, I wanted to say. Yet when I opened my mouth to protest, what came out wasn't what I'd planned. The words started out slowly, deliberately. A cadence then began to develop, and as effortlessly as my father would tell a Holyman tale that he hadn't practiced beforehand, the opening of what would be my first novel emerged, much to the satisfaction of my wife, who recorded the moment on film.

"It seems as if anniversaries have a way of letting spirits loose, and they don't respect boundaries any more than viruses do, so the only way to fool yourself into thinking you can control them is to make others believe that they can see them as well. A conjurer uses sleights-of-hand, feints, and mis-directions, which can succeed because you're willing to suspend visual disbelief. However, an author only has one dimension to work with, as well as a disconnected audience, which can be a disadvantage. But on the other hand, there's no one to say that what you're reading is false.

"Today marks the fifteenth anniversary of a momentous event in my life—the day I was sent to jail. It's the obvious time for me now to tell my story. My guess is that you're going to believe this is fiction; that would be a delusion."

ACKNOWLEDGMENTS

I'm immensely grateful to *Ann Streger Price*, who read every word of each draft, pushed me relentlessly to raise my standards, and offered words of encouragement when I needed them most. In this regard, she is, as they say, a "tough cookie," which is exactly what this author needs as he attempts to perfect his craft. I wouldn't have it any other way.

Heartfelt thanks to:

Shulem Deen, whose editorial guidance was nothing less than superb. I'm indebted to this craftsman whose only standard is excellence and whose methods of assistance should be a model for others to follow.

DJ Schuette, for extraordinary editorial and copyediting skills. His unusual ability to understand what an author wants to do enables him to provide the most insightful and helpful critiques.

Asha Hossain of Asha Hossain Design, LLC for the elegant cover, jacket design, and advertisements, which exquisitely captured the essence of the book.

Pauline Neuwirth, Beth Metrick, Jeff Farr, and Aubrey Khan of Neuwirth & Associates, Inc., for the general design as well as the classy interior look of the book.

Rachel Tarlow Gul of Over The River Public Relations, for excellence in publicity.

Alison Sheehy of Alison Sheehy Photography, for distinctive photographic gifts.

Thane Rosenbaum, prolific author, attorney, and true twenty-first-century Renaissance Man, whose singular gifts of advice and friendship are treasured.

Ellis Levine of Cowan, DeBaets, Abrahams & Sheppard LLP, for ever-present wise counsel.

Peter DeGiglio of St. Lawrence Publishing Consultants, for superb assistance in navigating the book world.

Jennifer Gardella, PhD, whose social media design and content talents are second to none.

Matthew Price of Design by Price, for first-class website designs and IT wisdom.

Heather Cameron and Jennifer Wickboldt of Publishers Group West, for unstinting distribution efforts.

All authors should be so fortunate to be surrounded by such skilled, unselfish people with whom it is a delight to work.

It's important for me to recognize the extraordinary efforts of individuals and groups (such as StandWithUs) on college campuses who bravely push back against anti-Semitism and anti-Zionism from those whose ignorance, calumnies, and blasphemies are directed at Jewish students in general and the State of Israel in particular. Your bravery inspired me as I wrote *Jacobo's Rainbow*.

Finally, I'd like to let the following friends know how much I appreciate their enthusiasm and interest in my writing endeavors: Karen Levin, Yoel Magid, Fran Scheffler-Siegel, Steve Siegel, and Bill Robbins.

AUTHOR'S NOTE

This book is a work of complete fiction; no characters or settings are remotely related to anything that deals with me, my family, friends, or acquaintances.

Neither the scenes that take place at the University of Taos (a school that does not exist) nor the actions of characters in them are intended to portray actual events or people associated with the so-called Free Speech Movement at the University of California, Berkeley.

In a similar vein, the description of the action in Vietnam is made out of whole cloth.

For the avoidance of doubt, I have had no interactions (i.e., verbal, electronic, or written) with any person who was at the University of California, Berkeley or who was in Vietnam during the 1960s.

To avoid any misconceptions, no character is based on any real person.

The book that is referred to—*The Dimming of the American Enlightenment Bulb: lights out due to anti-Semitism?* by Helen Karlstein—is not real. Similarly, the *Albuquerque Tribune* is a fictitious newspaper.

I do not speak Ladino; all Ladino words used in this book are from the *Ladino-English/English-Ladino Concise Encyclopedic Dictionary* by Dr. Elli Kohen and Dahlia Kohen-Gordon, Hippocene Books, copyright 2000.

ABOUT THE AUTHOR

ALISON SHEEHY PHOTOGRAPHY

DAVID HIRSHBERG is the pseudonym for an entrepreneur who prefers to keep his business activities separate from his writing endeavors. He adopted the first name of his father-in-law and the last name of his maternal grandfather as a tribute to their impact on his life.

He is the author of the multiple-award winning debut novel *My Mother's Son* and has published two short stories—*A Gift* and *Tikkun Olam*.

Hirshberg holds an undergraduate degree from Dartmouth College and a master's degree from the University of Pennsylvania. He lives with his wife and two setters in Westchester County, New York.